ASHLEY MACK

Elmwood Year One

First edition

ISBN: 978-1-960161-17-8

This book was professionally typeset on Reedsy.
Find out more at reedsy.com

Contents

Foreword

The Elmwood series takes place at an imaginary college in upstate New York, and the tales that follow are between consenting adults. These stories include graphic sex and sexual situations, and some of them contain d/s dynamics, sexual harassment, attempted sexual assault, mentions of abuse, cheating (not by the leads), forced and arranged marriage, and there is a more detailed warning in the final story about CNC. Please be aware of what you're reading. Otherwise, enjoy.

OFFERINGS

Elise

July

The air is hot and sticky, heavy with the humidity of summer. We've been free of the confines of high school for three weeks and my best friend, Rosie, is hosting her absolute blowout of a graduation party. The giant sprawling lawn that is her backyard is packed with bodies - pretty much our entire high school and the last three graduating classes are here. It's a drunken bacchanalia.

I've spent every minute I can here since graduation because for the first time since we were 5, Rosie and I won't be in school together. She's off to California and I'm headed to upstate New York and Elmwood College. The same place her brother attends.

If Rosie is my lifetime bestie, Colin is my lifetime crush. The first time I came over, Colin told me he liked my t-shirt, and I've been head over heels ever since. His soft brown hair was in a floppy bowl cut and he was missing one of his front teeth, and he was still the most beautiful boy I ever saw. Then he had to grow into a frustratingly sexy man.

I'm doing everything I can not to acknowledge him in any way tonight. I've been distant since he came home for the summer, trying to save myself from heartache.

Pretending like I don't know exactly where he is, I'm sitting with Rosie on a lounger near the pool.

"I love you," she leans her head on my shoulder, breath smelling of watermelon seltzer.

"I know." I take a drink of my own, trying to feel any sort of buzz. Rosie and her brother don't look anything alike - he's tall, dark hair, hazel eyes, pure muscle these days. Rosie is slight with auburn hair and dark brown eyes, fit but doesn't look it. They just barely look like siblings when side by side and sometimes you can only tell because they both inherited their dad's dimples.

She flashes them at me now. "This would be the perfect time to make a move on Colin."

"No." It's not our first time having this conversation. It's not even our first time having it tonight.

"He's going to be a junior at the same school - you can finally get him under your thumb and go to school with your hot older boyfriend."

"Colin doesn't see me like that," I counter her. "I'm his kid sister's bestie. That's it."

Rosie frowns and stares at the people causing a ruckus in the water. A bikini top goes flying and we both tilt our heads, unable to look away from the unexpected flash of nipples. She grunts and looks away, deciding it's not her business and everyone seems to be okay with what's happening.

"I'll talk to Colin if you finally make a move on Eli."

The frown deepens. "You're the worst friend."

"So are you." I drain the rest of the can and shimmy away from her to stand up. "You want more?"

Rosie nods, not looking at me. I follow her gaze to wear Eli stands with his friends further along the concrete apron on the back of the house. He's in the crowd that's playing beer pong on the ping pong table. I shake my head and walk away.

The crowd parts easily, everyone in a good mood. I cut across the area that's been deemed the dance floor, bouncing between bodies as people jump and grind to whatever is playing on the massive speakers. The tables near the house are loaded down with food and alcohol, her parents not giving a crap - not even being present - as we engage in all kinds of underage shenanigans. They told her as long as no one dies, Rosie could do whatever she wanted.

A warm body steps close to me, heating my back. I know from one deep breath that it's Colin. He always smells like spearmint with a hint of evergreen – his chewing gum of choice and a hint of his soap.

"Hey, Mouse, you having a good time?" He reaches around me, caging me between his arms, as he grabs a beer and a seltzer. I turn around and step back, and he hands me the seltzer. It's raspberry lemonade. My favorite. His golden eyes are so earnest, focused on me and waiting for an answer. It's what I've always loved about him – he talks to me like I matter. I'm past being annoyed that he still calls me Mouse, accepting it for the affection that it is.

When we were kids, he used to sneak up on me and scare me, and he started calling me Mouse after the squeak I made every time he did it. He remembered the squeaking, I remembered the feeling of his hands on my waist, diving in to tickle me.

"Good enough," I answer, honest. "Hanging out with Rosie while she pines."

"Eli Ward, still?" Colin smiles and shakes his head. Rosie and Colin are close because their parents are so in and out of their lives. They make money and take care of them, but they are hardly present. I'm not as rich as they are, but at least my parents are home and know what's going on with my life. Colin is two years older than us, but way more mature because he gave Rosie room to be a kid while he was always there for her.

She confessed to me one night that she was relieved when he went to college, not because she had less supervision, but because it was the first time he got to think of himself first. They almost make me wish I had siblings.

"Still." I get distracted looking out over the party because it's too hard to look at him, and I speak without thinking. "Although teasing her about it is no fun, then she calls me out on not talking to my crush."

Colin laughs but it sounds weird. "Ooo, who's your crush, Mouse?" He steps closer to me and his voice drops an octave. "Need me to help you make him jealous?"

I turn my gaze and shiver at how close he is to me. I can't control the way my eyes drop to his lips, my imagination spinning out all the possibilities of what he would be willing to do to make my non-existent crush jealous. I wonder what he'd do if he knew it was him? When I meet Colin's eyes, they're burning into mine.

"You'd do that?"

He takes my chin between his thumb and forefinger. "I'd do anything for you."

It would be sweet, sexy even, if I couldn't also smell the alcohol on his breath. Colin is the most affable drunk - friendly, affectionate, and at times grandiose, making big wild promises and letting his good nature get away from him. This is drunk Colin trying to be my friend.

"It doesn't matter," I answer. "I'm going to Elmwood. High school crushes won't matter anymore."

Something shutters in Colin's eyes, and he lets me go. "Whatever you say."

I grab a watermelon seltzer and tilt my head in Rosie's direction. "Going back to the queen. I'll see you later?"

Colin grins. "Of course." Before I turn to walk away, he stops me. "Don't forget that if you need anything at all next year, I'm a text away. You don't even need to text - show up at my door. I've got you."

I smile back, meaning it. I'm scared as fuck to be at Elmwood - it's exclusive, elite, difficult, and competitive - knowing that I can, and probably will, count on Colin takes a huge weight off my shoulders.

"I know you do. Thanks, Colin."

"Anything, Mouse." He repeats what he said earlier, tone and expression serious. I turn away before he can see how it affects me. Goosebumps break out along my skin and my nipples tighten and get hard. I love when his voice drops into that serious tone. The same tone he used the first time I cried over a boy and he told me that I was worth more than the idiot who rejected me. Colin promised I'd find someone who would appreciate me for everything I was, and would never make me cry.

Colin might be the only male who hasn't drawn tears from me. He's been my rescuer from bullies, my advisor and tutor on school and my future, and often our chauffeur until Rosie got her license. It's no wonder that I can't get over him - he's perfect.

And probably sees me like another little sister.

I sit back down next to Rosie. She's glaring at a girl in the grade below us who's playing beer pong with Eli. The girl keeps touching his shoulder after he throws, and every time she does I see Rosie's shoulders sneak closer to her ears.

"Let's make a deal," I snap her out of it. "If you go talk to Eli right now, I will tell Colin sometime in the next school year how I feel. I'm sure they'll be an opportunity while we're at Elmwood."

Rosie sits up and turns her head so slowly to look at me that it's almost creepy. Her eyes are wide.

"Seriously?"

"An unbreakable vow," I say, holding out my pinkie. "You go, right now, talk to him, and I will follow through."

She stares at me, warring with herself. "Fine." Rosie hooks her pinkie through mine. "An unbreakable vow. Just don't tell me what my brother is like in bed. I only like the idea of him pounding your brains out to be a vague, positive notion."

"Like that'll ever happen. I'm already preparing myself for the 'you're like a sister to me' conversation."

Rosie gives me a smirk and shakes her head. "I think you'd be surprised."

She doesn't let me ask her what she means by that because she gets off the lounger and heads over to where Eli stands waiting for his turn. He stills when he sees that she's approached, watching her like prey hoping that it's predator can only see movement. Eli snaps out of it when it's his turn to throw, but he quickly and spectacularly loses. The girl makes herself scarce.

I see Rosie and Eli say something to each other, and then walk off across the yard.

Part of me didn't think she'd follow through. I guess I have a year to make things awkward with Colin, get over it, and then we can both move on with our lives. Maybe telling him will help me let him go, and find the person who's meant to be my future.

Elise

October

Elmwood is everything I ever dreamed it would be. Our sprawling, isolated campus in the middle of nowhere in upstate New York is a dark academia dream. The buildings are ancient, the grounds are full of secrets, and I'm being challenged academically in all the ways I ever wanted. I argue with my classmates, I get to talk with faculty who are experts in the things that I care about, and I've found a group of friends who walk the same line as I do between partying and nerding out.

I've also successfully avoided Colin. He texts me once a week or so to check on me, and I keep him updated without asking anything of him. Since Colin is an initiated member of the Cavalry, he's fairly known on campus, and I've been careful not to use my association with him. I want to earn my own reputation.

Colleges like Elmwood - old, elite, private - are always home to secret societies. Although the ones at Elmwood aren't very secret. Their existence is well known, as are a lot of their traditions and practices, and they are a way bigger deal than belonging to any of the fraternities or sororities. Collectively, they're the Elmwood Trinity: the Cavalry, the Castle, and the Magistrates. All of them have existed since the founding of Elmwood, and they all serve a different purpose.

The Cavalry is exclusive to men, although they've opened that up a bit in recent years by expanding their definition of man. Same with the Castle, which is exclusive to women. The Cavalry and the Castle work together to throw events on campus, do a lot of fundraising, and are generally for networking and building relationships across cohorts. It's more social than anything.

The Magistrates are the ones with a more distinct purpose. Anyone can be chosen to be a Magistrate, but their purposes are generally to run student government and work on campus rules and policies, shaping the way that Elmwood runs and recruits, and act as the student voice to the administration. You don't have to be a Magistrate to be on student government, but it helps.

My closest friend at Elmwood, Maeve, wants me to try and be a Magistrate like her, but I've got my heart set on the Castle. I've been trying to think of ways to convince Colin to sponsor me. That's the easiest way to get chosen - if a member of one of the other groups nominates and sponsors you. Since he's always been hesitant about me and Rosie partying, I'm worried he won't think it's a good idea for me to join. Not to mention, he knows I'm avoiding him, so asking for a favor out of the blue won't go over well.

The few times I've seen him at parties have made my heart ache, and it reinforces that I need to follow through on my agreement with Rosie soon or I'll never be able to move on.

My eyes always find him, drink in his smile, his body, his intensity. The only relief has been that I haven't seen him with any girls. It was hard enough in high school, I don't know if I could survive it now.

In a weird way, I've never been happier.

During the day I love my classes, I spend time with my friends, I feel like I fit.

At night, I explore Elmwood. Slowly, the campus is revealing her secrets to me. The secret doors, hidden passages, unused or forgotten rooms, unlocked windows, and hiding places. Even though it's my first year, I already know that I'm going to do an analysis of the architectural evolution of the campus for my final capstone. I'm a history major but my area of interest has always been architecture and buildings, and what the changes in styles reflect about the societies that built them.

Elmwood is also know for it's expansive gardens and hedge maze. It took me two weeks to memorize it. I can find my way out from any place in the maze as long as I can orient myself on a compass. It's become my comfort place on campus, especially as the weather has gotten colder and other people stopped exploring it. Sprinkled throughout are clearings with benches, fountains, and seating areas. All my best papers so far have been written in those clearings.

I wonder if anyone else has discovered these places. If they've been trusted with Elmwood's secrets.

Right now I'm excited because it's almost Halloween. The smell of decaying leaves and bonfires is constantly in the air, I was personally invited to the best party by members of the Castle, and my costume is almost ready. For the next few days I'm focusing on homework so I don't have to worry about anything when I'm sleeping off my hangover. All I want to do is let go and dance, and enjoy where I am in my life right now.

Maybe that will be my chance to tell Colin how I feel, and then I can avoid him until we drive home together at Thanksgiving. Given my costume, it might just be perfect.

I'm in the library studying when my phone buzzes.

It's a photo text from Rosie - she's going as a bumblebee for Halloween and it's her finished costume. I reply: *Bee-utiful.*

Rosie: *Nerd. What are you going as?*

Me: *Not telling. I'll send you a pic night of.*

Rosie: *Snooty college has made you mysterious.*

I send her back a wink face and check the time. It's almost midnight, so the library will be closing. Not that it's ever closed to me. It was the first building I thoroughly explored on campus because it's also the oldest and has been everything from housing for administration to classrooms to it's current state. There are two secret passages and a secret entrance. The secret passages aren't anything special - one that's a staircase that takes you from the first floor all the way to the top, which I have a sneaking suspicion was how the first Chancellor carried on an affair - and the other leads to a small room on the third floor in one of the towers. It's empty, and I don't know what it was used for, but I did find an unreadable old journal that I gave to my roommate Cynthia to work on.

The secret entrance was the real find. Like any self-respecting creepy place, the library is covered in ivy. The grounds staff keep it trimmed and I happened to notice a change in the brick after a trim that was actually the top of a door. It's heavy, metal, and covered in a thick draping of greenery that's heavy and wet to lift, but gets me into a small alcove. The alcove opens - a whole wooden wall panel - into the reference section of the library. No one is ever there. Other than the first time I found it, I've never used it again. The library is most definitely haunted and I don't want to be there alone in the dark.

I pack up my bag and head out with the other stragglers. The night is windy, and a huge thunderstorm is on the forecast for tomorrow. Nice and spooky to get us all in the mood for Halloween the day after that.

My phone buzzes again as I start the long walk across campus to the hall I live in. I picked Harwood-Locke Hall because it's the oldest residence, and the rooms are enormous. Old windows, high ceilings, loud plumbing, but I don't care. My roommate Cynthia and I got lucky with a corner room, so we have two walls with windows, and it's so old school we even have a fireplace. They've replaced it with gas to keep it safe, and I love it. I love the cozy place we've made for ourselves. The downside is that it's on the opposite side of campus from the library - the entirety of Elmwood is between the two buildings, and it can be a half hour walk.

I lift my phone, expecting another text from Rosie, or maybe Cynthia asking where I am, but it's Colin. It's late for him to be texting and my stomach drops with worry.

Colin: *Will I see you at Beastly?*

The Halloween party is one of the big events thrown by the Cavalry and the Castle. This year's theme is the name of the party: Beastly. Everyone is encouraged to come dressed as an animal. Colin actually inspired my choice of costume: I'm going as a mouse. A slightly sexy mouse, but a mouse nonetheless.

Me: *Of course.*

Colin: *Will I actually see you, or will you pretend like you don't see me like you have at the last few parties?*

I cringe, guilty and embarrassed. I assumed he didn't see me, and assumed that he'd approach me if he did. Apparently, I over-estimated how protective he'd be once I was in college.

Me: *I didn't realize you saw me.*

Colin: *I always see you.*

I don't know what to say to that, so I say nothing. I lock my phone, tuck it and my hands into my jacket pockets, and speed up as I walk to my building. The temptation to explore is high, but I need sleep. It's going to be a long, crazy weekend and I want all the energy for fun with my friends.

Colin

Usually I enjoy the weekly meeting of the Cavalry, but my head is just not in it tonight. I've got a midterm essay to finish before the weekend, and Rosie has been texting me non-stop about Elise. As if I could stop thinking about her, but I'm trying to respect the boundaries she's clearly setting since coming to Elmwood. I won't say it doesn't fucking hurt, but I also know that I have no one to blame but myself.

Peter, this year's General of the Cavalry, is droning on about specifics for the annual Halloween party and what our responsibilities will be. I always volunteer to do the work upfront and the heavy lifting so that at the party itself I'm free, and I never have to drag my ass out of bed for clean up. I've been a servant for the Castle for the last week helping with decorating and anything else they wanted. My duty has been met.

When a hush falls over the room, it snaps me back to attention. Peter is about to cover the reason this is the most well-attended meeting all year: tomorrow is the Hunt.

It's one of the oldest and wildest traditions of the Cavalry. Each year, 5 names are drawn from the membership to be "offerings" and starting at midnight on October 30, they have to run and hide until sunrise. If they're caught, it usually results in some kind of humiliation and extra work. If the offerings survive, it's all the glory and one of the highest recognitions a member of the Cavalry can get. It's a weird balance - you do and you don't want your name to be drawn. Is the glory worth the exhaustion, and the potential for humiliation?

All we have left tonight is to draw names, and then tomorrow at midnight...I'm not sure I'll even join. I might hang back and let the others have their fun chasing the offerings, and I'll be there to help celebrate come sunrise on Halloween.

Rosie texts again, calling me the usual stream of names and insults because she knows that I'm holding back and beating myself up when it comes to Elise. It's hard enough having my little sister know that I've been obsessed with her best friend, but it's even harder that Elise is completely oblivious. I've fucked things up so thoroughly and I've been waiting for the right moment to basically lay my heart at her feet and hope she forgives me. Rosie says she will, and that everything will work out, but she's too positive for her own good sometimes.

"Colin Larson."

My head snaps up and I see Peter standing on the dais in our meeting room, holding a black bag in one hand a card in the other. He's picking offerings and called my name. Shit.

There are some "oohs" and a few teasing jabs at me. Not to sound arrogant, but I'm popular in the Cavalry and on campus. I've made a lot of friends - I'm reliable, loyal, and I show up when people need me. I also spend a lot of time at the gym, working out the things in my head by pushing my body. I'm a good offering - they'll see me as a challenge to catch.

Peter grins and laughs, telling everyone to calm down. He resumes picking, and when I drop my eyes they snag on Mathias Talmadge sitting across the room from me. He's grinning too, but it's nothing but malevolence. I sneer back, challenging him when this isn't even something that I wanted. Mathias will be gunning for me and I vow right then I'll give him the chase of his life.

The fact that I have a nemesis is as unbelievable to me now as it was when I came to the realization at the end of my freshman year of high school. Mathias was new and we were friendly enough at first, until we weren't. We constantly found ourselves vying for the same things - the same positions on teams and clubs - and then somehow it grew into something bigger and darker. Picking at each other over grades, over who threw the best parties, who we dated and who we hooked up with, and even which one of us got notified first about getting into Elmwood. We couldn't stop ourselves from running our mouths and got into way more fights than we should have.

Rather than being myself and exploring what I was interested in during high school, I spent all my time trying to beat Mathias. Most of the time, I did. In the mental tally of wins I keep, I know I'm ahead. Some of his continued animosity is because he knows it too. Other than being in the Cavalry together, Mathias and I don't cross paths at Elmwood. We're in different majors and I stay away from him.

Part of me blames him for putting distance between me and Elise, for a lot of reasons. First, because I shoved my feelings for her aside to be with other girls in order to look better than him. I should've realized all I needed was her, and what I'd have with her, to be better off than him even on the best day of his life. Instead I fucked around and boy did I find out. The first time Elise called me a man-whore it felt like I'd been stabbed. It was why I stopped caring about all the bullshit with him senior year. He didn't matter, and I'd failed to pay attention to the people who did.

The problem was, Mathias could see what Elise couldn't. He noticed that I'd pulled back on him and it was because I was spending more time with her and Rosie, and even time with just me and her. To Mathias, "getting" Elise was going to be his great conquering of me. Watching him flirt with her and her shy, unaware interactions with him nearly killed me. I thought that if I let my possessive feelings for her out, it would make her even more of a target, so I backed off again.

That was also a fucking mistake when he nearly raped her at a party. Rosie found me in time and I laid that fucker out and humiliated him in public. No girl would touch him for the rest of the year, and somehow that's when I finally, truly beat him. It was sick that he'd go to that level to prove something to me. Elise was a 16 year old girl I was supposed to protect and take care of, and instead I put her in the line of fire.

I told myself after that I'd try to get over her, and feel like a big brother towards her, but it never worked. The events of that night changed me in ways I didn't understand for years - I can't even imagine how they changed her.

I've tried to hide the fact that Elise goes to Elmwood from Mathias, but if she's coming to the party, he's going to find out. I guess I'll have to keep her with me just in case. It might finally be the opening I need to show her how I feel.

I text her to make sure that she's coming. I know some of my friends in the Castle personally invited her - they're already considering her for membership and asked me about her since they knew we were from the same high school. Elise answers my text quickly, and I taunt her about ignoring me at parties.

She wouldn't even look at me. It ripped me open.

Peter finishes picking the offerings and reminds us of the rules.

"You can run and hide anywhere you want as long as you don't leave campus property. Caught doesn't mean seeing you, it means laying hands on you." Peter glares at the room, "Don't get rough or I'll make you pay for it. Keep it classy." The guys laugh, but Mathias doesn't react at all. If he catches me, it's going to get violent and we both know it.

"Get your shit together, prepare, and tomorrow...the hunt begins." Peter grins and a bunch of guys start howling. I can't help but smile, even if this is inconvenient.

I'll survive the night, and then I'll finally claim Elise the way she deserves.

Everyone trails out of the Cavalry House and I walk down the street to my building. The lights in the library are being put out, the campus quieting down to nothing as the minutes pass after midnight. I was never the most outdoorsy guy, but since coming here I started hiking the trails around the campus, and the few miles between the Elmwood campus and the closest town, Direwood.

People don't leave campus except for holidays. Even though the parking lots are full of our fancy cars and most people come from rich asshole families like I do, it's like once you're here, you're in a separate world. A bubble that we create for ourselves that keeps the rest of the world hazy and distant. Sometimes it sucks because you can't make a midnight run for food or catch a game that isn't one of our teams, but nobody seems to mind. We have everything we need.

"You're going down, Larson," a voice snaps me out of my reflection. Of course it's Mathias. He lives in a building that's the opposite direction from me, but it doesn't surprise me he'd go out of his way to talk shit.

I sigh and turn to face him. One of my roommates gives me a look that clearly asks if I'm good, and I give him a nod. They'll be waiting when I get back. They know our history.

"Sure, Mathias. Whatever."

He gives me a mock frown. "Don't be like that. I want you to put up a fight." Mathias takes a step closer and drops his voice. "You know I like it when they fight." Images of Elise fighting him off, the sound of the smack across his face she gave him when he got distracted by my interruption, float across my eyes. Fury roars through me but I swallow it down. The time will come for true revenge.

"I'm not going to waste energy on you. I'll see you at sunrise." I give him a shrug, feigning disinterest, and take a few steps back before I turn around and start walking.

"I'm going to fuck you up!" He shouts. I don't acknowledge him in any way, and keep my head down.

It's when I'm safely behind the closed door of my bedroom that I let out my fury, punching at the bag I have hanging in the corner until my knuckles are throbbing because I didn't wrap them. Someday he's going to pay for what he's done. I will find a way.

I sit down on my bed and look over at the glass habitat where my pet mouse lives. She sneaks out of her little cardboard hut and sticks her nose in the air, whiskers spiked and searching.

"It's okay Leesey." I open the top and feed her a treat. She squeaks at me and then grabs it to go hide in her house to eat it. "Mathias doesn't matter. Only Elise matters."

Then I sit down at my desk, pull up a campus map, and try to make a plan to beat my brothers at their own game. If I'm going to win, I'm going to do it well.

Elise

Thunder has been rumbling for the last hour, but the rain isn't supposed to hit until closer to 1am. By then, me and my insomnia will be tucked up in bed with a book and listening to Cynthia's snores as a soundtrack.

Right now though, I'm scrambling to finish the last details of the probability project we were assigned for extra credit. I'm hit or miss when it comes to math so even though my grade is fine so far, every bit of extra credit matters. I keep watching the same YouTube video where a very cute nerd is explaining it, and it keeps sliding out of my head with every peal of thunder.

It's Devil's Night, and I think the sky is trying to scare the hell out of us. I can feel the building shake as the storm gets closer. I think for my own safety and sanity, I have to call it a night and get out of here.

As I make my way down from the third floor, I don't see anyone. Like they locked up and left me here, and it gives me a shiver down my spine. The lights are still on so there has to be someone, and we're too competitive academically for anyone to let a storm scare them off from serious studying. Maybe I'm seeing what I want to see - abandoned in an old building in a storm, like the start of a horror novel.

I shiver and it isn't from the cold. I bundle myself up in my thick, warm raincoat, double check that nothing important is exposed to the weather just in case it does start raining, and head out into the wild wind. It's work to press open the door, and as soon as I'm free of I have to take two steps to the side to keep my balance against the wind. The storm is coming in hard and fast.

My breath gets pushed back at me by the collar of my coat, keeping my face warm, as I try not to look stupid by running down the sidewalk.

Luck leaves me as the sky opens up. I'm immediately drenched from toe to hip, my coat doing what it can to keep the rest of me dry. I start moving faster but the rain is so heavy I can't even see - I step out into the street before I even realize I made it to the corner. There is no way I can make it back to Harwood-Locke I'm also only near residential buildings and can't see anything.

Except a sign on the other side of the street: Cavalry 3. The building Colin lives in.

Crap.

I'm desperate. I run the rest of the way across the street and up to the front door. It takes the flat of my hand to pound on it hard enough to be heard. I've thrown back my hood, semi-guarded from the weather by the overhang, but I'm decidedly wet and windblown when someone opens the door. It's one of Colin's friends I've seen a few times, I think his name is Tate.

"Can I help you?"

"Is Colin home?"

A weird grin crosses Tate's face. "Are you here to be his good luck charm for tonight?"

"Sure," I agree, and step in when Tate moves aside.

"Up the stairs, last door on the left."

I thank him and follow his directions. The butterflies in my stomach wake up into a riot with every step I take. I always tell myself staying away from Colin will be easier, but instead it makes the impact of his nearness more powerful. Memory dulls him, and reality shows me he's even more spectacular.

I knock softly on the door.

"What?" He sounds angry, and now I'm second guessing myself.

"Hey - it's - it's Elise."

The door whips open a second later and I am treated to the delicious sight of a shirtless Colin in dark jeans hanging low on his hips and showing blue checkered boxers. His chest is heaving, his abs are defined and lickable, and his Adonis belt is an arrow straight to the very spot on him I am most curious about. I know his mind, his dreams, a lot of his thoughts, but damn do I wish I knew what he looked like naked.

"Are you okay? What's the matter?" Colin takes me by the hand and pulls me inside enough to shut the door, and then unintentionally crowds me against it as his eyes scan me, looking for injury.

"I got caught in the storm and needed somewhere to go." My voice is small. It sounds like an excuse now. Colin turns to look out the window and his eyebrows raise like he hasn't even noticed the floor shaking thunder and bright cracks of lightning.

Then he drops into a frown. "That changes things." He shakes himself and focuses back on me. "Are you okay?"

"Just wet."

Colin licks his lips and his eyes drop down my body. "I've got clothes, if you want to change." He steps away from me and checks his watch. "I should have just enough time."

I stand still as he moves around his room, talking to himself. He gets another pair of joggers, a t-shirt, and one of his hoodies out and hands them to me, then turns back to the pile of things that are currently collecting on his bed. There's layers of clothes - I'm assuming the shirt he plans to wear - as well as a compass, a knife, a balaclava, and a small pile of protein bars. I don't ask. He pulls his rain jacket off a hook next to the door and adds it to the pile.

Since he seems distracted, I drop my backpack and shimmy out of my jacket, thinking that I can change quick before he pays attention to me again. My shirt did get wet through the jacket, that's how intense the rain was, so I change into the t-shirt and then the hoodie first. I glance his way and he's focused on the bed so I take a second to lift the neck to my nose and inhale the smell of him. It's not a clean hoodie. It doesn't smell like laundry soap, it smells like Colin - spearmint and evergreen. My pussy reacts, clenching, and a different kind of moisture pools between my legs.

Why does he have to be so perfect?

I shimmy out of my jeans, and my underwear is just as drenched. Slowly and silently, I let them drop. Except when I go to hide them under my coat, I bump his dresser.

Colin glances back at me and then stills. His eyes trace up from my socked feet, across my bare legs, to the rest of me that's drowning in his hoodie. I'm frozen and aroused from that look, feeling exposed and vulnerable.

"Fuck, El." It's nearly a growl. He turns back around and does something that almost looks like he's adjusting himself. I watch for a second as he reaches across the bed for his shirt.

I take the opportunity to pull on the joggers before my vagina has a chance to embarrass me by finding a way to be visible. Colin's clothes are warm and cozy and wearing them makes me feel like his girlfriend. It makes that fantasy real for a second, and I already debate with myself if I'll ever give this sweatshirt back. Probably not.

There's a squeak that draws my attention away from Colin's ass. On a small table next to his bed is a glass habitat. A little gray mouse is drinking from the water dispenser, it's pink nose wiggling between gulps. I can't believe he has a pet mouse.

"Oh, how cute! What's it's name?"

There's a long, long silence and I straighten to look at him. Colin's cheeks are pink and his mouth is opening and closing like he can't find the words. I've never seen Colin blush in our entire lives, and I've known him since he was 7 years old.

"Elise."

"What?"

He looks down at the floor. "Her name is Elise."

"You named your mouse...after me..." I don't know whether to be flattered or insulted.

"She's my mouse, you're my Mouse...it made sense at the time. And to be fair, I usually call her Leesey when we talk."

I have to hold back the grin that wants to steal across my face. I'm his Mouse. It hits different when I hear him say it like that. Also that he admits to talking to his mouse and having conversations with her. I decide that

I'm flattered by the shared name because it's adorable. I like knowing that he thinks about me, even if it's not quite in the way I want.

Colin grabs a treat and opens the top of the habitat, running a finger between her pink ears when she takes it from him. I've known Colin so long I thought he'd lost the capacity to surprise me, but I was wrong. This is precious.

He turns back to the bed and continues getting dressed.

"Listen, you can stay here as long as you want, I don't think I'll have time to walk you back."

"I don't need you to walk me back."

Colin whips around and steps up to me. "It's Devil's Night, El, and it's the Hunt. I think you'll be safer if you stay here."

The Hunt sounds vaguely familiar. "What's the Hunt?"

"Every year the Cavalry picks five offerings and hunts them across campus starting at midnight. If I make it to sunrise, I win."

Panic clutches at me and I grab onto him. "You're one of the offerings? Oh my god, Colin, that's awful."

He looks at where I'm touching his arm and then smirks at me. "I'm going to be fine, Mouse."

The rain has slowed considerably in the half hour I've been here, the storm leaving a torrential downpour before the harsh wind blew it farther away.

"I can get home - it's slowed down." I take a few steps back. "Thanks for the dry clothes." I turn my back on him, feeling oddly rejected. Also very tempted to stay in his room and wait for him. I want to crawl under his soft covers that smell like him, sleep all night, and be there for him when he makes it back after sunrise, warming his cool body with all the heat I have to give him.

Colin frowns and shakes his head. "Never mind, I can walk you home. No one is going to start hunting right at midnight. Let me walk you, Mouse. I've never even seen your room."

I don't know why that makes me blush, but I can only nod in response.

"I'm glad you came to me," he zips up his heavy black jacket as I slide back into my boots. He picks up my backpack and holds it out for me. "I meant it when I said anything you need."

What if what I need is you?

God I'm so pathetic. I slip my bag back on, feeling it's dampness at my back and glad it's mostly empty. We make our way out of his room and out of the house. We're barely up half a block, about to cross back onto the main body of campus, when someone screams his name.

Colin

Elise is going to kill me, and it's not the night to lose my focus. I was happy to see her. Elated that she came to me when she needed a safe place, except the rain on her skin and hair made her scent take over my room. My dick was already half hard but when I turned around and she was all disheveled and looked like she was wearing nothing but my hoodie?

Fuck. That was pure torture and I was immediately steel. I had to turn around and adjust myself, talking to her over my shoulder until I calmed back down. Thinking about the fact that I was going to be chased down by almost 60 insane college guys tonight probably helped.

Most of the members of the Cavalry don't hunt. It's usually the sopho-mores and juniors - the seniors stay at the main Cavalry House and get shit-faced while they keep score. Freshman don't get recruited until the end of the spring semester. It's a long, judgmental evaluation process.

Maybe having my Mouse in my room, seeing me before this, is my good luck charm. I'm going to win this for her. I'm going to keep her safely tucked away in her room and off of Mathias's radar, and then I'm going to devour every inch of her. I'm going to show her that life is good, but it'd be even better if we were finally together. The past won't be allowed to get between us anymore. She has to know how I feel - it's so fucking obvious. I'm practically the heart-eye emoji every time I look at her.

Mouse is perfect. Since we were little kids it's always been easy to talk to her, she knows a little bit about everything and a lot about what she's passionate about, she's crazy supportive, makes me laugh, reads my mood better than almost anybody, and everything with her feels right. As we got older, I noticed her differently. I noticed her body, her curves, the softness of her skin, the plushness of her lips. But being younger than me made careful about her, and then I was too wrapped up in the hormones of high school to think better of my choices. It took me way too long to realize everything she meant to me, and that I was in love with her. That I always had been. That no one else ever felt like love because I only felt that way about her.

Tonight I'm short on time, but nothing is more important than taking care of her. If we walk out this door and I get caught immediately, I'll live with it if it means she knows I'd put her comfort above anything else.

We don't get far, and my stomach sinks when a booming voice yells: "COLIN LARSON!"

It's minutes after midnight. The Hunt has begun.

"Come on." I grab her hand and we start to run. Across the street is the gate to campus - a huge black iron gate with black marble pillars struck through with lines of gold. The school motto is worked in metal on the arch at the top: non ducor, duco...I am not led, I lead. Very elitist of us.

We run down the long avenue surrounded by dense bushes and heavy, dark trees that are starting to lose their leaves. I don't hear anyone coming after us, but that doesn't stop me from looking over my shoulder. Someone is chasing but they're obscured by the hood of their sweatshirt, and the leisurely pace they're walking makes me nervous.

I pull Elise into a break in the bushes, and we find ourselves at the back of the library.

"This way." She takes the lead, pulling me now, deep into the ivy. I'm stunned when she lifts thick green vines and ducks under them. After a second, her head pops back out. "Come on. We need to regroup."

I follow her into the opening, and we end up in a small alcove. It's dark, only the dim light from outside penetrating our hiding place.

"Where are we?" I whisper.

"Shh." Her finger drops softly onto my lips and I'm tempted to take it into my mouth and bite it. Tempted by the chance to taste her skin.

Elise moves close to me and then past me, oblivious what that brush of her body against mine does to me. Or so I think, but then she shivers and shifts, and I wonder if it's the chill air or if it's us. Close like this.

She looks out from behind the ivy. "Coast is clear. I have an idea."

I'll do anything she says.

 Elise

I'm so close to Colin that it's almost distracting, but right now the competitive fire is ignited in my chest. I want to make sure he survives the night, and I can definitely help him stay hidden. I know all the best places. It's like Elmwood herself prepared me for this.

"We have to run, but I know where we need to go. Come with me?" I slide out from the alcove and offer him my hand. We ran most of the way to the library like that, clinging to each other so we didn't get separated. I'm in the game now, and I hope he'll let me stay.

"Yeah. Where are we going?"

"Newton Arts."

When Colin climbs out from behind the ivy, I close the metal door to the library secret entrance and make sure that it's secure. We step back up to the end of the grand avenue and look across the quad. It's dark and the streetlights across campus are struggling to fight the fog that's settled in after the rain. The golden glow is warm, but not exactly helpful for seeing things.

Colin slides his hand back into mine and we start walking across the quad. It's an open space and we're vulnerable.

"LARSON!" someone yells, and then we're running again.

Colin is faster than I am, but follows my silent instructions when I yank him around the side of the Arts building to the loading dock area. The dock itself is open, usually unsecured and allowing unfettered access to those of us who want to explore the buildings when they're empty. I jump up and grab the concrete lip of the dock, and then Colin's hands are on my ass pushing me up the rest of the way. I turn around and reach for him, pulling until he's up with me.

We both turn to look at a group of five guys – all dressed in black, all obscuring their faces, running down the drive that leads to the dock.

"Come on!" I whisper shout, tugging him after me. They'll catch up, but not soon enough to see us disappear into the hiding spot I have in mind.

The doors to the theater are closed but unlocked and I whip them open. We tear down the aisle, the thumps of our footsteps muffled by the carpet. When we reach the front of the stage I run my hands across the panels in the front, trying to find the catch that will swing one open and give us access to the tunnels.

We hear voices echoing in the hall.

"Any second now," Colin urges.

My hand finds what feels like a knot, but I press down and a panel swings open. I let Colin drop in first, then slide the door shut as soon as I'm in. It's solid timing because the whoops and shouts get louder, and then I hear their feet pounding the carpet.

"Where are we?" Colin whispers.

"We used to do more special effects in our shows – trap doors and stuff. Someone got hurt so we stopped, but the space beneath the stage is still here."

I put my finger to my lips and crawl deeper. The guys outside thump up the stairs onto the stage, calling out for Colin. They jump and stomp, trying to be intimidating. I pull Colin with me until we're right beneath the main trap door, and through a small crack we can see them.

"We're soooarin' flyyyyyin," one of them sings off key. They others laugh.

"Larson...come out, come out," another voice croons. "You can only hide for so long."

There's more laughter, and I wonder if they're a little bit drunk. That only works in our favor. There's a sliver of light shining down on us, and when I look over at Colin there's a smirk on his face. For the moment, we've outsmarted them. Oh, he has no idea how well.

I tug on his jacket sleeve until he looks at me, and then tilt my head to indicate that he should follow me. We half walk, half crawl through the underside of the stage until we get to the door at the back. The sounds of our pursuers fade as they either get bored, or we put that much distance between us.

A door swings open to a small, cramped office. I dust myself off as I step out, and enjoy watching Colin stretch as he gets to stand up to his full height. Neither of us says anything until I have the hatch shut again.

"How do you know about that? About the library?"

This time I blush, furiously, but he's looking at me with such flabber-gasted amazement I'm less afraid to explain.

"I don't sleep a lot, so I explore."

"Campus?"

I nod. "I've found some things."

Colin stares at me. "Will you show me?"

"Yeah," I reply, but it's barely a sound because I'm breathless. He's looking at me like I'm wondrous. I clear my throat. "What time is sunrise?"

"7:43."

"What time is it now?"

"12:38."

I blow out a breath. "That's a long time."

Colin shakes his head. "Yeah. And I think it's going to be harder than I originally planned. I was going to keep moving until morning, but I think I need to find somewhere to hide they wouldn't think to look."

"I know lots of hiding places, but I know somewhere comfortable," I offer as an idea comes to me. "My room."

"You think we can make it there without getting caught?"

"Maybe," I reply, "but I know how we can burn time in other hiding places on the way."

"You'd do that for me?"

Time slows when I look up into his face, his eyes intense. "I'd do anything for you," I tell him. Colin steps close, his mouth opening, but before he can say anything we hear a noise. Now his body is pressing mine into the wall, one hand dropping over my nose and mouth to muffle my breathing. We wait, bodies aligned, and I notice *exactly* how well the two of us work. His hips press just above my pelvis, my breasts brush his chest as I breathe. We're the perfect height that I'd barely have to tilt my head up to capture his mouth with mine.

I can't look away from his burning hazel gaze as it stares at the door, so intense I'd almost believe he could see through the wall.

The sounds of footsteps fade, and Colin looks down. He seems to realize what he's doing because he lets me go, and steps away.

"We need to get to Manderly," I whisper. "Come with me."

Colin

The Elise I'm with right now is not the one that I grew up with. This Elise is more confident, determined, and competitive. This Elise has secrets, and is surprising me in the best ways.

I'm a big believer in timing and I'm starting to wonder if my previous feelings about needing to be careful with her were right. Even though I'm only two years older, two years in high school is a big gap. Two years when I'm in college and she's still in high school can be stifling. Two years now? Maybe we're ready. Maybe all along I was holding back because this is the version of her that's meant for me. We had to finish growing and becoming ourselves for our pieces to fit the way they're supposed to.

I know in my heart that I could ask her to come hiking and exploring with me in the woods, and she'd not only say yes but be excited about it. That I could wake her up at any hour to head into the woods or explore campus and we'd have the time of our lives. Elise doesn't need me the way she did growing up anymore - while I'll always do whatever it takes to make her feel safe, she doesn't need to be protected in the same way. I used to want to stand in front of her, and I guess I still do, but now I want to be the guy that gets to stand next to her.

Even though I definitely never saw her in a sisterly way, I saw her as a kid. That's not the case anymore. Pressing against her in this tiny office, I am more than aware that she's all woman now. A woman that I love and trust, and will follow anywhere.

"Why Manderly?" I whisper.

She rolls her eyes and I love every time she can't hold herself back and gives me sass. It wasn't just the sounds she made that had me calling her Mouse, it was her demeanor too. Always timid, always holding back, always too careful, especially around me, but every once and awhile that other side would come out and it drove me wild.

"I want to make a deal with you." Her voice is measured and controlled, like she's hiding nerves. I don't know why that makes blood rush to my dick but I'll have to pick it apart later. I'm otherwise occupied right now.

"What kind of deal?"

"If we get to my room, if I help you survive the night..." Elise trails off and looks away. Whatever she's about to say makes her feel guilty and I don't understand why. I take her chin in my hand and turn her face so she can look up at me.

"What do you want, Mouse?"

Elise takes a deep breath and meets my eyes. "If you survive, I want you to sponsor me to join the Castle."

I blink a few times in surprise, and try to process this. Does she think I wouldn't have sponsored her anyway? Does she not realize that I'll do it no matter what, even if I don't make it through the night, because it's something she wants? I'd do anything to make her happy. I don't want to let it slip that she's already high on the recruitment list. If it keeps her with me tonight, I'll keep that to myself.

"You want to join the Castle?" I ask. She nods. "Then stay with me tonight, and I'll sponsor you." The innuendo in my statement can't be missed, and I see the faint blush on her cheeks. Elise nods in agreement.

"Are they gone?" she asks. I can feel her breath across my lips. I listen closely and don't hear a sound.

"Sounds like."

Elise shimmies away, leaving a her shaped space between me and the wall. I follow after her as she opens the door, looks both ways, and then walks out. I catch up with her and we move quietly through the back side of the Arts building. This is where all the classroom spaces are, so it's quiet and creepy.

Before she can turn the last corner toward the side door, I grab her hand

and yank her back. We watch as three guys in black hoodies walk past the door, looking around but not seeing us.

"How did you know?"

"They're circling the building. Now is the perfect time."

We get through the doors and start to walk quickly. Running would draw attention to ourselves and I love that she's so into this we don't have to talk about stuff like that. Our instincts on how to handle this are the same, and we're crazy in sync right now.

"Larson..." someone sing-songs. It sounds a lot like Tate and if he joined the Hunt and chased me, specifically, I'm going to kick his ass when this is over. I don't think they've seen us, I think they're calling out trying to mess with us.

We start moving faster, our hands finding one another and gripping tight. We're almost across the quad, and the trees that surround Manderly are in sight. Elise grips my hand tighter and we keep moving. My head is on a swivel.

"Got him!" Definitely Tate's voice yells from behind me, and then the pounding echo of footsteps on concrete starts. Elise and I break into a run, turning into the arbor that surrounds the administration building. We dive into a giant bush and I pull her around to the back of the tree, away from the direction our hunters will be coming from. My body is pressing hers into the bark and I don't let up or give her space. It's immediately a distraction and I know I should move back, but I don't.

I hold Elise right where I want her, and give in to my urges. I shift my hips against hers and delight in the high huff she lets out. Her eyes squeeze shut and I bite my lip imagining her face when she's feeling pleasure. My hands slide up her arms, her neck, until I'm cupping her face in my hands.

Her soft blue eyes snap open, and I am drawn to that small gap between her lips as they drop open slightly. Her dark hair is soft and damp beneath my fingertips and I want to dive into it, yank her head back, and kiss her like we don't have a care in the world.

"What are you doing?" She whispers.

I don't answer. I trail my thumbs across her cheekbones, then let one drop down to her mouth, pressing against her plump bottom lip. My fingers flex and dig into her neck, kneading the tense muscles there. All of her is tense. She doesn't know what to do right now and I want to take away her uncertainty.

I lean in and relish her sharp inhale as I ghost my mouth over hers, then up to the tip of her nose. I drag my own across her cheek and bury my face in her hair. I use it to muffle my groan as the soft, sweet scent of her barrels through my body and straight to my cock. Below it, I can still smell me on her – the sweatshirt hood is pulled up above her coat as extra protection. I want her to smell like this all the time – an undertone of me, marking her. Owning her. Fuck. My hips roll into hers and she gasps, her head snaps back, eyes wide open to meet mine.

"You smell so fucking good, Mouse." My whisper is pained, my cock throbbing even though it's the worst god damn time. "I want to know how you taste," I whisper quietly. So quiet I'm not sure she hears me, but then her eyes close and her head falls back against the tree. Her neck is exposed to me and I take that as an invitation.

I tilt my head and lean in, inhaling her again, before tracing the point of my tongue across her pulse. Elise's hands tighten on me and she arches. Her body presses against mine and I have to believe she wants me too. That it's because it's me that's touching her, and not just because she's being touched.

I lick her again and smile against her skin when she muffles a moan. She tastes like salt and peaches. Her sweat and her body wash. That same body wash might be in my shower because I've used it to jerk off when I'm feeling desperate for her. Tasting it straight off her skin nearly makes me come in my jeans.

Elise moves her hands to my chest and pushes me back. I go. She's breathing hard, conflict and confusion clear on her face.

Oh baby, I think, *can't you tell how I feel about you?*

"We need to keep moving. Do you have your keys?"

If this is how she wants to play it, fine.

"Yeah, why?"

She cocks an eyebrow at me. "Every member of the Trinity has a key to Manderly. We'll need yours."

My jaw drops in shock. "How do you know that? And it only gets us into one room."

"That's what you think. Have it ready, they've got keys too and we need to be fast." She stares at me until I reach in my pocket and take out my key ring, then move the heavy security key into my hand, ready to use. Elise nods and then makes her way out from the bushes.

We dart from tree to tree in the arbor, making our way to the side of the building. There are three black doors. Over each is a chess piece - the knight, the bishop, and the rook. The Cavalry, the Magistrates, and the Castle. I don't know where the hell she thinks we're going, but I run with her until we get to the door, get inside, and lock it behind us.

Elise

I don't know what Colin's doing and it's driving me out of my mind. He's choosing a really weird time to make a move but maybe it's because it's the first time we're in close proximity since coming to Elmwood. Maybe it's the tension of the experience and he's losing his mind.

Because there's no way the Colin I know licked my neck and pressed an erection into my hips. There's no way that he's being driven to distraction simply from the way I smell.

So before he can do something insane like kiss me and shatter my well-being forever, I push him away. We have to run, and I am oddly excited to show him my favorite secret place. While also showing him that I know more secrets than he can fathom.

We run, and I know we're seen, but it won't matter. The Trinity doors are ahead of us. We dive to the left and Colin quickly unlocks the door, pushes me inside, and then closes and locks it behind us. The room looks the same as I remember - a plain, windowless space with a small table against one wall, a candle on the table, and a tapestry of a horse on the wall above it.

The room's existence isn't a secret, but one of few secrets the societies have kept us what the rooms are used for. No one has let it slip, and I'm sure it's something completely benign.

"How do you know about this?" Colin asks, something like fear in his voice in addition to his curiosity.

"I found the other entrance."

He frowns. "That is the only entrance."

I step to the left of the tapestry and the wood paneled wall. I press hard against the big panel and it swings open, leading to an antechamber. We step through and I close the door behind us. I stop and look back - Colin can see all three entrances to the other rooms.

"I don't know what you do in there, but don't abuse the privilege of what I just showed you." While I trust him with my secrets, I don't want to violate the Societies either.

Colin nods, and follows me to the door into the main hallway of the basement of Manderly. It was the first residence hall on campus and then converted to the administration building after the old building endured a scandal. They built new residence halls, refit Manderly, and few people know it was ever anything else.

The hallway is dark but small high windows let enough light in for us to see. Our footsteps are muted but quick, and the biggest risk is ahead of us - we have to walk past the main doors and up the main staircase to get to where we're going. Colin grips my hand tight and takes the lead, correctly assuming we're heading up the stairs.

He watches out the windows, and flicks his head that we can go. I don't know why we're not talking right now but it feels like the right thing to do. Still holding hands, we run up the main staircase. I tug him to the left and we don't stop running. At the end of the hall is a huge pillar in an alcove. I pull him into the alcove and then around the pillar.

Colin's gasp when he sees the door is satisfying. I open it and he follows me to the ancient but sturdy iron spiral staircase. We don't say anything until the door closes. I use the light on my phone like I usually do and tug him along.

"How?" Is all he asks, and I laugh, secure that we're well-hidden here for the time being.

"People take things at face value - I don't. Why put a pillar in an alcove?" I shrug and we start up the stairs. "So I looked around the pillar. The door was unlocked, I went up the stairs. I found my favorite place on campus."

"When did you do that?"

"One of the first nights I was here."

He stops me with a tug of my hand. It felt so natural and comfortable I hadn't even realized we were still connected.

"How did you get in?"

Heat crawls up my face. "I was using the study room on the second floor and fell asleep. When I woke up, all the lights were out. So I went exploring."

Colin smiles at me and my embarrassment dissipates. "Of course you did." He shakes his head and we resume our ascent. "Remember the time we went to that Victorian house?"

Of course I do. Crenshaw Manor was one of those historical Victorian mansions that was restored and turned into a museum. It was a massive estate, still owned by the family, but they no longer wanted to occupy it. There were rumors in the early 1900s that Evander Crenshaw was some kind of criminal or vigilante, and that he had a secret lair in his house like a vintage Batman.

"If you'd read about Evander you would've come with me."

"I swear I thought you were fucking with me to play a prank," he laughs. "After that whole black dog thing..."

He trails off but I still shiver. On that same trip, Colin convinced Rosie and I that a black dog had been following our car and that it was an omen someone was going to die, and that it was going to be one of us. Then we stopped a gas station and a black dog really did come out of nowhere and bark and growl at us. The guy working at the station chased it off, said they had a tendency to get strays.

"I'm still mad at you for that."

"It's been 6 years."

I frown at him, but we're almost there. There's a landing that leads to the third floor, or another flight that leads to a trap door. We keep going up to the trap door. I have to let go of Colin's hand to open it, and he seems reluctant to let me. The door isn't heavy, and I may have come back with some oil to make the hinges work more easily. I climb through and onto the platform. Colin follows, and I close the trap door.

We're in the bell tower of Manderly. The huge unused bell looms over us, slightly ominous, but when you look over the railings at the campus - the stunning view can't be argued with.

"Holy shit," Colin breathes, and reaches back out for my hand. I take it, and stand next to him. Even with the overcast weather, we can see out over the grounds. Across the quad to the avenue, and the library, even his apartment building and the Cavalry house. To our left are the other academic buildings, and behind that we can see the looming stretch of the hedge maze. In the distance, what seems impossibly far right now, is the old gymnasium and then even further are the residence halls. They look warm and cozy, since they're vague shapes with golden lights.

Beyond the campus is only the woods. Miles of trees between us and civilization. A fog hovers, and with the mix of dying leaves and pine trees it's definitely ominous. A shiver of excitement runs through me and before I can stop it I'm grinning. I look at over at Colin and he's looking at me, a similar expression on his face.

"I'm glad you're so happy here, Mouse," he whispers, even though no one could hear us up here. "You belong here."

"I do," I nod and look back out. This is my happy place for a reason. The view, the spooky atmosphere, knowing that I'm seeing without being seen. I feel both small and enormous when I stand in this tower. I'm above everything yet still a part of it. I'm tiny in the scheme of the massive forest, another life hiding among the trees. Every time I look out, there's this twinge of fire in my chest that I can't explain.

"Sometimes I find myself wandering in the woods, and it's so primal," Colin's voice is quiet. I keep my reaction to myself that he's gone out there. That he's talking about it like he does it all the time. "I feel like I rose from the ground, or came from one of the trees. I feel connected when I'm out there - a part of something so much larger than myself."

"Will you take me sometime?"

Colin turns to me, a hard look on his face. "I will." Even though it's an answer, it sounds like a command. Like he'll drag me into that forest if he has to, and show me what he means. That connection we feel to this place is part of our connection to each other. For a moment I imagine running through the forest and Colin chasing me, catching me, and feasting on me.

I shiver again and breathe in sharply.

I don't miss that his eyes dilate, and drop down to my mouth again.

And again, I break the moment. I step back from the railing and sit down on the ground, shifting until I'm comfortable and leaning against the brick part of the tower. I pat the spot next to me and Colin joins me, pressing his body against mine so that we can keep warm.

"What time is it?" I know that I could look myself, but I want to distract him.

"2:38. Five hours to go."

Colin

It might be a hit to my manhood, but this building would be scary as fuck if I was in it alone. Having Elise here makes it exciting - an adventure. While I've always loved the area surrounding campus, she's showing me the place I've been for the last two years through entirely new eyes. There have been things right in front of my face that I missed.

I have no idea how she found the ceremony rooms, and I'm relieved she hasn't asked what they're for. The Cavalry and the rest of the societies are pretty open about most of our traditions because it keeps people from looking too closely at the things we don't share. The few mysteries that are only ours, unique to each one, the secrets we keep that bind us together. I have no idea what the Castle and the Magistrates do in their room.

Ours is used for initiation. An act of trust between members. The outgoing seniors are each assigned a freshman initiate. They share our history, talk about our responsibilities and goals, what it means to be connected to each other - a connection that's meant to go beyond the bounds of Elmwood. One of the phases of initiation is to kneel in that room and let your brother, the one you're replacing, hold a knife to your throat. I knelt and Alex Kelley held a blade at my neck. We held eye contact, his hand shaking, the metal nicking my skin, until enough time had passed that I had apparently demonstrated both my trust and my worthiness.

Alex was General his year. The fact that he picked me also means he marked me as the likely successor. If Peter follows protocol, I'll be named at the end of this year. It's a big responsibility, but one I knew I was taking on when Alex approached me just after winter break my freshman year. It never occurred to me I'd be considered to join the Cavalry, let alone lead it. I'm not a legacy, I don't think of myself as anything stand out or special. Maybe it's that I'm steady. I can be trusted to get the job done.

"Tell me more about how the year has been for you. Now that you can't avoid me," I give a huff of a laugh, but it's forced.

"If it makes you feel any better, you're not the only one I avoid." She gives a small smile but doesn't meet my eyes.

My stomach drops. "That makes me feel worse. You're putting me on the same level as Mathias."

Elise panics and turns to me, putting her hands on my thigh. "No. I'm sorry I didn't mean it like that."

"I know. I don't think he knows you're here."

"I've worked very hard to keep it that way. I don't know what he'd do." Her eyes shift away into the middle distance. "I can't tell if he hates me or you more." It's said softly but she might as well have screamed it in my ear for the way it makes me flinch. Elise knows that his enmity with her is tied to me, but I don't think she understands the whole of it. I don't even know the whole story of what happened that night, even if I know the reason why.

"What happened, Mouse?" I can't stop myself from asking this time. I need to know.

Elise blinks a few times, her eyes glassy, and it kills me but I wait. I can't back down.

"I knew when he started talking to me all of the sudden that he was up to something. Everyone knew you two were enemies, and everyone knew I was Rosie's best friend. There was an ulterior motive to him trying to flirt with me." My stomach twists with jealousy, remembering the way he'd lean over her, one arm on the locker above her head, touching her skin or twirling her hair. I remember the way she blushed and stammered, the relief I felt when she'd dart away from him. The leer he gave me when he knew I was looking.

"I assumed he was using me to get to Rosie, in order to get to you." Elise looks down at her hands. "There's a lot you don't know about that night."

"I know." I take one of her hands into both of mine and run my thumb over her knuckles. "So tell me. I'm here." I ride out the silence, waiting until she's ready.

"I lost Rosie," her voice breaks. "I couldn't find her, and when I did, she was passed out in the bedroom and Mathias was there." My entire body freezes. "He hadn't done anything, but I knew he was going to - before I could leave the room and get you, he grabbed me." Elise's free hand goes up to her neck, rubbing at the skin like she can still feel his touch. "I was up against the door and he had me so tight I couldn't speak, I could barely breathe." A tear drops down her cheek and lands on our joined hands.

"He said that it was me or her and I had to choose." My heart cracks open as her voice breaks. "So I chose me."

"Mouse," my voice is weak. "Can I hold you right now?"

She nods and I open my arms, relieved when she climbs into my lap. Her head rests in the crook of my neck and she fits perfectly there. I don't ask her to keep going, she will when she's ready. I kiss the top of her head.

"Things get kind of...choppy, after that. I remember him holding me down on the bed and touching me, and it hurt. I'd never done anything with anyone. All I wanted was to leave my body so he could do whatever it was to me and not hurt Rosie. He was so caught up in what he was doing to me that he didn't see her wake up. I remember her turning her head and meeting my eyes...and then her running away. The next thing I remember is you."

Rosie had run to me, and the second I'd seen her face I'd known something was wrong. Her eyes were glassy with intoxication but the fear in them was real. She didn't even have to say anything to me - I'd gotten off the chair where I was sitting and followed her to the bedroom.

Mathias had been holding Elise down by the throat as he used one of her hands to jack himself off. Her eyes were closed, her face was red, and I could see the tear tracks down her cheeks. He looked up when he heard us come in, and I remember the sound Elise made, a squeak of terror, and her slapping at his face. Everything for me went black after that. Rosie had to tell me what happened.

I'd dragged him out of the room, thrown him on the floor in the living room, dick still out, and shouted for everyone to hear that he'd tried to assault a drunk sophomore. It was a shitty move on my part because it wasn't hard for people to guess it had been Rosie or Elise, and it wasn't my story to tell. I'd yelled that anyone that talked to Mathias and any girl that touched him was dead to me. Any space they occupied would be empty in my eyes.

Then in front of everyone, I'd beaten the hell out of him. The videos of it made the rounds through all the group chats but no one ever turned it in. I never got in trouble for knocking out one of his teeth and giving him a chest full of bruises.

"You picked me up from the bed," she continues. "I remember you holding me for a really long time, just like this. Until I came back to myself."

I close my eyes and try to hold it together, but I crack. It's my turn to cry. A tear lands on her cheek and she looks up, searching for the source until she realizes it's me.

"Colin," she says, and brings her hands up to wipe them away. My eyes close at her touch. Elise never touches me. "I'm okay," she promises. "You were there. Rosie was there. I took care of myself."

"It never should have happened." I shake my head and open my eyes again. "I put a target on you and Rosie, and I didn't watch out for you."

"How did you put a target on me? It only happened because I caught him."

"No. It happened because he knew how I feel about you, and knew nothing would hurt me more. Not even hurting Rosie."

Elise stills, blinks, and frowns. "One, Mathias made his own shitty choices and used you as an excuse, but two, what do you mean how you felt about me?"

"Feel, Mouse. Present tense." I sigh. "I put distance between us because I thought it would keep you safe. I thought if I was indifferent he'd stop thinking of you as leverage. Instead, I should have had you with me. I should have protected you."

"I can protect myself," she huffs. "You didn't answer the question."

I look down at her, and slide one of my hands along her cheek and into her hair, holding her so she can't look away from me. I know she's going to try. She's going to dodge facing the way that I feel about her, or try to downplay it, but I won't let her. Elise can try but she's not going to pretend like I don't know myself or my feelings.

Her eyes drop when I lick my bottom lip, and lean in close so she can't see anything but me. It's a challenge - she won't drop her eyes from mine because that's weakness.

"Mathias saw that I was in love with you." Elise opens her mouth to protest but I drop my thumb over her lips and she stops. "Don't say anything, Mouse. I want you to sit with that knowledge and absorb it. Believe it. Know that the way I feel about you is constant and unshakable, and you've always been mine. I've always been yours."

She shakes her head, dislodging my thumb from where it rested on her plump lips. Before she can say anything, I close the distance between us and press my lips to hers. It takes only a moment before she melts into me. My insides are lit up from my toes to the top of my head. After another moment I tilt my head slightly, pressing deeper, and groan when she relaxes her mouth and the tip of her tongue touches mine.

There's no holding me back. She gave me an inch and I'm going to take a mile. I fucking devour her, holding her close to me and taunting her tongue with mine until she's whimpering. I swallow every sound. Her arms are wrapped around my neck as she clings to me, and I grab her around the hips and shift her until she spreads her legs and straddles me.

I let Elise have me. She's in control of the kiss now, grinding on me and driving me crazy as she learns the inside of my mouth and the shape of my lips. It's everything I ever wanted it to be the first time I kissed her - addicting, dangerous, perfect. As always, she is perfect.

When I grip her ass she moans, and it drives me to the edge. We're grinding on each other, my hard cock desperate for the heat I can feel through her sweatpants - through my sweatpants that she's wearing.

"Please," she whimpers.

"Please what, baby? What do you want?"

"I don't know." She sounds frustrated.

I've never asked Rosie about what Elise has done, and especially not with who. I don't deserve to know and I don't have the right to be upset about it because she watched me be with others without giving her the thought she deserved. But that answer is so fucking innocent it makes me wonder if she's ever been with anybody. If anyone else has ever made her come. I want to hate the darkly possessive feeling that rears it's monstrous head because I'm going to be the first to make her feel this. A further feeling of ownership over her settles deep into my bones.

I don't want to be a hypocrite but I love the idea that there's only going to be me. She will never know pleasure from anyone else. I'll own all of it, forever.

We rock into each other and I pull her down, grinding the ridge of my cock against her center.

"Oh." It's the softest, sweetest sound I've ever heard. I keep doing that, letting her reactions guide me until she's gasping and moving against me.

"Colin," she moans as she comes, shuddering over me and clinging tight to my jacket. I pull her to me and seal our mouths together, loving her with my tongue as she comes down, holding her close to me. Elise breaks the kiss and presses her forehead to mine, eyes still closed.

"Oh," she says again, an embarrassed smile on her face. When she opens her eyes and looks into mine, there's still uncertainty there. But it's okay, we have time. She's going to be with me all night, and then I'll convince her we're meant to be together the rest of our lives.

 Elise

Well. Okay then. I'm still straddling Colin, having destroyed his joggers with the first orgasm ever caused by someone other than myself. It's surreal, and I don't trust it. We'd had this huge emotional moment, when I'd finally told him everything about that one night - of course it brought us together. We were both vulnerable and we're in an intense situation right now.

Of course Mathias was aware that Colin cared about me, and that using me or Rosie would hurt him. That would be obvious to anyone. Despite what Colin said - which my brain shies away from acknowledging - I can't help but feel like a lot of it is guilt. He's let his guilt convince him that he owes me something, when he doesn't at all.

Except...why am I being such a pessimist about this? It's what I've wanted for as long as I can remember. I'm doubting this and myself for no reason. The only time I ever question my instincts and feelings is when it comes to him because I'm terrified to lose him.

I look down into his face. I know it so well. Probably better than my own. When I put my hands on him, his mouth lifts in enough of a smile for his dimples to peek out. I trace them with my thumbs, and give in to letting myself touch him like I've always wanted to do. The faint rasp of his scruff beneath my palms feels good. I smile when he shivers as my cold hands find his warm neck, and I imagine what it could be like if this was us all the time. If he was mine the way he says he is.

Colin talks about us like he's felt the way I have for as long as I have. Like we've been inevitable all along, we just had to see it. The thing is, I've put distance between myself and guys because I knew that until I got over Colin, I'd never be true to them. Physically, yes, but my heart would never really be theirs. Until he let me go, it would always belong to Colin, and that wasn't a show I was willing to put on. Thoughts chase across my mind.

"If you've felt this way about me - if you knew - then why - you never said anything. You were with other girls." Our history catches up to me all at once. Suddenly, I very much do not want to be on his lap or touching him, and I scramble to get up and put distance between us. It's so much colder without his body against mine.

Colin moves to stand and step close to me but I put my hands up to stop him. Hurt flashes across his face, and I don't regret it. He should hurt. If he supposedly loved me, then he should feel even a fraction of how much it killed me to see him with other girls. To hear him with them, on one particularly horrific occasion.

"I was, and I'm sorry. I wasn't ready for you, and I let my ego and my reputation get in the way. It took me too long to realize and stop what I was doing, and I hate that I hurt you. Remember when we did that big cabin trip like Rosie wanted?"

Of course I fucking do. Fall of sophomore year of high school, Rosie rented this huge cabin on the nearby lake for a weekend, invited a bunch of people, and we all got drunk and hung out. We swam, played board games, roasted marshmallows, and I accidentally heard Colin fucking Lola Talbot's brains out only to hear him tell one of his guy friends later that she was only his "hookup for the weekend."

My answering frown indicates that I do remember, and he continues.

"After it, the three of us were hanging out and talking about the trip and I said I was enjoying being single, and I'll never forget what you said to me - "There's a difference between being single, and being a man-whore." And I was shocked. It hurt so fucking much for you to talk about me like that, and even worse because I'd earned it. I was sleeping around, and that wasn't the kind of guy I wanted to be. It definitely wasn't what I wanted you to think of me. I stopped, after that. It took me awhile to figure out why, but it was because of you."

"I heard you. That weekend."

Colin pales. "What?"

"With Lola. I went upstairs to get something from my room. At first, I thought it was funny, then I heard your voice. I wanted to die, right that second, and then you made it worse."

"How?" His voice is hoarse.

"You told Ben she didn't matter. It was just fucking. Casual fucking for the weekend and that you wouldn't have touched her except she was there. It was like a week after she broke up with..." It hits me then that Lola had just broken up with Mathias. "Wow. Wow. That's fucking low."

"I know. I know it was. I haven't been with anyone since."

That catches me off guard. "What?"

"We got home, you said that to me, and I was done. I didn't want to be that person, and it's when I realized, truly, how I felt about you. That I needed you, and I needed to be worthy of you." Colin steps forward and takes my hand. I let him. "I've spent the last two and a half years waiting for my moment."

I frown at him. "And it's right now, in the middle of this?"

He smiles at me and I have to hold in my own at the absurdity of this situation. I haven't quite forgiven him for everything, but he's given me a lot to think about.

"It wouldn't have been if you'd actually spoken to me this year. You set up boundaries, I wanted to respect them."

I roll my eyes. "I didn't want you to get over-protective."

"Oh, I would have." He tugs me closer and his body heat envelopes me. Colin puts his arms around me. I don't return the gesture but I don't move away. He leans in to talk right into my ear, causing my skin to break out in goosebumps and my nipples to tighten. "Except I would've been protecting my hot girlfriend, and carrying her off like a caveman because I was tired of sharing her."

I lean back and arch an eyebrow. I'm going to make him work for this. "Who says I'd be your girlfriend?"

Colin blanches and then glowers at me. I take a step back and check my phone. It's almost half past three - we should get moving if we want to get to my room. There's a lot of campus between us and there. Even though we could stay here all night, my warm bed is calling to us.

I grab my backpack and open the trap door. "Come on. We have to go."

Colin follows me down the stairs without saying anything. I can feel the grumpiness radiating off of him, and to be honest, I'm amused. While the hurts of the past were re-opened by that conversation, I feel like they're healing in a new way. A way that has a lot of information I was missing.

We get to the ground floor and to the back door. There's no glass, so we can't see outside.

"We have to get to hedge maze," I tell him. "I can get us through, and then we're almost there."

"Stay close." He takes my hand. "Is this okay?"

"Yeah." I give him a soft smile and squeeze. He squeezes back, a little of the tension leaving his body.

We run from the door to the closest building, moving from shadow to shadow until we reach the science building. There's a concrete mall with an obnoxious fountain, and beyond it is the entrance to the maze. Colin looks around for anyone and listens carefully, but there's only silence. Maybe we hid for long enough that they gave up.

"If we get separated, put your right hand on the wall and follow it. If you get to the clearing with the Hecate statue, go straight past her left shoulder, take the first right, the second left, and you'll be out."

"How do I know if it's Hecate?" Colin asks, perplexed.

"She's wearing a spiky crown and wrapped in a snake."

"Got it. Let's go."

The silence was too good to be true, but the voice that calls his name sends a chill down into my soul. Colin yanks me behind him and turns to face Mathias.

"Well, well you've been keeping secrets, Larson." Mathias's grin is lecherous. "Hey, Mouse, I've missed you. It's a shame no one told me you were here."

"Don't call her that, asshole."

"I've had my fingers in her cunt, I can call her whatever I want. Can you say the same?" His laugh echoes across the empty mall. I desperately wish someone else was here, anyone else from the Cavalry to see how he's behaving. Not that they would stop it, but they need to know what kind of filth they let in.

"We have to run for it," I whisper to Colin. "Into the maze and split up. He can't catch us both."

"No," Colin growls, "I won't risk that."

"We have to. We have to get away somehow and you know that it changes nothing if you surrender. The only way we can be safe is to run."

"Fuck." Colin turns us. Go." Without any further discussion we turn and run into the maze. It starts with a long path with no branches. When we get to the end, it's left and right.

"Go right. Hand on the wall. I can get out this way."

"Be careful," Colin says, and then yanks me to him by the front of my jacket and presses his mouth to mine. I kiss him back, communicating that it's okay.

"How precious," Mathias coos from the mouth of the maze. "The pussy finally caught his mouse."

We push away from each other and run. I'm hoping that Mathias's desire to beat Colin will overpower his need to mess with me. That he'll think it's more important to catch the Cavalry's offering for the Hunt than it is to settle a high school grudge. Except something inside me truly doubts that Mathias is capable of moving on. I got away from him, was part of his humiliation at Colin's hands, and now he knows something is going on between Colin and I, even if we don't know what that is.

When I hear footsteps behind me, I know my instinct is right. He's coming after me.

I run faster, my heartbeat audible in my head as panic and genuine fear rocket through me. Adrenaline scrambles me, and I make the wrong turn. I try and correct, visualizing the maze and how I can get to the Hecate statue. I send up a prayer to her, hoping for a little witchcraft to save me.

It seems she's not on my side because Mathias tackles me from behind as I reach the clearing with her statue. The hazy moonlight shines down on the pure white marble as I thump to the ground. Mathias rolls me over and straddles my chest.

"You're supposed to catch him if you want to win," I taunt.

"Oh, catching you is winning a much better game," he laughs. "Plus, we have unfinished business. Things were going hot and heavy until you left me hanging." The amusement in his eyes drops, and only cruelty shows. "Maybe he'll find me fucking you, debasing his little mouse while she cries around my cock."

"Fuck you," I spit at him.

"Exactly." Mathias starts to slide down my body and I fight back, pushing him off with my hips and kneeing him in the back. "Don't make me hurt you, Elise." He reaches up and caresses my face. "I could make it feel good, if you behave."

"Not a fucking chance," Colin says, and I tilt my head to see him standing behind us. I'm stunned into paralysis when Colin grips Mathias's hair, yanks his head back, and punches him right in the face. There's an audible crunch, and a heavy, sickening thud as Mathias falls to the ground when Colin lets go. He's unconscious.

I scramble up and run to him, burying my face in his chest. Colin keeps me tucked under his arm as we walk across the clearing toward the exit from the maze. We keep moving because there's no telling how long Mathias will be knocked out. I was only semi-relieved to notice that he was still breathing.

"How did you find me?"

"I realized pretty quick he wasn't following me, so I went your way. It took me too long, I'm sorry. Fuck, I'm sorry. I let him hurt you again." He holds me so tight our legs are tangling together. We're almost out of the maze, and I pull him into an alcove, hiding for a minute before we have to run to our next hiding spot.

"You saved me again. I don't blame you."

"I keep pulling you into this shit," he grunts. "My mistakes keep punishing you."

I tug on his jacket until he looks at me. "I chose this tonight because I wanted nothing more than an excuse to be with you. I was waiting for my moment too."

"What?"

"I made a deal with Rosie, and my side of it was that I had to finally tell you how I feel. That I've been head over heels for you since the first time we met." I go up on my toes so my lips can meet his, and the kiss is sweet and dirty at the same time, our tongues dancing as we share breath.

"That's to be continued," he says after breaking the kiss. "We have to go."

"To the old gym, the side door. I have a key."

Colin shakes his head and smiles, learning another one of my secrets. We clasp hands and dash into the darkness.

Elise

Colin and I don't encounter anymore hunters before we reach the door. I make sure it's locked behind us, then walk through the hall to the main pool doors.

The scent of chlorine and old stone soothes me. While Elmwood joined the modern world and built a big fancy athletics building a few years ago, they kept the old gymnasium going. The upstairs is random offices and study spaces, but the bottom floor is still the pool and the locker rooms. The first time I came here I saw a sign that they were hiring lifeguards. I immediately applied. Two nights a week I hang out with the mostly unused pool. It meant I got keys to the building and the pool.

I unlock the door to the pool and make sure it's locked behind us.

"How?"

"I lifeguard." I laugh at his shocked expression. "It's relaxing."

"You're incredible."

I blush and walk along the pool. The only light comes from inside of it, but it's bright enough. I put down my backpack and unzip my jacket, relaxing for the first time since I walked into Colin's room earlier tonight. We only have a handful of hours left to survive. I collapse on the bench and start taking off my boots.

Colin sits next to me and takes off his jacket, but freezes when I stand up and remove my shirts. I have no idea what I'm doing, but I know that right now I need to run with my impulses. My impulse is to give in to what I've always wanted, and that's him.

"What are you doing, Mouse?"

I look at him over my shoulder as I reach behind my back to unclasp my bra.

"Skinny dipping." It's immensely gratifying when I watch his eyes drop down my body, and the hard swallow he does as he meets my eyes. "Are you coming?" I drape my bra over the bench and then turn to shimmy out of his joggers. I'm bare underneath, and when I step out of them I'm standing naked in front of the only boy I've ever loved.

I don't look at him. Instead, I step up to the edge of the pool and dive in.

The water is always ridiculously warm in here, barely below bath water temperature. It feels good to be warm and weightless right now. I hadn't realized how much all this running and tension had messed with me. There's a splash nearby and I feel the water move as Colin jumps in too.

I pop my head up above the water and take a deep breath. At this part of the pool I can just reach the bottom. Colin is waiting, watching, the water hitting him at mid-chest. My thighs squeeze together and I shift. Even though we're feet away from each other, knowing that we're naked together in the pool turns me on.

I start backing away toward the shallower end of the pool, and Colin matches each step, tracking me. He gets closer, and I slow down, watching the water get lower and lower on his body until it's at his hips. Slowly, I stand up. The water races down my body and reveals all of me to him.

Colin's eyes don't leave mine - they're intense and dilated, and the expression on his face is fierce. Hesitant, I step forward until I can feel his body heat.

"I've only ever been touched in anger," I whisper, and put my hand on his bare chest. "Make me feel good."

In a second, he has his hands on me, yanking my body against his. All that hot skin pressing against me makes me whimper, and he captures the sound with his mouth. Colin drags us back into deeper water, then grabs my thighs and wraps me around him. I can feel his cock but he's focused on me, devouring my mouth in a way that has me squirming and grinding against his abdomen.

I squeak when he lifts me up further and sets me on the edge of the pool.

"Do you trust me?" he nearly growls.

"Yes," I answer immediately.

Colin's hands rest on my knees, and now his eyes move away from mine, trailing along my body. They linger on my breasts, and he licks his lips, which makes me squirm again. Gently, he pushes my legs open and I take a deep breath as he sees my wet core. I'm wildly aroused, even if I'm still upset with him, and I want him to touch me. So, so badly.

"You've got such a pretty pussy." He steps closer and slides his hands beneath my legs. "I think I should give it a kiss, don't you?"

I can only nod, vehemently. Colin's grin is absolutely filthy, and I spread my legs open wider in invitation. I don't take my eyes off him when he starts kissing down my inner thigh, or when he runs a finger softly over my slit. I flinch from the sensitivity but it's not a bad feeling.

Colin lowers himself, moves my thighs to his shoulders, and looks straight into my eyes as he licks me with the flat of his tongue. The wet warmth of it feels amazing. I can't look away when he dives between my pussy lips, the tip teasing my clit.

"Oh," I gasp. It's a soft sound that echoes in the large space. That triggers something in him and his eyes close as he presses in, his shoulders spreading me as wide as I can go, and he eats my pussy in earnest. I've never felt anything like it, and it's not anything like I imagined it would be.

It's better.

I lean back, resting one hand behind me while the other dives into his hair. My hips rock against his face and I don't know if anything I'm doing is right or wrong, I only know if it feels good. Colin doesn't stop me. My reactions seem to make him even hungrier for me.

When he stops and looks up at me, his lips and chin are shiny with my arousal. He presses a finger against my entrance.

"Is this okay? I'll be gentle."

I nod. "I know."

"You taste so good, Mouse, but I need more. I need you to come for me." As he talks, Colin slides his finger inside me. I hear how wet I am as he slides it back out, then in again. "Do whatever it takes. Move your hips, ride my face, put me where you want me. I'll do anything you want." There's something desperate and supplicating in the tone of his voice and the way he's looking at me. His eyes are soft but his body is tense. I gasp when he slides two fingers inside me, and my hips roll, trying to take them deeper.

"Keep going," I beg.

When he puts his mouth back on me, alternately sucking and licking my clit, I do what he said. I thrust my hips against his face as I lean back on my hands for leverage. The view of him between my legs is enough to bring me to the edge of an orgasm all by itself.

"Colin," I breathe out his name, thinking of all the times I cried it out while touching myself. Now I'm saying it to him, about him, making me come for the second time tonight.

"Please don't stop," I beg again, thrusting hard and then tensing as I start to come. I don't hold back my moans, and he presses his fingers deep, moving against a spot inside me that I didn't know I had.

I'm out of breath when I come down but I want more. I slide away from him, back onto the pool deck, and tug at his arms until he's climbing out with me. As soon as he's out, it's my turn to attack him. The taste of me is on his lips and I love knowing that. I press myself against him, seeking more, and not sure how to ask for it. Afraid to ask for it.

"Elise," he moans, breaking our kiss. "We have to stop, baby."

"Why?" I genuinely mean that. There's no reason to stop.

"You really want your first time to be here, like this?"

That makes me laugh. "It's perfect. I promise."

I pull away until I'm standing and stepping toward one of the benches that run along the outside of the room. After a second of hesitation, he stands up and I don't have the control that he did to keep eye contact. Mine immediately drop to his hard cock. Again, not like I imagined, but even better. It's long, thick, and smooth. My mouth waters.

When he wraps his hand around it and starts to move, my whole body reacts - an electric tingle goes through me, tightening my nipples even further, and more arousal floods my core.

"You like to watch me do this?" Colin's voice is heated and my mouth parts on a sigh. "I wish you'd been there to watch all the times I got off like this, thinking of you." He steps closer and I step back, and then he moves around me to sit down on the bench. The idea that he's come thinking of me, the same way I have of him, is intoxicating. My eyes flutter as I start to lose my sanity.

I step between his legs and look down at him, aware that he's still stroking his cock. Colin leans in and kisses across my collarbone, then down to my breasts. He takes one nipple into his mouth and sucks before lathing his tongue across the sensitive tip. My back arches into him and I don't hold back the moans he pulls from me.

I'm breathing hard, getting worked up, and pull his mouth off my chest so I can kiss him again. There are so many things I want that I can't make up my mind. His hands are everywhere as I taste him, already addicted to it.

Letting go of the rest of my inhibitions, I drop to my knees and wrap my hand around his cock. Colin stops stroking himself and groans as I take over, moving along his velvety flesh. I take a deep breath, try and remember what I've learned from watching porn, and lean forward to take the head of him into my mouth.

The skin of his cock is warm and smooth against my tongue, and I am overwhelmed with the scent of evergreen and the unique scent of his skin. I take him as deep as I can, breathing through my nose, and exerting pressure with my lips and tongue.

"Fuck, Elise, fuck," Colin groans as his hands dive into my hair. I keep going, enjoying the feeling and the way he's letting me explore even as it teases him. "I've thought of this a thousand times - watching you take my cock in your pretty mouth." As he talks, my hand moves to my clit and I make slow, firm circles, turned on by his words. "Every time you mouthed off, I'd end up in my room jacking off to the thought of getting you on your knees and skull fucking the sass out of you."

I moan, and the vibration of my voice causes him to groan again. He tugs at my hair and I release his cock, looking up at him. He's so turned on he's furious, and it gives me a thrill through my entire body. Colin pulls my face close to his and takes over for my hand, teasing my clit with his rough finger. He's holding me so tight I can't move. I like it.

"Colin," I whimper. I'm shaking I'm so turned on, and even though it's going to hurt, I want him inside me as soon as possible, as deep as possible. "Please."

"This is only the beginning, Mouse." He lets me go and leans back. "I'm all yours. Fuck me how you want - you're in control."

I swallow hard but stand up and move to straddle him. I'm wetter than I've ever been in my life, but still a little nervous as I move him to my entrance. I start to push down, hissing a little at the stretch and burn, but I slide up and down, gripping his shoulders, taking more of him in with each stroke until my ass is resting on his thighs.

That's when I notice Colin is holding his breath.

"Are you okay?" I'm afraid I've done something wrong. Colin lets out his breath and rolls his hips, hitting even deeper. It hurts and feels good at the same time.

"You're so fucking tight. You feel perfect." He takes my face in his hands. "I haven't been with anyone in over two years, waiting to get inside this perfect pussy, but I don't want to hurt you. You told me to make you feel good. I'm trying to keep control."

I dive forward and suck his bottom lip between my teeth. "I didn't say it couldn't hurt," I whisper, revealing something about myself. "Show me how much you've wanted me." I roll my hips, following the instinctive ways my body wants to move. "Let's lose control."

Colin groans and brings my mouth to his, and starts to move. My legs are on the bench, and I start pushing myself up and down, riding and grinding and repeating whatever feels good. We're shifting against each other, fast and hard, and it hurts in the ways that I want. I feel fuller than I ever have, a kind of fullness I didn't know I was missing.

Every time my clit hits his pelvic bone, I get closer and closer. The orgasm is building again, and I'm so sensitive it sends shocks through my body. My movements turn primal, uncoordinated, and I'm digging my nails into his back and shoulders, chasing the edge I want to reach.

"Colin!" I scream it again as everything around me blanks out and all I can feel is where our bodies meet.

"Elise," he groans before wrapping both arms tight around me and pounding me down, hitting so deep I cry out. His hips roll beneath me, drawing out his own release.

When he lifts his head, the kiss he gives me is unimaginably gentle. This was everything I wanted it to be, and with the person of my dreams.

Colin

It might be a couple years since I've had sex, but I know that doesn't explain how amazing it felt with Elise. The only explanation I have is that it feels better when your emotional attraction is deeper than your physical attraction to them. The connection with her was as important as fucking her. Feeling her come on my cock was multiple layers of satisfaction.

We stay joined for a long time before she slides off of me.

"How do you feel?" I ask.

There's a tightness in my chest that lets go when she smiles, and it lights up her whole body. "Fucking amazing."

I laugh and then grab my boxers from my pants, and hand them over to her. "Use these to clean up. We'll both go commando the rest of the night."

She laughs in return and takes them. I can't look away from her body, and I definitely want to watch as she wipes away my come as it drips from her sweet pussy. The possessive, monstrous feeling that rises inside me has my cock rising again too. Elise notices, watching with heat in her eyes. I don't want to hurt her, so I grab my pants and cover myself, tucking my dick away.

When we're both dressed, I pull her to me, needing to feel her body against mine.

"This changes everything, Mouse."

She breaks eye contact and shifts to stare over my shoulder. "It doesn't have to."

"I want it to. I can't let you go after this." I pull her closer and lean in to breathe against her neck. The possession inside me takes over, and without thinking I sink my teeth into her, biting at the juncture of neck and shoulder. Elise cries out, but not in pain.

"I'm the only one who gets to hear you sound like that, the only one who gets to know how that greedy pussy feels when you come. I'm the one who owns you, Elise." I pull back and hold her by the nape, not letting her look away. "I'm the one who gets to give you pleasure, and pain." I lean in and bite her lip, not breaking eye contact. "I'm the one who gets to love you."

Her eyes search mine. "You don't love me."

"I do," I disagree with her. "And you love me. You've always been my someday. Someday is now."

Her eyes flutter shut and I let her go when she moves to bury her head in my chest, clinging to me as her reality shifts. Now is the time for me to put it all out there between us.

"I've seen all of you for so long, Elise. The way you make me laugh, your endless curiosity, the way you dwell on the macabre without ever being dark yourself, the deep way you care for people. You'd do anything for them, without expecting anything in return. I want you to expect things from me. I want you to expect everything from me, and I'll give it to you. I've been trying to figure out how to tell you since the summer."

She laughs, and looks up at me. "Does Rosie know?"

I blush because the reason Rosie knows is embarrassing as fuck. "Yeah. She's known for awhile. You?"

"That bitch," Elise hisses, but there's no real heat behind it. "She's known since 4th grade when she found a notebook that was pages of MASH with your name."

"That's less embarrassing than what happened with me, I promise you."

Elise doesn't say anything, just lifts her eyebrows and waits. I can't keep eye contact. I look away and bite my lip.

"She caught me masturbating to a picture of you."

I feel Elise freeze, and the terror that I've truly fucked this up comes over me. I chance a glance at her, and she's somewhere between shocked and turned on.

"When? What picture?" The intrigue in her voice has me relaxing slightly.

"At the start of the summer...it was that one you sent me on your birthday." The thing is, I know she was tipsy when she sent it. Elise had been wearing a fitted gold dress, showing off her body, and in the picture she'd sent it was slipping off one shoulder, revealing her black lace bra. Her hair was disheveled like she'd just been fucked, and the lazy smile on her mouth and slightly mussed lipstick...fuck it had driven me crazy.

To my surprise, she laughs, so hard she has to put her face back in my chest. "I guess it worked then." There are almost tears in her eyes when she looks back up at me.

"What are you talking about?"

"Rosie dared me to send that to you. It was my last dare of the night."

"I'm not sure how to feel about that."

"It provides some clarity on your answering text," she glares at me, "which just said: damn."

Now it's my turn to grin. I slide my hands down her body until I'm cupping her ass, then lean in to talk right into her ear while grinding myself against her. Even thinking about that picture gets me hard, and knowing she took it just for me makes it even more intoxicating.

"As in, damn, you look so fucking sexy I want to get my mouth on every inch of your body." I slide my hands into the joggers so I can feel her soft skin and tease her lower back and the top of her ass. "Damn, you're the most beautiful woman I've ever seen in my life. Damn, I would give up food and water if it meant I could eat that pussy for sustenance instead. Damn, what I wouldn't give to be the guy you send sexy selfies to, to be the guy who makes you come, to be the guy that gets to taste you every day for the rest of his fucking life."

Elise reaches up and turns my head so she can kiss me. We're pressed up against each other, moving and grinding, getting ourselves all worked up again. I've needed her for years, and trying to hold back now that I can have her is an exercise in self-control that I deserve a damn trophy for. I pull away from her.

"We have to go."

"You're right. I know." She smiles at me. "I can send you better pictures than that if you need spank bank material."

I growl at her. "Who did you send pictures to?"

"Nobody. They don't exist yet. But I'd take them for you." With that pronouncement getting me to the absolute edge of my control, she steps away from me and gets her coat on. I take a deep breath and do the same. We get everything together, and leave the pool.

I follow her through the building until we get to the back door.

She freezes, and when I follow her gaze, I see why. Mathias is out there, leaning against a low wall. I don't think he knows we're here, but he's probably guessed we were trying to get to the residences.

"I don't want him to get away with it anymore," her voice cracks and it kills me.

"Away with what?"

"Being an asshole. I think...I think we should trap him."

"Where are we going to do that?"

The grin on her face when she turns to look at me is pure evil. "I know exactly the place."

 Elise

Colin keeps pouring his feelings out, saying everything I ever fantasized about, and yet I can't say anything back. The words aren't making it from my brain to my mouth and I'm not sure why. It might be fear, or doubt, or the very real concern that I have a head injury and this is the beautiful hallucination before I die. It's all as possible as the reality that he is as in love with me as I've always been with him.

He certainly keeps demonstrating it for me.

We keep an eye on Mathias while I go over the plan.

We are next door to the absolute scariest building on campus - the old infirmary.

Being as isolated as Elmwood, it was to the College's benefit to run their own mini hospital for about a century. It hasn't been a hospital in two decades, but they kept using it for other things until five years ago. It took me weeks to talk myself into getting inside and having a look around.

The first floor was the only one recently used, so the upper floors are all abandoned and straight up scary. They also have psych rooms on the third floor that can only be opened from outside.

If this is going to work, we need a head start. Colin and I go back to the front of the building and I send up a wish to the universe that no other hunters are out there. It also wouldn't surprise me if Mathias had called dibs on getting Colin and threatened anyone who got in his way. While Colin says Mathias has stayed low key since they've been here, that level of cruelty can't be hidden forever. I'm sure he's revealed himself in subtle ways already.

There's no one in the front of the building. We look around the corner and Mathias is still sitting on the wall, arms crossed, unnaturally still. If I didn't know him, it would seem like some hot demon was waiting in the night, maybe even the Devil himself. Golden hair, light eyes, a tall, fit body, and a face so chiseled it would cut. He's intimidating. His beauty is empty though, and full of malice.

Colin turns to me. "Are you sure?"

"We have to show him that we aren't afraid of him. I don't want to hide from him anymore."

"Okay." We share a quick kiss, and it already feels natural. A thrill goes through my stomach.

Colin takes my hand and then we run. We aren't quiet. The plan only works if Mathias notices us, and doesn't think we notice him. There's a window to the right of the main door that doesn't lock. I keep my eyes focused ahead of me, looking like I'm not terrified at all that my nightmare is coming for us.

"He's following," Colin says quietly.

The window is ahead, and I chance a quick glance over my shoulder. Mathias is standing in the shadow of the building, watching us. It's not about catching us, it's about cornering us. Mathias wants to play with his food, and it looks like we're walking straight into his plans.

The window slides open and I boost myself inside. Colin follows, and closes the window behind us. We're in an office suite that used to be campus counseling. Even they found the building to be too creepy. They were the final holdouts before the college gave up and moved everybody out. Last I checked, there's still no plans for this space and I think that's odd. A mystery for another day.

I lead Colin out, and we wait. Mathias has to be able to follow us if this is going to work. When I hear the window open, I start walking down the hall to the main staircase. We talk quietly about nothing - class schedules, dining hall food - enough to make Mathias believe we don't know he's there. Loud enough that it seems like we're not afraid.

In actuality, my heart is pounding out of my chest and I'm sweating. I'm scared out of my mind, even with Colin right beside me. For this to truly work, I have to be bait.

We walk up the stairs and Mathias follows. The third floor is looming when he breaks the silence. The plan is working.

"Going to play Doctor?" He taunts. I jump and scream, honestly scared even though I knew he was there.

"Run!" Colin yells. We race up the last few stairs, share a look, and then run in opposite directions. Colin will do what he did in the hedge maze - circle back as soon as he knows Mathias is following me.

I run, hoping I'm not caught until I get where I need to be. The building is shaped like an L, and I need to get around the corner to get to the psych rooms. Why they felt they needed so many when they made the building is disconcerting, but tonight it's going to save me.

Mathias grabs my backpack and it sets me off balance. I wiggle out of it, relieved when I hear him swear and stumble. I'm almost to the first room.

I jump inside and make a show of trying to pull the door shut. Mathias dives at me and wrenches it open. He's breathing hard, his eyes so dilated I can't see the color, only black. He's high on the chase. When my eyes flicker down his body, he's also hard. Delightful.

"Little Mouse, caught in a trap," he rasps. "About to get eaten by a ravenous predator." Mathias licks his lips. It's salacious and terrifying. I'm shaking but holding strong as I wait for Colin.

I keep stepping back until I feel the covered wall behind me. Mathias crowds me, his body heat like lava in the cold room as he traps me. I can see the sheen of sweat on his skin and the bite marks in his bottom lip.

"I'm going to give you one chance, Elise."

My head rears back in surprise. "A chance to what?"

Mathias leans in and inhales me, then presses his hips and hardness into my body. I still, and try to control my panic.

"Fuck, you smell so good. Fear and innocence." He laughs to himself and then focuses on me again. "A chance to choose me."

I'm stunned into silence.

"I didn't mean to hurt you that night. I truly wanted you." He grips my chin in his hand so I can't look away. "I dream about you. You haunt me." There's actual pain in his voice and a desperate look on his face. "I understand why he's obsessed with you - but he had your whole life and never made a move. The first time I got close to you, I tried. I tried to show you." He shakes his head. "I'm sorry it went like that at the party, I just...got my hands on you and lost my mind. It's hard to keep control when you're under me."

"So that's why you threatened to rape me in the maze?" I snap out, done with this pity party.

He skims his lips over mine. "It was an empty threat. I don't want to hurt you."

I pull back as much as I can. "Too late, asshole." Then I bring up my knee and hit him in the crotch. He lets me go but doesn't go down. I run, trying to get to the door and get away, plan be dammed.

Mathias growls and tackles me, and I go down on the padded floor. We wrestle, pushing and holding, and I try and scratch him.

"Colin!" I scream, wondering where he is, afraid he got hurt, afraid for myself. I focus on fighting Mathias.

Suddenly, he's ripped off of me and goes flying back into the padded wall. I crab walk back into the hallway, then stand up to watch as Colin shoves Mathias back.

"Stay down, or I'll give you a fucking concussion," Colin threatens. Mathias glowers, but doesn't get up. Colin walks backward out of the room. When he's clear, I close the door. Through the window we see Mathis get up and run at it, but other than the thump of his hit, it doesn't move.

"We'll send someone to get you when the Hunt is over," Colin shouts, and then pulls me away. It's almost 5:30. He'll be fine for a few hours.

"Where were you?" My voice cracks and Colin yanks me to him.

"Somehow I walked past you. I was looking like crazy and then I heard you. I'm so sorry."

"It's okay. I held my own. It was...weird." As we walk out of the building, I tell Colin what Mathias said. I can see his fury building but appreciate that he holds it back. I squeeze Colin's hand. "I'm okay."

We get back to the office window and climb out. The sky is already getting light.

"Almost there," I smile at him, weirdly excited now to show him my room and where I am on campus.

Colin guides us through the shadows. We don't see anyone else. Harwood-Locke is within sight, and we run across the street and don't stop until I'm swiping us into the building.

When we get to my room, I'm relieved that Cynthia isn't there. She's been dating someone new and staying with them a lot even though she's being super secretive about who it is.

"This is it," I say and turn to look at him. He's not looking around, he's only looking at me.

Colin

The part of me that wants to see my Mouse's space is dominated by the part of me that recognizes we're finally safe and alone and I can have her. I unzip my jacket and let it fall to the ground. I slide out of my shoes, never breaking eye contact with her.

I step up to her, enjoying the way her breathing picks up and her skin flushes. I unzip her jacket and let it fall like mine. She's still wearing my clothes, and smells like the perfect mix of us both. I'd given her a sweatshirt I'd been wearing lately because I wanted to mark her with my scent.

She shivers when I pull the tie on the joggers and slide them over her ass and hips until they drop down her legs to pool at her feet. Mouse steps out of them, watching me with heat and patience. I grab the bottom of the sweatshirt and the t-shirt, and she lifts her arms so I can remove them.

"When I saw you earlier, it looked like you were only wearing my sweatshirt. I liked that." I slide my hands up and down her sides, enjoying the way her sensitive body reacts.

"You're not getting it back," she nearly moans.

"I don't mind. I like it." I lean in and kiss her, parting her lips and dipping my tongue into her sweet mouth. I kiss her slow and deep, sensual but teasing. Her hands dive underneath my shirt and I only break the kiss to remove it when she pushes. Her little hands dive down and tremble as she removes my pants, forcing them down my body.

"I want you," she begs. "Please."

I follow as she walks back to her bed, touching her everywhere. When she falls back on it, I kiss down her body until I'm lip to lip with her pussy, and don't hesitate to take and taste her. Mouse let's her legs drop wide open, offering herself to me. She tastes so good, heavy and sweet, and I keep going, sucking and biting, until her legs clamp shut around my head and she's bucking against me.

Now she's ready.

I move over her, looking down into her dazed face.

"Tell me you're mine." It's a command, and it's not sweet. I need to know. She's admitted to having feelings, but not what she wants to do about them. I tease the head of my cock over her clit, torturing us both.

"Tell me I own this pussy." I slap my cock on her and she moans, hips bucking. "Tell me, Mouse."

"You do," she breathes out.

"Say it," I grit out and suck on the bite mark I've already left on her neck.

"You own my pussy." Her little voice is hesitant, maybe embarrassed, but she said it, and unleashed the monster. I glide inside her tight, soaked cunt, and groan at the satisfaction of it. I hold myself deep inside, letting her adjust, struggling to maintain control.

"I'm okay," she whimpers and starts to move against me. That's permission for me to move, and I do. I press myself against her body, keeping our faces close, and snap my hips. Her pussy grips me, and I know that I'm not going to last long. Every time I thrust deep, I grind and roll my hips, hitting her clit and giving her pressure that she seems to like. Soon, I'll know every reaction, every tiny tell that will help me give her maximum pleasure. When we've recovered from tonight, I'm going to spend hours making her come.

I have years to make up for.

"Colin," she gasps, "harder. Please."

"You want me to fuck you harder, Mouse?" I do it, but love taunting her. I'm slamming deep into her and I can feel my body tighten, ready to explode. "Come for me, Mouse. If I own this pussy, you come when I tell you."

Her nails dig into me and she rolls her hips. It hits her hard and she starts to scream. She bites down on my shoulder and the pain of it barrels through me and makes me come immediately.

"Fuck!" I shout and pound her into the mattress, my orgasm chasing hers. I spill inside her as she cries and whimpers into my skin. It feels so damn good.

We're both breathing hard when I lift my body from hers. "That was insane." I look to my right and can barely see the teeth marks on the meat of my shoulder.

"Sorry," she blushes.

"I marked you too," I shrug and run a finger over the bruise I left on her. "I like it."

She moans when I slide out of her and move to the side. I run my hand over her stomach. "Sore?"

"A little. I'll...be right back." She gets up and won't meet my eyes as she throws on a bathrobe and leaves the room. Anxiety twists in my gut, and I steal the joggers she borrowed from me and slide them on. They smell like her pussy, and I feel smug about how I made her come tonight, and kept her turned on. Whatever she's thinking, I can reassure her. We're meant to be together.

Elise steps into the room, her face slightly more relaxed. She sits next to me on the bed and takes my hand.

"I've been having trouble figuring out what to say to you."

"About what?" I tease her knuckles with my thumb.

"We've both had feelings for a long time, apparently," she swallows and continues, "and I'm scared that reality won't live up to your imagination. That I'll give you what's always been yours, and you'll realize that now that you've had me, you don't want me."

She sniffles and it breaks my heart.

"Mouse..."

Elise shakes her head and cuts me off. "If I let myself fall the rest of the way in love with you, I'll never recover if you leave me. I've never loved anyone else. I don't think I ever will." She finally looks at me, her eyes swimming with tears, and I take her face in my hand.

"I don't ever want to love anyone else. Tonight has already outstripped my imagination by miles. I love you, I want to be with you. You're going to be my hot college girlfriend, and then my hot wife, and then the hot mom to my kids."

"Yeah?" she grins at me, and then a laugh breaks out. The tension dissipates. "So you're my hot college boyfriend?"

"If you'll have me."

She dives at me, crawling into my lap and kissing me. It's the best feeling in the world. Finally, finally I have her.

The alarm on my phone goes off, and when I turn it off, we both look out the window. Sunrise. I won.

Elise

7 months later

I'm kneeling in the Castle room inside Manderly. It's my turn for initiation. I've been waiting for the night for a month, ever since I got my official invitation. Obviously, Colin sponsored me, but he did tell me that I was already being considered. It felt good to know that I was chosen for myself, and not because I was his girlfriend.

Things between us have been amazing. When we called Rosie and told her, she laughed, said I told you so, and hung up on us to finish getting ready for her Halloween party.

The night we went to Beastly together - I was a sexy mouse, and Colin was a hawk. He "hunted" me back to his room in the Cavalry house and fucked me doggy style for the first time. It's become my second favorite position.

We fell into place like we were always together. It was only our own hesitations that kept us apart. It was all in our heads.

Now, I've got a few days until finals, I'm acing my freshman year, and I've discovered even more of Elmwood's secrets. I'm about to become part of one.

The buzz of the tattoo gun makes me nervous - it's my first. Every initiate gets a small tattoo of a feather on their body. It's a common enough thing no one questions it, and every person gets to pick where it's tattooed. I like the game of it - the castle in chess is called a rook, and a rook is a bird. It's the symbol of our membership.

The artist brings the gun down and it stings, but I hold still. I'm putting my feather behind my ear. I hold my breath as he works, and then force myself to breathe. It's a weird kind of pain, and I understand why people get so many tattoos. The control of modifying your body is kind of intoxicating. It's powerful.

When the gun lifts for the last time, I wait as the artist, who's name we're not allowed to know, cleans up my skin and puts salve on it. He shows me the tattoo in a handheld mirror and I smile. I love it.

"Thanks."

I step away and the outgoing Steward of the Castle waits. She gives me a hug.

"You're going places, kid," she says in her very Boston accent.

"Thanks, Gwen."

"Go join the party...someone's waiting for you." Gwen winks, and then lets me out. The next initiate steps past me and into the room.

I walk across campus to the Castle house, where the party is already raging. It's the members of the other societies and their new initiates, as well as any non-members we personally invite. The Castle is the last society to go through their ritual, so the party is huge. The outgoing and incoming classes overlap this one night of the year.

I barely step inside the basement when Colin grabs me around the waist and pulls me back into his body. I melt right into him. He kisses me on the opposite side of my tattoo.

"Well, hello General," I purr at him and burrow into his kiss.

"Did it hurt?"

I shrug.

"You want more don't you?" He laughs as I nod and I turn in his grasp, offering my mouth. He kisses me and then smacks my ass. "I'm proud of you. Now let's go dance so you can get your teasing done with and I can take you home and do unspeakable things to you."

I laugh and start pulling him toward the place filled with grinding bodies. "Deal."

Colin

Three years later

Elise's graduation ceremony was yesterday. I watched her walk across the stage, sitting with her parents and Rosie as she got her degree. She's already gotten a book deal to expand on her history of Elmwood, and the architecture of some of the country's oldest campuses. She's delighted.

It means a lot of travel, which I wasn't looking forward to until some unexpected changes at work. The last two years we've been doing long distance while I worked in NYC, but now - now everything is going to change. My position is moving to remote, and she's done with school. I've been waiting to ask her this question since the night of the Hunt.

From her location on my phone, she's on the way here from her house. She thinks she's coming to have dinner with me, Rosie, and my parents, but the house is empty. I pace anxiously as I watch the little dot of her location get closer and closer, until it's turning into my driveway.

I open the door and lean against the jamb, waiting for her. I got a lecture the first time she came to our house after we were a couple that she doesn't want me to open her car doors because it rushes her. She'll get out herself when she's ready.

Elise steps out and she's wearing my favorite navy blue dress. It's the one she wore the night of her Castle initiation. We didn't make it to either of our rooms after the party - I pulled up that very same dress and fucked her in the shadow of the library, hidden by ivy. We might be the only couple in Elmwood history to have sex in every building – after the first few, she made a checklist just to make sure we got to them all. Even the infirmary.

She knows that dress drives me crazy.

"Hey, Mouse," I pull her to me and kiss her when she gets close.

"Hi." She walks past me into the house and calls for Rosie. All she gets is silence. I follow her in and close the door. "Where is everyone?"

"It's just me and you."

Elise frowns at me, and I take her hand and lead her through the house to the back living room. It's the one off the kitchen, with the easiest access to the backyard, where Rosie and I spent most of our time at home and with our friends.

It's the first place I ever saw her. I guide Elise over to the couch she was sitting on. The exact spot. I remember walking into the living room, ready to ream out Rosie for playing with my Transformers, but instead I saw Elise. Her brown hair was messy, and she had her head thrown back in laughter. I was smitten, even if I didn't know that.

Both girls snapped their heads down to look at me.

"This is my big brother Colin," Rosie introduced me. "This is Elise. We're best friends." I'd noticed the way Elise preened at the pronouncement, and I wanted her to do that for me.

"I like your shirt." I did like it – it was black with a robot cat – but I also said it to say something nice to her. When Elise's eyes met mine, they absolutely sparkled.

"Thanks," she replied, suddenly shy. I was sunk.

When she's seated, I get down on one knee. Elise stills. I take the small blue velvet box from my pocket. It's an odd ring, one I had custom made for her. It represents all of our adventures together.

I open it and turn it toward her before I start talking. She gasps, and looks at me.

"The first time I saw you, you were right here. You entered my life and my heart, and you never left it. I love you with everything I have, I'd do anything for you, and I will never let you give my heart back to me. I'm yours, and I want to be your husband. Be my wife?"

"Yes!" she laughs and holds out her hand. I take the ring from the box and slide it on her finger. The stone is a black diamond but the metalwork around it looks like tree branches. It looks delicate and fierce against her hand, exactly how I imagined.

I pull her to her feet and she leaps into my arms, kissing me.

"Does Rosie know?"

I shake my head, and her grin gets bigger. "I kept it all a secret. This is one we can tell her together."

"I love you," she whispers, staring up at me. "I know I don't say it as much, not the way you do, but since the first day I saw you there's never been anyone else for me. Only you."

The monster in me rises up to devour her, and takes and takes until she's a writhing mess on the floor. I can't wait to do that to her for the rest of our lives.

PRESERVATION

Epigraph

"I love you as certain dark things are to be loved/in secret, between the shadow and the soul."
   -Sonnet XVII, Pablo Neruda

Rome

The lie they tell you is that the further you get in college, the more you like it. That's when all your classes are supposed to be in your major and your focus is on nothing but what you came here to do.

What they don't tell you is that while your time is no longer wasted on shit you don't care about in the classroom, your extracurricular obligations increase. At least, if you want to get the right attention and support and start building connections for when you're done.

So here I am, at the fall mixer for all the students in the Archives and Preservation program and all the potential students. The email always says it's optional, but not going is not an option. Especially not if you're me. I was told very clearly by the program director, Dr. Cunningham, that my presence was required. I know why, and I'm already dreading it.

Juniors are assigned a freshman to mentor in the program. We take them under our wing in whatever lab work we're doing, help them prepare their formal application materials to be accepted into the program, generally get them acclimated to Elmwood and answer questions only upperclassmen can. Since this is my junior year, it's my turn to carry on the legacy.

My mentor, Jonas Deveaux, had been helpful while also being completely disinterested. When it came to getting to know Elmwood, he was great, but when it came to the program I was miles ahead of him before I ever set foot on campus. I'd been doing chemical work in preservation and restoration since I was 11 years old. I had no need to become familiar with what the program did. The program was using a technique that I created.

People are mingling around the yard. The program director has a house on the outskirts of the campus, and her garden is nice. Dr. Cunningham is over by a table, chatting with the other faculty. We make eye contact and she glares at me, clearly telling me to start talking. I'm supposed to be networking with the people who will either be my colleagues, or fund my work when I graduate from here. Dr. C and I have been through a lot together. She knows my struggles better than anyone, and I have an immense amount of respect for the way she recovered her dignity after the shit show that went down at the end of my freshman year.

My chest twinges, the pain still stronger than I would like it to be. A fresh wave of anger has me looking away and walking across the yard as if I have a destination.

I go to the table that's set up with snacks and drinks, and move to refill my cup of punch. Someone else reaches out at the same time and our hands bump together, neither of us grabbing the ladle.

"Oh, I'm sorry. After you." Her voice is soft and musical, and when I look up at her every thought or sharp response that formulated in my head is gone. This girl has to be a freshman, I would remember having seen her before. She has long blonde hair, dark brown eyes, and she's wearing a yellow sundress that makes my mouth water, the way it shows so much of her lovely skin and yet it's innocent in its shape. The temptation to reach over and slide one of the straps down over her shoulder takes me by surprise.

"Sorry," I say gruffly, and walk away without looking back or getting more punch. My reaction to her disturbs me greatly, and I need some time to get myself under control. I find a corner to post up in, giving nods and minimal responses to people I see that bother to interact with me. I don't mean to be grumpy, that's just my default setting.

I keep having to force my eyes away from her. She's somewhere else every time I look, meeting people, smiling, laughing, ingratiating herself with students and faculty alike. People already like her, I can tell. The guys all went to fuck her, and I can't say I blame them. As much as I hate it, I do too, against my better judgment. The more I see her sunshine temperament, her relentless joy, the more I dislike her. People with that kind of blatant happiness can't be trusted. It's always a lie somewhere. Still, her beauty is sweet and sensual at the same time and I've always been a sucker for that. I hate her because I want her and that's not her fault.

Dr. Cunningham calls everyone's attention to the small patio where she stands, and we quiet down to listen.

"Welcome to a new year at Elmwood College, we are so happy to have you."

Everyone claps and cheers, and I hold in my sneer.

"Our program is going strong, garnering national attention, regular publication and research development, patent work, and our graduates move on to amazing things." More whooping. "We believe one of the reasons for our success is our mentor program - we pair a committed freshman with a junior student already accepted into the program to teach them about our work, our expectations, and help them find their place. We are so excited for that tradition to continue, and to announce this year's mentors and mentees."

I know I'm not the only one who isn't a huge fan of this, because I can see the rest of my cohort giving forced and pained smiles. It is a beneficial program, but it's also a lot of work. I know I was a lot of work for Jonas at times, but if this is what I have to do to keep the program happy, and keep my lab going, then I will.

I'm sure I can give my mentee distraction projects so they don't interfere with or screw up my work. My temperament alone will scare them off eventually anyway. If whoever is assigned to me lasts the entire year, I'll know they can handle anything.

Dr. Cunningham starts reading the list of mentors and mentees, the parties named making their way to the space in front of her to meet one another and go off to talk. She hasn't called my name, and we're getting to the end of my cohort. My stomach twists, fearing she decided not to pair anyone with me. Not to subject anyone to my moods, even though I'm one of the most brilliant students the program has ever had. I don't brag about it, but in my mind I know it to be factually true.

"We are once again blessed this year to have a recipient of the Van

Hornen Legacy Fellowship choose to attend Elmwood. As you know, the Van Hornen fellowship is not given out every year, and is awarded to a high school student who shows promise and capability in archival and preservation work. This year's recipient is Cynthia St. Clair."

Everyone claps dutifully until they see her, and then the applause gains enthusiasm. It's her. The beautiful, peppy blonde. Of fucking course it is. A stone settles in my stomach because I know where this is going.

"Cynthia has a large and active social media following where she teaches DIY preservation techniques on her YouTube channel and her Instagram. The attention she's drawn to the importance of preservation, and timely preservation at that, made her a perfect candidate for the award, and an excellent addition to our program."

Cynthia blushes, and quietly thanks Dr. Cunningham.

"It felt like fate that the years should line up that I can pair Cynthia with our other Van Hornen fellow, Jerome Dwyer." Dr. Cunningham looks at me and gives me a come hither motion.

Trying not to grumble, I make my way to the space in front of her. Cynthia is standing there expectantly, probably waiting for me to drop down at her feet and worship her for being smart and beautiful and all that other bullshit. The second I heard her last name I knew this was all fucked - she comes from one of the oldest and richest families on the East Coast. Unlike me, she didn't even need the fellowship to pay for college. She could've come to Elmwood on her own dime and done the same work.

Then she also wouldn't have been paired with me, and I could seethe about her brightness in peace.

We stare at each other, and her smile dims. Dr. Cunningham closes her speech, prompting us to get to know our mentees and enjoy the rest of the party.

"Hi."

"Hi." I glare. "I'm in the lab every day from 4:00 to 8:00 on weekdays, weekends when I feel like it. I'm working on the project to restore the first Elmwood president's documents. I expect you to email me your intended schedule by the end of the day Monday, and I'll make adjustments as needed. You'll be added to the security for the lab, and no one is ever allowed in without my permission. We'll go over expectations on the first day."

"Okay," she nods. "Anything else?"

I step closer to her, invading her personal space, but I need to say this quietly.

"I've worked hard to be where I am, and I take this work incredibly seriously. I appreciate that you're getting laymen to understand our work, but I'm not sure you're up for this. It's science, not scrapbooking."

Cynthia immediately frowns at me, and it makes me like her more. Or at a minimum, feel more respect for her.

"I can handle the work," she smiles, and I feel like she did it knowing it would piss me off. Damn it, why do I like that?

"We'll see," I shrug at her and take a step back. There's nothing else to say and I don't want to talk about Elmwood in general right now. I want to put distance between me and her. I don't want her to think I care.

"I'll be waiting for your email." I lean in close for a second, enjoying making her that little bit uncomfortable, before I back off and walk away. My obligation is done. Without saying goodbye to anyone, including Dr. C, I get the hell out. This year is going to be the hardest yet, on every single level.

I know that I have my own personal issues with social media and influencers. It's not surprising considering the only time I ever allowed myself to love someone, she hid all her ugliness behind the persona she put on for her followers. Everything about her was a lie, a web she wove to make her life seem perfect, her decisions always appeared to be made from a place of care and kindness, when really she was the most self-centered, selfish person imaginable. My chest throbs again when I can't keep the memories at bay.

The way she smiled at me when she'd open her eyes in the morning. The look she gave me the last time she kissed me. The wild mess of her hair as I walked in on her getting her face fucked by our professor. The eager way she bent over his desk and lifted her dress so he could fuck her. The way she wasn't even sorry when I confronted her, and almost five years of our lives went up in flames.

Cynthia

I've got this. It's what I've told myself repeatedly since the mixer on Saturday, since I emailed Rome my schedule that same night, since he responded back in a few minutes with some minor adjustments, and since he told me he expected me to start Tuesday night.

I'm thrilled I have a roommate who is, frankly, amazing. Elise and I connected immediately and I know that she's going to be one of my best friends. We were brutally honest with each other and have an obsession with all things old and secret. When I came home from the mixer, obviously distressed, she called our group of friends together and they gave me a pep talk. I got the Van Hornen fellowship based on a lot of hard work, and I was going to show Jerome Dwyer that I knew my stuff.

It would take persistence, communication, and consistency. Those were all things that I was great at, he would see. By the end of the year, he'd be so damn grateful to have me as his mentee that he'd ask me to come back to the lab next year.

I was beyond thrilled to be on this specific restoration project. The first president of Elmwood was also one of the founders. He'd moved his whole family out here to run the College he and his associates built. There were lots of anecdotes about what happened in the years he was president, most of them scandalous, and it was going to be fascinating to be a part of that project. A lot of his documents hadn't been kept well, and we were slowly seeing what could be restored and revealing even more of his life and his secrets.

I couldn't believe they were trusting the project to a student, but then again, that student was Jerome Dwyer. He was a brilliant scientist, and had created a method for ink restoration that changed the game. It's literally called the Dwyer method.

I get why he's judging the work that I do. On my YouTube channel and my Instagram I do crafty DIY projects that help people preserve photos, keepsakes, documents, and photographs in ways that might withstand time. I do projects that show people how to do basic restoration work like fixing damage to photos, countering water damage, and tracing the source of items. I've also done a lot of work on helping people create their family trees. I can imagine that it seems cheesy and unscientific to someone like Rome, but I know science as well as I know scrapbooking. I'll prove it to him.

The work I've done on my channel won me the Van Hornen because it got more people interested in preservation and restoration, and interest generates money. People will see the value in museums and archives when they understand the work that goes into those places, and the work that goes into keeping the ancient fresh. Jerome will see my value. I'll make sure of it.

After class, I change quickly into clothes appropriate to the lab. During the class day, I wore a pink sundress and white sandals. For the lab, I'm wearing comfortable black pants, a pair of tennis shoes, and a fitted long sleeved shirt. One of his emails let me know that it's cool in the lab and to dress accordingly. Despite his terse demeanor, he also says things that come across as very considerate. Maybe there's a nice human behind those glowering eyebrows.

He's also stupidly fucking hot. Dark eyes, dark brown hair with the kind of volume and natural wave that makes women jealous, high cheekbones, defined jaw, and he's tall and strong, which I didn't expect since he has a reputation as a major nerd. The way my body reacted to him when we bumped hands at the punch bowl at the party was downright embarrassing, and then finding out who he was made it even worse.

It frustrates me how attractive I find him because I don't want to be distracted by his face and his oddly sexy voice when what I really want is to be learning from him. Even saying I worked in Jerome Dwyer's lab is going to be a huge win on my resume, and I'm a freshman. Except when I looked at him I didn't think about his mind, I thought about his lips. His piercing eyes. His heavy eyebrows and the depth of his frown, which appealed to me for some perverse reason. I thought about how I was oddly attracted to his teeth and had the weird fantasy of what it would be like for him to bite me.

So not what I need to be thinking about.

My phone buzzes with a text. From dad.

Make sure to post on Instagram today.

He doesn't ask how I'm doing, how school is going, if I'm settling in okay. The worst part is that if I don't post in what he decides is a timely fashion, he'll post for me. That always blows up in my face because it's always something too private for my public, professional page. Like the time he made a post on the anniversary of mom's death, sharing private thoughts and grief for everyone to pick apart. Some people shared sympathy, while others accused me of using the loss of my mother for attention. I make a quick post of a photo I took earlier this week of the small photo collage I did on my wall. I tagged the right vendors. Hopefully that's enough for him.

I finish getting dressed and run across campus to the library. There's a separate door to the lab spaces, which requires one code, and once inside there I enter the code to his lab room. It's 5:00 on the dot. I ate a very early dinner and brought a few snacks in my bag in case I need to sneak out and eat.

Rome is sitting at a computer in the far corner, and the only indication I have that he's aware of my presence is his jaw clenching. I look around the lab - three long tables covered in Plexiglas containers and bright lights, documents sealed inside a bookshelf, and along one wall are other computers. There are cabinets full of chemicals and other lab equipment, some with locks. It's bare but full at the same time.

To the right of the door is a small row of lockers. I step toward them and see there's a lab coat hanging in one and assume that it's for me. Rome is wearing his and I'm annoyed it makes him look sexy. The comfort with which he wears it makes him look so damn competent, and demonstrated competency is my freaking catnip.

I hang up my backpack, put on the coat, and walk over.

"Jerome?"

He cringes. "It's Rome. Just Rome."

"Oh, good, because I go by Cyn. Cynthia is an old lady."

"Cyn? As in pray for our?"

I laugh, even though there was no humor or even sarcasm in his tone. "A name like hell, a personality like heaven." I grin at him, but he doesn't smile back. "I'm very excited to work with you. I understand why you're not enthused about me but I hope you take a genuine chance to see what I'm capable of because yes there's the channel but I'm a scientist first. I want to do things right and I want to do things well, and I think that I can be the assistant that you need in the lab."

"That will do, Cyn." Rome snaps.

I was looking around while talking to him, anxious but excited and when he cuts me off my eyes move back to him. He looks livid, crimson on his cheeks, chest heaving, and fury etched in every line of his face. I don't know what I did.

"We need to go over my expectations, the deadlines for the current materials, and what your primary duties will be." His voice comes out even, despite the appearance of anger.

"Great," I smile at him, letting my excitement filter back to the forefront. I will win him over.

"Your primary duty is to clean all the tools I'll use. Once I know you can take care of things to my expectations, you'll be doing transcript work. If I feel like things are progressing positively, you'll be scanning. I need to know that you can handle the delicate materials we're entrusted with. This isn't something you can throw money at if it's destroyed."

The progression seems reasonable, but I'm curious exactly how long the progression will take, and what that weird comment was about money. Most students at Elmwood come from money. Even if he doesn't, he's surrounded by them. His fixation about this can't only be focused on me. Weird.

"That sounds totally cool," I respond. "I'm still excited to work with you, and I hope you find me helpful." Trying to bridge some of the grumpiness, I keep going. "Where are you from? Why'd you choose Elmwood after winning the Van Hornen? Someone with your skills could have written their ticket to anywhere."

"Those questions aren't relevant to the work," Rome snaps and it's so harsh I take a step back and away from him. For a second there's a flicker of regret on his face, and then it smooths out into a cold but neutral mask. "I'll walk you through the lab. Take notes."

He gestures to where a pen and notepad wait for me, and I follow along behind him as he tells me where everything is, what it does, and if I'm allowed to touch it or not. Most things are off limits to me. Fine.

If Rome wants to keep things very collegial and formal, that's fine. I need to learn to keep professional boundaries and act accordingly. This is an exercise in expanding my professionalism, that's what I tell myself. There's nothing that I can't turn into a positive opportunity. Everything I do here is working toward a larger goal. Everything is a lesson to learn.

Despite my excitement, I need to be respectful of him and being respectful is recognizing his boundaries.

Rome's showing me the journal he's currently working on that belonged to President James. It's from the second year of Elmwood's existence, and it's where he kept notes on all of his appointments and the general running of the school. The ink is faded in places, and even for a time where everyone wrote in cursive, he had exceptionally sloppy handwriting. I get caught up trying to read the lines, something about hiring a new professor, and the possibility of expanding with another building.

"Are you listening?" Rome's voice cracks through my awareness.

"Yes, sir," I straighten up quickly and face him, that tone so familiar that I respond automatically, the same way I responded to my headmaster and to my father. The two people who pushed me beyond my limits and demanded excellence of me no matter what it cost. My headmaster who made it his personal mission to keep me at a 4.0, and my father who demanded I pour all of my energy and creativity into growing my channel and expanding my influence.

Rome stares at me, seeming unsettled by that answer.

"Sorry," I try again. "Yes, I'm listening. It's very fascinating."

"It is," he agrees. "We can't get caught up in the story though, it's our responsibility to objectively report the findings. Correct?" He challenges me.

"Yes, sir," I respond and wonder why the hell that flew out of my mouth again. Rome's eyes widen, and I swear to god they darken before sweeping over me quickly.

"You can start cleaning. When the items on the counter are washed, you're done for the day."

I nod. "Yes, sir," I say for the third time and I see it again. His eyes darken, his jaw clenches. Rome reacts when I say that, and it gives me a brief shiver. I want to make him react. It gives me a weird thrill of joy, and something else that I refuse to name, when I get on his nerves.

Rome opens his mouth to say something else, then turns away from me and goes back to his work on the computer. I go to the sink and start cleaning the materials he used. Chemical restoration is risky, and things have to be done absolutely perfectly or you risk ruining what you're trying to fix. There's only one chance at it too. If it goes wrong, that's it. It's gone. Having exceptionally, perfectly cleaned equipment is where that starts.

A song goes through my mind and even though I don't hum out loud, I know that I'm swaying to the beat and dancing a little as I clean. Every once and awhile I glance over at Rome, but he's never looking at me. He seems focused on his screen, and I get momentarily distracted by his hands when he stops to take a note. They're large and well-veined, his fingers are long with prominent knuckles, and I want to put one of those fingers in my mouth.

That's a weird thought. I focus back on the washing, and find that I finish quicker than I expected. I check and examine the glassware and tools, but they're all as clean as can be.

I step to the desk and clear my throat to get Rome's attention. He doesn't look at me. "I'm done."

"You can go. I'll evaluate your work and give you feedback."

"Okay. Thank you again, Rome. I'll see you tomorrow."

"Tomorrow, Cyn." His voice sounds odd as he says my name. It's not negative, but it's something I can't quite articulate. For the barest moment his dark eyes flick to me, hot and hard, and then move away again. Just that look and I feel like my panties are getting damp.

Damn it, I hate this, and I don't hate anything. I will have to be nicer and more positive than my attraction to him. I have to overcome this. He's going to be frustrating, I feel that down to my core, and I'll have to find a way to stop him from getting to me.

I give him a nod and go back to the lockers, getting my things to leave. One endless night down, so very many left to go.

Rome

Cyn did what I asked, and the work was good. Every night she came in, she cleaned, and there was nothing for me to criticize. I wanted to find something wrong with her work. I knew I couldn't keep her washing dishes forever, even though she did it for an entire week without complaint.

I could feel her eyes on me. When she wasn't looking, I looked. At first, I was furious that she was appearing to dance while working to whatever song was in her head. Except when I checked, everything was sparkling clean. I couldn't penalize her for that because dancing while working was not something I could overtly forbid just because it annoyed me or we'd turn into some kind of *Footloose* situation. I was trying to accept that she was different from me, and that I was obligated to make space for her in the lab.

After a week of dish washing, I had to let her move on. It felt punitive to hold her back because I was possessive of my work, and mistrustful of her. I gave up a day of chemical work to train her and observe her doing document scanning, rendering, and transcription.

Cyn would scan each page of the journal, run it through the rendering program that digitally restored the ink, and then type the contents into a document. I preferred this to only scanning the items as I think legibility is an issue in the renders - they aren't always accurate. I show her the gloves, the cases we use, the tools to handle the papers with, and after demonstrating my exact method for handling the papers, I let her take over.

"Touch as little of the document as possible, and use the lowest brightness you can tolerate," I advise her. She has to stand close to me as I show her the equipment and the heat from her body is making me uncomfortable.

"You get one chance here. One strike. Do you understand?"

Cyn meets my eyes. "Yes, sir."

Fuck. I'm looking down at her and she's looking up at me and that feeling like I need to destroy her rises up. Like I want her on her knees saying that to me before she sucks my soul out through my cock. I know she knows it does something to me but I doubt she understands the extent. The borderline violent sexual impulses she raises in me. So fucking shiny I need to darken her.

I observe Cyn handling the pages. Even focused on the work, she's got a little smile on her pink lips.

"Stop," I snap, and move behind her. Without thinking, I take her arm and adjust her position and grip. It's a moment before I realize my chest is up against her back and she's caged in my arms. Shit. I step away.

"Try again." This is the first page of this journal, and it lists the dates of the entries. It's a safe page to train her with.

Even though I try to soften my delivery, I snap at Cyn every time she does something slightly less than perfect. It doesn't seem to bother her at all. She adjusts, does it again, and I never have to correct her more than once. I will grudgingly admit she's competent, though inexperienced. I might have to watch some of her videos to see what I'm working with when it comes to her skill set. She seems to have more of a preservation than restoration focus and that would change how I approach teaching her what to do.

My focus is totally fucked because she keeps saying "yes, sir" and I keep imagining bending her over my knee and spanking her perfect ass in order to correct her mistakes. God I'm an asshole.

When she has things the way I want, I back off.

"When you get in to the lab from now on, scans first, and manage your time so you can do the washing before you leave. Understood?"

Cyn nods, already absorbed in the slow, methodical scanning of journal pages. I like that she never complains about what we're doing. It's slow and tedious, and she shows up every day excited and smiling. She genuinely finds this interesting. It annoys me to have that in common with her. It annoys me that she can appear to have fun while doing this work, where I drop into a well of serious focus that I sometimes can't escape from.

Things settle in to a pattern for another few days. She still tries to talk to me. More like she talks at me and asks questions that I don't answer. I learn things about her against my will.

Like she got into preservation work because she found her great-grandmother's diaries in their house, and they were still in decent shape despite being stored without care. That's how she started her YouTube channel - by documenting her self-taught journey of restoring and caring for her grandmother's journals. She also created projects that could highlight certain entries, or how to make copies of them to turn into items that she shared with her family. After that rant, I did grudgingly look through her YouTube.

I went back to those early videos, and super young, awkward Cyn was disarming. Her curiosity was sincere, and I can feel that same sincere curiosity in the work we're doing now. It lowers my guard toward her - not on a personal level, but a professional one. I'll never entirely trust anyone to get involved in my work, but at least I'm feeling reassured that she takes this seriously.

Her money might have gotten her a lot of opportunities and access, but she doesn't appear to be wasting the privilege on things that are frivolous.

The more recent videos on her channel set my teeth on edge though, their familiar fakeness burrowing into my brain. Five years later, Cyn has an entirely different persona in her work. It's a more extreme version of who she is every day, and an overly confident version of who she was in those early videos.

The thing is, she looks dead in the eyes. Like this is so much work and she doesn't care about it anymore. It feels oddly good to know that the glimmer of excitement and life from the early videos is there when we work together in the lab. I wonder why she keeps doing the YouTube channel when it clearly brings her no joy anymore. Then again, I have no idea what it's like to feel a responsibility towards a fanbase, and I don't want to know.

I'm considering letting her move on during our third week together and start teaching her my methods of chemical restoration, but then she fucks it all up.

"What are you wearing?" I snap at her. The scent is strong enough that I can smell it from across the room, but I also have a sensitive nose. It's lightly floral, but stronger than she should be wearing before coming into the lab.

Cyn pulls on her lab coat and dashes over to me, panic on her face. I feel no sympathy.

"It's lotion, I'm sorry, I didn't realize it would be this strong."

"Seriously, lotion? Even with gloves you should know better than to put a substance like that on your hands, and a scent that strong around sensitive documents. What the fuck, Cyn? Here I was thinking that you could be trusted and then you break one of the most obvious fucking rules. Get out. Come back tomorrow."

Her shoulders droop and I don't want to feel bad.

"I'm sorry – I didn't have anything else and my skin has been cracking from washing. I'm – you're right, I know better. It'll never happen again." Cyn meets my eyes, and hers are wet with unshed tears. I respect her for holding them back, as much as I acknowledge that seeing them and knowing I caused them feels like a stab in the gut.

Of course her hands are all fucked up from washing if she didn't know how to properly take care of them. My tongue is swollen in my mouth, I can't say anything else, I only nod in acknowledgment. Cyn turns around and hangs up her coat, then leaves the lab.

Part of me wants to apologize, and the other part of me is convinced I need to stand my ground. I do something in the middle. I don't apologize, but I do buy a tub of unscented salve for her to use after washing.

Cyn doesn't say anything the next day, but I can see her smile when she notices it sitting next to the sink. That smile does dangerous things to mind and runs through my body with the same power as when she calls me sir. Fuck.

Friday night my roommate Del and I go to dinner. We've known each other since we were 12 years old, before my family betrayed me, before they transitioned to non-binary, and before my heart was ground into dust. They are, to use the sappiest term, my person.

They plop down into the seat across from me, and as usual I assess their outfit. Del says I have a "strong sense of aesthetic" and never takes my criticism personally. They're wearing a pair of fitted, flared black pants, a tight army green t-shirt, a fuck ton of chains in mixed metals, and their long hair is up in a messy bun. Big silver hoops swing from their ears. It's slightly feminine but their muscular arms and lack of makeup today walks a fine line.

"That's a good color on you."

Del grins. "Ah, a compliment. I've won the week." They laugh. "How about you? How's the lab assistant?"

"Perky." I grumble.

"Do you think her personality affects her body? That perky smile makes perky tits and a perky ass?" Del is the most openly sexual person I know, and I don't hold that against them. I am holding it against them that they talked about Cyn that way.

"Shut the fuck up." There's more heat than I intended. I want to defend her from a collegial standpoint. Locker room talk will not be fucking tolerated about women in our programs. It creates a toxicity that's impossible to break, and I won't put her in that position no matter how much she annoys me. Protecting her from being objectified is the minimum respect that I owe her.

Except there's more there, and Del hears it.

Their eyes get round. "Holy shit. You like her."

"No, but you know my standards, asshole. Meet them."

Del lifts their hands in surrender. "Sure, but I still think you like her."

"Of course not. She's a rich kid who social mediaed her way into a prestigious fellowship, has to be taught everything down to the smallest details, and wore fucking scented lotion into the lab the other day. I was so livid I almost blacked out. She talks at me relentlessly as if I have any reason to give a shit about what she has to say, and keeps asking questions about me even though I've never answered a single one. She doesn't get the fucking hint. She just talks. And now I know all this shit about her that I can't get out of my head. She dances when there's no music while she washes the dishes!"

Del bursts out laughing. "How dare she have a song stuck in her head."

"You know her type. I know her type. I'm never going near that again."

"Not everyone is her, Rome." Del's voice is quiet and sympathetic. "Maybe sunshine is your type, and maybe there's sunshine out there meant for you. You're a fucking thunderstorm, you need a little clear skies."

Nausea swoops through my stomach. "I'd rather be alone."

"I know, that's why I can't stay mad at you. You're that damn protective of your heart, and you're not casual with anyone else's. Honestly, if it was anyone but you, I'd tell you to fuck her, break the tension, and go about your business."

"Even if I wanted to do that, I wouldn't cross that line with my mentee." I swallow thickly. "There's no reason to believe she'd be interested."

"She's interested," Del answers immediately. "Have you seen you? I know every gross detail about you as a human being and I'd still consider it if you caught me in the right mood."

That's the first thing they say that makes me uncomfortable. I don't like thinking about my looks. A lot of people have made assumptions about me based on my appearance and when they find out that I am exactly as much of an asshole as my glowering appearance shows, it gets me into a lot of trouble. I'm like a predator in the wild - everything about me should be warning people away, except it's pretty enough to be enticing.

I think it's why Hannah put up with me so long. I was good looking, and a contrast to her sunny persona. We made an interesting story, pieces that could be manipulated to show what she wanted to show, without her caring about who I was as a person anymore. I became a set piece to her, and at some point I wore out my value.

"Could you at least try being nice to her?" Del finishes their food and practically begs me.

"No. At the very least, I'll make sure she ends her year in my lab as a fucking rock star of skill and detail. I'll teach her. That's what I'm supposed to do."

Del rolls their eyes, and I can't meet them when they stare me down. Even I know how full of shit I sound. They can read between every line of what I'm saying to what I'm not saying. I'm already stating a plan to do more for Cyn than I ever planned to do for my mentee, which Del knows because I ranted to them about it over the summer. I really do want to shape her into a stellar applicant. I want her to succeed because from what I've observed, I know she's capable of it.

But I'll never admit that I like her.

Cyn

On Friday nights, Rome lets me leave early. He tells me I'm allowed to have a life - like I need his permission - and only frowned when I pointed out that he was staying in the lab. It seems I'm not allowed to point out his lack of social life even while he encourages mine. Although, when I see him around campus, he's rarely alone. He doesn't talk or interact much, but he's always surrounded by other people in the program. The jolt of jealousy I feel when he almost smiles around other people is completely irrational.

I'm staying in and having a girl's night. My roommate Elise, and then our corner neighbors, Maeve and Tati, are hanging out in our room. We have the better fireplace and it's already cold here at night. Maeve is painting my nails and talking about some tension with her family about if they're going to follow through on a marriage agreement.

I might come from money but my dad is dreading the day I get married. He wants me to become a single old spinster who leaves all our money to my cats. I'm not sure why or where that comes from, but he's always loathed every person I've ever dated. Maybe I'll have to dig into that someday because it's sure worked to make me apathetic toward romantic relationships. I wonder if it would be different if mom was alive.

"You'd really marry someone your family chose for you?" Tati questions, laying a mask across her face. She lays down on the floor next to the fire and closes her eyes.

"I mean, I have a choice, but I want to see how it pans out. I don't think my family would ever choose someone for me they couldn't see making me happy. They're being really secretive about it though, like I'm going to stalk him before I meet him." She rolls her eyes and moves to my other hand. "I'm not creepy."

"Speaking of creepy," Elise butts in, "how's it going in the basement with the grump of darkness?"

I sigh, not sure how to answer. "Nothing is ever good enough and if he isn't actually telling me to be quiet, he's always giving off that impression. The work is awesome but I feel like I'm suffocating down there. It doesn't matter what I do, I get nothing from him."

"What do you want to get from him?" Maeve waggles her eyebrows suggestively.

"He is pretty hot," Tati chimes in.

"He's so hot," I groan. "He's so hot it's distracting, and he's as much of an asshole as he is sexy. If I'm not drooling over him, I'm mad at him for existing."

Elise is quiet, looking into the fire. "Are you learning anything? I mean he might be unpleasant, but is he teaching you?"

I reflect on that. When Rome shows me how to do something, he's very thorough. He stays with me and corrects me over and over until it's exactly right. He checks everything I do and tells me what's good and what needs improvement. While he isn't effusive with his praise, he does make a point of telling me when I succeed, or when I no longer need supervision.

"Yeah, I am. He expects me to be capable, and demands it of me until I am."

"Wow," Tati murmurs from the ground. "That's intense."

"It is, but I don't mind. In case you missed the life story, I'm used to intense. At least he doesn't want anything from me except to not screw up. And to stop talking. He won't get that though. I kind of live for annoying him."

We all laugh, but I know they don't understand. Rome is like no one I've ever met before. I know nothing about him. Most people are so eager to volunteer information about themselves, to define to others who they are, and Rome is like a black hole. Information goes in, nothing comes out. The way he reacts when I annoy him is the only way I know he notices me at all. It's the only time I know for sure that he's as human as I am.

"Here's how I see it," Elise stands up and puts her hands on her hips. "He might be grumpy, and he might not vibe with your personality, but he's still teaching you. It would be so easy for him to be a true asshole and punish you because he doesn't like you. Instead, he teaches you anyway. So stand your ground. Be yourself. If he crosses a line, set an expectation for how you want to be treated."

"We know that there's lots of stupid sexism in our programs," Maeve continues. "I'm not saying he's doing this because you're a woman, I doubt it, but I think it makes a difference if people see different kinds of personalities and different shades of professionalism. He can learn from you, too."

"You're right," I agree. "I shouldn't have to change myself to be in this field."

"Damn straight," Tati holds up a hand and then drops it down to cover her yawn. We all laugh at her, and the mask moves as she smiles underneath.

"I'm so glad I have all of you," I sigh. Because of the academic demands from school, and the influencer demands from my dad, my friendships were few and shallow. I was invited to parties because everyone was invited to them, but I never had anyone I spent significant time with and really got to know.

I've never had the chance to be relaxed and not feel the pressure to record every moment, or turn it into something for social media. I don't think any of us have even touched our phones other than skipping the song for over an hour. I'm disconnected from the internet but plugged into my friends, and I love that. No matter what happens, I'm keeping these three. They'll have to kill me to get rid of me.

"You said that out loud, hon," Maeve whispers.

"And we have no plans to get rid of you," Elise adds.

"Especially not now," Tati laughs.

I blush fiercely. They let me drop out of the conversation and recover as

Maeve finishes the fast dry top coat on my nails. Because my channel is a lot of focus on my hands, I've always kept my fingernails very clean and basic. I didn't want to scandalize the Karens who definitely watch for ways to preserve their kid's things. Maeve painted my nails a bright purple, and they make me happy.

I'm going to take their advice and not change myself. I'm not going to even try and stifle who I am in front of Rome because I don't think it changes anything. He's still going to be insanely surly, hypercritical, and hold me to high standards. I should at least feel like myself while going through all of that.

There's a part of me I don't like to acknowledge that loves how controlling and bossy he is in the lab. This little thread of something that makes me call him sir before I can think about it, that hardens my nipples when he gives me a sharp command, and that has the filthiest fantasies about the things I want him to tell me to do. I like it when he bosses me around. I like it when he breaks and snaps at me, causing my entire body to react to him.

The other night when I was alone in my room, I got off to fantasizing about him putting me on my knees and bossing me around while I sucked him off. I didn't even get to make him come in my imagination before I was orgasming. It was nearly embarrassing because it wasn't about how well I know my body, it was about how aroused I was by that scenario. I wanted him to have control over me.

Rome would probably be horrified. On the one hand by my attraction to him because he sees the mentor/mentee line as very serious, and on the other because I think he'd be frustrated that I was attracted to him when he's worked very hard to make sure I'm not.

It's just that sometimes I catch him looking at me, and I don't understand the emotion in his eyes. There's always heat and intensity, but I'm starting to wonder if that's not his regular state and that's an expression that's just for me. That I bring out his heat and intensity the same way he brings out mine.

That's crazy.

The next morning, Elise and I are getting ready to meet the girls for a late breakfast. We stayed up really late watching movies and Tati gave us all henna tattoos on the tops of our feet. I'm tired, but I'm also so, so happy.

"Uh, can I ask you about something and you need to stay absolutely chill about it?" Elise asks without looking at me.

"Yeah, of course." I get nervous, and a small shiver goes through me.

"You know how I disappear at night?"

No idea where this is going. "Yeah."

"And I tell you to let it happen?"

"Yeah."

"I found something the other night, and it only occurred to me now that you might be able to do something with it."

I frown, confused. "Okay..."

Elise goes to her desk and opens the bottom drawer. She takes out a large Ziploc bag with what looks like a bundle of old cloth inside it. I take it from her and sit down on my bed, opening it carefully.

"I put it in the Ziploc to protect it, I didn't know what else to do."

I slide out the material - it's very, very old silk, probably a white or cream faded to a stained yellow. Slowly, I unfold the silk to reveal a leather bound book. It's a dark russet color, and it looks familiar. It looks like President James's journals.

"Did you open it?" I ask her.

"No. It didn't seem like a good idea."

"That was the right choice." I get up and dig around in my desk until I find my letter opener and a pair of tweezers I use for preservation projects for the channel.

Carefully, I open the cover of the journal. On the first page, barely legible, is the inscription of who it belonged to - it's faded badly and I can't see anything except the years. It would be the third year that President James was in charge of Elmwood - could this be a lost journal of his? A family member? His alleged mistress? I'm immediately intrigued.

"This is amazing, Elise. Where did you find it?"

"Um...I'm going to say the library, and you're going to say okay."

"Okay. Can I keep it? Look into it?"

"Have at it. It's not my thing."

I wrap it back up, slide it back into the bag, and hide it in a drawer for now. Maybe I'll start going back to the lab late and work on this. It's unlikely Rome would notice as long as I take care to make sure everything is where it belongs when I'm done. This could be a huge discovery. It would also make an amazing video. The trickle of excitement that runs through me at that prospect is nearly unfamiliar it's been so long since I actually wanted to film anything.

I'm lost in my thoughts as we head to the student services building in the center of the halls, which includes dining, the health center, student counseling, and various other things we might need during our time here.

Maeve and Tati are already waiting for us, heads bent together in excited chatter.

"What's up?" I sit down, and feel paranoid when they jolt and share a guilty look. "Seriously, what?"

Maeve blushes a little. "So my older sister was a senior when Rome was a freshman."

"Yeah..." I don't know what that has to do with anything but my stomach pools with dread.

"There was a big scandal that he was kind of a part of - it might explain a lot."

The dread deepens and my voice is weak. "What happened?"

"He was dating someone." I hate this story already even though I have no reason to have feelings about this. "It was serious." I hate it even more. Jealousy is irrationally roaring through me. "She's some big influencer now and they were together for years before coming to Elmwood together. Apparently, while they were here she slept with a professor and he caught them."

"Oh my god, poor Rome." I clutch my hands to my chest, feeling pain for him over that kind of betrayal.

"The professor was married to Dr. Cunningham. He's married to the girlfriend now."

"Holy fuck," I whisper. "Who was she?"

"Hannah Mearitt?" Maeve says. "I've never watched her videos."

That hits me like a physical blow. I used to love her videos - they were focused on the concepts of kindness and positivity, talking about how we should treat others, and she had a whole series about honesty. I remember seeing her wedding to her silver fox husband and thinking it was so sweet. Now thinking of it makes me want to vomit.

It kind of makes sense now why Rome immediately disliked me. I probably remind him of her - social media following, generally sunshine personality - he must think the worst of me because of her. I hate that. I feel both guilty and furious at the same time.

"What a bitch," I hiss. "The whole catchphrase for her channel is "kindness is a culture" and about how we should treat others. That fucking hypocrite."

"Yeah. Poor guy," Tati chimes in. "You're pretty mad about this, huh?"

"I didn't even know you could frown like that," Maeve teases me.

"It makes a lot of things make sense," I sigh.

"But what we told you last night stands," Elise chimes in. "Don't stop being yourself for him."

"Of course," I agree out loud, but in my heart I know otherwise. If he's harsh because I remind him of his ex, and yet he's still taught me so much, I'll do my best to dial it back in order to spare his feelings. He might be over her, but it doesn't mean reminders of her don't hurt.

My phone has been buzzing during the entire conversation, and I know it's my dad. It's Saturday. I'm supposed to film today so he can edit footage and post a video Sunday. When I open the text, it's a list of vendors and products I'm supposed to try and use in the video. I respond that I understand and try to focus on being with my friends before I have to work.

Cyn

Monday night, I stalk the lab by hanging out in the library until I see Rome leave. I get momentarily distracted watching him move - his long, strong body, the dark clothes that make him look mysterious and vaguely threatening, the way he brushes away the lock of hair that falls across his forehead. He's intense and demanding, but I can't imagine anyone finding a reason to cheat on him. He brings that same intensity to everything he does and I bet he'd be insanely committed in a relationship.

Maybe that's too much for some people.

I sneak downstairs, afraid of anyone seeing me, especially if they already know Rome left. He's never told me that I can't be in the lab without him but it's always been implied by the schedule we agreed to keep.

No one sees me, and I quickly get myself set up. My goal for tonight is to start small. I'm going to work on the title page and find out who the journal belonged to, and that will determine what I do next. If we ever find anything significant about the history of Elmwood, we're supposed to turn it over to the administration right away. I understand why, but part of me wants to hold onto this secret and explore it for myself.

Elmwood is a weird place. It's full of secrets and hiding places, layers of history piling on top of each other as it changed with the world and the needs of the student body. It isn't weird to find hidden journals, surprise art, even secret rooms. People talk about the campus like it's a person with feelings and emotions, with an agenda, even. There's no telling what anyone will find or experience while they're here. There are no coincidences at Elmwood. She always has a purpose for her students. Even the non-believers eventually believe.

Maybe I feel like I have something to prove to myself or to Rome when it comes to this journal, but I don't want to reflect on that too much.

First, I take a bunch of footage of the journal without any talking. I'll narrate over it if I decide to move forward with this as a project. I want to show a restoration from start to finish, and this might be my only chance. The President's journals is too big of a project. I put down my camera and get to work.

I start simple and use the hand scanner. Once the page is scanned, I use a program to read for indents in the paper and fill them in, digitally restoring the written words. I'd rather use electronic means than chemical, as it will be a lot less noticeable. I also don't feel comfort with chemical restoration yet. Rome has barely started teaching it to me, and I understand why we're going slow.

I get lucky as I watch the page render and the title page becomes legible. I film it in real time, and allow myself to react during recording.

Charity James.

Elmwood College.

Holy shit. Charity was the president's eldest daughter, and she has an insane legacy here. While she wasn't allowed to attend the college as a student, she did marry one of the first alumni, and her descendants are still active supporters of the institution. Not a lot is known about her because her wedding and the documentation that should have surrounded it was overshadowed by her father's affair coming to light.

Even though he didn't lose his job, his family left him behind in Elmwood and moved back to the city. Charity's life after being married is well-documented, but who was this girl before becoming an influential woman?

This could be everything, or it could be nothing. It could be an accounting of the early days of Elmwood and the scandals, or it could be the recording of the daily life of a young adult woman in an age where she didn't have a lot of opportunities. It could be filled with social gossip and recipes, which also have their historical value.

The thing is, if that was the case, why did she hide it? There are so many ways it could've ended up in a hidden place, but I don't think Elise will tell me where she found it. I don't think it's the first secret place she's found. It's why the rule about turning over found items exists, because they're never quite sure where something is going to turn up. This journal definitely falls under that category, but I don't care.

I want to make sure Charity James finally gets the attention she deserves, instead of drowning in her father's scandalous shadow. No matter what this contains - the simple or the significant - I want to give her a chance to speak for herself. This is my project now.

I film what I can, and make notes on my initial thoughts for video narration later. Energy thrums through my body and I'm relieved I can get excited about this.

I stick to my goal when it comes to Rome - I tone it down. While I still ask him how he's doing and how his day was, I give myself five minutes to ramble before trying to keep it together. I comment on my classes, saying only the good things or highlighting something I learned so he knows how seriously I'm taking my education. There's no more idle stream of chatter during our hours together. When I speak, it's to ask him questions or answer them, or to talk about the work we're doing.

It's hard work to be quiet when I'm so excited. The restoration work is easier to do than maintaining my silence. I'm bursting with things I want to tell him, things I want to know about him, and honestly extremely tempted to tell him about Charity's journal. I feel like Rome would understand my motivation and I feel like he would help me. Whenever we're talking about a technique in the lab that I think would be useful for the journal, I make us spend a lot of time on it. I won't have him there to ask questions when I do it on my own later in the night.

I'm thanking my lucky stars he hasn't caught me in this last week. I've been here every night, late, and I'm surprised that he hasn't been. Rome has given off the impression that he doesn't do much outside of school obligations, including the lab. I've never seen him at any parties or events, and at this point I'm attuned to his presence. I swear I can feel him enter a space, even when he doesn't see or acknowledge me.

Since I've started pulling back talking in the lab, I do feel like I'm learning more. Rome seems calmer when he talks to me, his tone is softer when he's going through an explanation, and I feel like he's been snapping at me over mistakes a lot less. I can't tell if I'm making fewer mistakes or if he's correcting me before we get to the point of him snapping.

The quiet isn't the worst thing, but this fierce desire to connect with him is still burning inside me. I want to pull something from him, anything, anything that isn't about our work. Any tiny real detail will do, but I don't know how to get it.

We're packing up on a Friday, early even, when Rome is the one who breaks the silence.

"What did you do with the journals?"

I flinch, thinking he means in the lab, but he watched me put them away. When I look over, I see the calm, questioning look on his face, and I put together what he's actually asking.

"You watched my channel?" I'm surprised and embarrassed at the same time.

"The early videos. I wanted to see how you got here. It was interesting work."

"It was. She was really involved women's rights back in the day and it was interesting to read about all of those things through her eyes. She got cancer when I was young, I don't remember her as well as I wish I did."

"Cancer can suck a dick." His words are harsh, and I blink over at him.

He blinks a few times, reining himself back in. "Sorry."

We stand in silence for a second, staring at each other. Understanding passing between us. "Who?"

"My father." His jaw tics. "I was 15."

Without thinking, I step closer and take his hand. It's even more unexpected when his fingers weave through mine as if his body sought comfort before his mind could stop it.

"I'm so sorry. That must have been difficult for you. I lost my mom when I was 3, lymphoma. I don't know if it's worse to be me and not remember much, or be you and remember almost everything."

Rome looks down at our joined hands and then looks away, but he doesn't let go.

"It changed a lot of things. Some I didn't expect, but I'd rather remember. I'm sorry you don't."

I shrug, knowing we can't change the past. "I'm sure he'd be proud of you. Look what you've done. Look where you are." I gesture to the lab.

He nods his head at that. "True." Rome sighs. "Why are you being so nice to me?"

"That's who I am as a person."

"Okay," he says it like he doesn't quite believe that. His hand squeezes mine and then he let's it go and steps away. "You can leave. I'll finish up." Then Rome turns his back on me and starts washing the tools we used today. Part of me wants to say something else because for a second he let me in, and I don't want that door to close.

Then again, he gave me a centimeter, I shouldn't take a foot knowing that he wouldn't appreciate it.

"Goodnight," I say softly, a little bit defeated. This is the most I've been able to be myself around him in a week, and it's been exhausting. Holding myself in is burning me up. I need to find an outlet or I'm going to lose my mind. Maybe the girls are right, and I have to push him to get over it. I'm not his ex, I'm my own person, and I deserve to be myself while working for hours a week in this room. There's got to be a balance somewhere.

Rome

Del and I sit down to eat, and I look around carefully before speaking. All the students live on campus so the chance of running into Cyn is high. Or running into someone who knows her. We're eating late, so the cafeteria is mostly empty but it's still risky.

"I think I broke her."

Del has half a taco in their mouth. "Who?"

"Cyn."

Del finishes their bite and chews, thinking before answering. "What do you mean?"

"I mean she's been quiet. No chattering, no dancing, she keeps her head down and works, and then leaves. She literally bites her lip to stop herself from talking. Who does that? Who needs to do that to be quiet?"

Del raises their eyebrows at me. I'm mesmerized for a moment because their eyebrows are currently covered in blue glitter to match their blue dress, which is far too showy of an outfit in my opinion, but that's not the focus right now.

"Isn't that what you wanted?"

"Yes." I frown, staring at my food.

"And now you're grumpy about it?"

"I'm grumpy about everything."

I don't meet Del's eyes. I know what they'll see, and I know that I won't hear the end of it for years. The other day in the lab, I told more about myself to Cyn - revealing that one personal fact - than I have to anyone since my freshman year. Del already knows my baggage, but the only other person I've told anything about myself to is Dr. C. She earned my secrets because I feel like I ruined her fucking marriage, even if he was a jerk.

"Holy shit." They crow, and I flinch as the sound echoes. The few other people turn and look our way, and I try and kill Del with my eyes. "You really do like her. I was kind of being sarcastic before, but you do."

"She's competent. I respect her." I try and keep my face neutral as I meet Del's eyes.

"No," Del shakes their head, "you genuinely like her. You miss her babbling at you."

"No," I deny. "I'm concerned she's going to injure herself biting her lip like that." I want to bite her lip for her, but I am absolutely not allowed to think that.

"I bet you liked watching her when she danced. Did she commit the ultimate sin and make you smile?" Del laughs at me.

"I told her about my dad."

Del's mouth drops open. "What do you mean?"

"I asked her about something and cancer came up and I told her that's what he died from."

They sit back in their chair, worry taking over their expression even more than shock. "That's a big deal, dude. I know that you compare Cyn to she-who-is-faithless but it's got to be telling that you told her something that huge."

"I know. I don't like it."

"Fine, don't like it, but maybe take my first advice to you - be nicer to her. She hasn't earned your unpleasant snarling, and if anything, she's earning your trust."

"That might be taking it a little far. She's decreasing my mistrust."

Del laughs and eats another taco while I still pick at my food.

"This is a fabulous development." They laugh, I frown, and things are the way they always are, and that's comforting.

It takes an hour - our walk home, following me around our suite, and demanding my opinion while they get ready - for Del to convince me to come to the Magistrate party tonight. They have their eye on a sophomore who got inducted last year, and it's the first party she's agreed to go to so they want to try and get to know her better. Always willing to be wingperson, I grudgingly give in.

As soon as Del gets us in the door, they disappear. This is typical for when we go out together, so I don't get mad about it or take it personally. Del never ghosts me, and they never will. If they're getting lucky with the sophomore, they'll find me and tell me, and release me from my obligation to get their ass home.

Despite the supposed wokeness of our campus, Del has gotten trouble from time to time. They're about 6 inches shorter than me, so when I step up by their side, people back the fuck down. While I might have the emotional capacity of a shot glass, Del is my constant person. They've never let me down, and I'll do my damnedest to never let them down either. If anyone wants to give them shit for being who they are, I will make whoever it is regret it.

A laugh that I feel down into my bones pulls my attention to the other end of the Magistrate house, where they have a serve yourself bar setup. It's Cyn. I think I'd know her laugh from it's vibrations in the air even if I couldn't hear her clearly. She makes herself laugh while she's talking in the lab and I fucking hate that it's cute. I hate that she's stopped doing it as often, and I hate that I miss it.

I hate that everything about her is cute. All blonde and perky and smiley, like nothing has ever dimmed her light. It probably never will. There isn't a hint of darkness in her, and that's why I hate her. Not because of her light, but because she wouldn't be able to handle my darkness, and that rejection of myself fills me with self-loathing. I hate her because she makes me hate myself. It's something I'm familiar with and good at, but wanting Cyn takes that to a whole new level. It returns me to a sense that I'm not good enough, and if I even tried to connect with her she'd see it, and she'd leave.

That doesn't stop me from fixating though.

Cyn becomes my project for the night. I keep my distance but keep an eye on her, checking in with Del every so often to make sure they're safe.

Things seem to be going well with the sophomore, so I grudgingly give them a high five when they demand it of me.

Things do not seem to be going as well for Cyn. She's had more to drink than I would've expected, but mostly spends her time dancing with her friends. They're a tight little circle in the middle of the dance area, ignoring anyone who tries to break in and single them out. It's kind of sweet, and I like that she's got a group of people who care about each other and take care of one another.

Cyn breaks away from the group to head back to the bar. I'm thinking about approaching her, saying something to tell her to slow down without sounding patronizing, but then she takes a bottle of water. I can hear the crack of the seal from where I stand, and get lost in the way she moves as she drinks. The silky pulse of her throat swallowing, the way her breasts raise when she takes a deep breath after drinking, and then the sound of her laughter as she giggles in relief.

She starts to walk back to the group when a guy grabs onto her from behind, pulling her back against his body. Cyn keeps a smile on her face as she turns around to reject him, but it's not a real smile. I see her gesture toward her friends, who are too far away to see what's happening.

The guy doesn't listen, pulling her into him again, pressing his hips into her backside. She tries to step forward and away, but he's a lot stronger and she's under the influence. Cyn stumbles, falling back into him.

My feet move on their own, eating up the distance between us. Without thinking, I pull her to me and push the guy back.

"Fuck off," I snarl. "Or can't you tell when a woman is trying to get away from you?"

"Whatever," he rolls his eyes and holds up his hands. "I don't need that kind of drama tonight."

I step closer to him, pushing Cyn behind me. "If you ever touch her again, I'll break your fucking fingers."

Cyn gasps behind me, and I know she heard, but right now I don't care. The guy looks freaked out enough, and that's all I need to see. I'm intimidating as hell when I want to be, and in this moment I really, really want to be. When everything blew up freshman year and I was beyond angry all the time, Del started calling me the Dark One, and the nickname got around. Even if people don't know me, they know my reputation.

It's not the one I wanted in college, but sometimes we have to live with the titles we've earned. I'm short with people. I'm not nice on the first pass. I'm passionate but I'm rigid in my pursuit of that passion. I don't trust people not to hurt me or hurt others. The circle of people I care about and let see the softer side of me is so small it might as well not count. If this drunk meathead tells his meathead friends what happened, they'll all leave her alone.

At least then I'll know she's safe, even when I can't be around to protect her.

Done intimidating him, I turn to Cyn as if they don't exist and focus on her.

"Are you okay?"

"Yeah," she nods, expression confused. I'm too big for her to look past me to see the guy, but her eyes keep moving around me instead of focusing on me as she bites her goddamn lip. I'm stone sober and theoretically should have complete control of my body, but apparently that's untrue. I reach up and run my thumb down her chin, popping her bottom lip out from between her teeth.

"Are you sure?"

"No," Cyn sighs. "I'm not used to things like this." She waves her hands around her, indicating the party. "I feel a little overwhelmed."

"Should I walk you home?"

Cyn nods, then pulls out her phone. I watch as she pulls up a group message and see her texting her friends that she's leaving, and that she's leaving with me. They immediately respond, and I look away to respect her privacy. Though I'm sure her friends don't have the highest opinion of me based on our lab dynamic, I hope they know I would never hurt her. Cyn smiles at something in the chat and then tucks her phone into her pocket.

"Let's go," she keeps smiling, and loops her arm through mine. For some reason, I let her.

I start to maneuver us through the party toward the door. It's hot as hell in this house, packed with bodies because there isn't much else to do in Elmwood on the weekends. We're jolted around against drunk and inattentive people. As we pass through the front living room, I see Del in one corner, whispering in their sophomore's ear. Her eyes are closed and her cheeks are flushed, so I think there's a good chance they get lucky tonight.

I pull Cyn to the side. "Sorry, I need to text someone before we go."

Cyn nods, her smile fading a little and her eyelids drooping.

I text Del, and they look over at me when they get the message. We share a nod, confirming they feel safe on their own, and I leave the party. My hand once again moves on its own, this time to rest over Cyn's where it's tucked into my arm.

The air is cold and refreshing, and I hear her inhale sharply. She leans on me a little bit and I can't even pretend to mind. She lives on the other side of campus from where we are in the underclassmen buildings, so I start heading in that direction.

"I don't feel so good," she moans. Her face is pale and her forehead is sweaty.

"Do you need to puke?"

"I think I should," she murmurs. I guide her off the sidewalk and behind some bushes in front of one of the Cavalry houses. After a few deep breaths, Cyn bends over. I wrap both hands around her soft blonde hair, holding it back while looking away and trying to let her keep some of her dignity.

A few minutes later, she stands back up and I let her hair go. She digs in another pocket and surprises me when she comes up with a pack of gum.

"You good?"

"I feel like I got hit by a car." She pops a piece of peppermint gum in her mouth, then leans on me again. I make an impulsive, but kind, decision right then.

"Come on, we're going to mine." Cyn and I walk back to the sidewalk and head the opposite direction from before, to the buildings behind the Cavalry houses. Del and I live there, even though they could live in the

Magistrate house. Del says its because they can't abandon me but I think it's because they hate the idea of sharing the bathrooms with that many people.

Cyn's eyes are blinking long and slow by the time we make it to my door, and I know I made the right choice. I'd be carrying her about halfway to the residence halls if we'd kept going that route. That's a danger I don't need to experience.

I don't even bother turning on the lights in our suite. I take Cyn's hand and lead her to my room. She sits down heavily on my bed, and doesn't even protest when I kneel down to remove her shoes. Without letting myself think too hard about it, I tuck her beneath my covers and leave her there to sleep it off. I get a bottle of water and a bottle of ibuprofen and leave them on the table next to my bed.

"I don't know how to drink," she mumbles before I can step away. "They never let me do anything so I don't know how to do anything."

I perch on the bed next to her and listen. "Who?"

"My dad and the headmaster. It was grades and channel, grades and channel, no life unless it benefits one of those two things. No friends, no boyfriends, no drinking, no parties, no one to fuck me. It all had to be a secret."

I stiffen. "What?"

"What am I saying?" She rubs her hands over her face. "No one wants to fuck me."

I reach over and brush her hair out of her face. "I'm sure that's not true." It seems like the most neutral answer to her last statement. It's not like I'm going to tell her I'd fuck her because one, she's drunk, and two, she can never, ever know that.

"My life sucked, Rome. I didn't have a life. I only do the channel for my dad anymore. He applied for the Van Hornen. I didn't even know."

"You're telling me a lot of things right now, Cyn, that you might not want me to know."

Cyn frowns, her eyes hazy as she meets mine. "I know there's a sunshine under there somewhere. I believe that. I have to believe that." She reaches up and pokes me in the cheek and I almost smile because it's so absurd. There's nothing I can say to her pronouncement because I don't agree with it, and I'm not about to argue with a drunk person. That's a rational human rule. There's no sunshine in me, and there hasn't been for a long time. If there ever was at all. This is who I've always been, I can't even blame Hannah.

It all makes me more frustrated for and with Cyn, knowing these things. She never stands up for herself and is letting other people tell her who to be and what to do. It's easier for her to be happy and positive, to smooth things over, rather than to rip them up and plant new roots. That will never be the way I live my life. I will never let being comfortable overshadow what's right or what I need.

Perhaps I have been too hard on her though. Some people aren't built for confrontation, and I shouldn't force her to be something she's not. It's not fair for me to be another person trying to make her be anything other than herself. My problem with it should only be my problem. With a sigh, I leave her to sleep it off.

Then I settle onto the short, awkward couch in our living room area, and try to get some sleep.

When I wake up in the morning, Cyn is gone, and I'm unexpectedly furious.

Cyn

When I walk into the lab Tuesday afternoon, the atmosphere is so tense I can feel it pressing down on my shoulders. The thing is, I'm not even sure what Rome is mad about this time, but I know for sure he's mad at me.

I woke up early Saturday morning, still a little drunk, and extremely embarrassed. I didn't even take the time to be nosy and look around Rome's room. I took two ibuprofen and the bottle of water he left for me, and did my best to sneak out quietly. When I walked through the living room and saw Rome curled up on their small couch, I felt guilt in addition to humiliation.

I was vulnerable and he came to my defense, then he took care of me when I was drunk. He even held my hair back while I threw up. Then he has to go and be all sweet by letting me sleep in his bed. My dignity and reputation around him is completely shot. Rome already thinks I'm an airhead and doesn't take me seriously, I'm sure that's even more true after he experienced me not being able to get a dumb guy to go away and that I can't handle my liquor. I know we talked when I was in his bed, but I don't really remember what I said.

At this point, I can only hope I didn't tell him how sexy he is.

Split second decision, I decide to play it off like Friday night never happened.

"Hi, Rome!" I sing and smile at him, trading my jacket for my lab coat. I check that everything is in its place and out of my way. "We're supposed to get thunderstorms all week, so I'm going to keep a pair of shoes here so I don't have to work in my rain boots, hope you don't mind. I love thunderstorms, how about you? I even bought a brand new umbrella before

I came here!" My laugh is forced.

I start walking over to my station, and the tension gets sharper. I haven't looked at him, but I can feel him staring at me. Now, after my usual semi-lab related greeting, is when I force myself to shut up and get to work.

The squeak of the feet of Rome's stool as he moves it out to stand up is echoing and ominous in the large lab.

"That's all you have to say?" His voice is deceptively cool. I'm terrified to look at him.

"What do you mean?" I put extra energy and bravado into my voice. I still don't look away from my station, arranging my tools and preparing my computer program.

Rome comes up behind me. Not close enough to touch, but definitely in my personal space.

"A thank you would've been nice."

My shoulders come up to my ears as I wince. "I am grateful for your help." I glance at him over my shoulder. "Thank you."

Rome is glowering down at me, nearly seething. It makes the butterflies in my stomach riot and I have to ask again, what the hell is wrong with me? Why does his fury turn me on?

"What are you thanking me for, Cynthia?" He uses my full name and I don't think I like it. It feels threatening. Now I turn around to face him because if we're going to keep going down this road, I think I need to see his expression to gauge what I should say. I don't want to fight with him.

"For getting that guy to leave me alone, and giving me someplace safe to sleep when I drank too much."

"You told him to leave you alone with a smile on your face. Why?"

"I was trying to be nice."

"Where has being nice ever gotten you? Where has being nice ever gotten anyone?" He takes a step forward, and I take a step back, until my body is pressed up against the work table. Rome leans over me and I bite my lip for a second, the pain centering me so I can answer his question. I'm going to try for honesty.

"It's not about other people. It's about me. That's who I need to be for my own happiness."

"Happiness is a myth, Cyn. People are going to think they can walk all over you if you keep being so damn nice."

"Happiness is important. I'm sorry you don't feel that way." There's a slight snap to my words, and I immediately pull back, upset with myself. "We see the world differently, and I choose to respond by being happy."

Rome snorts. "Whatever."

For some reason, that casual disregard for my opinion is the thing that breaks me. Yes, I am positive, upbeat, and choose to be happy over feeling anything else. I'm doing his damn lab work to his standards, he doesn't have to make me a grump like him. He doesn't get to tell me how to live my life.

"Why do you hate me? What is your problem with me?" I basically shout it in his face, and immediately bite my lip again, needing to calm my anxiety. I don't take it back though.

Rome gets up in my face, glowering down at me, and even furious I can't help but notice how incredibly hot he is. The intensity of his gaze lights a fire over my entire body, and I hate the fact that I'm getting aroused by someone who has been such an asshole to me. My nipples are hard in my shirt and my mouth is watering feeling him so close to me. This is the part of me that's broken, I swear.

"My problem?" he growls and sneers. "My problem is that I don't trust relentlessly positive people because they're just as selfish as every other asshole except they're in denial about it. My problem is that you "influenced" your way into a prestigious fellowship while I killed myself for the same opportunity doing science, and you didn't even want it." I flinch at that, but he's not wrong. He steps even closer, and I can feel his breath on my face, and his chest brushing mine. I bite my lip to cover my emotions, almost hard enough to break the skin.

"My problem is that I watch you bite your fucking lip and all I want to do is replace your teeth with my own. My problem is that even though everything about you makes me want to burn the world down, I am dying to devour you, Cyn." His voice is so soft for the last sentence that if I wasn't centimeters away I probably wouldn't have heard him at all.

"Do it," I whisper, giving him permission. The challenge is clear in my voice. I don't think he'll do it, and I want it. I can't believe how bad I want it.

Rome darts forward and does what he promised – he takes my bottom lip between his teeth and bites, then sucks, causing my mouth to drop open. He takes the opportunity to shift upward and seal his mouth over mine, his tongue invading me and sweeping across my own with ruthless, erotic precision. I feel myself melt into him, and his hands land on my hips and squeeze, bruising me. I let him attack my mouth, submissive and pliant, begging for his punishment.

After a long moment, Rome breaks the kiss. His eyes are hazy as he looks down at me, but they clear up when they drop down to my mouth. They widen with something like horror. He drops his hands from me as if I'm on fire.

"Cynthia," he murmurs, before turning around and running from the lab.

What the fuck? I reach up and brush my hand across my lips. When I pull away, my fingertips are pink with blood. He bit me hard enough to make me bleed, and while that should bother me, it doesn't at all. It was the best kiss of my life, and it wasn't enough.

To center myself, and because I'm fairly sure he won't come back, I work on Charity's journal and film a little.

My phone buzzes repeatedly. When I finally look at it, I see I have a bunch of notifications from Instagram. I didn't even post anything today, so it doesn't make any sense.

I open the app and slide over to profile. My stomach drops to the floor. A picture was posted today. I'm maybe 2 years old and my mom is holding me, her nose pressed to my cheek as she smiles. The caption talks about losing her to cancer, being too young to have many memories, and then talking about keeping journals and diaries for the ones we might leave behind someday. Dad listed three brands I frequently use.

The comments section is a disaster. Thousands of people offering comfort, or criticism that I'm using a picture of my dead mother to sell products for a company. I appreciate the former, but have to agree with the latter.

I don't even bother calling my dad. I turn off the comments section.

I debate on posting an apology in my stories. Instead, I pull up a photo on my stories that's of a journal from one of the companies that was tagged. It was what I'd been working on for this purpose this week, but dad jumped the gun and invaded my privacy again. I hit post on a video on the channel about journaling prompts, and then add a photo and link in my stories.

I feel sick to my stomach. One of the wildest, most intense moments of my life has been ruined by my invasive, asshole dad. I've asked him repeatedly not to use photos of mom or bring mom up in posts and he never listens. Apparently my brand is more important than me. That's not new, but it hurts every time.

I clean up and shut down the lab, all motivation gone now.

It's misting outside but I don't bother covering up. The cool rain covers my face, drips down into the neck of my coat, and dampens my hair.

Rome hates my existence, but he wants me. I can work with that. I'm not a huge fan of his attitude or his approach to the world, but my body still wants him. I also know under all that snarling fury is a good guy. I can trust that guy, and maybe chasing the annoying attraction between us is how we make it through.

Before going inside, I tilt my face up to the sky and breathe in the icy rain. I've got this. I can choose to be happy about these other avenues opening up in front of me. Or I can find a way to walk away, and be happy with that too.

Rome

I'm pretty sure I blacked out for the rest of the day because other than kissing Cyn, I don't remember anything until I wake up on Wednesday morning. It was incredible. The best kiss of my life.

It was also wrong on more levels than my brain is allowing me to think about right now. I kissed her because even against my will and better judgment, I'm intensely attracted to her. I kissed her because part of me hates her and wants to punish her, and savaging her lips was the best way to show it. She is my mentee, and I took advantage of our strained relationship to take this from her.

There's no rules about mentors and mentees fraternizing. It's happened plenty of times before, and even though the area is murky, it's not technically an issue. We don't have any grading authority over our mentees, even if we do supervise them in our own labs. I have no power over her, not in any formal way.

But the power differential exists. I'm accepted into the program, I have a good reputation, and it's not an exaggeration that I can open doors for her. Not that she'll need me to, she does excellent work, but it's a reality. It's a reality that women in academia are coerced by shitty men because they get beaten down and don't believe they can do the work without help.

The fact that even for a second I crossed that line makes me want to bash my head in.

Del wakes up and finds me sitting on the couch, staring at nothing.

"Uh, don't you have class?"

I look up and then frown. Del is dressed more masculine than I've seen them in awhile. Baggy jeans and a t-shirt, which even though it's fitted, covers all their skin. Their hair is down and straightened, but there's little to no make up on their face.

"Are you okay?" Usually when Del gets reserved, it's because something happened. Someone said something to them that makes them feel like they have to pull back and hide. Del has forbidden me from calling it "turtling" out loud, so I only say it in my head. Generally, when Del is dressed more masc, they're turtling.

"You first."

I sigh. "I have class. I'm not going."

"Obviously. Why? What happened?"

"You tell me first and then I'll tell you because we're going to get sidetracked."

Del perks up a little, sensing something big. "I've been doing more reading lately and I think I've fallen into a trap. I'm gender fluid but then why do I always present as feminine? Why do I feel the need to do that, to prove something? So I'm trying to find my masculine identity, too, or what the middle ground looks like for me. The happy place, so to speak."

I groan, thinking about the stupid shit I said to Cyn about happiness. I was so angry with her, it's unreasonable. Happiness exists, I'm just not a happy person. My instinctual reactions are annoyance and dismissal. I refocus on my friend.

"That's good to know. But if it's anything else, you'd tell me, right?" I check in, making sure they keep looking in my eyes. Del has the most obvious tells. They nod, and look relaxed, so I think everything is okay.

"Tell me." Del comes over and sits down in the chair next to me.

"Cyn and I got in an argument - I confronted her about leaving and then it turned into something else and then I kissed her." I say it quickly, hoping Del will blur it all together and not catch the last part.

They say nothing, and I look over. The look on their face is indescribable. Something like shock, horror, and extreme amusement. Like they ate something sour and their face is reacting even though they liked it.

"You did...what?"

"I kissed her," I mumble.

"Holy shit I thought it would take me a year to convince you to make a move. What happened?"

"She was biting her fucking lip and I couldn't take it anymore. I said some things and she said some things and then we were kissing."

"How was it?"

"Perfect. I ran out of the lab in panic."

Del laughs. "And then?"

"Oh," I continue, angry with myself. "I blacked out. I don't remember anything until about an hour ago."

"So you have no idea how Cyn feels about this because you kissed the hell out of her and ran away?"

I put my head in my hands and groan. "I'm such a fucking idiot."

"Yes," Del agrees.

"She should report me. I'll talk to Dr. C and get her assigned somewhere else. I can't believe I crossed a line like that."

"Wait," Del shakes me, "you have to talk to Cyn. This is about what she's comfortable with, don't make assumptions. Let her talk, and listen to what she says. Promise me?"

"You're right." That makes me feel a little bit better. Cyn and I will be able to talk like normal people and clear the air. I can apologize, and if she wants to transfer to another lab, I'll do everything I can to help her. This is more complicated than I ever expected. Something about her gets under my skin and drives me out of my mind.

The feelings I had while kissing her were so strong that even replaying the memory of it in my head makes me get dizzy. I have to blink a few times to clear my thoughts because the emotions that roar through me are powerful and confusing. I want to tell myself that I don't know her, that I've made it a point to not get to know her, and yet she wouldn't let me push her away.

I know things about her every day life because she doesn't stop talking about them. I know her friends and their majors, I know where she lives, I know her favorite food from the cafeteria, I know her coffee order. I know that her favorite holidays are New Year's Eve and the 4th of July because fireworks are her favorite. I know that she has strong feelings about conservation and she's trying to hit all of the National Parks before she finishes college. I know she wants to work in the Boston Public Library after she graduates. I know how she lost her mom. I know she keeps doing YouTube because of her dad and I know she does things that her unhappy for the sake of other people. I know she's kinder than the world fucking deserves. Than anyone deserves, especially me.

All she knows about me is the Dwyer method, and that my dad died of cancer. That I'm grumpy as fuck and don't talk to people. Excellent.

I'm sure by now someone has told her about Hannah. It's the kind of lore people who aren't involved in it like to spread, because they forget that the people it hurts are still around. I get it, it's full of angst and betrayal, and I'm over Hannah. I'm not over the way it all went down. That's always going to hurt.

We'd been together for five years. If she'd broken up with me, I would have let her go. At that point, we were more friends than romantic partners anyway. We'd even had conversations about our relationship fading and if we thought we were ready to go our separate ways. When we had those deep, emotional conversations, she was already fucking her future husband behind his then-wife's back. I'll never understand her choices, and I never gave her the chance to explain herself.

Hannah knew my ethics. What she did spat in the face of them. There was no explanation she could give me that would justify what they did. For a woman who had built her entire brand around kindness, she did the cruelest thing imaginable.

She knew my past with my family, my struggles with abandonment, as well as my intense beliefs in loyalty and commitment. Hannah betrayed us in private while espousing a false ideology to her millions of followers. I could expose her, but I don't.

The only time I met with her after catching her in the act was when the College facilitated an agreement between the four of us to keep what happened quiet. Hannah agreed to leave Elmwood. Dr. C got her no contest divorce with no alimony. I got nothing. I guess I got to stay here, and that was enough. Of course, it got out, but not like it could have if any of us had talked.

"I'm going back to bed. I'll talk to her in the lab tonight," I promise Del.

They nod, pat me on the knee even though I know they want to hug me, and get up to leave for their class.

I'm waiting at the lab table by the door when Cyn comes in. She stops, looking surprised to see me so close. With a small smile, she reaches up and takes off the hat she's wearing. Her golden hair stands up with static and when she feels it, she laughs. Her laugh hits me in the chest, sparking both horror and hope. I don't want to notice her laugh.

"We need to talk." My voice is weak, so I clear my throat. "About yesterday."

"Oh?" She grins and steps closer to me. "What about yesterday?"

I take a step back away from her, and for some reason that makes her smile wider. I'm on unsteady ground here. She's not reacting at all like I expected. I replay Del's advise in my head, which is to talk, and actually listen to her. To try hard not to make assumptions.

"I'm sorry - I crossed a line. It was inappropriate and if you want to report it, or work in a different lab, I'll do whatever you'd like." The words come out rushed, and I know the anguish in my voice shows on my face. "I'm your mentor and I should never put you in a position where you might feel like I took advantage of you. I'm sorry."

Cyn's smile dropped while I spoke, and it makes the pit in my stomach grow larger. Maybe she hadn't thought about it that way until I pointed it out, and now I've upset her even further. She looks down for a long time, the silence stretching between us.

When she looks up, I don't know how to read the look on her face. She takes another step closer to me, backing me up into the lab table. It's the mirror scenario of what happened yesterday. I don't like it.

"You didn't put me in any position that I didn't want to be in," Cyn's voice is soft but her words hit me hard. "I told you to do it, Rome. There's nothing to be sorry for."

She puts a hand on my chest and I flinch, wound so tightly I might spring apart from the tension at any moment. Cyn leans closer, and has to tilt her head back as I move mine down in order for me to keep eye contact with her.

"I think it was kind of inevitable, don't you?" Cyn's voice is soft and husky, and it makes my cock twitch. Her eyes drop down to my mouth and then back up. "The tension had to break."

Then she grabs my shirt and uses it as leverage to lift herself up. Cyn's lips crash into mine, and immediately I lose my sense of self and control because I kiss her back. I dive into her mouth like I'm dying of thirst, sipping at the cup of her. She tastes like sunshine and fresh air. Right now nothing but her could stop me as I grasp her to me, my hands diving into her hair, my fingers digging into her nape to keep her where I need her.

Cyn drops her head, breaking our contact, and slowly, I let her go. We're still close, still breathing each other's air, but not touching anymore.

Her cheeks are flushed, and I can tell she's trying hard not to smile. "I'm going to give you some space today. I'll see you tomorrow."

I swallow hard and nod. She's right to do it. I have a lot to think about.

I don't move as she puts her hat and coat back on, and quietly leaves the lab.

This is as good a place as any to think, so I lean against the table and close my eyes. First, I replay this second kiss in my mind, allowing myself to groan out loud at how fucking good it felt. I've been with people over the last year and a half since things imploded with Hannah, but those were quick hookups that scratched an itch for both of us. There was none of this explosive chemistry. I didn't feel anything when I kissed them. Not like when I'm with Cyn.

She makes me feel so many emotions in such big ways and my body doesn't know how to handle any of it. It's not used to feeling anything, let alone this intensely.

No work is going to get done tonight, and we're far ahead of our deadlines, so I pack up and shut down the lab. A walk in the cold October air is exactly what I need right now.

Campus is dark and blustery, the sun setting and light spearing through the trees and appearing from behind buildings. I'm not sure where I'm going, so I follow the footpaths through the quad, not getting too far from the library. At some point, I sit on a bench in the green space. I've been thinking about nothing, really, only keeping my mind calm and clear until I'm ready.

I'm not sure what Cyn wants me to think about - if I want more? If I want to keep kissing her? Even if I think I shouldn't, the answer to that is a resounding yes. My body is basically screaming at me how much it wants her. My heart is afraid of her, but wants her all the same. She makes me feel things, and I'm still not sure that's something I want. My brain is a hard no, and even as it tries to shout all the reasons doing it again, and doing anything further, are a terrible idea, it's still drowned out. I want her. I want her so much it makes me furious.

I want her in a way that spins out dark fantasies. I want to do terrible things to her. I want to own her so hard and so deep that she'll cry when she comes. I want to punish her for being so bright and so beautiful, and for warming me when I'd gotten used to being cold. I'd made a lot of assumptions about her and she was always proving to me that she was more. That only makes me angrier and I want to take it out on her body. Imprint it on her fucking soul.

It made me even more aggravated that she did it without rubbing it in my face either. Cyn was smart, capable, and rigorous. She knew what she was doing and what she was talking about. I respected her, maybe even liked her if that was a feeling I allowed myself to have, and couldn't deny that I wanted her badly.

At some point I cross campus to the dining hall and grab food to go. I eat it on the way back to the library. The only way to really clear my mind is to do some work.

The light is on in the lab. I notice as soon as I step into the hallway. I know I turned it off when I left.

I look through the window in the door, and Cyn is there. She's at one of the lab tables we don't use, working with the computer.

Quietly, I put in the code and open the door. Luckily, Cyn has headphones in so she doesn't hear me come in. It's another thing I've never explicitly said she can't have while working, but one she intuited.

I walk up behind her and look over her shoulder. She's scanning pages of a journal - it looks like the ones we've been working on, but the handwriting is totally different. Clearly more feminine, and the dates are not for a journal we've been working on. The initials at the end of the entry she's working on read "C.A.J." Who would that be?

"What are you doing?" I ask with a slightly raised voice, not wanting to seem like I'm yelling but needing her to hear me over the headphones.

Cyn jumps and screams and turns to look at me with terror on her face. The kind of apprehension I expected when she came into the lab today as a result of me crossing the line, not me catching her working on her own project. She snaps the laptop she was using shut and turns to me, pocketing her earbuds.

"It's my own project I'm sorry I should use somewhere else I didn't think you'd be here but if you leave me alone I'll pack up and go." Cyn says it quickly, in one rushed, desperate breath.

I don't say anything. I stare at her, waiting.

She keeps eye contact with me, hoping that I'll break first, but honestly, she should know better. I can wait her out. Cyn feels the pressure to fill silence when I do not share that compunction.

"My roommate found a journal in a hidden room and it belonged to Charity James."

In shock, I say nothing, only raise my eyebrows.

"I've been working on restoring it in secret." Cyn hangs her head in shame. "Are you going to turn me in?"

"Let me see it." I step closer and she moves aside. The journal isn't in great shape but it's not terrible either. There are strong indentations on the pages and I can see she's been careful to only do digital restoration so far. She's been doing a thorough scan of each page and then allowing the program to render the entries. It's a slow process, she's only a quarter of the way through the little leather book.

"I'm not going to turn you in," I look at her and surprise myself by smiling slightly. I don't actually know the last time I smiled, even a little. "I want to help you."

Cyn nods in agreement, relieved. Something just changed between us.

Cyn

Our schedule changes without us really talking about it. I work with Rome on the President's journals from 4-7pm, and then we pack everything up and switch to Charity's journal for at least another hour or so. For the moment, we're focusing on scanning the entire book and having the pages rendered. If we learn there's historical value or specific value to Elmwood and its history, we agreed we'll stop and turn the journal in to the department. Rome seemed pretty confident Dr. Cunningham wouldn't penalize us for only engaging in digital work.

It makes all of my days extra long, but I'm also spending them with Rome. Since the intense kisses we shared, and since he caught me, something about him has loosened up a little. He's still grumpy and serious all the time, but it's like he's no longer shielding me from his excitement about the work.

The tension between us is high again. It snapped for a few days, and now it's building up. By the time we leave every night the butterflies in my stomach are exhausted and my muscles are sore from holding myself still. Every time we brush against each other, even unintentional bumps, I feel it through my entire body.

Sometimes I catch Rome watching me instead of watching the screen as the render processes.

Every time a page is complete, he has me read it to him out loud.

The early pages are pretty basic. Charity talks about moving to Elmwood, about helping her mother host dinners and parties, and a distinct dislike for her father. Charity keeps making reference to his "plans" for her. There was one entry in particular where she said she believed he wanted to make her disappear, that he was ashamed his oldest child was a girl, and she feared that when she married he'd keep her away from her family.

Nothing about what we knew of Charity indicated she was a troublemaker by the standards of the time. She married at 19, had many, many children, and a descendant of hers even went on to be another President of Elmwood. She was New York high society and connected to a lot of people. Some descendants of the James family are current Elmwood students here, but the only reason they're connected at all is because Charity had such a large family. President James owed Charity's existence and her marriage for his enduring legacy. Neither of his sons went on to do much with themselves, and one of the branches died out entirely.

Poor Charity. She seemed feisty.

Rome and I agreed to come in and spend a Saturday in the lab, trying to get a huge chunk done at once. We both expressed concern that we were more invested in Charity than in President James, and that some of the excitement might go away if we finished the rendering. The priority has to be our actual funded lab project, and I know how much completing it and leading it means to Rome.

I arrive at the lab first, and I'm braiding my hair to get it out of my face when the door opens. I turn as Rome steps in and nearly swallow my tongue.

It must've started raining in the minutes since I walked in the building because there are drops on his jacket and he shakes his head, his dark hair dripping water. A drop slides from his sharp jawline and down his neck and I want to taste it off his skin.

"Cyn," Rome says sharply, and I get the feeling he said it more than once before I heard him. "You can't look at me like that." There's barely restrained fury in his voice. "We've been doing so well."

"Well?" I scoff. "If 'well' is feeling like I might die of sexual tension at the end of every night, we've been doing spectacular."

Rome closes his eyes, a pained expression slashing across his face before he hides it away behind his stony mask. "We shouldn't."

"I think we have to, Rome," I nearly whisper, and his eyes fly open.

There's so much heat and torment there it makes my knees weak. "Unless we keep breaking the tension, we're never going to get anything done."

"What do you suggest?" He raises an eyebrow. I take a step toward him and watch him tense, bracing himself.

"Kissing you isn't going to be enough," I murmur, moving into his personal space and inhaling. He smells like the rain and the cinnamon scent of chai, which I know he drinks the few times I've seen him get coffee from the cart outside the library.

"Then what is?" Rome reaches behind me and wraps my braid around his fist before he uses it to pull me in closer to his body. "If we go further, I don't know if you can handle what I want to do to you."

My body clenches, my core feeling aching and empty. I look from his eyes, down to his lips, and then back. "What do you want to do to me?"

"I want to punish you, Cyn." He leans close and nips at my bottom lip. "I want to drag you into the darkness with me and see if your brightness can withstand it. I want you on your knees and begging for me to give you another orgasm even if you don't think you can take it. I want to show you your dark side; the sweet, hungry slut who will do any fucking thing to please me."

My breath comes out in a stuttering gasp. "Yes. I want that."

Rome rears back slightly, searching my eyes for the truth. I let him see my desperation. I don't hold anything back.

I've always been a more submissive person, it's why everyone in my life has had so many opportunities to take advantage of me. I don't put up a fight, I don't engage in conflict, some of it because I don't think it's worth bothering, and some of it because I'm not built that way. The idea that Rome wants my submission to pleasure us both feels like the right use of it, rather than an abuse.

I lift up on my toes and run my tongue between his lips. "I'm yours, sir."

Rome groans and his eyes close. "I knew you were doing that on purpose."

I bite my lip to hide my smile, but let it go when he snarls at me. I didn't realize biting my lip got to him so badly. It's a nervous habit I can't break.

"Maybe a little," I admit. "I know we're supposed to work on the journal..." I trail off. "I can't take it, Rome," I nearly whine. "I can't go through a whole day like this."

Rome searches my face again, his dark eyes blazing over me, taking me in. I know he's weighing his own decisions and the possible consequences. Oddly, I know he's also trying to consider what's best for me. He lets go of my braid and steps back. My heart falls for a second.

"Grab your coat." I jump into motion at his words and get my coat and hat on. We don't say anything else as we exit the lab, and when we get to the door that leads out of the library, Rome reaches back and takes my hand. I'm not even sure he realizes that he's done it, but I cling to him as we step out into the windy, misty rain.

We walk past the Cavalry houses and to the small buildings behind it. I remember leaving here on Saturday morning but was still too out of it to pay attention to what room number and what building were his. Rome says nothing, just pulls me along the hallways.

He still says nothing when we enter his apartment, and I follow him into his bedroom. He closes and locks the door.

Rome turns and stares at me, and then I don't know who moves first but we collide in the center of the room. If I thought our kisses had been intense before, they were nothing compared to this. He's in the safety of his room now, he's in control of his anger, he's made a measured decision to take me and he has my permission to do it. Rome has unleashed himself.

While one hand cups my neck, keeping my mouth sealed to his, the other efficiently strips me out of my hat and jacket, removes his jacket, and as he swirls his tongue around mine in a move that feels so filthy my body shivers, his hand slides into my leggings.

For a second he breaks the kiss, meeting my eyes, waiting before going deeper. I nod and then dig my hands into his shirt, pulling him closer. Rome's long, talented fingers slide into my sex and I moan into his mouth. His middle finger finds my clit, swirling and pressing softly at first, then harder. It feels so good, and at some point I'm barely holding myself up. His hands are keeping me upright as he plays with my drenched pussy.

Rome yanks away from me, and when he removes his hand I whimper in disappointment. A flicker of a smirk crosses his face, and I think I would die to experience that expression fully. To see him give me a full, sexy smirk of satisfaction.

Rome sits on the edge of his bed and beckons me with a finger. I step between his knees.

"Take off your shirt." I do as he says. Rome looks me over, nothing but desire in his gaze. "Now your bra." I unhook it and let it drift off my body and down to the floor. Rome reaches out and slides his hands up my sides, his thumbs sliding underneath my breasts, then along the outside of the soft flesh, massaging away the remaining feeling of restraint.

His hands slide back down and into my leggings. Teasingly slowly, he starts to slide them over my ass, grazing his hands along my thighs, then letting them drop on their own when they get past my knees. I step out of them, and now I'm naked before him. I'm so aroused his gaze feels like a touch.

"Rome," I whimper again.

"Get on your knees," he replies. I do as he says, and watch as he removes his own shirt, revealing expanses of muscle that I want to sink my teeth into. Rome stands, the bulge beneath his jeans right in my face, and I'm panting as he unbuckles his belt, flicks open the button, slides the zipper, and lets them drop down his legs.

"Do you want it, Cyn?"

"Yes," I breathe, desperate to see his cock.

"Take me out."

I reach into his waistband and wrap one hand around him, pulling his boxers down with my other hand. He's thick and hot and the second he's in my face the desire to let him use my throat rises inside me. I've never wanted to do that. I've never wanted to beg to taste anyone the way I want to taste him.

I look up at him and open my mouth, sticking out my tongue, begging with my actions instead of my words.

"Fuck. What a pretty slut you are, Cyn. Are you wide open for me, baby?"

I nod. Rome slaps my tongue with his cock and I moan. He does it again, the slaps getting wetter as more saliva pools in my mouth.

Rome sits down on the bed and beckons me over again. I shuffle forward on my knees, and he wraps my braid in his fist like he did in the lab, and my body becomes alert.

"Take me as deep as you can, and hold there."

"Yes, sir," I respond and shiver at the flash of fiery pleasure in his eyes.

Rome's cock is long and thick, and I open my mouth for him and slide down. I let saliva drip from my lips, making the path slick, and keep going until he hits the back of my throat. I can fit more of him in my mouth than I thought, and I swallow. His hips thrust up, taking him even deeper, and I'm surprised to find I can take it. He tastes amazing, a little like soap from the shower he probably took this morning, and then that primal musk we all have. My pheromones fucking love it.

"Good girl," Rome praises. "Suck my cock."

I do as he says, sliding up, and then back down. Rome's grip on my hair is tight, but the little bit of pain keeps me engaged and keeps making me wet as hell. The sounds I'm making as I move on him would embarrass me if he wasn't constantly telling me how good it feels, that he knows I can take him deeper, and god I want to please him so I do. I gag on him and find that I don't mind it.

"Stop, Cyn," Rome groans and I pull off of him, my lips abused and swollen. "Get up."

I stand and then so does he. "Bend over the bed."

"Yes, sir."

That earns me a smack on the ass and I chirp, but realize that I kind of liked it.

Rome, ever observant, gives me that hint of a smirk again. "I'll give you more if you want it, but do what I say."

"Yes, sir." I bend over on his bed, resting on my elbows. All of me is exposed to him now. I've had sex before but I've never done anything like this. Never in the light or where I revealed so much of myself to the other person. To be honest, in the past I did it because I was bored, and wanted to see what the big deal was. It had been okay, nowhere near as good as what I could do myself, but nothing earth-shattering.

I know that Rome is going to shatter me. Down to my mitochondria. It might even alter my damn DNA by the time he's done with me.

Rome's hand smacks my ass again, and then a few more times. The vibrations of the slaps zing through my pussy and make me clench around nothing.

I hear Rome shift and then feel both of his hands on my ass cheeks, massaging the stinging skin before he spreads them apart. When his tongue spreads me open and he licks from my clit to my asshole, I gasp in pleasure. He repeats the stroke of his tongue, again and again until everything is wet. When I'm shaking with the need for him to touch me more intensely, his face presses into my pussy and he sucks my clit into his mouth. His tongue and teeth swirl around it, driving me higher and higher. When his thumb presses against my entrance I push back, seeking more. Rome obliges.

He fucks me with his thumb and sucks on my clit, relentless, never stopping, never changing, terrifyingly consistent in the way he's playing with and devouring me. My thigh muscles start to shake as I get closer to coming, and my hands are gripping his comforter like I'm going to fall down if I let go.

My pussy clenches and it's enough to send me over the edge. "Rome!" I shout as I grind against him, taking what he's giving me. He doesn't stop until I'm breathing somewhat normally again, and even then he pulls out his thumb but continues to lap at me, licking me clean.

"That was good, but I think you can do better. I think you have more sunshine to give me, baby." Rome smacks my ass, then stands up and flips me over. He's stronger than I thought he'd be, and I don't mind at all that he's manhandling me around on his bed.

He gets back on his knees and dives between my legs, using his hands to spread open my pussy lips so he can attack my clit more directly. When his eyes flick up to meet mine, the sight undoes me. The sight of his eyebrows drawn together, giving my pussy that same intensive, nearly violent focus he gives his work is too much. Right now I'm his work and I love it.

My head crashes back on the bed and I roll my hips, chasing the over-whelming pleasure as his insane tongue moves back and forth and around until he finds the rhythm that makes my hips pump all by themselves. Fuck he's good at this.

I'm getting close and he knows it because one hand moves to press my thigh open, and he starts licking the tiniest bit faster. I moan something unintelligible trying to tell him I'm coming but then it doesn't matter, I'm seeing stars and grinding my hips on his stupidly handsome face.

My orgasm isn't quite done when he pulls away and stands over me. One of his hands is on the bed by my head, and the middle two fingers of the other are sliding into me, hooking hard on my g-spot, building me up again before I'm even done with the last one. He leans in close to my face and I can smell myself on his breath, on his skin. I love the idea that he's tasted me, is still tasting me, and now he wants more.

"Come for me one more time, get that pussy ready for me," he whispers while looking straight into my eyes. The anger is still there but it's all part of the desire too. He doesn't want to want me, and that should bother me. Except his want is overruling everything else, and that makes me feel so damn powerful. I make this intense, beautiful asshole weak, and I love it.

"Fuck my fingers - show me you want it. Show me how much you want me to fuck you, Cyn. That you're a needy, hungry little slut and will do anything for my cock."

"I will," I promise, moving my hips in time with the thrusts of his fingers. "I want you," I confirm. The pleasure on his face when I say it is enough. I cry out sharply, body bowing as another orgasm rolls through my body, my hips undulating as I ride his hand.

"Good girl," he says before kissing my forehead and pulling his fingers out. Rome gets a condom and I watch as he rolls it on. "Get on the floor," he commands. "All fours."

The carpet is short and harsh, and a part of me feels oddly pleased I'm going to have rug burn from this. A reminder for a little while of the first time Rome fucks me.

He gets behind me, grabs my hips, and thrusts all the way inside me with no warning. My back bows and then my body falls over, face pressing into my arm where it rests on the rough carpet. Rome gives me a second to adjust, and then moves his hips. He isn't slow, he doesn't warm me up to anything, he pounds into me with all the fury he holds for my existence and his attraction to me. He's punishing me with his cock and I already know I will never, ever get enough.

"Yes," I cry out. "Please."

"Please what."

"Punish me, sir," I respond without thinking.

"Sweet Cyn. I will, and you'll take it all, won't you?"

I can only cry out something that sound like yes. I'm so damn sensitive I know I'm going to come again and I'm afraid I won't be able to stay conscious.

"Take it. Come all over my cock like you did on my mouth and my fingers. Give me all that fucking sunshine, Cyn." Rome nearly growls at me, both hands digging into my hips now, pounding faster and harder, my hips jolting forward, my face smashing into my arm. I squeeze my pussy around his invasion, and my next orgasm starts. I close my eyes and hold my body tight, drawing it out as he groans against me, feeling the pulse of my pussy as I fade from reality for a little bit.

"Good girl," he praises again, and pulls out of me. I can't move. Rome lifts me up and puts me on his bed on my back. "You good?" he asks, concerned for a moment.

"Yes. More," I beg. "Give me more."

Rome's mouth smashes into mine and he kisses me, swirling his tongue around mine, teasing the nerves in my mouth. I bite down on his lip when his cock presses into me, slow and insistent, filling me up. I tilt my hips so I can wrap my legs around him, and open myself up for him to give me what I asked for.

He raises up over me, grinding deep inside and torturing me with pleasure. The expression of lust and fury making me clench around him and his eyes lose focus for a moment.

"I'm going to hold you down and fuck you until I come now, Cyn. It won't be about you. It won't be about making you come. It will be about using you," he leans forward and nips my lip, "like the happy little slut you are, taking from your sweet, tight pussy until I get what I want. Do you understand me?"

"Yes," I nod and roll my hips, turned on by his words. I'll tear myself apart about liking it so much later.

"If you say stop, I'll stop."

"I won't," I promise. Rome looks at me again, trying to read my mind with the power of his gaze.

He wraps one of his hands around my throat. Not cutting off my air or restricting my blood flow, but hard enough to keep my where he wants me. I feel his fingers flex, getting comfortable against my skin. I take a deep breath and brace myself. He knows it. Rome is drawing out the moment to mess with me, to see how long I can be patient when I want to get fucked. My hips squirm against him, seeking friction, and I earn myself another half smirk.

It drops off his face as he looks at me again, something more serious I can't interpret in his expression. He leans close and drops a soft kiss to my lips, unexpectedly sweet in the dark heat of what we've been doing.

When he leans up the moment is gone, replaced by only hardness and desire. Rome moves. I cry out at the harsh slam of his pelvis against my clit, and then tilt my hips so he can hit deeper. His cock pistons in and out of my body, slamming into me so hard I know that it'll be hard to walk later. I relish the future discomfort already. I slam my hips back into him, loving the way he's using me and enjoying my body.

I didn't think I'd come again, I didn't think it was possible, but I can feel it building already. I don't think I'll be able to take it. I don't know what he'll do if I actually pass out from an orgasm. I can't stop myself from seeking it out though, grinding my clit against his body as he continues to slam in and out of me.

When it hits I tense and I scream, the ecstasy nearly agony, and tears fall from my eyes and down into my hair as I lose my sense of everything except him. Rome is in every sense right now, he is all that I can perceive.

My hands clench and my nails dig into his skin. When he leans forward and groans, his nose grazing my cheek, I get aftershocks of my orgasm as he presses deep while releasing his own.

I flinch when he licks the tear from my temple. "Such a good girl," he murmurs, and then presses feathery kisses across my cheeks, my nose, and the corners of my lips.

A whimper escapes when pulls out of me, both from the ache and from the loss. I'm surprised when he doesn't let me go, holding me to him, stroking my skin as I come back into my body.

When I look over at him, he's looking at me. I watch his fingers trace over the contours of my form, something worshipful in his gaze I didn't expect. It's the most relaxed expression I've ever seen on his face, and I wonder if he ever decompresses. Rome's eyes raise to meet mine, and a ghost of smile appears.

"Are you okay?" his voice is gravelly.

"Well, I think the tension is broken," I laugh lightly, a little anxious. "And I'm happy to repeat the process whenever needed."

The smallest smile raises his lips, and he crashes back on the bed for a second before pushing himself up. I admire Rome's naked body as he takes care of the condom, surprised by the harsh, muscular contours of his body. He spends so much time in the lab I wonder when he works out.

Rome grabs a bathrobe from the back of his door and walks it over to me, unashamed of his nudity.

"If you want to go to the bathroom," he holds it out. I take it and wrap it around myself, sinking into the soft material that smells like him.

"Thanks." I sneak away, out of the room and to the bathroom next door. I take care of things quickly, treating myself gently because I'm definitely going to feel this for a few days.

When I get back in the room, Rome is back in his bed, one hand resting on his stomach and the other behind his head. He's moved over to the side of the small twin bed, clearly leaving space for me. I did not expect that. I don't want to leave, but I was already plotting how to protect myself when he kicked me out, or rushed us back to the lab.

Instead, I hang up the bathrobe and crawl beneath the covers with him. He surprises me again when he turns on his side to face me, draping one arm over my side and pulling me closer to him.

Rome watches me for a second, that relaxed, almost dreamy expression on his face again. Then he tucks my head under his chin, and I close my eyes.

Rome

I drift off to sleep for a bit, relaxed and exhausted. When I wake up, I almost fear for a moment that Cyn left again before I fully come up from sleep. She's still wrapped in my arms, her nose pressed to my chest and her soft breaths tickling my skin.

The tension that was there before is gone, she's right, but there's a different tension now. It comes from me recognizing that this frustrating woman makes me feel things, brings out a side of me I've kept careful control over, and god help me, she likes it. Cyn has always liked me and I find it inexplicable. I've never given her a reason to like me.

Then again, I seem to be drawn to her because she's everything that annoys me in another human being and by a perverse twist of fate it also gets my dick hard. Maybe it's the same for her - our opposition is also our attraction.

She doesn't actually annoy me though. Hasn't for awhile.

Cyn shifts away from me and blinks a bit before focusing on my face. Hers splits into a wide smile and I almost smile back. She makes me want to smile at her in return. I don't, but I consider it, and that's worth more than she'll ever know.

"Can I ask you something?" There's hesitation in her voice, and I have some idea what's coming. My body doesn't tense like usual, still humming with pleasure from earlier.

"Yes." I readjust so I'm still holding her, but there's enough distance between us we can see each other's faces.

"Why did you stay at Elmwood? After everything?"

"You mean after Hannah?" I haven't said her name out loud in over a year, and it doesn't hurt at all. It doesn't even make me feel a flash of anger and betrayal. It's an echo of something painful, but not painful in itself.

"Yeah. You're Jerome Dwyer, you could've gone anywhere."

I stare past her for a second, wondering how much I want to tell her. It's a story that few people who know me now have heard. I feel like she'll read too much into some of it, and that it will reveal more of me to her than I am comfortable with. There's a part of me that also feels like I owe her. No one has ever been such a direct victim of my ire before, and while I'm not offering an excuse, this might be an explanation.

"It's a long story, if you want to hear it."

Cyn's hand finds mine and she tangles our fingers, intuiting the magnitude of this. I don't know the last time anyone but Del offered me physical comfort this easily, or knew instinctively when I needed it. Of course it would be her.

"My father came from a good family. Old money. They were furious when he married my mother, but he fought for us. He fought for me to belong, and get everything I had a right to as a son and heir of his family." I swallow, working hard before I continue because this is the thing that is still freshly painful to say. "Then he died."

Cyn squeezes my hand and waits, her gaze soft and open.

"They cut us off. Every privilege I had access to, out of the home we lived in, because dad didn't leave a will. He thought he was too young, and they had the means to fight for every single cent. My grandmother set up a trust so I could stay at the private school I went to because they 'support education' but made it clear it was the last money we would get from them. I was suddenly a normal kid among the rich, and to some of them, that mattered. A lot."

Cyn lets go of my hand and reaches up to stroke my cheek, and then slides her hand into my hair, massaging my scalp. My eyes close, but I keep talking.

"Dad went to Elmwood and was part of the program. He taught me things. I've always been good at science and loved working with documents, so I started offering my services to families to work on their personal archives. One of them told me about the Van Hornen, and that became a huge part of my life. It felt like I owed it to him to win it, come here, and follow in his footsteps. To defy his family and show them what I was worth."

I sigh, and try to explain Hannah to someone who probably only knows her from social media. "Hannah and Del were the only people who stuck by me when everything crashed. We'd already been together for a year then, and she was steadfast. For a long time, those two and my mom were all I had. I'm a loyal person. I take commitment seriously. Even after her betrayal, I had committed myself to a path here. I was going to finish. I wasn't going to let her take away or tarnish a goal and a promise that had nothing to do with her."

"Did she ever apologize?"

"I never gave her the chance. I didn't need it to get my own closure, and I have no interest in offering any to her."

"That's harsh. Is it weird I find that sexy?"

I nearly laugh, and she knows it. "I don't think anyone finds me sexy."

"Excuse me?" Cyn sits up and pushes me back, straddling my hips. "For one, I do, and for two, you have clearly not heard the way people talk about you."

"I don't want to know."

"You probably don't," her voice drops and so do her hips, pressing her warm, wet pussy onto my rapidly hardening cock.

I raise an eyebrow. "Can you handle more, Cyn?"

"No. But I don't care. I want you to give it to me."

With something like a growl rumbling from my chest, I grab her braid and pull her down to me, savaging her mouth until she's begging me to fuck her.

We do eventually get back to the lab. I feel a little bit awkward, which I didn't expect. I've never crossed a line like this with someone I had to work with before. I'm not sure how to behave now.

"I'm not going easy on you," I warn.

Cyn slides her eyes over to me, amusement on her face. "I'd be disappointed if you did." The double entendre is clear in her words. "I want to learn from you, Rome. I can't do that if you go easy on me." That part was said seriously, and I appreciate that we reset this boundary so easily.

"I'm going to start cleaning up the renderings and transcribe them. You keep scanning. I'll check your work." I direct Cyn and move around the lab table we've set aside for Charity's journal. As I wait for the program and the images to load, I think of one last thing that needs to be addressed.

"I don't know if we should do that again," I say honestly, trying to keep any emotion about it, positive or negative, out of my voice.

Cyn frowns up at me. "If we don't, the tension will only build again, and distract us again. We have to keep doing it. It's the only way we're not going to kill each other."

I hold in a smile again. "You wanted to kill me?"

"I've never been so mad at anyone in my life."

I can't hold it back this time. It's perverse that this is the thing that gets me to smile, but fuck if it doesn't make me feel oddly good to know that I got under her skin as thoroughly as she got under mine. Apparently, we were both good at pretending to be unaffected by the other.

Cyn's mouth drops open slightly as she stares at me, her cheeks turning red.

"Don't ever do that again," she whispers, as I regain control of my expression. "That's a deadly weapon and my pussy is the victim."

My cock twitches, and I'm aroused and flattered at her reaction. "I'll keep that in mind." I clear my throat. "Do we want to schedule it, or...?"

I trail off when she laughs. "Minimally, every Saturday, but I'm open to every damn day if we need it."

"Fine," I agree, and then focus on the computer. Without looking up I continue. "You're welcome to stay over when we do. I don't keep secrets from Del, and they won't mind."

Cyn doesn't say anything, but when I glance up quickly, her cheeks are pink again. I like making her flustered like that.

I start reading the rendered pages, my fingers flying over the keyboard as I transcribe the digitally restored words. I try to make corrections where I can, fixing where the blurring or fading of the ink was too much for the scanner to catch appropriately. Charity James was sad, and the only thing I think we'll learn from this journal is that while her father was a good president of the college, he was exactly the horrible person the stories about him describe.

It's made very clear in these pages that he didn't think much of Charity's obvious intelligence, finding it a detriment rather than an asset. I know the way the world treats women, I saw it happen to my mom over and over again. She's a professor of economics, tenured, but still junior when she has more experience than a lot of the men in her department. They treated her like she was teaching for fun because she could fall back on dad's money instead of as an insanely smart and dedicated academic.

We don't see each other much because I don't have the means to leave Elmwood except over winter break. I think she'd like Cyn. Mom tolerated Hannah because she respected that Hannah took care of me, and was there for me when I needed it. I didn't get my grumpy nature from my dad, so Hannah's relentless positivity, something I thought I needed, grated on her at times.

Even though Cyn reminded me of Hannah at first, now I see them very distinctly. Cyn is happy and positive, but she's also real. While she chooses to see silver linings and bright sides, she acknowledges pain and darkness. She's never going to cover up bad things, or pretend they don't exist like Hannah did. She's never going to manipulate those situations for her own gain. Cyn's decision is about herself, and her approach to her own feelings and decisions. That's not the same. I've painted her with an unfair brush, I know that. It means I'll have to do the work to look past my annoyance to her true intentions.

I don't know where the hell this is going or what I'm going to do about it, but for right now, we're doing good work together. That's what has to come first for me.

I can hear Cyn's stomach grumble, and it brings me back to the surface.

We've been at this for a few hours, and it's time to call it a day.

"Do you want to get dinner?" she asks as she gets her things together. I am hungry, but I want to keep some of the boundaries I previously established between us.

"I'll eat at home. See you Tuesday?" I get on my own jacket, and make sure that everything is shut down and put away for me to work on Monday. It's my day in the lab without her.

"Yeah," she nods, looking like she's trying not to look disappointed. "Don't work too hard the rest of the weekend."

Cyn doesn't wait for me to walk her out, which I'd never really done before either. When I exit the library, she's already halfway down the street toward the residence halls. I watch her, almost hoping she'll look back and give me a chance to change my mind.

Why the fuck am I wishing for that? We're not dating. I'm not going to be her boyfriend. She's the mentee I got stuck with but actually got lucky to have, and I cannot let the amazing sex distract from the fact that she's not part of my plans.

Cyn

"It's getting juicy!" I crow to Rome. He's on scanning duty today, and I'm transcribing rendered entries. Rome looks up, a flash of amusement breaking through the mask. We've hooked up nearly every night since the first time, although they've been quick and dirty. Our clothes barely off, me bent over his bed, one of his hands pressing my head into the mattress as he fucks me so well and makes me come so hard I see stars. Then we walk back to the lab and into our usual flow like it never even happened. We've been getting a lot more done, and it's been damn good work.

It's Halloween tomorrow, so we're staying late tonight since we won't be doing any lab time this weekend. Rome said it was part of his job as my mentor to make sure I acclimated to Elmwood, and that Halloween weekend is one of the best. He grudgingly admitted that it's one of the only times of year he never misses going out.

I haven't asked him if he's going to Beastly, the big themed Halloween party thrown by the "secret" societies known as the Elmwood Trinity. Elise is going as a mouse, which is apparently an inside joke with her bestie's brother. It took me a few weeks to finally get her to admit she has a crush on Colin, and then it all came pouring out of her. She's pointed him out to me at parties and even though she refused to go and talk to him, I saw him watch her. I don't think her crush is as unrequited as she thinks. Plus, he's crazy hot. I'm thinking about getting Rosie's number from her phone and conspiring behind their backs to make it happen.

It took me awhile to decide what animal I wanted to be. I wanted a costume that would be comfortable and cute, and that's surprisingly limited. After a lot of internet searching, I found a cozy snake costume. It's leggings and a hoodie with a scale pattern, and the hood looks like that of a viper, even a little red tongue at the front where the hood comes to a sharp point. I got snake eye contact lenses and fangs to complete the look. Elise said it was sexy, but I think it's kind of awkward.

We also laughed our asses off at the fact that snakes eat mice. It's our sweet couples costume.

Rome comes around to look at the screen with me. I read the entry out loud to him. We've kept doing that for every entry, and I finally asked him why. He told me that hearing it in my voice, in a feminine voice, gives it dimension for him. That started an entire conversation about how he doesn't add inflection or tone when he reads in his head. It's why he doesn't enjoy reading fiction. My mind was blown.

"Father has decided who I'm going to marry. Ethan Carstairs, whom he claims is a gentleman of the highest caliber, a graduate of Elmwood's first class, and will be able to "lead me" as a husband should lead his wife. I have heard otherwise about Carstairs. Not that he is not a gentleman per se, but he thinks very highly of his person. Other ladies in my circle have been chaperoned with him and described the man as arrogant, to a degree that it outstrips his status."

We share a look, and I read the next entry.

"Carstairs is a boor. When we met in the front parlor yesterday, he looked me over in a way that bordered on lewd, then barely spoke to me. I made several attempts at conversation and he shut down each. Like many, his family works in shipping, and it has required travel from him in the past. He would not even discuss travel with me! After an hour had passed I dismissed myself and left him sitting with mother. Father was furious, of course, but my behavior did not, apparently, dissuade Carstairs."

"He sounds like a charmer," I retort, and click over to the next entry.

"Carstairs took me for a walk in the park, with mother and Mrs. Jewell as chaperones. After more attempts at conversation, he told me that I was not required in any way to entertain him, and that he was following social expectation for courting. He added that no word I said would alter his decision to marry me one way or the other. I told him I wanted to get to know him, and he said it would not be necessary, as other than producing heirs we would not interfere in each other's lives. Interfere! The man is contemptible. Yet, he's also beautiful. I cannot help but look at his handsome face, despite its repugnant mind. At least we will have handsome children."

I laugh, reading the end of the entry again to myself. In my mind, Charity is wistful. Wishing that her handsome fiance gave her any attention at all. It wouldn't be hard to get a loyal wife and companion from Charity. She came across as smart in her entries, looking for a purpose or belonging. Someone who appreciated her. The bare minimum from Carstairs and he would've had her forever.

We know they married. I'm so curious now what changed between them, as they had a productive marriage, going by the sheer number of babies they shared.

"What's funny to you?" Rome asks, serious.

"Oh," I blush furiously, embarrassed now at what that entry reminded me of. "It doesn't matter."

He quirks an eyebrow. "Based on that reaction, it definitely matters."

I cover my face and speak through my hands. "I need you to remember this conversation happened before I knew you better."

Rome looks concerned, but nods. I drop my hands.

"I basically said the same thing about you to my roommates. I may have said you were as much of an asshole as you are sexy. Sounds about the same." I can't look at him, but he says nothing, so I have to.

For the first time since I met him, Rome looks truly upset. Stricken by what I've said.

"Is it the asshole or the sexy part?" I whisper.

He blinks and turns to look at me. "I'm not sure." Rome frowns and looks down. "I didn't mean to be that much of an asshole. I was suspicious of you and didn't appreciate having someone I didn't choose in my lab. I wanted to keep you at a distance."

"The harder you pushed, the harder I tried," I murmur. Rome nods, agreeing with me. That's exactly what happened, even if I didn't see it at the time.

"I'm used to my demeanor keeping people away. The more you ignored it, the more I wanted you, and the angrier I got about it." He still sounds a bit thunderstruck, and I feel bad, but I also feel like this revelation might be good for him.

"I couldn't stop thinking about you. I was either imagining furious diatribes or slapping you or thinking about kissing your face off. I still don't understand."

"Neither do I." Rome steps around the table, takes my face in his hands, and gives me a hard, filthy kiss. "I'm still going to be an asshole."

I smile, and it lifts his palms where they rest on my cheeks. "I know. I'm still going to be confusingly turned on by it."

He nods at me and goes back to his seat in front of the journal. I watch as Rome stares at it for a moment before shaking his head. "We should call it a night."

"Okay," I agree. I save all the renderings, and save a back up of them to my personal school drive. We put everything away where it should be in silence, and get ready to leave the lab.

"Do you want me to walk you home?" Rome offers.

I hide my smile by putting on my coat. "No. I'm good. I'll see you...next week?" I trail off, chickening out about asking him if he'll be at Beastly. He probably will. I'm sure Del will drag him out, like they did the last time I saw Rome at a party. The one where he saved me.

"Alright," Rome shrugs, but he's tense again. We walk out of the lab hallway, and through the library to the exit. We walk together in awkward silence until the corner - he has to go straight, I turn left. There's a moment where we pause and look at each other. I'm not going to ask to come over. The boundaries around this seem to bother him more than they do me, so if anything is going to happen it's on Rome to bring it up.

"I'll see you," he says quietly, and then crosses the street.

I don't linger, my breath caught in my chest because I want to chase after him and demand more. Except I don't know if I mean more sex, or more of him. Rome lets me in and I know he doesn't do that often. I want to ask him what it means. I want to know if he feels more than attraction for me. If this could turn into something, or if I need to guard myself more carefully. I'm at a point where if he says this is only physical, and only for now, that I won't be too hurt by it. I've tumbled but I haven't fallen, and I have enough time to stop myself.

"Cyn," Rome's voice stops me, and I turn to face him as he jogs down the sidewalk toward me. "I'm walking you home."

"Okay."

"I forgot tonight is the Cavalry Hunt. I want to make sure you're safe before they start their shenanigans."

I turn to face him. "Are you sure I wouldn't be safer somewhere else?" Okay, I'm being all hopeful and pushy here, but he stopped me for a reason. The Hunt was just his excuse.

That hint of a smirk appears on Rome's face. "You're absolutely right, you should stay with me."

We turn around and walk back toward the corner, and cross the street together. Despite his invitation, I haven't stayed over yet. We always have somewhere to be afterward. Walking to his place is a habit now. It's easy to follow his steps because I know which building, I know which room, and the tension is there but it's not a driving madness like this past week. This feels new.

The lights are on in the apartment when we enter. Rome's roommate, who I assume is Del, comes into the room. Somehow we haven't crossed paths during the entire last week. They're wearing tight black jeans and a pale blue crop top. They're pinning their hair on top of their head and wearing long, long eyelashes.

A huge grin spreads across their face. "You must be Cyn."

"You must be Del."

They laugh with glee and then grab a bag off the counter. "I'm out. You kids have a very, very good time."

We step aside so they can go through the door. Del and Rome share a look, Del's full of amusement but I can't see the look on Rome's face. Del leaves the apartment, and Rome starts moving toward his room. I hang up my coat and leave my shoes by the door before I follow him.

Rome doesn't turn on the light, but closes the door. A streetlight not far from his window gives us enough light to see by. The pull between us is so strong, but so different from the previous times. I don't know what's different tonight, but it's doing something to me. It's making my heart race and my palms sweat. Whatever it is I want it.

"Come here," he commands me quietly.

I step up to him and he wraps his arms around me, pulling me tight into his body. Rome leans down and kisses my temple before he starts talking quietly in my ear.

"Do you like being my sweet slut, Cyn?" I can only nod in response, my core immediately heating and flooding at the way his voice changes when he's like this. "You're needy for more, aren't you?" I nod again. "You take me like such a good girl, you give me everything I demand of you. Are you going to be my good girl tonight?"

"Yes, sir," I breathe out, dizzy with need.

Rome steps away, letting me go, and I waiver on my feet. My brain is fuzzy and every nerve is awake and begging for stimulation. He sits on his bed and watches me. The moment draws out, torturing and arousing me. I hate it as much as I love it.

"Strip."

I turn so I'm fully facing him, and unbutton the flannel I'm wearing. I do it slowly, and let it drift down my body, closing my eyes at the feeling of the soft material on my sensitive skin. I undo the button and zipper on my jeans, but turn around before I remove them, bending at the waist to show him my ass, remembering the way he ate me from behind. I linger there, shifting needlessly before standing up and facing him again.

Rome has taken his cock out of his pants and is stroking it while he watches me undress. My eyes flutter for a second before I continue. I'm wearing a tank top and no bra, so I slide down one strap, then the other. I push it down slowly, revealing my breasts, before pushing it down my entire body and taking my panties with it. Once again, I'm naked in front of a mostly clothed Rome, watching him get off to the visual of me.

"What do you want, Cyn?"

"I want your cock in my mouth."

"Crawl to me and beg for it."

I drop down to all fours and cross the short distance between us. I rest my head on his knee and look up at him, biting my lip. "Please. Fill my mouth."

"Fuck," he hisses. "Fill it yourself."

I rise up and move over him, swirling my tongue around the head of his cock before taking him into my mouth. I work up and down his velvety length, going deeper with each stroke. Rome dives his hand into my hair and grips and pulls in a way that doesn't hurt, but provides a tense sensation that I like. I get lost in the feelings and flavors, loving the power I feel giving him pleasure. Rome slides his hand under my chin and pushes me off of him.

"On my lap," he directs. I stand up and straddle him, but don't make a move other than to hold onto him for balance. Rome starts running his hands over my skin, all the way from my ankles, over my legs, up my sides, then across my collarbones and down my arms. He repeats the movement over and over, my head falling back as tingles erupt across every inch of my skin, the pleasure radiating from my scalp and all the way down my spine.

I cry out when his tongue brushes across one of my nipples, the sensation pleasurable but unexpected. His hands don't stop moving over me as he sucks first one, then the other. He licks and sucks at my nipples, alternating and working me up.

One hand slides over my hipbone and his fingers dive into my wet pussy.

"My little slut is so ready." Rome nuzzles the space between my breasts and my hands move from his shoulders to his head, diving into his hair and holding him close. I hear rather than see Rome open and put on a condom.

One of his hands grips my ass cheek. "Sit."

My knees slide further apart and after a moment, I feel his cock at my entrance. I drop down, sinking as far as I can before I feel tension. Both of his hands are on my hips now, and I follow his lead and the pressure of his hands as he starts working me up and down his length until he's fully seated inside me. Rome holds me there, and I don't move, following the silent command.

Once again, he starts trailing his fingertips all over me, up and down my body, across my back, over the mound of my ass.

"Do you want to move? Grind on my cock like the needy slut you are?"

"Yes," I moan. "You feel so good."

"Do it. Be a good girl and make yourself come while I worship your soft skin. While I suck on your sweet tits. I'm going to mark you this time, Cyn. After I feel you come on my cock, I'm going to pound into you until you lose all sense of yourself. Until all you know is where I pleasure your body."

"Yes," I moan again, and start moving like he told me. There's so much sensory input as he never stops moving his hands, exploring and delighting every inch of me with his soft touches. My body grinds faster, clenching around him, and my breathing becomes tight and erratic as I get closer to the edge.

"I want to kiss you," I beg. "Please."

One of Rome's hands slides up my spine, over my neck, and into my hair. He directs my head down and I meet his eyes for a moment before our mouths meet in a reckless, wet kiss. One swipe of his tongue against mine and it's like it was the missing piece. I break around him, hips jerking as I orgasm, getting myself off as he devours my mouth. He swallows every scream as it goes and goes. I'm branded by him in a way I wasn't before.

Rome breaks the kiss, trailing his mouth down my neck and across my chest, nipping and licking in between kisses. I hiss when he bites into the soft flesh of my breast and sucks the skin between his teeth.

I gasp when he grabs my ass and stands, still inside me, and rearranges us so that he's over me on the bed. There's no time for me to react or adjust because as soon as he has me the way he wants me, he gets up on his knees, grabs my hips, and starts to fuck me.

Rome pounds into my body like he promised, watching my little tits bounce, eyes roving over my skin the same way his hands did. I feel it as if his hands were still doing it, as if seeing him look at where he touched me is raising the memory of the touch.

"Lovely," he murmurs, meeting my eyes. "My lovely, good girl."

I tighten around him at the praise, and finally, I see it. The devilish smirk I only got a hint of the first time. It's absolutely devastating, and I cry out because he's reached around my leg to play with my clit, getting me to the edge so fast. It's not enough, but I'm there.

"Beg, lovely."

"Make me come," I cry out, trying to grind harder against his cock and his thumb. "Please. Rome." Tears spring to my eyes and spill over, the tension and need coiling through my entire, wrecked body. "Rome!"

He presses his thumb down as he thrusts deep inside me, pressing hard and grinding. I break apart, and can do nothing but ride it out as he uses my body and gets off on my pleasure. Rome thrusts deep and holds himself there, groaning as he comes. His body crashes down over mine.

We lay there together, breathing hard. Rome slides out of me and gets up, disposing of the condom.

"Go to the bathroom, then get that ass back in here." It's the most playful he's ever sounded, and I follow his instructions.

Rome pulls me into his arms when I come back into the room, snuggling me down into his bed. He's like a warm octopus and I don't think anyone would believe me if I said the angry commanding man who fucks me like a devil also likes to cuddle afterward. He presses a kiss to the top of my head.

"It's early," I remind him. It's not even midnight yet.

"Are you going to stay?" Rome is doing that thing where he says something as neutrally as possible so it can appear like he doesn't have any feelings about it. I don't think he realizes how obvious of a tell that is.

"Yes. If you feed me."

"My cock wasn't enough?"

I whip my head up to look at him and he's smirking at me. "Pizza?" He asks.

"Pizza," I agree. We crawl out of bed and I watch as Rome puts on his boxers and t-shirt, and he hands me his bathrobe. When we get in the kitchen, Rome surprises me by picking me up and putting me on the counter while he starts the oven and gets a pizza out of the freezer. After he puts it in, he steps between my legs.

"Why do you do this?" he asks, and the question is sincere, and confused. I'm also not entirely sure what he's talking about.

"Do what?"

"I'm the opposite of you. The things that matter to you piss me off. I get angry at the things that makes you happy. Why the fuck are you here?" There's no anger in his voice. It's pure curiosity.

It's a really good question. "I must be a masochist," I reply quietly. It's the only explanation I have. I swallow. "Is this - usual - for you?"

Rome stares me down, considering his answer. "No. I've never been like this." He leans in, voice dropping. "I've never wanted to punish anyone before." I squirm on the counter, aroused by his words and tone. He leans in and bites my lip, just a nip, but it makes me gasp.

Then he pulls away from me and turns off the oven. "We'll come back for it. Get in my room and bend over the bed."

I do what he says. I always do what he says.

Rome

Dr. Cunningham is waiting for me in her office with bagels and coffee. We do this once a month to check in with each other. I am lucky as hell she's my program chair, and even without our shared history I would be fond of her. Part of me wonders how she tolerates me at all because I have to be a reminder to her about Hannah, just as she is for me. Then again, Dr. C forgave and forgot far faster than I did. She's moved on with her life in every way.

I'm trying, but I get stuck in my own head. It's why we started doing this. I get to vent about things that are bothering me, talk about work that excites me, and I think she gets to make sure that I haven't been ruined by a selfish girl.

"How are things? Have they gotten better with Cynthia?"

It's a good thing I don't blush, or we'd have a problem. This is the first time I've ever kept secrets from Dr. C, and now I'm keeping two of them. Not only the change in my dynamic with Cyn, but also our discovery of Charity's diary.

"They're better. I still don't like having to share my lab," I frown and drink my coffee. It's better to keep everything close to the vest.

"It's an ambitious project to be given to a single student. You're lucky you're you or I'd be having you supervise a whole team of eager young archivists."

My stomach actually twists in horror. I don't say anything in response to that.

I'm a little jittery this morning. It's the annual Halloween party tonight, this year the theme is Beastly, and I'm oddly excited to be going. At first, the usual plan was in place to keep an eye on Del, but now I'm kind of hoping to see Cyn tonight. I want to interact with her outside the lab and see what she does. I want to know how she treats me in front of her friends. I can deny my feelings to myself all I want, but there's a part of me that wants to know what this is to her without asking that question.

"If you're really that miserable, I can find something else for her next semester."

"No." I sit up straight in the chair, almost spilling coffee. "It's fine."

Dr. C looks over her cup at me, eyes narrowing. She's in her forties with gray and blonde hair, a soft round build, but young, sharp blue eyes. It would not be the first time she's made me feel like she sees through me. Dr. C can intuit a lot, especially about me. About anyone. It's what makes her an amazing educator. She knows exactly how to push or motivate, how to make someone understand a concept from a new angle, and how to turn learning into an act of exploration.

"Have you warmed up to her? Her Van Hornen materials were quite impressive."

"Cyn is tolerable. She learns well." She also obeys my every command and calls me sir when she begs me to fuck her brains out. She's crawled inside my head and stays there more often than she should. I hold her in my arms and she pulls out all my secrets.

"I see." Dr. C raises an eyebrow. "This might be good for you."

"What?"

"Being interested in someone. There's no rules against mentors and mentees, you know."

"I know," I snap before I can catch myself. I wouldn't know that unless I'd thought about it. She nearly laughs but manages to keep it in.

"You don't trust people easily, Rome, and I understand why, but if you keep closing yourself off you're going to lose perspective and that's essential to have in this field. If you're going to be analyzing people and preserving what mattered to them, you have to understand them. You have to value them. It's important that you form connections."

"I'm preserving myself, Dr. C." I shake my head.

She gives me a sad smile, one she's given me a hundred times before. "I know, but I worry."

"You always worry."

Dr. C shrugs in response, and lets our conversation shift to more academic topics, and away from my lack of emotional or social life. It's livelier than she knows at the moment, but I also want to keep Cyn to myself for now. Until I know what's going to happen.

Del is going to Beastly as a giraffe and I have never been more embarrassed to be by their side. It's a creative costume and they look great, but they keep yelling, "I'm a sexy giraffe!" and hip-checking me every chance they get. I am not showing up at this party with a thorn in my ass because they knocked me into a bush.

Maybe I'm annoyed because they laughed at me for a solid minute when I came out in my costume. For me, I went all out. Black jeans, black tee, and a black hoodie that looks like bat wings when I spread out my arms. I'm even wearing fake fangs on my teeth. Del felt the costume was too close to my actual personality to count, and that they were sure to catch me wearing the hoodie on a regular day.

Del might've pre-gamed a little too hard. Apparently they have plans with their sophomore tonight after the party, and they're a little nervous. They might laugh at me again if I tried to give them a pep talk, so I leave it alone. Del will read too much into it if I try and talk about sex, emotions, and relationships.

Beastly is held at the Castle because they're the only Trinity house with a huge ballroom and a big back garden that could accommodate most of the campus. There are smaller parties scattered around the buildings and the houses that line the campus where students live, but at some point tonight everyone is going to be inside this house.

We aren't there long when I see Del's sophomore run up to them. I'm surprised when she grabs them, dips them to the floor, and passionately kisses them. Everyone around stops to watch the giraffe being dipped and tongued by a crocodile, and break into applause. When they end their kiss, both of them are blushing.

Del gives me a shrug and walks off.

I'm almost jealous. I don't want to be, so I let the feeling sit for a moment before wiping it away.

Hannah didn't go to parties with me, and to be honest, I didn't want to go to them. Whenever I went to parties with her, even when things were good, I'd end up sitting somewhere alone until it was time to go. She always accused me of hovering if I stood next to her while she talked.

I wonder what it would be like with Cyn. If I was at this party with her instead of only hoping to run into her. Would she think I was hovering, or be glad for my silent, if glowering presence? Would she let me drag her into a dark corner to steal a kiss, or more? Would she be proud to have my arm around her, or to have me kiss her in public? I know what my reputation is like academically, so I also know my social reputation leaves something to be desired. I know people don't approach me. Would Cyn care?

No one talks to me as I get a drink and lean against one of the pillars in the well-decorated ballroom. From this position I can watch the door, see who goes in and out.

Someone leans on the other side of the pillar, and I look over to see a sharp beak and feathers. I look past it to the face, and recognize Colin Larson. I don't detest him, which he takes as high praise. We TAed for the same history professor and shared an office; I didn't want to kill him.

"Dwyer," he nods at me. "Didn't think you'd be here."

I shrug in response.

"Waiting for someone?" he asks, never taking his eyes off the door.

"Are you?"

"My girl," he grins like he can't help it. "She told me her costume was a surprise."

I nod at him and turn back to watch. A group of girls walks in the door, and I know she's one of them before I even narrow it down. Then I can tell only from the shape of her mouth beneath her hood, a hood that makes her look like a snake, that it's Cyn. The fact that I think "that's *my* girl" should make me panic, but it doesn't.

Colin straightens up next to me. "Later." He pats me on the shoulder and makes his way toward them. My heart stills in my chest, watching him approach the girls, panic that he's going for Cyn fighting to break free from it's cage in my brain.

Except he doesn't even acknowledge Cyn. Colin scoops up a small brunette girl dressed like a mouse, lifting her up until her legs wrap around his body, and kisses her like there's no one else in the room. Jealousy rockets through me again.

I start making my way slowly toward the door, watching as Cyn and her other two friends - a dog and a cat, respectively - watch and laugh at their friend. They basically write off the girl as Colin walks off with her. I notice other people watching them. Part of me thinks I should walk away, let her have her night at the party without having to worry about me. I have no claim on her except in my mind.

Cyn says something to her friends and then turns to go back into the dark of the house. I follow her, creeping closer with every step she takes. When she stops at the table along the wall to look at the drinks I step up behind her but don't touch her.

"I know it's you," she murmurs. Cyn grabs a can of soda and turns to face me. Her eyes flick up to mine and she has yellow contacts in. When she bites her lip I see she has fangs to match my own. It's weirdly hot now that she's got this vaguely threatening look when she normally appears so sweet.

"Gorgeous," I say before I can stop it, and her cheeks turn pink.

"I kinda like the fangs on you, too," she taps my lips and then moves around me.

"I'm not a partier, so if you need me, come find me, okay?" I stop her with a hand on her hip, coming close.

She looks over her shoulder at me. "What if I need you to dance with me?"

I give her a bland look and it doesn't take long for her to crack and laugh, turning to face me. Cyn grabs the front pocket of my hoodie and sticks her hands inside. It's an intimate move and my stomach swoops. "Don't go far." She rises up on her toes and presses her lips to mine. For a second we're trapped in our own dark cave, the hoods of our sweatshirts hiding us from the world.

It ends too soon, and she steps away with a small smile on her face.

I move back toward the door to the ballroom and find a wall to hold up, watching everyone go crazy for Halloween. Even I can admit that I'm impressed by the creativity and ingenuity of my classmates in coming up with different animals to turn into costumes. Despite their popularity during this season, I don't see another bat. I do see a caterpillar, a few bears, multiple deer, a moose with what I suspect are real antlers, an ant, a rhino, and a a praying mantis. I give that one a wide berth.

Del checks on me a few times and finally introduces me to their sopho- more, whose name is Everly Kramer. The name dings in my brain because Charity James, later Charity Carstairs, gave birth to Eleanor Carstairs, later Eleanor Kramer. If I remember the family tree right, this is one of Charity's descendants, and one of the descendants of President James. I'm weirdly fascinated. I'm also a little chagrined to have that man's family tree nearly memorized.

"Did you know you're related to the first president of the college?" I ask her, loudly over the music.

"Yes! But family lore says he was not a good dude."

I nod at her. "He was not. What else does it say?"

Everly starts telling me everything she can remember about her family tree. Her grandmother, Eleanor's daughter, was very interested in their genealogy, especially after Everly got accepted to Elmwood. Talking to her helps me understand what Dr. C was saying earlier about perspective. I have to contextualize what people remember and learn from the things we restore and preserve. I know I'm already giving Everly more of a chance because Del likes her, but it's a reminder it's possible to be open with people without actually letting them in. I can't save what matters if I don't know what matters to people.

When I look up from the conversation, Del is frowning.

I step back from Everly. "I'll let you two get back to the party. It was nice to meet you." I toast them both with my nearly empty cup. Everly takes Del's hand and leads them away, into the crush of bodies dancing. They don't look back so I can safely assume Del is mad at me. I didn't mean to monopolize their date's time.

It's been awhile since I've seen Cyn, so I start wandering through the ballroom looking for her. She's dancing with her friends, but there's a guy behind her dressed as a wolf. His hand is on her hip, and I see her turn and say something to him. The hand drops, but I'm already pissed. The anger and possessiveness are not rational, I know that, but that doesn't stop me.

I move through the crush of bodies, and bump smack into the wolf. When he looks up at me, I see it's that same asshole from the party a few weeks ago. Touching my girl. Again.

"I thought I warned you," I sneer at him.

He rolls his eyes. "Didn't see you with your hands on her."

"Didn't see her giving you permission to touch her."

"Whatever. I'm done."

I step up to him and our chests brush. He's shorter and smaller than I am.

"I think I promised you broken fingers."

"Rome," Cyn's voice cuts through my fury. She forces her way between the two of us, her back to him, pressing her hands into my chest. "Leave him alone. I told him to fuck off, he listened."

I glare at him for a moment longer before looking down to focus on her. "You sure?"

"I'm sure. Let's go."

No one and nothing else matters as soon as she says that. Not the guy, not her friends, or my friend. I tuck her under my arm and we maneuver through the crowd. The air is biting once we get outside, the wind harsh and filled with the scent of rain. It's been downpouring on and off for the last few days. I don't let her go, keeping her warm with my body heat until we can get inside.

The further we get from the party and the crush of all those people, the more I calm down.

"I'm sorry," I tell her.

"What was that about?"

"Honestly, if it hadn't been that same dick from the party earlier, I would've let it go. You brushed him off once already and that kind of persistence is fucking rude."

"I didn't even notice."

Discomfort takes over, but I push it down. Cyn leads us into my building and to my front door. My emotions feel out of my control right now. It's been a long time since I spun out like this, since I let myself be anything but detached. I'm remembering why it's healthier for me to detach - when I let myself feel, I feel a fucking lot.

I get attached to people. I get too excited and too focused on what I'm excited about. I get passionate, I get possessive, I fall hard and inescapably. I have to fucking pull it back or I'm not going to survive. The one thing I learned from being with Hannah is that while someone like me intrigues the sunshine type, I can't sustain them. They can't withstand my darkness forever. As much as what I have with Cyn matters to me, I know I won't be able to keep her. I'll only bring her down, and ruin her in a way that I don't want.

Now is all I have, and fuck if the anger that causes doesn't make me all the more desperate for her.

Cyn

I can tell Rome is feeling really off right now and I'm not sure what to do about it. At first things seemed fine at Beastly, and I did have fun, but part of me didn't want to be there. I know that I'm getting too wrapped up in this thing between us and we're in an obsessive honeymoon phase where all we want is to be around each other. It's not even a relationship. It's undefined but it's also undeniable.

That bubble is going to burst and it's going to be painful. Rome doesn't want a relationship. He's never said that specifically but I know that he has goals and I know that he's still gunshy about relationships because of his last one. If I would ever point out to him how scared he is, he'd think I was crazy. In so many ways he's the most confident person I've ever known, but I also see how every time he's vulnerable with me, he beats himself up about it.

I've kept a lot of things about myself from him because I know he's not in a place to realize how deep this is going. We have talked about the weird dynamic with my headmaster at school and how I pushed myself too hard too fast because I will put myself at risk if it means I don't let others down. It made him careful with me and the hours we were keeping. I don't know if he realizes how much he's changed and adapted to take care of me.

He even let me film a video in the lab for my channel, showing what I'm working on and learning about while at school. It blew up, and I got so many questions and some more collaboration opportunities. Just reading those emails exhausted me. I sent them to my dad. I'll do whatever he tells me because I don't care anymore. Rome hasn't outright asked me about

YouTube and my dad, but he knows something is off about it.

I haven't directly spoken to my father since the post of mom. I've kept up my posting and filming schedule and I'm surprised that views are still good given my obvious lack of giving a shit in all of them.

Apparently, I put on a damn good show.

Like the one I'm putting on right now for Rome, keeping it light, keeping the sexual tension high, as if I'm not one sweet word away from having my heart obliterated by him. I've gotten angry, horny, commanding Rome. I've gotten sweet post-orgasm Rome. This possessive, protective version of him might be the most dangerous.

"I didn't like seeing his hands on you." Rome's voice is harsh and deep. He pulls me to him, gripping me hard enough to ride the edge of pain. I wrap my arms around his waist and press my body into his, giving him what he wants. Reassurance.

"It meant nothing."

"It should have, but it didn't." He leans close to me and slides his tongue between my lips, opening me to him. I lose the thread of my thoughts for a second as he takes my mouth in a kiss that's deep and gentle, pulling me in. God I never thought that he would kiss like this, or that he'd kiss me like this. Rome's distaste for me was so obvious from the first moment we met I never could have imagined how much things would change, or how much I would want this.

"Fuck," he snaps, and breaks the kiss. He reaches into his mouth and pulls the fangs off his teeth, and then taps my lips for me to open up. With surprising gentleness he removes mine as well. "Now I've got you," he murmurs before attacking me again, plunging deep now that there's nothing in the way.

Rome lifts me up and my legs wrap around him. He breaks the kiss but his eyes snare mine and I'm unable to look away as he walks us back to his bedroom. The more intensely he touches me, the more my brain slows down and I'm no longer thinking. I'm only feeling. Feeling him.

I don't care about my costume. I don't care about anything right now. I reach up and take out one contact, flicking it to the floor, followed by the other.

Rome looks up into my eyes, that slight smile on his face for a second. "There's the real you. Let me see you, lovely." I might as well melt out of his arms at the words.

Clothes tumble to the floor between kisses and then his chest is pressing against mine, and feeling the hot expanse of his skin against mine everywhere is amazing. Rome isn't rushing anything, he's tasting and touching with thorough focus that's going to ruin me. No matter what happens, there's a part of me that's always going to be only for him. With every touch, I know there's nothing I can do to save myself. I thought I could hold back, but I was wrong.

"I need you," he whispers into my neck before nipping at the sensitive skin.

"You have me," I moan in response.

He kisses down my body, teasing and taunting. I watch as he leans back on his knees, cock hard and throbbing, weeping pre-cum for me. Rome puts on a condom, seeming frustrated that he has to stop touching me for the moments that it takes to do it.

Then he's over me and on me, my legs opening to accommodate his hips, and my soaked sex pulling his cock in to fill me up. Rome goes deep, pressing as far as he can get inside me. He hikes one of my legs up over is hip and grinds into me, holding onto my lips with his own, connecting us everywhere that he can as he moves inside me.

This isn't fucking. This isn't us keeping the tension at bay so we can get work done.

Tears well in my eyes and spear down my cheeks. All I can do is hold on and let him shatter me.

It doesn't take long before my orgasm hits and I cry out into his mouth. He doesn't let me go. He doesn't let me breathe. Rome presses and presses, never letting me find my way back down. It's a constant build and all I can do is cling to him, my nails digging into the skin of his back as I come again.

"My good girl," he groans against my lips. He starts to move in short, hard strokes, savaging my tongue and my lips as he chases his release. "Cyn," he says as he comes with such agony that I can't hold back the sob, or the last orgasm. My pussy clenches around him, holding him deep as he releases.

When he's done, his eyes clear and he looks down at me. At first, his expression is soft and open, but turns to shock quickly when he sees my face and my tears.

"What's the matter?"

"What is this, Rome? What are we doing?" My voice breaks.

If he'd been able to answer that, one way or the other, I think I could have kept it together. Except he doesn't answer. The silence is heavy, then he opens his mouth, closes it, and turns his head away. That's the answer. I nod to myself and gently push him off of me. Rome goes, sitting on the bed, watching as I get up and get dressed, sorting through the mixed mess of our clothes to find mine.

Tears are still pouring down my face and I can't stop them. It's not even that I'm crying, it's like I'm overflowing.

"This wasn't supposed to happen."

"I know," I agree. It wasn't. I didn't think it would.

"We can't be more than this, Cyn. I can't."

"I know," I acknowledge, having always known that to be true. He kept trying to put up barriers between us and I think he was trying to save me as much as himself. I take a deep breath and finish getting dressed.

"We shouldn't - anymore. We need to go back."

Rome's face falls and then he lets neutrality take back over. "Of course, whatever you want."

"What do you want?"

"It doesn't matter," he answers sharply. "Wants are irrelevant. There's only what I need to do, and I can't let anything get in the way of that." Rome blanches for a second, realizing how that sounded, but he can't take it back. The message was received: I'm getting in the way.

"Okay. Got it." I take a few steps back and he gets up from the bed, reaching out as if to stop me. Then he realizes he's standing there naked in nothing but a used condom.

"Cyn," he says, but it doesn't matter.

"I'll see you in the lab on Tuesday." I turn my back on him and leave as quick as I can, running as soon as my feet hit the sidewalk because I know he's going to try and follow me. I know he's going to try and smooth things over, or get me to understand, but I don't care. I need this feeling so that I can ice him out. I don't want to be kind and empathetic right now. I want to be hurt, and I want to form scar tissue and callouses around my heart when it comes to him. Rome almost got all the way in and I have to fight with myself to push him back out.

The wind carries the sound of my name to me, but I don't stop and I don't look back. I keep running until I'm safely inside Harwood-Locke. Until I'm curled up in my bed in my pajamas.

I wake up the next morning to the sound of laughter. I sit up, tense and alert.

"Oh!" Elise gasps, scared by my sudden movement. She and Colin are in the room and closing the door. "I thought you'd be with your secret boo."

The second she says it, I burst into tears. Elise runs across the room and hugs me. Colin stands awkwardly for a second and then sits down on Elise's desk chair.

"What happened?"

"I think we broke up, even though we weren't together and there was nothing to break, but whatever it is, it ended."

"Rome is an idiot," Elise assures me. "Do you want to talk about it?"

"You all knew?" I sob out, ashamed and frustrated with myself.

"Holy shit," Colin whispers, and we both turn to look at him. "Sorry," he shrugs, "I never saw that coming. He's a fortress."

"You know him?" Elise asks.

"Yeah, as much as anyone can. How do you know him?"

"I'm his mentee in the archives program, I work in his lab. God, how could I be so stupid? I should have known better."

"Rome isn't a bad guy," Colin assures me. "Maybe a little slow on the uptake when it comes to personal matters. He'll come around."

"To what?" I sob and throw my arms in the air. "I don't even know what I want."

"Maybe figure that part out first, so you'll know. When you're ready." Elise pats my hand and then stands up. "You wallow, we'll go get you donuts from the dining hall, and then I'll round up the girls, okay?"

"Okay." I swallow and wipe my eyes, trying to pull myself back together. "It's going to be fine."

"Hell yeah it is," Elise agrees. "You're Cynthia St. Clair, winner of the Van Hornen, DIY YouTube sensation, all around awesome human being. "

I give her a watery smile and flop back on my bed. I'm going to be fine. Except being with Rome, I felt better than fine. I'll have to move past that and find my way back to being the happy person I choose to be.

I'll have to find a way to cherish the experience while also feeling the pain. I'll find a way back to appreciating the opportunity working with him gives me, and know that this pain will be part of what leads me to the rest of my goals. I have to hope that I offered him a safe place for the time that he allowed it, and that maybe he won't be so afraid of connection in the future because I reminded him that it felt good to let someone in. Whoever they are, I'll fucking hate them, at least for a bit, but I want him to be happy and whole. I want him to fully heal from how Hannah and his dad's family broke him, and I will try and understand that the person to do that isn't me.

That no matter how much he feels like mine, he's not.

Rome

Of course the first day we're back in the lab together, Dr. C decides it's the day to visit and check on our work. That seems like something that would only happen to me. Luckily, we'd hid Charity's journal well and were not caught with our pants down in front of the chair of the department for keeping an important document to ourselves.

The only options I had for contacting Cyn were email since I never bothered to get her phone number and I never give anyone mine. I only sent one email offering to talk, and she didn't respond. To be honest, I wasn't even sure if she was going to show up today based on how we left things. I know she said she'd be here, but there was no guarantee.

I'm waiting with Dr. C when she walks in the door, trying hard to keep my anxiety to myself. It's less about Dr. C and more fear of what Cyn will be like when she comes in. If she's upset or obviously hurt, it's going to break me. I never intended to hurt her. It took me far too long to realize I was even capable of it. That she thought of me, or felt for me, in a way that could result in her being hurt.

I've never had anyone cry over me before. I didn't like it.

I'd always been preparing myself for her to be done because she got bored or tired of me. It never occurred to me that she'd end things because I didn't give her enough instead of because I gave her too much.

Cyn looks fine. Her long blonde hair is in two braids that trail over her shoulders. She's wearing lip gloss that makes her mouth extra pink and shiny and biteable, and with no falsity whatsoever, she gives Dr. C a big smile.

"I didn't know you'd be here today!" Cyn puts away her things and gets on her lab coat.

"I thought I'd see how the project was coming along and hear what you're working on. We want to make sure our mentees get true exposure to the rigors of the program."

"Rome is an excellent mentor. I've learned a lot."

"He can be a bit much," Dr. C jokes, but is also feeling out Cyn's response.

"We're working with a limited resource and we don't get second chances. I understand his precautions." Should I be reading into that? Is she talking about us? Is there an us? Holy fuck I need to get it together, and stop thinking about it. It's over.

"Excellent," Dr. C responds. "You two do what you need to do, and I'm going to look over your work so far."

I sit down at the computer in the far corner, working on transcriptions, and Cyn takes up her station near the current journal and starts scanning pages. The serenity on her face and the small smile on her lips shouldn't hurt me but it does. Despite her emotions last weekend, she feels nothing. She's over it. It was deeper for me than it was for her, and that's understandable. I'll get over her in time, it'll just take me longer than it's taken her. Cyn is still a good person, and an asset to my lab.

At least I didn't hurt her. This is one time where I'm glad I'm wrong. I'm used to the pain and I can use it. It's better if she leaves it behind and moves on.

I'm deep in transcription, my hands flying over the keys, when Dr. C interrupts us.

"Could you both come look at this?" The tone of her voice has me on edge, and my heart drops into my stomach. Cyn and I share a worried look, purely collegial, before walking over to where Dr. C is examining one of the journals. We'd done chemical restoration work and most of the ink returned. The journal itself was now legible without needing the scans and transcriptions.

She holds up the journal, showing us one of the restored pages. Immediately, I notice that the color of the page is off, the yellowed paper now a light green color.

"The chemical mixture was off on this page, the ratios too intense. It didn't do extensive damage, but it looks sloppy."

My body tenses. Cyn checks the logs of which day we restored that page.

"It was me." Her voice is so soft and yet so defeated that I feel it like a precise blade into my heart. "I'm so sorry. I followed the formula."

I move around her to check the date she worked on the page. It was only a week ago, when we were wrapped up in each other and Charity's journal. I got sloppy watching her work. I trusted her too much, and didn't double and triple check everything that she did. My feelings for her distracted me from my responsibilities, both to training her as well as to preserving and restoring the journals. Elmwood's legacy. My legacy.

"Apparently you didn't," I snap. "Or it wouldn't look like that. We should check the other pages."

"We will," Dr. C reassures. "It's alright, Cynthia." She looks between the two of us, sensing the tension and upset from me. "For now, both of you are done tonight. We'll meet individually tomorrow to discuss this." We all look at our calendars on our phones and confirm appointments with her.

Cyn leaves first, and I shut down the lab.

I open my mouth to talk to Dr. C but she raises her hand. "Tomorrow. Sleep on it."

I don't sleep on it. Del still isn't talking to me and when I came home in an obviously grumpy mood, they retreated to their room. In that case, I'm still not entirely sure what I did wrong other than have enthusiasm for their potential romantic partner. I'm sure they'll explain it to me in a way I understand later.

I sit in my room, awake. I go over the formula Cyn should have followed over and over until I understand where she went wrong. If I'd been watching, I would have caught her mistake and explained where things went wrong. But I wasn't watching, I was working, I was distracted by her, our trust outside the lab filtered into the lab, and threw everything off balance. I wasn't watching.

While I am frustrated with her, I am more frustrated with myself.

This is on me. I let the boundaries down between us, I let myself be convinced that this was the way to solve our problem, and I let someone in who could impact the things that mattered most to me. I can't say it was a mistake, but it was a misstep. One I'll never make again.

Getting my degree from Elmwood matters to me in a way I don't think anyone else can understand. I lost my father, and his family abandoned us like I never mattered to them. Like I wasn't their flesh and blood, too. My mother came from a regular background and worked her ass off to both attend and work at an Ivy league school. She's incredible, but had humble beginnings, and therefore she and I are less than them. I'm tainted in some way in their opinion.

In the midst of grieving my father, I lost any stability we had until mom could right our ship.

I have something to prove to the Dwyers, even if I hate myself for how much I need that. I need to show them that none of us ever needed their money because mom, dad, and I had our own intelligence and drive. I don't need their money to succeed. All I want is to honor dad's memory and make him proud. I want to show him that I defied his family in this way, the same way he defied them in marrying mom. I wouldn't be here if he hadn't been willing to risk everything for his love for her. We were a happy damn family, even with serious people like mom and I. He was cheerful enough for the three of us.

I let my feelings put that at risk.

Dr. C is waiting for me when I arrive for my meeting. Her face is serious, but less like I'm in trouble and more like she's worried.

"I think Cynthia should leave the lab," is the preamble I start with before sitting down in the chair across from her desk.

"Why?" There's a note in her voice I don't understand.

"I don't think she's ready, not for a project like this. While I agree with the assessment she has talent and promise, this project is important to Elmwood. She's a freshman. Cyn hasn't even found her place on campus yet, she hasn't settled down into the work. Maybe next year, or taking over the project when I graduate, but she's not ready."

"You'd recommend her to lead the project?" Dr. C sounds surprised.

"If she keeps up this level of work, she'd be ready by her junior year." I do mean that. It's a solid assessment of her skills, and based on the courses she'd have between now and then, her abilities would be honed to do this work. But maybe she'll be drawn to teaching or other areas. Maybe she won't want this project by the time she could lead it.

"Then why can't she remain your mentee in the lab?"

"She's a distraction. Our temperaments are simply too different, she's not yet developed her professional persona, and we get off track on the work because of her behavior. Cyn has promise but she's simply too immature for a project of this magnitude. Her time might be better served in the chem lab. Or running social media for the department," I offer, trying hard not to sound sarcastic about that. It really is an important part of recruitment, especially since recruitment to Elmwood for admission is an odd and mysterious process. Most people aren't even aware of this as a discipline, although it's perfect for a liberal arts college.

"If that's really how you feel," Dr. C frowns. "Neither of you will go to the lab until you hear from me and I decide what to do. I might choose to keep her with you. That might be the lesson you need to learn, Rome."

"I understand." My stomach pits because I don't know if I could survive that. I didn't want to throw Cyn under the bus but I wanted to say enough that was true to get Dr. C to move her. Fuck, it's such a selfish move but it's self-preservation too. I'll die every day I'm around her.

Cyn

I show up for my meeting with Dr. Cunningham early, and recognize Rome's deep voice immediately. Despite the closed door, it resonates and is easy to hear.

"She's a distraction. Our temperaments are simply too different, she's not yet developed her professional persona, and we get off track on the work because of her behavior. Cyn has promise but she's simply too immature for a project of this magnitude. Her time might be better served in the chem lab. Or running social media for the department." That last suggestion hits me in the gut, reminding me how little Rome thinks of all that I've done. How little he sees of who I am.

I know that I didn't show him everything, but I thought I'd shown him enough to respect me. I thought he respected the work I did to make people understand the value or preservation and restoration, to see it as more than scrapbooking. Apparently not. Even if my motivation to do my social media work has waned, that doesn't meant I'm not proud of it.

The thing is, I know I made that error, but I also know that I checked with Rome repeatedly about the mixture and ratios. We both made the mistakes that damaged that page. I'm sure he's blaming our attraction to each other, and I am too, but I didn't think that was enough for him to throw me under the bus. The last few weeks he'd been telling me how much I improved, he'd been trusting me with more, and that was before we hooked up. I was doing good work and he knew it.

I was capable of the work the President's project required, and the insult that he levied to the chair cuts me really fucking deep.

The rest of their conversation blurs. I turn away and leave the building, sending an email to Dr. Cunningham that our meeting is unnecessary and for Rome's convenience, I'd like to be reassigned. I make it clear that it's out of respect for his preference, and that it's not my own. I want to be on that project and in that lab. It's not in the cards for this year.

When I get to the library, my eyes tear up for a second. No more late nights here. No more hours in the caverns of the basement, flipping through the past. I take a deep breath before heading down into the lab.

It looks the way it always does, but somehow feels emptier to me.

It also surprises me how many of my things found their way here as I start trying to pack it all up. Some of my favorite pens and highlighters, my preferred post-it notes, a few notebooks worth of diagrams and formulas that I got from Rome. A stress ball that looks like a strawberry that Rome kept stealing from me to squeeze while waiting for renderings to process. I decide to leave that, and place it by his computer. He won't see it until he's sitting in front of it, and I hope it hurts a little.

I'm packing up Charity's journal when the door to the lab opens.

I stiffen, terror racing through me at the reality that I'm about to face Rome unprepared. Without having fully processed what he said, the email I sent, my decision to run away from this whole situation instead of facing it head on.

I finish wrapping the journal before I turn around.

"Aren't you supposed to be meeting with Dr. Cunningham?" he asks, appearing concerned.

"I declined my meeting. I'm leaving."

"Cyn," he takes a step toward me and I step back. He stops.

"This is your lab. Clearly, you feel like I'm not capable and I don't want to slow you down. Maybe I'll run the department's social media," I snap, unable to help myself.

Rome has the sense to wince at that. "It's up to Dr. C."

"No, it isn't, it's up to me. I don't want to be here." There's a venom in my voice that I've never heard before. Then again, I've never been hurt like this before. I've never had both my heart and my brain stomped on so thoroughly by another person. No one's ever had that power before, and I pray that I never experience it again.

Rome flinches, and I hate that a flicker of sympathy burns in my chest. I'm just another person abandoning him, but he's the one that keeps pushing me away.

"Thank you for everything," I say, retreating back into kindness and politeness for the armor that they are. "I've learned a lot working with you, and appreciate the time you took to teach me."

I turn my back on him and finish putting Charity's journal in the protective case I got for it. We finished the scan last weekend, now it's doing the work to render each page and work on the transcriptions. I can do that from my dorm room, and I'll figure out what to do after that.

"Are you going to turn me in?" I ask without looking back. Rome doesn't answer. I slide the case into my backpack and zip it shut. I swap out my lab coat for my winter coat, and put my backpack on. I still haven't looked at him, and he still hasn't said anything.

I have to walk by him to leave the lab. When I finally turn to him, he's looking down at he floor. When we're shoulder to shoulder I stop, and have to swallow hard around the lump in my throat before I can speak.

"Bye, Rome."

I leave the lab. My heart just got broken for the first time and I had a hand in breaking it. At the same time, I stood up for myself, and that's something I've never done before. I can still choose happiness, I can still seek silver linings, and I can demand to be treated the way that I deserve. I can confront situations that are bad or uncomfortable without losing the core of myself.

If I can stand up to the first man to own my heart, the sky is the limit.

I think it's time I have a harsh conversation with dad about my damn YouTube channel.

Cyn

The silver lining for my first broken heart is that I have amazing friends. That's a first too. Elise, Maeve, and Tati have my back in every single way. I wallow over Rome for a solid day. They stay with me the entire time, losing the rest of their weekend to drown in sugary foods and a bottle of vodka that Colin gifted me.

It becomes a hugely important time for all of us.

Drunk mouths speak sober thoughts, and we confess a lot to each other. Elise tells us more of the story about her and Colin, about the guy that goes here that assaulted her. Maeve revealed that because of her marriage contract, even though she doesn't know him, she's not allowed to have sex. Tati finally caves and tells all of us that she never wanted to come to Elmwood and she's here when she'd rather be somewhere else. That we're the only ones who make it survivable for her to stay.

I tell them I want to be done with the influencer bullshit.

"Yeah, of course you do," Maeve nods, taking a pull from the bottle. "You have school to focus on, not to mention the lab obligations. You're running yourself ragged, babe." Tati nods in agreement. I turn to Elise.

She turns pink. "We've talked about it before. We worried about you."

I know they'll think I'm upset they talked behind my back, but honestly, when it comes from a place of care there's nothing to be mad about.

"What do I do?" I rub my face, tired down to my marrow. "My dad has all these contracts, he pushes it so hard. If I don't do things, he'll do them, and that's always the worst. He shares personal stuff on my accounts that I don't want on the internet."

"Like what?" Tati asks, concerned with a hint of pissed off.

"In high school, he'd share things about my grades, my achievements. He'd share photos of my private journals and scrapbooks, the ones that I made for me and not for my social media work. My privacy didn't exist if it was for the channel. He uses my mom for posts even though I've asked him not to - it's the only thing I fight with him about, but he keeps doing it anyway."

"You're 18. All of this shit is in your name. Get him out. This is your life." Elise sounds so firm about it. "Take control."

"He's my dad."

"Doesn't sound like it," Maeve replies. "You deserve better. If he won't give it to you, demand it. Just like you did with Rome." She winces for a second and I wave her off, not bothered that she brought him up. "Maybe he was practice for you standing up to your dad."

I laugh and take another drink. "Silver lining."

Maeve holds up her cup, and we all follow suit. "Silver linings."

The next morning, after we eat breakfast and separate to go about our days, I change all my passwords. Every single thing I can think of gets a new password. And not the same password, ones that are specific to each site.

It takes 25 minutes for dad to realize and FaceTime me. Elise is there, and I ask her to stay and be quiet and be there for me. She nods in agreement.

"Dad," I greet him as I answer the call.

He looks furious. His face is red and he's frowning. "Have you been hacked?"

"No?" I force some confusion. "Why?"

"I can't get into any of your accounts."

"It's Sunday, dad, I already posted this week's video today."

"I wanted to prepare posts for the rest of the week. You have two posts from contracted ads, and it's your mom's birthday on Friday. That will be a good draw."

"No. I'm not posting about mom unless I want to, and not for an ad."

"Cynthia," he starts.

"I changed all my passwords. My social media is mine, and I'm cutting back.'"

He blanches. "You can't do that, we have contracts-"

I cut him off. "The only contracts I signed are up at the end of this year. I'll meet my obligations, and then I'm done. At least for now. I'm in college, dad. I need to focus."

"Your work is worth more than your degree."

"No. Not to me. I'm not your employee, I'm your daughter, but to be clear - this is me firing you, and it's also me quitting. I'll work when I want to, once the year is over. It's mine to make choices about, and I'm done."

"Cynthia. You can't do this, it's irresponsible."

"Actually, I think it's very responsible."

"I can't let you do this."

The tears that have been building slip out as I shake my head at him. "It's not up to you." There's nothing more for me to say right now, so I hang up the call.

Elise comes over to my bed and hugs me. "You good?"

I take a deep breath, reaching back for that light, hopeful feeling that took over when I changed the passwords and regained control. "I think I am. About this, at least."

"Not so much about Rome?"

"No," my voice cracks. "It could have been something truly amazing, Elise. I don't care that he's a grumpy asshole. I actually like it. It drives me wild to get under his skin and make him snap. I miss him already." I sniffle and grab a tissue from my nightstand.

"Don't give up hope. Colin is a pretty good judge of character and he likes Rome. He'll come around."

"I'm not in a rush to get over him." Because I don't want to get over him.

"Okay. Then you cry some more while I work on college algebra."

Instead of wallowing, I grab my laptop, and start working on Charity's journal again. The scans are all on my personal cloud, and it doesn't take much to start working. It'll be easy to fall into that project and find my way out the other side. This is unfinished business, and I know it will get to Rome the same way that it got to me. The mystery has to be revealed. The story has to be told.

I get to work on something that brings me joy, and that's all that matters right now. One half of my heart is broken, and the other half is trying to find it's way back into the light.

Rome

When I finally come back to myself in the lab, Cyn has been gone for awhile. I follow Dr. C's instructions and take what I need, then close it up. Del is waiting on the couch when I get back to the apartment, but whatever lecture they'd planned to give me is immediately abandoned by what they see on my face.

"What happened?" They stand up and grab me, pulling me over to sit down on the couch.

I open my mouth and everything comes out. My relationship or whatever it was with Cyn, having feelings for her, the screw up in the lab, what I said to Dr. C and that I'm pretty sure Cyn heard some of it, and that now she left me. On every level, and that I know the only person to blame is myself. I keep thinking if I'd never let her in, if I'd never crossed the line, we wouldn't be here right now. We'd be working in the lab, conquering our sexual tension, and eventually moving on with our lives.

"That would be terrible," Del tells me. I hadn't realized I'd kept talking and said that part out loud. "You needed to let her in, Rome. She was so good for you, and I think you were good for her too."

"Then why did it work out like this?"

"Because you're you, and you're complicated and damaged and afraid."

"Fuck you." I snarl and move to stand up. Del puts their hand on my knee and pushes me back down.

"You know why I was mad at you at Beastly?"

"No."

They almost smile at my furious tone. "I was jealous."

"Of what?"

Del sighs and collapses back on the couch. "I know I'm pretty, but you're prettier. You were talking to Ev with so much intensity and excitement and when you do that it pulls people in. Watching you go from grumpy to engaging is kind of intoxicating. I was terrified she was going to end up with a crush on you and I'd be her speed bump on the way to you."

"I'm not interested in her."

"Not the point," they frown. "At the same time, it was so long since I'd seen you that way. Casually engaging with another human being, not acting like the world was out to get you and everything was evil. I also got jealous because I thought it was about Ev, but when I thought about it later it was more than just your conversation with her. It was really about Cyn. The side of you she woke up."

"It's not part of the plan."

"Fuck the plan!" Del throws up their hands. "Your dad would already be proud of you, don't you think he'd also want you to be happy?"

That's a legitimate question and my gut does not like the answer.

"Listen, you do what you want, and I'll support you. Just don't throw something away because you didn't plan for it. I know it feels like she's abandoning you, but it might actually be the other way around."

That fucking stings. I'll have to think about it from that perspective for awhile.

"Now, I'm going to get inside Everly and have her tell me I'm the most beautiful person in the world, and I'll see you in the morning to make you eat breakfast."

"Too much information." I slump down. "Are you two official?"

Del blushes, and I smile to see my best friend so unabashedly happy. "Yeah. We'll do something, all three of us soon. Or maybe four?" They look at me hopefully but I give them nothing. I need time.

Time away from Cyn, time away from the lab, and time to process what I want and how the events of this semester might alter everything for me.

The next morning I get an email from Dr. Cunningham. Cyn has been reassigned to another lab, and I can get back to work the next day. Right.

Good. Everything is the way it's supposed to be.

I don't see or hear from Cyn for two weeks.

I go out to dinner with Del and Everly. We have a good time, and I try to be more open with both of them. I try to relax.

The lab feels empty but I'm getting the work done. It's a lot slower without Cyn. I'd gotten used to our pace together and didn't realize how much it advanced the work. I wish I could tell her that. I wish I could tell her I'd taken her for granted in the lab, and that I did trust her. That I would take back everything I said if I could apologize to her.

I'm such a fucking idiot. One mistake was not worth imploding our professional relationship. If I'd been honest with myself, one moment of panic was not worth imploding our personal relationship either. Sometimes I'm so wrapped up in doing the required thing or following the plan that I'm more machine than human being. I forget how to be a person and disconnect so thoroughly from others I can't always find my way back to my humanity. I let my heart and soul disconnect from my brain and I'm nothing but cold, rational thinking.

Del tells me it's my Capricorn energy. In return, I remind them that the placement of celestial bodies at the time of my birth has little do with who I am as a person, and that life experience has made me into this monster.

They always retort that it's such a Capricorn thing to say. At this point, we no longer have that argument. I won't win it.

It should tell me something that Cyn disrupted the pattern of my life. That's important. It never happened before her, or when it did it was always something bad. I can only think about my time with her as something good.

As something that made me happy.

Don't get me wrong, I still mentally sneer even thinking the word, but I also know it's the truth.

It's been two weeks without even a passing sighting of her when she sends me an email. My heart races and I'm terrified to open it. I decide to look at it on my computer instead of my phone so I can see the preview of the message. I also notice it has an attachment.

The preview starts: The rest of Charity's journal.

I open the email and there's only one more sentence: They fell in love.

I click on the attached pdf and start reading the rendered pages and Cyn's transcription.

Charity decided that she wasn't going to marry someone she had no relationship with, and was going to find a way to prove herself to Ethan Carstairs. She found out that President James was trying to get into a business deal with Carstairs, but it was a manipulation to get access to a source for a material. Before leaving one night, Charity stopped him at the back gate and told him the truth. It made Carstairs see her in a different light.

They started meeting at the back gate after every visit. She would sneak out the back door and meet him there, and they would talk. He saw her as the asset her father did not.

A month before their wedding, he kissed her for the first time and told her that he loved her. That nothing would separate them now. He confessed to her that he'd had a failed engagement and relationship before, and that he'd been hurt and his trust broken. That he wanted to be married to move to the next stage in his life but was hesitant to trust again. She was overjoyed to have earned his trust, and seen for her value.

Of course, her father got wind of their relationship and tried to end the engagement. Charity finally got to stand her ground and told her father that she'd ruin him if he tried to stop them. She basically told him to stay in his little world running his college, and that once she was married to Ethan he'd never have to see her again.

The last entry is on her wedding day. Charity is happy. She writes that she's leaving her journal in the ladies' reading room in the library. That must have been blocked off during one of the renovations, and I wonder where. I wonder if any of the ladies ever found it, if they read it, and if it changed anything for them.

The parallel between our situation and the relationship between Charity and Ethan is obvious. Elmwood has a way of doing that though. Some kind of magic on these grounds leads people to exactly where they're supposed to be, to experience something that will change them, heal them, solve a problem, or reveal one to them.

The only reason I was going to Peter Cunningham's office that day was because a librarian had caught me on the way out the door and asked if I'd deliver some articles that had arrived for him. The universe conspired so that I would see him with Hannah, and know that I was betrayed, and that it was time to move on.

Elmwood is telling me that this journey isn't over. There are some things to let go of, and maybe, there's something to hold on to if I can find a way to fix it.

Rome

I'm waiting outside Dr. C's office first thing in the morning. We stare at each other, and her eyes narrow at me before she opens the door and lets me in. I sit down, tense and anxious, preparing for the reaming of my life that I will definitely deserve.

"Cyn was a distraction in the lab, but not because of her work."

Dr. C stares, waiting.

"I mean, at first it was, but she caught up well. She did good work. There was something between us and we decided to explore it." I try and explain that we fucked each other to the point of passing out in a way that preserves everyone's dignity. "It was more than I was prepared for, and when I thought it was getting in the way of my work, I reacted poorly."

"A mistake was still made," Dr. C points out.

"I know, but she and I are equally responsible for that. I let my trust in her outside the lab alter my trust inside it. She should have checked with me, and I should have been more diligent."

"I see." She sighs. "What happened, Rome?"

"She earned my trust. I wasn't expecting to have feelings for her. I didn't handle it well."

She stares at me so intensely for so long that I start to squirm under her scrutiny.

"I say this with the highest respect for your intelligence. You are an idiot."

I half smile, and she seems stunned by that expression. Until Cyn, I hadn't been aware of how little I smiled, or how much people noticed the absence of that expression on my face.

"I'm aware."

"Are you going to correct your mistake?"

I bend my head, already feeling defeated. "I'm going to try."

"Good. It'll be up to the both of you if you want to work in the lab together again, and I want some serious thought on that."

"I understand."

"Get out." The words are harsh but she says them with a smile. I wait a moment, surprised that I didn't get lectured, but I think Dr. C knows there's nothing she could say to me better than what I've said to myself. At least she's giving me a chance to fix this without penalizing either of us.

I leave feeling lighter. I fixed one piece of the mess that I made, and it's time to work on the rest. It's going to mean talking to people, which I generally dislike, but there's really no choice. If I want to find her, and if I want to make things up to her, then I have to show her the work I was willing to put in.

Luckily, the first step in finding her won't be that hard.

Colin is already in the TA office when I get there. I'm not doing it this year since I'm running my lab, but I know he likes taking the morning classes. He looks up from his notebook, surprised to see me, and then he frowns. I'm guessing that he knows about Cyn and I from her roommate, who is his girlfriend. It took me longer than it should have to put that together.

"Larson," I greet him, and close the door to the office. I lean against it and wait him out.

"Dwyer. What's up?"

"I need a favor."

"If it has to do with Cyn, the answer is no. You've done enough." The fact that he sounds so firm about it makes me scared. It makes me fear that she's been as miserable and destroyed as I've been the last few weeks. The thought makes me sick that I'm responsible for that. It also fills me with relief that she might feel the same as I do. That the loss of what we were becoming is hitting her as hard as it hit me.

"Please."

Colin sighs and pulls out his phone, tapping the screen and putting it to his ear. "Where are you? Can you come to the TA office?" For a second he laughs. "Not for that. Serious thing. See you soon." He hangs up the phone. "Elise should be here in a minute. It's up to her."

"Okay." I take a step into the office and sit on the empty chair. I try to think of anything to say to him while we wait. "So, Elise."

Colin grins. "Yeah. That's been a long time coming. We grew up together, she's my sister's best friend, and I couldn't wait anymore."

"What changed?"

"I told her how I felt. I didn't dance around it or hint at it, I said it. Even if she hadn't felt the same, it would've been worth it. Just for her to know."

I nod, and we sit in silence, both lost in our thoughts. His probably a lot more pleasant than mine. A soft knock on the door disrupts us before his girlfriend pokes her head in. She's got a smile for him but as soon as she sees me her pleasant little face drops into a furious frown.

"What do you want?"

"Hear him out," Colin soothes her, and takes her hand.

"I know that you have no reason to help me, but I'm asking anyway. I need to know when and where Cyn has lab now."

"Why? To yell at her some more?"

"I never yelled." That's the wrong thing to say based on Elise's face and I backtrack quickly. "I need to talk to her."

"To apologize?" Elise snaps.

"As a start, yes."

"What else?"

"That's only for her," my voice is quiet and nearly breaks. I know she hears it. Elise's face softens. "Please?"

"She's in the general chem lab starting at 2:00 today. Don't fuck it up."

I nod. "Thank you." I stand up to leave, but pause. "Will she – did I – can I come back from this?"

Elise tilts her head and looks at me with an expression I can't read. "I don't know, but I think you have to try anyway."

I hate that answer, but for the first time in my life I'm holding onto hope.

I have until 2:00 to figure out what the hell I'm going to say to the only person worth ripping my heart out for.

Cyn

This lab is boring.

It's mostly cleaning, doing basic mixes, and doing work that any other professor on campus requests if they don't have time to run their own experiments. Mostly, I'm spending my time checking formulas because I don't have to think too hard to run the math. The upper classmen students running the lab were unsurprised at my arrival. One of them even mentioned I lasted longer than they expected.

While I understand it, I also hate that people see Rome that way.

Despite his serious demeanor, life has been boring and colorless without him. There are things I want to tell him about life, big and little things, chatter I want to share with him while watching him frown at his computer screen. I want to talk about Charity's journal with him. I want to talk shit about President James with him. I want to tell him about everything that's happened with my dad and my channel, that I stood up for myself and that I couldn't have done it if I hadn't been able to stand up to him first.

I want to talk about our feelings, and sort out where things went so wrong between us. I want him to apologize and explain himself. It only took a day for my anger to dissipate and leave sadness behind. When I put everything that happened between us into the context of his life experience it couldn't be anything other than sad. He panicked. If I hadn't gotten so upset I probably could have talked him out of having me leave the lab. What's left in the wake of all of this is disappointment, frustration, and pure hurt. This could have gone so differently.

We both reacted poorly. Instead of taking criticism and making change, we took it out on each other in different ways.

I miss him. I expected to miss him while I got over him, but this is like a piece of my memory got taken away. I can feel the shape of where it used to be and I know there's something there but I can't access it. I need to find a way to fix this, or move on. I need closure and I'm not sure he'll give it to me.

Trying to focus on my work, I'm rewriting a formula that was incorrect when complete silence falls in the lab. It's usually quiet but this is pin drop quiet.

The door to the lab closes, echoing in the silence, and I look toward it.

Rome is standing there. Dark hair wet and windblown, dark jacket, dark clothes, looking like a crow come to life and searching for something shiny. His eyes are roving the lab and change when he sees me. His gaze softens, all of the sharp angles of him blurring when his eyes lock with mine. Like I'm his something shiny

He crosses the lab to get to me and everyone watches. Rome steps close as I turn to face him, closer than I expected, and his proximity makes me want to cry.

"Do you like it here?" he asks. Not what I expected him to ask.

"No. It's boring." I whisper, afraid of being heard.

"Do you want to come back to my lab?"

My head snaps back and I stare at him. "Excuse me?"

Rome takes my hand, but I don't hold it back. My fingers rest limply in his palm. "I'm sorry for what you heard, and what I said. Blaming you was a terrible thing to do. I've explained everything to Dr. Cunningham - my part in what happened, what was going on between us. The mistake was both of ours, but it was my responsibility. Your work has been beyond adequate and I need you back in the lab."

My lips twitch because to anyone else that might sound like an insult, but coming from Rome it's definitely a compliment.

"Do you only want me to come back to the lab?" My voice is weak, but I have to know.

"No," his voice is quiet, and when I meet his eyes again I can see the torment there. Rome lifts my hand to his mouth and kisses my fingers. "I want you with me where you belong."

It's such a sweet, sappy thing that I almost can't believe he said it. I wait him out though, knowing that Rome will take his time saying everything that he wants to say if I give him the space to say it.

"I was afraid of what I felt for you, afraid that you would be the next person to abandon me, and I let you go when I should have held on."

"I won't abandon you."

"I know. I won't let you." There's a hint of a smile on his face. "Come back to me."

I look at him for a long time. As apologies go, it's pretty good, but I need more.

"What are we doing, Rome?"

He pulls me against him, our bodies lining up, the connection and comfort between us unmistakable. Against my will, I melt. This feels perfectly right.

"We're falling in love." He leans close and waits for me to make the next move and accept what he's offering to me. I press up on my toes and our mouths connect in a deep, sweet kiss. He lets my lips go but doesn't put any distance between us. "I might already love you."

"That's good, because I love you too."

Rome smiles, a full, big, joyful smile and it's absolutely devastating. When he kisses me again, I can feel that smile against my mouth and I don't think I've ever felt more power in my life.

"Come to my place when you're done. We'll figure everything out." Rome starts to let me go but I hold on to him.

"I'm done." I take off my lab coat and throw it on the table, not caring about anything. "I'm coming back to your lab, they don't need me here."

Rome gives a hint of a smile again. "Okay then. To my place."

"Yes, sir," I smirk at him. Rome glares, but in a sexy way.

He holds out his hand for mine, and we walk out of the lab together. It's still pretty silent, everyone watching us in complete shock. Even if they knew I was working with Rome, they had no idea how close we'd gotten.

I doubt any of them had ever even seen him smile before. They'd talked plenty of shit about him the first day I showed up, assuming that I was as afraid him as they are.

We don't talk on the way to his apartment. There isn't anything more to say. Not with our words, anyway. The tension is building between us with every step closer to his apartment. I've missed him touching me and commanding me. The power behind his actions and the devastating release I get from the way he uses my body.

No one is there when we arrive, and I wonder if Rome hoped this was the way things would go and told Del to make themselves scarce. While he is a confident person, I don't think he's confident in this arena so I doubt that's the case. I'm sure Rome was as certain that I'd slap his face and tell him to go as that I'd tell him I loved him back. We discard our shoes and jackets, the action still familiar and comfortable even thought it's been weeks since I was here.

We walk to his room, and Rome locks the door behind me.

He steps up to me and takes my chin in his hand, making me look up at him and keeping my gaze captive.

"I'm going to make you cry, Cyn, and you're going to like it."

"Yes, sir." There's no other answer. He can do whatever he wants to me because now I know he loves me, and he wants to control me in order to pleasure me.

"Take off my clothes." That's a new instruction, but I listen. I start with his shirt, peeling off the long sleeved black tee and revealing his beautiful, sculpted chest to me. Before my hands can drop to his jeans, he catches them and presses my palms against his chest.

"I've rushed you, in the past, greedy to get my hands on you. Touch me. Explore me, lovely. Take your time." I look up at him, at the intensity radiating from his gaze. He's still in control, but he's making himself vulnerable to me. Reminding me that he is mine, too.

I run my hands over his tight, smooth skin. The tips of my fingers trace each dip and curve, and when I run a finger between his abs the muscles jump and he jolts away.

"Are you...ticklish?" I ask with wonder. Rome grimaces and says nothing. I smile up at him and do it again, laughing when his muscles jump. I don't tease him too much, eager to touch him. When my hands slide up and I pinch his dark nipples, he cuts off a groan. I file that information away for later.

I drag my nails firmly down his torso to the waistband of his jeans. I undo the button and the zipper, but don't push them down. Instead, I run my fingertips along the waistband of his boxers, dipping in and out to tease that sensitive skin. His cock grows beneath the cotton, aroused by my touch. Power thrums through me again. I push his jeans down.

I tease his body over his boxers, dragging my hands over everywhere except his cock. Rome bites his lip and throws his head back, fighting to maintain his control. I want to give it back to him, so I take a few steps away.

It takes Rome a minute to realize that I've stopped, and his head drops down, his eyes hazy with lust. He watches me as I take off my shirt, then my yoga pants, until I'm standing in my bra and a thong. I twirl on my toes so my back is to him. My bra drops to the floor, and then I bend over as i drag my thong down my legs.

Rome groans. "Fucking perfect. So goddamn beautiful, Cyn. The most beautiful woman I've ever seen."

I stand up and look over my shoulder before I step over to his bed and lay down on my back. Bending my knees and resting my feet on the edge of the bed, I spread my legs open in invitation.

"Please, sir," I beg lightly, desperate to feel him.

Rome doesn't need to be asked twice. He walks over, drops to his knees as he hooks his hands around my thighs and drags me to his mouth. It happens so abruptly and smoothly that I cry out at the invasion of his tongue against my clit. He eats me like he's been starving, and maybe he has. His thumb takes over as he moves down to spear his tongue inside me, spreading me wide open and fucking my entrance with the tip and teasing me to the edge over and over.

My hands fly up and dig into his thick, silky hair, pressing him hard against me as I careen toward my first orgasm since the last time he fucked me. While we were apart I couldn't even bring myself to masturbate because I'd always end up thinking of him. My memories and fantasies never compared to the real him.

I start to come, pressing my hips against his face, screaming as my pleasure takes over my entire body.

As it starts to dissipate, Rome rises over me, licking his lips. "You're not done, lovely," he tells me. I cry out when his fingers slide inside me, pressing against that deep, intense spot that makes my eyes cross. He moves his fingers, beckoning against my body and leading me over the edge.

"Again, Cyn. I need one more from you like this. I want to give you more but I can't wait to be inside you. Come on my fingers so I can fill you with my cock, my love."

That does it. The swelling of my heart when he calls me that matches the swelling of my pussy and I explode. My eyes squeeze shut as I dive into the darkness, nothing but a raw nerve wracked with pleasure. I scream his name, my body bows, and he doesn't stop until I'm whimpering from the sensitivity.

Rome pulls out of me and I watch as he gets out a condom and rolls it down his thick erection. His cock is as fierce and angry as he is most of the time, and as desperate for me as the rest of him. I move deeper onto the bed as he climbs over me, lining himself up with my throbbing pussy.

"You're mine, Cyn," he rumbles at me as he starts to split me open on his cock. "I will fuck you until you think you can't take it anymore, but I know you can. I know you can handle whatever I want to give to you. My lovely, good girl, made to break for me."

"Yes!" I scream as he's finally seated all the way inside me.

Rome slides out, then slams back inside, repeating the motion over and over and picking up speed. He grabs my hips and tilts them up, his cockhead now hitting the same spot his fingers did. My hands dig into his comforter and I can only brace myself for the explosion that's coming. I'm panting, gasping for air as I get close to the edge.

"Rome!" It's more of a rasp than a scream, all the air leaving my body as my orgasm rolls through me. Before I can finish he drops over me, one hand pinching my clit while the other grabs my chin, keeping me from moving too far. The tears falling down my cheeks run over his fingertips.

"Another, Cyn, one more. One more." Then he kisses me, devouring my tongue and teasing the pleasure circuits along that muscle that seem to go straight to my pussy. Rome presses hard against my clit as he slams deep inside me and I go off again. Everything goes white, lightning rocketing through my body.

"Good girl," he murmurs against my lips before burying his face in my neck and groaning as he comes. Everything fades for a moment.

When I come back to myself, Rome is laying next to me and stroking his fingers through my hair. I don't remember how he got there.

"You passed out," he whispers, but I hear the satisfaction in his voice. I turn to look at him, trying to glare. I can only laugh.

"That's a first."

"Not a last," he promises and then kisses my temple before laying down and yanking me to him. "Will you stay tonight?"

"Yeah." I get up to go to the bathroom, but he catches my wrist as I steal his shirt.

"Is there anything else I need to apologize for? The last thing I want is for you to feel like you can't tell me when I've upset you."

I step to him and run my hand across his cheek and up into his hair, holding him like that. "I'm not expecting you to stop being who you are, Rome. I know you'll always be a bit of an asshole, and I don't want you to stop teaching me and holding me to high standards. Push me to be better in the lab, and support me outside of it. I'll do the same."

Rome turns his head to kiss my wrist, and I shiver at the sensation. "I've always got you, lovely. I trust you've got me too." Then he smiles at me again, easier than ever before, and the last piece of my heart leaves my body and goes to his.

Cyn

I'm in the small sitting area outside Dr. Cunningham's office, waiting. Rome wanted to talk to her first and explain everything. Not only how we cleared things up between us, but it was also time to come clean about Charity's journal. Even though I was the one that found it and didn't turn it in, at the end of the day it was his lab and he agreed with me that we should keep it to ourselves. He wanted to take responsibility for that.

Last night while he fed me my weight in pizza, we talked about everything that had happened in the last two weeks. I finally told him everything about my dad and my social media, and how I cut him off. I thought that would be it, but it ended up my dad had done some pretty shitty things regarding my public persona. Like sign contracts with my name without my knowledge. Using money that I inherited when mom passed, I've hired a lawyer to sort through it all and determine the next steps.

Rome was furious for me. So mad he had to leave the room for a second before coming back and asking me what I needed from him. I kissed his nose and reminded him I had it. He'd already given it to me. That earned me a hint of a smile.

It was my decision to tell Dr. Cunningham now, even if he's the one taking the lead. No matter how much he's assured me that we aren't going to get in too much trouble, I'm still nervous. He might have the security of a good relationship with her and he's earned some leeway in the demonstration of his skills. Aside from winning the Van Hornen, all she's really seen of me is that I messed up a page in the restoration of the journals. I haven't earned this.

I flinch when her door opens, but she gives me a soft smile and invites me in. My eyes jump to Rome's as I step inside and he manages to give me a smile with only his eyes. I don't know how he does that.

Dr. Cunningham looks between the two of us and smirks, but tries to hide it. I can see the affection she has for Rome and I'm glad that when he's felt so alone he had someone like her on his side. The pain they share brought them together rather than making them enemies, and I think that has everything to do with who Dr. Cunningham is as a person.

I sit down in the unoccupied chair across from her desk and next to Rome. His hand twitches like he wants to reach out for mine, but he refrains. Even though we'll need to comfort each other when this is done, we agreed to put professionalism first in this conversation, as much as we can given everything that's happened.

Dr. Cunningham sits down in her chair. "First, are you sure you want to go back to Rome's lab?"

"Yes," I rush out and feel myself blushing. "I'm invested in the project and the work. To be honest, I wasn't challenged in the chem lab. I want to keep learning."

She looks at me for a moment that's slightly too long. "I can imagine that's true, given your experience. I'm approving it, but I need you two to understand that if there's any further issues, you're done. No matter what the reason is, I'm not allowing people to lab hop. So if this doesn't work out," she gestures between us, "you still have to work together. At least until the end of the year."

"I wouldn't worry about that," Rome replies, full of confidence. Not only in our ability to work together, but I can tell he's that confident in us. I smile down at my hands.

"The easy part is settled then." Dr. Cunningham writes a note on a page in front of her, and then turns back to me. "Where did your friend find the journal? How did it end up with you?"

I sigh. "All she would tell me is that she found it in the library. I can press more if you need me to, but that's all I know right now. She put it in a Ziploc bag when she brought it home, and gave it to me a few days later.

I took it to the lab right away so it's been in a safe environment since."

"When did you know it belonged to Charity James?"

"Um, the first day I worked on it. About a month now."

Dr. Cunningham frowns. "And you rendered the entire journal?"

"Yes. Nothing chemical, only scanning. It was in decent shape and the renders were very good."

"I see." She frowns and looks down at her desk. "Why keep it to yourself?"

That's a much harder question to answer. "I think we all know that President James wasn't the best person. I wanted Charity to have a chance to be heard, especially once I read the first entries. Charity's legacy is as important to Elmwood as her father's, maybe even more so, and I know how women's stories get treated in academia." I breathe in sharply. "That wasn't a critique of you, but it might've been out of your hands."

I can feel the heat of Rome's gaze on my face, and the pride for me radiating out of him. It makes me feel more confident. It reassures me that this is going to be okay.

Dr. Cunningham sighs. "I won't disagree with you. I do think if you'd come forward this would have been put off for years, and I think our true history as a college would be incomplete. Since the work is all done, and was done in the appropriate lab, I'm not going to penalize either of you. The best people to have their hands on it other than me would be the two of you."

"However," she continues, "pull a stunt like this again and you'll be out of the lab. Any lab. You hear me?"

"Yes, ma'am," I answer immediately.

Rome smirks a little. "Understood. Thank you."

Dr. Cunningham sits back in her chair with a small smile. "Now, tell me what's in the journal."

Rome

3.5 years later

We have one last thing to do before Cyn officially leaves Elmwood. After I graduated, I started my own company doing personal restoration and preservation. Cyn took over the President's project from me, just as I planned, and got her dream job working for the Boston Public Library with their rare books and manuscripts collection. We move next week.

That first year, Cyn made me take her home for Thanksgiving. Mom loved her. Still loves her. Maybe more than me. Apparently she's got the secret to making two very grumpy people happy.

I take a deep breath and look at myself in the old, hazy mirror. Mom appears over my shoulder.

"You look fine, stop it." She bats my hand away from my tie. It's dark gold and matches the pocket square I'm being forced to wear. It stands out against the black shirt and the black suit. Since she won't let me mess with my tie, I start working on my hair.

"Nope, not that either." Mom grabs my hands and holds them, pulling my attention to her. "Other than fidgeting, are you okay?"

"I want it done. I don't even know why I'm anxious. The hard part is over."

Mom laughs. "Asking her wasn't the hard part. Today isn't the hard part. The rest of your lives, making it work, that's the hard part."

"Was it hard with dad?"

"No," her eyes wet with tears and I feel bad bringing him up, but she waves me off before I can say anything. "Not even at the end. Loving him was the easiest thing I ever did."

"Then the hard part is over," I raise an eyebrow at her in challenge. "I want the rest of our lives. Right now."

Mom smiles a little. "Then let's get out there."

We exit the small room where I got ready and my side of our wedding party is waiting in the hall. Being with Cyn meant I gained friends even when I was reluctant to do so. Trusting her restored my ability to trust overall, and we found people worth having and keeping in our lives.

Del is my best person, of course, but we're joined by Colin and his best friend who became one of my best friends, Tate. I was in Tate's wedding last year and he still won't stop giving me shit for not smiling in a single picture. They'll be lucky if they get a picture of me smiling today.

"I'm going to be honest, I never thought you'd get married," Del whispers. That almost gets a laugh from me. "I'm glad it's her. That you got your head out of your ass."

"Me too," Colin chimes in.

"Thank you. All of you." I grimace. "Now shut up, I want to get married."

Colin signals our wedding coordinator that we're getting started, and on her signal, I escort my mom down the aisle of the small chapel on the Elmwood campus. The college had been restoring it for almost a decade, and as soon as I knew that Cyn was it for me, I put our names on the list to be married there when it was complete. She loves Elmwood as much as I do, and adored the history and beauty of this place.

It's dark but intricate, a lot of wood and stone work. No stained glass windows, all clear, bright glass. The inside is lit up by the bright sunshine from outside and the candles all around. We kept the invite list small, so it's about half full.

We didn't invite her dad. Even though everything was cleared up on a legal level, nothing could repair the harm he did to her and her reputation.

Mom hugs me before going to take her seat. I stand next to the pastor and try not to fidget as I wait for the love of my life.

Del and Elise come first, both grinning at me, both knowing me well enough to know that I'm about to burst out of my skin with impatience.

They break off after Elise gives me a cheeky wink. I vow right then to give her so much crap when she gets all antsy at her own wedding. A taste of her own medicine. Based on the darkly shining diamond that recently showed up on her finger, that'll be sooner rather than later.

Colin and Maeve follow, then Tate and Tati. My woman's friends stuck together all four years, and even though I'd never say it out loud, I love them too. I love who they are for her, and that they bring out the best in each other. We all have varying degrees of relationships with our families, but we're also our own family. We look out for each other like family.

I wouldn't have that without Cyn.

The music changes and I lose my breath when Cyn comes around the corner and into my view. Nothing else exists in the universe except her in this moment. The dress she's wearing is cream colored satin and it would seem simple except for the way it runs down her body, cascading over her curves. My mouth fucking waters. She looks so damn good in it that I can't wait to get her out of it.

My eyes meet hers as she walks herself down the aisle. She doesn't need anybody to give her away. She gave herself to me years ago. This is just making it official so the rest of the world knows she's fucking mine. So they all know that I'm hers.

We're still darkness and light. Cyn is smiling the biggest I've ever seen her, and I know that I'm glowering so hard I might pull a muscle in my face, the intensity of my feelings for her drawing out that same fury it did when we met. That fury that makes me want to punish her for being so pure and perfect. The fury that she loves, and the punishment that she craves.

Cyn hands her flowers to Elise and then takes my offered hand. I yank her up to me, pulling her closer than she should be but I don't give a fuck.

The pastor starts speaking but I don't hear much. I can't focus on anything except her. On the way her body still flushes and reacts to me like it did in the beginning. How our desperate want for each other hasn't faded at all.

We decided not to write our own vows. The things I want to say to her and the promises I'll make to her are private, only between us, and some of them would not be appropriate to be spoken in this chapel. I repeat after the pastor, and so does she.

Cyn slips a ring onto my finger, and I'm surprised that it doesn't feel odd or foreign. It's black titanium. I already like the weight of it, the meaning of it, on my body. I put my ring on Cyn, nestled next to the engagement ring that belonged to her mother, and before that, to her grandmother. The one whose journals started it all for her, and I believe, led her to me.

"You may kiss the bride."

I yank Cyn to me and devour her. I barely hear the cheers and teasing of our friends and family as I run my tongue over hers, feeling more than hearing the little moan she lets out. I'm kissing my fucking wife.

I let her go to let her breathe, and stare into her bright, brown eyes. "Good girl."

She touches the tip of her nose to mine and smiles. "Yes, sir."

TRANSFIGURED

Epigraph

trans.fig.ure /ˌtran(t)sˈfig(y)ər/

  (verb)

   "transform into something more beautiful or elevated."

Tate

In a perfect world, I'd get to spend this entire party holding onto Halle, and then I'd get to take her home and bury my face between her thighs until she came on it. Then I'd fuck her until we were both sated and exhausted, and fall asleep with my hand cupping one of her perfect tits.

It's not a perfect world.

I get to hold her and dance with her, both of us dressed as sea otters, while Beastly rages on around us. I'll probably get to take her home and sleep with her cold nose buried in my chest all night. We'll go to bed best friends and we'll wake up best friends and I won't do anything to change that because she doesn't see me as more than her friend. I work to be okay with that every fucking day.

So for now, I'll enjoy slightly drunk Halle leaning on me with her arms around my waist.

"I can't believe you hunted me, you fucker," Colin punches me in the shoulder, jolting Halle and I back a step. We're a single entity at this point in the night.

"What else was I supposed to do? It was hilarious," I offer in return. "Your face when your name was drawn was priceless. Had to get in on the fun."

Colin shakes his head in disgust. I've known Halle my whole life so she's my best best friend, but I met Colin when I came to Elmwood and he's a close second. The best guy I know. I think I'd have turned into a giant asshole in college without him. He keeps me humble and focused.

"Plus, I think it worked out for you." I flick my chin at him, prompting him to turn around. A small brunette dressed as a mouse comes bouncing up. After a second of hesitation, she snuggles into his side and beams up at him. Colin looks completely lovestruck and in awe, and presses a quick kiss to her temple.

"I mean, if I hadn't chased you," I continue, "would you have gotten to run away with her? I did you a favor." Elise laughs and Colin frowns. He showed me who she was on the first day of move-in this year. Didn't hold back about the fact that he wanted her and he was going to figure out how to get her, but mostly he was asking me to keep an eye out for her at parties and make sure she was safe. That wasn't a problem. I envy him for his ability to step across the line and go for what he wanted.

"Keep telling yourself that, champ," Halle slaps my chest and then slides away from me. "Bathroom. Be right back."

I watch her walk away, admiring her curvy body and how she even looks adorable wearing a fur otter suit. Listen, I know how far gone I am. I also know better than anyone that it's pointless.

My grandpa and Halle's grandpa are best friends. That meant our dad's were best friends. It meant that growing up, we became best friends. Our families are intertwined by best friendship and loyalty. I don't have a significant memory in my family that doesn't also involve Halle and the extended Bridger family. Every holiday is the Daniels and the Bridgers, every vacation, every celebration.

I don't know when my feelings for Halle started to change, but the first time I tried to kiss her she rejected me so soundly I didn't try again for a year. We were 12, there was mistletoe, and she put her hand over my mouth and said it would be like kissing her brother, and she didn't want the memory of her first kiss to be followed by vomiting on my shoes.

She really knows how to make a guy feel good.

It didn't matter though - I was hers. While I was the popular jock in high school, Halle was the ambitious nerd. She kept me in line with classes and I made sure she had a social life. We went to every school dance together, even the Homecoming where I had a girlfriend, and the Prom where she had a boyfriend. Halle was the one who wore my football jersey to school every Friday, and it was Halle who wore my backup baseball jersey in the stands at my games. The best friend who unabashedly wrote my number on her cheek and screamed every time I did something good.

Mine but not mine enough.

While I'm distracted, someone comes up behind me and slides their hands over my waist and rubs them on my abdomen. The hands are tiny with long fingernails that are sharp like claws and painted blood red. I know those hands, and I cringe inside.

"Marin," I say with a fake smile, turning in her embrace. "Hi." I take her wrists and withdraw her grip on me. We slept together one time, and don't get me wrong it was wild, but the kind of wild that a man lives through and then runs the fuck away from. Someday she'll find her kinky submissive prince, but it is definitely not me.

I try to take a step back and she clings to my furry onesie instead, claws digging in. She's wearing some sort of skin tight outfit with a scale design - a lizard or something. I wrap my hands around hers and step back again.

When I look to my left, Colin and Elise are watching this, their heads tilted slightly and matching expressions of amusement. Doesn't look like I'll get much help from them.

"Tate," Marin purrs. "You look tasty."

"Thanks. Nice costume. Iguana?"

"I'm a raptor, darling," she hums and runs her claws up and down my chest. I can't even lie, I'm terrified of this woman. It took two weeks for the marks on my back to heal from her and that's not even counting the paddling she gave my ass. I'll try most things once and once was enough with Marin. I don't know why she's still trying with me - we aren't compatible, and I made that clear. I've been rejecting her every time I've seen her since. Playing hard to get and running away in terror are not the same thing.

"It's good to see you, but I should be, uh," I falter, desperately looking around for an out. Colin shakes his head at me, and Elise doesn't know me well enough to help. Fuck.

Suddenly a body bumps into us, dislodging Marin's grip. A drunk, wavering Halle is leaning on me like she's about to pass out.

"Tate," she moans, and it sounds like she's about to throw up.

"Sorry, you know how it is," I say to a glowering Marin. Then I pick Halle up in my arms bridal style and start walking through the party.

"Can she see us?" Halle whispers against my neck, driving me unintentionally crazy.

"Home free," I whisper back.

"Good." Halle rearranges her body and wraps her arms around my neck, but makes no move to get down. "Are you sure you don't want to go there again? She's determined."

It pained me to ask Halle to put antibacterial ointment on the scratches on my back but there was no one else I trusted to actually help me. I know she sees me as a player, although I'm less of one than anyone would believe. It's a reputation I have whether or not I've actually earned it. The flirt, the closer, the Casanova, that's a side of me Halle's never seen, only heard about. I've tried dating other people to get over her, but it only ends up with me hurting them. When we're only hooking up and having a good time together, that's me playing it safe with everyone's heart.

"I can't believe you'd ask me that." I carry her out of the Castle house and when we get to the end of the walkway I put her back on her feet. "Another party, or home?"

"Home. We put off *Trick r Treat* for too long and we're out of time."

"Fair point," I agree with her. Halle loops her arm through mine and burrows close to me as we walk down the street to my building. It's a companionable silence, one neither of us ever feels the need to fill. I spend a lot of those silences getting my feelings under control and keeping my imagination in check. Halle is almost always touching me and killing me while she does it, but I'd never ask her to stop.

It would be so damn easy to shift things and be more than friends.

Halle hasn't dated at Elmwood, and hasn't had a relationship since high school. Sometimes I wonder if she's waiting for me, too. If we're by ourselves, pining for each other, waiting for the other one to figure out how we feel. Waiting for one of us to say something. Someday I'll test the theory.

We get into Cavalry 3, my building, and upstairs to my room. It's across from Colin's, and I stop and make a note on his whiteboard while Halle uses my keys to open the door. She's as comfortable here as if it were her own.

Halle strips off the furry onesie. Underneath she's wearing a tank top and tight black running shorts that make her ass look incredible. Her thick, muscular thighs jiggle a little as she jumps and shakes her body, free from the uncomfortable fake fur. She twists her dark brown hair up on top of her head and clips it, and now my eyes run up her body - the soft curve of her stomach, the sensual curve of her breasts, her bare collarbones, and the smooth line of her neck. Fuck I want to worship her with every part of my body.

I shake my head, snapping out of it, and strip out of my furry onesie, too. I'm in boxers and a t-shirt and don't feel self-conscious at all. I might not play sports in college but I still work out regularly and I've kept my muscle. Halle peeks over at me and then looks away.

She plops down on my bed and uses the remote to find the movie. Halle and I have traditions for almost every holiday, and waiting until the last possible second to watch our favorite Halloween movie is one of them. We only let ourselves watch it this one time.

The robot and the spaceman are walking down the street to their house when I crawl over her and get comfortable. I know that I won't make it more than 15 minutes into the movie. I know that Halle will stay up and watch the whole thing, shut it down, and go to sleep in my bed like she does at least one night a week.

At some point, I wake up to Halle moving around, turning off the TV and arranging herself for sleep. She moves toward me under the covers in the dark. I lay my arm down, offering it as her pillow, like always. Halle snuggles her face into my shoulder, her cold nose against my pec, and I fall back asleep with the girl who's not my girl in my arms.

I'm fucking hopeless.

The actual ringing of my phone wakes me up. There are only a few numbers that are setup to override silent and make a noise, and all of them mean bad news. Halle shoots up from the bed and scrambles to grab my phone for me.

It's her grandfather calling. Halle's eyes get wide and round, and when I take the phone she grabs my hand.

"Hello?" I answer.

"Tate." I know the second he says my name why he's calling, and feel my chest crack, the air leaving my lungs. "He's gone." My grandpa, my second favorite person in the world, is dead.

Halle

The death of Raymond Daniels is national news. Once it gets out, I take away Tate's phone. I field declining all the calls from the people coming out of the woodwork to offer condolences, or the reporters trying to get a comment from a grieving grandson. To the world it's the death of a billionaire and philanthropist. To Tate, it's his grandpa, his mentor, his favorite person. He's taking it hard.

When the call came in, I went into business mode to take care of him. There's a reason I'm in line to be the next Steward of the Castle: I get shit done. I use his laptop to email his instructors, then I switch over and email mine. I pack for him while he's in shocked pain. My heart throbs every time I look at him but I have to keep it together.

As much as Ray's loss hurts me, my feelings are irrelevant. Tate is all that matters.

I text Colin, afraid to even leave him to go knock on the door across the hall. It only takes a minute before there's a soft knock on the door and Colin goes to sit with him. Tate's still in just his boxers.

"I'll be back as soon as I'm packed."

I literally run from his apartment to the Castle house. It's a disaster after last night's party and I know I'm going to get some flack for leaving. Luckily, I run into Gwen when I'm only a few steps through the door. The look on my face stops her from saying whatever was going to come out of her mouth.

"Tate's grandpa died. I have to go."

"You got it. Let me know if you need anything." She turns around and gets back to bossing everyone around who has cleaning duty. Since I'm the chair for the Founder's Ball I got out of pretty much everything that has to do with Beastly, and I can't say I'm not grateful. Halloween is a disaster.

It takes me minutes to grab what I need, but longer to get to the parking lot where I keep my car. When I pull up outside Cavalry 3, Colin is outside with Tate. He must've needed air. Colin gets him inside the car, throws Tate's bag in the trunk, and raps the hood to let me know I'm good to go.

Tate's terrifyingly silent. We've been an unbreakable duo our entire lives and I've never seen him so shut down. Neither of us has ever had a loss like this that we can remember. We were too little to really remember his grandmother dying. It's uncharted territory.

I was born to be Tate's best friend. He's a month older than me, to the day, and our families were so close we were raised together. I feel as comfortable with his family as with mine, as free to be in his house as I do my own. Sometimes even freer in his house than in mine. Tate has been by my side for everything, ever. I keep no secrets from him and I'm pretty sure he doesn't keep them from me. I think there are things as a guy he keeps from me as a girl, but if I wanted to know, he'd tell me.

He's the other part of my soul, and even around my own pain losing a man I loved and respected, I am breaking knowing how much this is hurting him.

We're an hour into the drive before he cracks. "What do I do, Hal?"

"Show up, champ." I reach across the console and take his hand. He curls in on himself and presses his forehead to the back of my hand, and finally, he cries.

For the next few days, if I'm with Tate, we're holding hands.

Sitting with family, reminiscing about Ray and making decisions about details of his funeral and celebration of life.

Walking into the church, during the service, walking behind the coffin bearing one of the best men I'll ever know. That's when I lose it. When it feels so final. Tate and I stand together in the vestibule of the church and cry into each other's shoulders, mourning him in private before we have to face the onslaught of media.

When I can breathe again, I look up at Tate. He takes a handkerchief out of his pocket and fixes my running mascara. Even waterproof couldn't conquer the grief.

"I love you, Hal. I couldn't," he stops himself and then swallows heavily. "I need you."

"You have me." I take a deep breath and slide his hand into mine. I don't let go as we get in the car, as we drive to the cemetery, as we stand with his family as Ray is lowered into the ground.

I remember the last time I was with him for one of our random chats. It was in the summer and I was waiting for Tate so we could go play golf, which was code for make stupid bets while day drinking. Ray brought me water and sat with me on the window seat in the front room of their giant ass mansion. It's my favorite spot in their ancestral home.

"Halle girl, are you happy?"

Ray never asked questions lightly, so I thought before I answered. "Not quite. But I'm satisfied, and I think that's a start."

"What's the finish? What's the dream?"

I stared out the window across the bright green lawn. "Finish school, work for dad but not with him," we both laugh at that, "start a family. I want to find my person. We have so many good examples of relationships that sometimes I think my standards are too high."

Ray stared at me for a long time, like he was willing me to understand something. "When the time is right, you'll know."

I hope he was right.

The reception celebrating Ray's life is a blur, but also like a depressing high school reunion. Tate was popular, people knew him, knew his family, and Ray was wealthy and powerful. People show up. They want to be able to say they went to the funeral, that they were known enough to be allowed into the reception.

It makes me think of a quote from one of mine and Tate's favorite movies: they're suckling at the power teat.

It's exhausting for Tate. He might be the extrovert, but this isn't the kind of restoration he needs. I'm already planning for how I can take care of him tonight. Even though my parents live 5 minutes away, I've stayed at the Daniels estate since we got in from Elmwood. Other than going to get the dress I wore for the service from my closet at home, I haven't left.

When the reception is finally shut down, everyone goes their separate ways. Tate's dad is taking it hard, and everyone is trying to be respectful of each other. Ray would want it that way. I follow Tate upstairs and make him change into pajama pants and a t-shirt. I do the same.

I leave his room briefly to get food because I know he hasn't eaten, and then we crawl into his bed and watch every National Lampoon *Vacation* movie. They hook Tate in enough that he eats without thinking about it, sustaining himself out of habit. The first time he laughs, something unwinds in my chest. We're going to be okay. He's going to be okay.

I'm watching him more than I'm watching the movies. He's working through things in his head, I can almost feel it. Tate won't say much out loud, he rarely does even to me, but he knows I'm here.

At some point, I fall asleep with my head on his shoulder. I wake up when the tips of his fingers run along my forearm until they weave between my own. Tate presses a kiss to the top of my head.

"Hey, champ," I murmur and wake up. We're already on *Christmas Vacation* so I must've slept for a decent amount of time. It's after midnight when I glance at my phone. "How are you?"

Tate's eyes meet mine, and he looks so lost. My confident, powerful, secure best friend looks shattered. "I'll live. But what do I do now?"

"What he would want you to do. Finish school, get to work, do good, find happiness. That's what he always told me."

Tate smiles, and the coil in my chest unwinds a little more. This wasn't exactly a shock. Ray had been sick, his heart had been a problem for years, but I think we all believed there would be a little more forewarning. A final goodbye or conversation that none of us will ever get. He died in his bed, quietly, and hopefully without pain. Rejoining his wife in wherever we go after this.

"We should get some sleep," I prompt him. I clear the food off the bed, turn off the lights, and crawl in next to him. The movie is still playing but that's fine. Tate rolls onto his side and I snuggle up against his back, wrapping my arm over his waist. He's not normally the little spoon but I know he needs this. I press my cheek between his shoulder blades and inhale the comforting scent of my twin flame.

 Tate

Halle's still sleeping when I slide out of my bed and get dressed. Dad wanted to talk this morning and I'd rather get it over with. There's an exhaustion deep in my bones that won't leave and I know it's going to be around for awhile. I think I would have crawled into bed and stayed there, ignoring every obligation, if it wasn't for Halle making me get up and go.

My body goes through the motions while my brain feels numb and empty. I shower, I get dressed, I make my way to the office downstairs. It's been dad's office since Grandpa retired, but it feels more official now. That's where I could always find Grandpa when I needed to talk, and he was there for me. Dad loves me but he's busy, focused on keeping our empire alive and thriving, focused on the future instead of the present. I'm sure he'll be a great grandfather one day too.

As expected, dad is sitting behind the massive wooden desk in front of the large windows that show the back lawn. He's not working, but sitting and staring down at nothing, still as a statue. Dad and Grandpa had a strong relationship, even though they disagreed loudly and often. I know dad still went to Grandpa for guidance or outside perspective, and I know that loss will hit him hard, and will keep hitting him for the rest of his life.

I know it will for me.

"Dad?" We both jump when he flinches, snapping out of wherever his mind went.

"Tate. How are you?"

I shrug and he nods, understanding me exactly.

"I needed to talk to you about the will."

I frown and move to sit down in the deep leather chair across from the desk. As far as I know, everything was pretty clearly laid out. Grandpa was not cagey or mysterious about his intentions. The majority was left to dad, but there was a trust and assets left to me, as well as some other relatives not in the direct line. He was clear he intended to be generous to everyone. I wait dad out, because whatever this is, it's distressing him.

"It's possible to leave requests in a will that are not legally binding, but some people put them in the will anyway. To a certain extent, it's up to the executor to enforce them."

"Okay..." I'm still confused.

"Grandpa left a request regarding you." Dad swallows, moves around some papers, and then finds what he's looking for. "In the event that Tate Daniels is not engaged to Halle Bridger within 3 months of my death, his trust shall be held in abatement until he turns 40." Dad clears his throat. "There's also a note."

I'm stunned into paralysis. Not only that Grandpa Ray would do this, but that he would give me so little time to convince Halle. She's always been oblivious to the way I feel about her, and I'm going to have to rearrange her worldview to make this work. I don't need the trust, not really, but it's kind of the principle of the thing.

Snapping out of it, I take the note and open it, reading silently.

Tate,

I love you, and there is nothing in the world I want more than your happiness. I wouldn't even trade it to live a little longer. You've been waiting for your sign that it's time to get your girl – this is your sign. Good luck. Love her the way she deserves.

-Ray

"Technically, I can't make you do this, and I can't change the terms of the trust to include you being engaged or married to a specific person."

"Right." I have no idea what to say right now. The love of my life is sleeping upstairs in my bed right now and thinks we're only friends. Despite my borderline obsessive commitment to her, she's oblivious to the way that I truly feel about her.

I talked to Grandpa Ray a lot about waiting for a sign that it's the right time to change our dynamic, and I always thought it would be something from her letting me know how she thought about me. Apparently, it's time to stop waiting for a sign because it's arrived. There's no time like the present, and I'm not going to ignore the very last ass kicking he'll ever give me.

"You're not legally bound to do anything, Tate. We all know how you feel, so don't rush this because of a deadline imposed by a man who wanted the best for you, but was not always reasonable." Dad's very serious, but I laugh.

"I know. But I work best on a deadline."

Dad nods and goes back to staring at the papers. I think about trying to say something to him, but he's always done best handling his feelings alone. Despite the distance in his relationship with me, I know that he's got an amazing one with mom. They work together, they rely on each other, and as a kid I was kind of grossed out how often I'd catch them kissing. She told me once he keeps his distance from me because he wants to give me a chance to by my own person, and not feel weighed down by our legacy.

Maybe losing Grandpa Ray will change that. Halle and I might not be the only dynamic that evolves into something better because of our loss.

Halle is awake when I get upstairs. She's walking out of the bathroom, her golden brown hair freshly blow dried and the scent of coconut wafts toward me. I love how comfortable she is with me, and with my space. She belongs here.

"You okay?" There must be a look on my face because concern washes over her. "What did your dad want?"

I shake my head and tuck my hands in the pockets of my pants, holding myself back from grabbing her. For now.

"Grandpa left a note." My voice breaks because the finality of that hurts. Halle comes rushing over and hugs me, her arms wrapping around my neck and pulling my head into her shoulder and her still warm hair. I rest my hands on her lower back, keeping some distance from her.

"It's okay. It was a reminder of some things I need to keep in mind about my future."

Halle pulls away and looks up at me, but doesn't move from our embrace. "He was so proud of you, and he knew exactly how bright your future is."

I follow my impulse and lean in to kiss her forehead. Halle breathes in sharply. It's not that I've never done that before, but not during a situation as emotional as this. When I'm a whirlwind of grief and hope, trying to calm my racing emotions to find a way to make Halle see she's always been mine.

We stand like that for a long time, arms around each other and my mouth resting against her forehead.

"Do you ever think about us?" I ask against her skin.

Halle stiffens. "What about us?"

"Why we've never been more than friends?"

She gasps like I've hurt her, and I don't understand. Without looking at me, Halle pulls away and starts putting her things together, stuffing them in her bag. We don't go back until tomorrow and she's not leaving this house without me, so I think she's trying to keep her hands busy.

"You're hurting, Tate. We all think crazy things when we're hurting."

"It's not crazy. I've been thinking about it for a long time."

That stops her. She drops what she's holding and turns to me, putting her hands on her hips. Halle is going into serious mode, and it's a defense mechanism. A way to put up walls between the present and her emotions. I'm not going to let her do that.

I walk across the room to her but I don't stop at a reasonable distance. I get up in her space, and I follow her when she backs away from me until her back hits the wall. Halle is tall but I still loom over her, and I'm enjoying having her trapped. At my mercy. Uncertain about me for the first time in her life.

Halle knows almost everything about me, has seen me in almost every way except like this. I've protected our friendship by rarely flirting with her, and never making a real move. Not since I was 12. I've only been what she needed me to be because what she needed was all that mattered. She knows Tate the friend. It's time she meets Tate the man.

"I don't want to be friends anymore, Hal."

"Tate," she breathes out, but I don't let her say anything else.

"I might be thinking crazy, but that doesn't mean I'm not right. I've been waiting for a moment, and I realized the moment is mine to make."

Halle closes her eyes and takes a deep breath. I can't tell if she's afraid or aroused right now, and it's probably both. I'm throwing it out there right now. I'll be patient with her, but I'm not going to dance around the fact that I'm changing the game for us.

"This is going to happen, Hal," I run a finger down her cheek, and enjoy the confusion dancing across her face when her eyes snap open. She's conflicted and I like it. "I'm going to spend the rest of this year showing you how happy I can make you, how perfect we are for each other, and how I can make you feel so fucking good." I hold her chin, and feel a rush when her cheeks get a hint of pink. "I've always held back when it comes to you, and now I don't have to and I hope you're ready, Halle, for what I'm going to do to you."

"What - what are you going to do to me?" Her voice is high and breathy, and I've never heard it like that before. It gives me a semi, and I want to press my hips into hers but I hold back. Patience.

I lean in and whisper in her ear. "Tease you." I pull back and move to the other ear, noticing that her eyes are closed again. "Seduce you." I pull back again and bump my nose into hers. Halle's mouth drops open slightly on a gasp. "Satisfy you."

"Tate," she whispers, and I hear the panic and longing in her voice. I let her go and take a step back, giving her room to breathe. Halle's chest is heaving, and I know all of this is unexpected. To her, it's going to feel like I flipped a switch. She swallows heavily.

"I know what you want. I've heard your dreams our whole lives. You think I don't know how to give that to you? That I haven't been waiting for my chance? You'll see." I can't stop myself from reaching out and running a finger down her cheek again. Touching her because I can.

Halle blinks a few times in confusion, then shakes her head. "I should go."

"If you want. I've given you a lot to think about. What time are we leaving tomorrow?"

"Early. I'll text you." She steps around me and finishes packing her things. I don't want her to leave, I hate it, but I think she needs it.

I step away from her and make myself look busy, like I'm gathering my stuff to do laundry before leaving, but really, I'm giving her time. There's always the hope that my feelings are reciprocated and she's about to throw me down on my bed and have her way with me. Given the shell-shocked expression she's rocking, I doubt it.

I hear her sigh and turn around as she lifts her bag to her shoulder. I walk over and take it from her because she should know I'm walking her out to her car. Everything has changed and yet nothing has changed. I'm going to do the same things to take care of her that I always have, but now they have a different meaning.

Halle reaches out and takes my hand, and it soothes the anxiety that was trying to build inside me. While I'm going to show her what we could be, I also want to make sure I protect what we are. She'll always be my best friend first.

"Are you going to be okay tonight?" she asks. I know without question that I could tell her I needed her to stay and she would despite the current awkwardness. I know that she would put me first if I needed it.

"I'll be good." I squeeze her hand but let it go as we walk to the front door in silence, and when I put her bag in the trunk of her car. Halle turns to get into her car but I grab her shoulders and pull her into me, my chest against her back.

"When you're thinking about us tonight," I drag one hand down her side until it can wrap around her hip. I squeeze it and she arches slightly. "Don't forget to say my name."

Halle freezes for a second and then steps away, shaking her head. There's more amusement than heat in her gaze when she glances at me, but the heat is there. Hope springs.

"Sure, champ."

She gets in the car and drives away, and I watch until she's out of my sight.

Halle

The drive back to Elmwood was a mixed bag of tension and normalcy. Tate talked like he hadn't thrown me completely off guard with everything he said in his bedroom, as if it was the two of us like normal.

Except every once and awhile he would reach over and put his hand on my thigh.

A gentle touch, a soft squeeze, letting it rest for a few minutes before taking it back. Like he was testing the waters of new ways to touch me.

Then he would rest his arm along the back of my seat, toying with the ends of my hair or running his fingertips over my nape. A shiver would run through me that I would try and control, but I failed.

It doesn't help that thinking about everything he promised did turn me on, and I did orgasm thinking of him last night. It's dangerous. It's sudden, at a time of huge upheaval in his life, and it could break what we have forever if it went wrong.

I've done my best our entire lives to ignore any feelings for Tate other than pure friendship. Mom was always very intentional about pushing me for more with him while simultaneously telling me that I'd never be good enough. Thin enough, pretty enough, friendly enough, popular enough, girly enough. It was safer to never risk her being proven right because what we already have is amazing.

I can't help but struggle to believe anything that he said to me. In his room he was talking like he's always had feelings for me that he didn't act on. I know what an uncontrollable flirt he is, so I didn't believe it for a second. Tate is latching onto this to focus on something other than his grief.

Tate will move on from it when he remembers who we are to each other. When he remembers that he's got a few more years of sowing his wild oats before he has to settle down. I have no doubt that Tate loves me, but he's not in love with me.

When we got back to campus he stayed with me to park my car in the far lot and walked me to the Castle house. Before I could walk in the door, he grabbed me and pulled me flush against his body. It's not like I hadn't been there before but that was for a hug, this was something else. Fire spread through me and I was breathless in a second.

Tate held me to him, pressing his body against mine with a firm hand on my lower back just above my ass, and his other hand caught my chin so I was forced to look up at him.

"Did you think of me?"

I don't answer him but I blush so he already knows the answer to that. Rather than smirking at me like I expect, his gaze heats and he clenches his jaw.

"Let me show you how good it can be. Go on a date with me." He whispers it, and I feel his breath across my lips. I'm so mesmerized being this close to his deep green eyes that I answer before I can catch myself and put up any resistance.

"Okay," I whisper back.

Tate smiles, that big real smile that I love so much on my friend, the first one I've seen since we got the call. It makes everything inside me go soft and loose because if chasing this charade was what he needed to be okay, then I will let it happen. I'll keep boundaries up until he's over it.

He leans close, his nose nuzzling my cheek, his breath tickling my ear, and kisses the corner of my mouth.

I gasp. I can't help it.

Tate lets me go and walks backward for a few steps, that sweet smile turning into his cocky flirt grin. It hits me right in the stomach, and butterflies riot. This is bad.

"I'll see you Thursday night."

It takes me a second to remember. "Right, friend date."

"No," his face turns serious, "just a date, baby." Then he walks away before I can say anything else. I stand here for a solid five minutes, watching him, confused and flustered, and frustrated that I'm kind of turned on. I have to get used to this new proximity and guard against it.

Thursday comes faster than I'm ready for. Normally, friend date involves me wearing pajamas and a face mask, stuffing my face while we watch movies or play video games. Tonight, out of sheer nerves, I'm wearing leggings and a baggy sweater, my makeup is still on, and I did my hair. It's shiny and a little curled and at least I had the excuse that I'd given a presentation in one of my classes today. The idea that I'm trying to look pretty for Tate feels weird in my chest.

It also means I've been hearing my mother's voice in my head, but I smothered it pretty quickly.

Our usual pizza is ready from the kitchen downstairs, the bed is set with pillows, and I have the Goonies ready to play because it always gets Tate in a good mood.

I jump when he knocks on my door, but settle myself before he opens it and walks in. Tate appears to have put in some effort too. He's wearing black joggers and a white hoodie, but his hair is freshly washed and still a little wet. More surprising is that he's holding a giant bag of wild berry Skittles. He would have had to drive into Direwood to get those since on-campus only has regular or sour.

"Hi," he smiles at me, puts the Skittles on my desk, and then walks over to give me a kiss on the cheek. "Let's eat." Like always, he tackles me onto the bed and sets me on my side of it to get comfortable.

For a little while, we fall into our normal pattern of hanging out.

"So what's the hang up?" Tate asks. I've been ranting to him for a solid half an hour about issues with planning the Founder's Ball. It's a big deal and most things are set, but there's so many details and I've only got 2 months left to work on it all. It has to be perfect.

"The vendor doesn't want to come out here in winter, basically. They want to drop everything off super early and charge me for the extra time. At some point, isn't it their responsibility, too? I get that it's a bit of a trek but they'll make a lot of money either way."

"Let me ask around and see who else might be available."

"It's too late of notice to switch vendors."

"Capitalism has taught you nothing," Tate laughs and taps my nose. He's been casually touching me the whole time, but nothing overly intimate. "Pit the competition against each other and they'll be falling all over themselves to help. Not to mention the sheer number of rich bitches like us who throw parties that will see their work. I've got this for you."

"Okay," I sigh. "Give it a shot." In the back of my mind though, I'm rearranging the budget to accommodate the ridiculous demands of the party supply company. Tate can dream big but I've always been the grounded one.

We move the pizza off my bed and arrange ourselves to start the movie. Except Tate doesn't do what I expect. He moves behind me, and I find myself laying down, pulled against his body, feeling every firm line of him against every soft curve of me. His hand rests on my hip, his thumb resting on the bare skin just above the top of my leggings. The heat from that single digit scorches through my body.

Tate leans in and inhales, burrowing his nose into my neck. His breath on that sensitive area gives me shivers, and I squirm against him before I can stop myself.

"Did you do your hair for me, Hal?"

"Don't flatter yourself, champ, I had a presentation today."

"Sure," I can hear the smile in his voice. Then that freaking thumb starts moving up and down on my bare skin. "Keep telling yourself that."

It's been awhile since I've been with anyone, and I know that I'm weak. Especially weak for him. He's unearthing the feelings I buried and I don't think he has any idea how much he'll hurt me when he moves past this and wants to be friends again. I have to figure out where the line is that we can't come back from.

We quiet down and watch the movie, pulled in despite the fact that we've seen it a hundred times. Or maybe it's just me, because it takes me a moment to realize that Tate's hand has moved up and is now under my sweater. The large span of his fingers stretches across my stomach, and he pulls me more firmly against him.

I don't want to like this. I don't want my body to like this. If I give in, he's going to break my heart, and he'll never forgive himself.

"I've thought about this. Watching movies with you like we always do, but being able to touch you the way I've always wanted. Your soft, smooth skin," he breathes over my neck again. "Inhaling you, tasting you." I gasp when I feel the barest hint of his tongue grazing my ear. "Knowing that I could touch every fucking inch of you because you belong to me. You're mine. Instead of watching the movie, I could roll you over onto your back and get your leggings off, then eat that sweet pussy until you begged me to fuck you." Tate's hand moves down now, over my leggings, his long fingers stretching dangerously close to my rapidly dampening core.

"Do you know how often I've gotten myself off thinking about eating you out?" Tate's hips press into my ass and I am now very aware of his erection. I squeeze my eyes shut, begging to stay strong. "Holding your legs wide open while I devour you. You on all fours and feasting on you from behind," he groans, "but nothing gets me there like thinking about you sitting on my face, squeezing me with your thighs while you orgasm." His hand drifts down, massaging those very thighs as he speaks.

I am fucking drenched. I don't know what to do.

"Tell me you feel it, Halle," he says and he presses his hard cock into my ass again. The insane urge to roll over and attack him is barely restrained. "I know your body is reacting to me. I think you held back, just like I did. Let go."

"Tate," my voice is more moan than cry. "Please stop. Please. I'm not ready." That declaration was more emotional than I realized. What he said and my reaction to him gave me a lot to think about, and I am not an impulsive person. I know things are a mess right now, but I don't think he could fake any of this. His emotions are complicated but the physical attraction is real, on both our parts. I can accept that, but I can't accept that only. My emotions are already involved even if I don't want them to be.

Tate takes his hands off me, and moves his hips away from my body. After a few seconds, he reaches around my side and slides his hand under mine.

"This okay?"

"Yeah." I squeeze his hand over and over as my breath and body calm. As the adrenaline washes out of my system. We watch the rest of the movie and things are mostly back to normal. We comment on our favorite parts and the things we know are too improbable, even for a movie.

When it's over, Tate gets up and grabs the giant bag of Skittles. He feeds them to me while I talk more about my vision for the Founder's Ball, and then we argue about which math professor is actually the hardest. We're both getting liberal arts degrees with an emphasis in mathematics. We've always connected over understanding numbers.

Most friend date nights Tate crashes here with me, but I know on instinct he's not going to do that tonight. Things are changing, and I have to try and keep up with it all. I have to stay in control or I'm going to get hurt.

Tate gets off the bed and stretches, revealing his lower abs and I let myself look. Trying to give this new dynamic a chance, or at least the appearance of it, I give myself permission to appreciate his body. The way the joggers sit low and I can see the V of his muscles leading into them. The way his broad shoulders make that hoodie look extra cozy because he's big enough to wrap me up in his arms.

I'm tall and I'm curvy and I won't lie that I've never been with anyone that made me feel as safe and surrounded as Tate does. He carries me around like it's nothing. He can disappear me with his arms in a big ass hug. It's like my own little bubble when Tate hugs me. Insecurities, worries, and stress can't get to me in there.

Indulging, I climb off the bed and smash my face into his chest, wrapping my arms around his waist. He hugs me back immediately, surrounding me with his warmth and his amazing smell like usual. Except he drops a kiss on the top of my head and I want to swoon.

"What's the matter, baby?"

"Just needed a hug from you." I let him go and step back.

He smiles again. "Any time."

I walk him to my door, another first, another thing that I'm unsure about between us right now. He opens the door and steps into the hall, and I lean against the door jamb. Tate worries his lip with his teeth and then turns back to me, stepping close and talking quietly.

"If I'm going to treat this like it was a date, and not a friend date, then I'd be making a move to kiss you goodbye." His gaze is heated and my stomach riots when he takes my chin like he did the other day. I think I like that move.

"Except I don't think you're ready, so for now..." Tate leans in close, his lips almost touching mine, the barest graze. He keeps his eyes open and on mine, so close that I could tell you every dot and line in his iris. Tate rubs his nose over mine, back and forth a few times, and then draws back.

Still holding me, locking me into looking at him, his expression is fierce. "Goodnight, baby."

I blink a few times as Tate walks down the hall, hands in his pockets, strolling as if he didn't just get me to the edge of my sanity and my control by brushing noses.

Holy shit. I'm in danger.

Tate

If there's one thing my family knows how to do, it's how to throw a wild fucking party. We're talking specific themes with intricate decorations, performers, games, even prizes. It takes very little work for me to get that information from our usual planner and start making calls to find someone who can work with Halle's budget, as well as meet the demand for her vision.

When she talked last night I couldn't miss the fact that she was always saying what her vision was and then there was always a "but" because the vendor she was using wouldn't do what she wanted. I couldn't understand it because doing an open event at Elmwood like the Founder's Ball was basically courting rich people to use you for their parties. This company was treating Halle like shit and I had a lot of suspicions why.

Fridays are quiet for me - one class early in the morning - so I spend the entire day making calls, demanding estimates, and describing what we're looking for. I also have all of them commit to delivery time frames and charges related to early delivery and late pickup. That kind of shit should be done up front and I think it's unethical as hell that the douches she's using don't put it all out there. Things shouldn't be mysterious.

When all is said and done, I send Halle an email with the details of each company, and because I'm honest with her whenever I can be, which ones I think she should use.

Last night was more than I imagined. I expected when I made a move on her she'd stiffen up and push me off immediately, but instead she let my hand stay. It had not been my intention to tell her that I think about her when I masturbate, but at least I hadn't gotten too detailed in that arena. Like I hadn't blurted out that she'd been pretty much my exclusive spank bank since we were 12. I can get close but I can't finish unless I'm thinking about her.

Even when I've been with other women. Even when I've tried really fucking hard not to think about her, and even when guilt about it eats me alive. Everything about her does it for me. I need her. I crave her. I can't hold anything back anymore. The dam has been broken and she better prepare for the flood.

In her pussy.

I smirk to myself and get some homework done before I go to the dining hall with the guys.

My computer dings, alerting me to an email. It's Halle, writing back: *I never should've doubted you. You're the best.*

I respond quickly: *Doubt me? For shame. Can I get a reward for good work?*

A few minutes later, she replies: *What kind of reward?* I know I threw her off with the flirtation in that response, but I'm delighted she replied in kind.

I type back: *Depends on how much I helped. A little help? A kiss. A decent amount? Let me make you come with my fingers. A lot? Let me eat, baby.*

After five minutes without a response, I feel a little bit of anxiety. Halle is cautious and if I push too hard I'll break her trust, and she'll curl inward on me. Every move I make with her has to be intentional and strategic. She's doubting what I feel for her, and I understand that, but at the same time it's aggravating. There's no reason for me to fake anything. I'd be crazy not to be attracted to Halle. The problem is I've been strangling my love and need for her so tightly that I can't put it back in the box now that it's out. My control keeps slipping when it comes to us and I told myself I'd be patient.

There's a knock on my door and for one insane second I think it's her, but that hope leaves me before I even open it. Of course it's not her, it's Colin. Disappointing but also someone I need to catch up with. He's the best guy I know.

"How're you doing?" He sits on the edge of my bed while I plop back into my desk chair.

"Good as I can be. It's easier when I'm at school and don't notice he's gone." I sigh, feeling a tug in my chest that I think will be there for the rest of my life. I know Grandpa Ray was proud of me, and I know he loved me, but he'll never get to see me truly succeed.

"It's a hard time of year for it too. Everything go okay? No drama?"

"Uh..." I can't look him in the eye because I know that to anyone outside of my family, explaining the request from Grandpa's will is going to sound odd. Then again, I need to talk to someone. I trust Colin.

"There was something in the will that threw me for a loop." I pause and Colin waits. "If Halle and I aren't engaged in three months the maturation of my trust is being altered."

Colin laughs for a second and then sees that I'm serious. "What?"

"I'm going to do it."

"Does Halle know?" Colin looks perplexed.

"About the will, no, that I'm going to pursue her as more than my friend, yes." I look down at my hands and prepare to confess. "I always thought I'd marry Halle anyway. That someday she'd be mine. There's no time like now."

Colin blinks slowly, eyes wide. "Someday she'd be yours?"

"Did I really hide it that well?"

"No," Colin smirks, but then shakes his head. "Everyone knows there's something between you, but it's not like you've been sleeping alone, dude."

I wince at that. "I kept trying to get over her. It didn't work."

He raises an eyebrow and shakes his head. "So now what, full on player Tate seduction mode? Go straight for the home run and hope she gets dickmatized enough to agree to marry you?"

"No." I tilt my head as I think about the idea, but then shake it out. "No. I'll get there. First I want to remind her what we already have, and slowly add the soul shattering orgasms to our repertoire. She's already my best friend, my favorite person, is it really that big of a change to add sex?"

"Yes and no," Colin rubs his neck. "Elise and I weren't nearly as close as you and Halle are, but the fear that you'll lose them, or that compatibility might be an issue, is valid. I hate to bruise your ego but it is possible she's not into you."

Fear clenches my stomach. I've considered it, but given the way she reacted last night, I doubt it. "Shes afraid of changing our dynamic, or that I might not really be into her and I'm just grieving. That's not the case though. It's about her. I want her. I love her. I'm in love with her. I always have been."

Colin gives me a shrewd, analyzing look. "Your grandpa's condition on your trust has nothing to do with it?"

"No. I've felt this way about her for as long as I can remember. It was more important to be her friend, so I was." I don't bother telling him it can't be enforced, and that dad has no intention of even trying.

"Well, good luck. What are you doing to show her, other than trying to get in her pants?"

I glare at him, but then start outlining my plan of all the things I'm going to do to show Halle what I'd be like as her boyfriend, fiance, husband. That I'd help her, take care of her, do sweet things for her - the things I don't let myself do now. Flowers, text messages, presents, anything that will make her smile and relax because she overthinks all the time.

"That sounds good when you're trying to woo her, but you're trying to show Halle that you can be this guy for her all the time - don't do anything you can't keep up with."

I smirk at him. "I can keep up."

"Gross." Colin shakes his head. "Be patient. I'm here if you need me."

"I know. Thanks, man."

When Colin is gone, I decide to take a page from Halle's book: if there's a plan to be made, write it down. I write down everything I want to do now that nothing is holding me back. Starting with the most important thing and that's keeping me on her mind at all times.

Even though she never responded to my email, I pull up our messages.

T: *Thinking of you beautiful. Party tonight?*

H: *Staying in and getting to work. Breakfast?*

T: It's a date.

I see the indicator that she's replying, and it starts and stops multiple times before a reply finally comes through.

H: Will it end like a date?

I grin at my phone and reply: *If you want it to.*

No use holding back. I might not have played basketball but I'm familiar with full court press, and now is the time.

Halle

I spend all afternoon when classes are done going through Tate's vendor list. It's everything I needed and saved me hours of work. Tate always comes through when he says he will but I did not believe that this was a problem he could solve.

I should know better. If there's a connection he doesn't have, he knows someone who does, and he can charm anything out of anyone. It's why I'm so damn scared about him charming me.

It feels really, really good to send contracts to the two new vendors I'm using, and then call to cancel with my original vendor. Listening to the jerk I've been working with panic and splutter and try to get my business back is immensely satisfying. I make sure he knows everything that was an issue for me, and that I'll be making his boss aware of the way that I was treated.

Knowing Tate has my back in this makes me feel a lot more confident.

Thinking about the last email he sent has me feeling less confident, and more like I might combust. What would he do if I answered either of the last two options? Would he show up at my door and read it as permission to take me? A shiver runs through me but it's definitely not from fear.

As much as he turned me on, I'm nervous. I have some experience but it's limited compared to him. While I don't begrudge Tate anyone that he's been with, the idea of going up against all those experiences is really intimidating. Then again, I don't know why I'm worried about it. Tate is going to give up the chase long before I have to worry about having sex with him. He'll get over this and we'll go back to normal.

Tate texts asking me to go out tonight, but I focus on homework instead. He basically said he's going to kiss me after breakfast tomorrow and I'd be lying if I said I wasn't nervous. I watch his Instagram stories and he's at a party with a bunch of guys and keeps giving me updates on the beer pong winning streak he's on. The more he drinks, the more he tells me he misses me and can't wait to see me. The other guys tease him, but he doesn't care. He never cares what other people think.

I get his last message when I wake up in the morning. Tate is shirtless, wearing a hat backwards, and crashing face first into his pillow. He turns his drunken, smiling face toward the phone screen. It's so stupidly cute.

"I'll see you in a few hours, baby. Miss you." He's so out of it he falls asleep recording the message, and the last seconds of it are me watching him pass out, and then at the last moment a twitch of him waking up. That must've been when he sent me the message.

I'm getting ready when there's a knock on my door.

Tate steps in before I can reach it with a paper bag and a carrier with 2 cups of coffee. Even though my hair is done and I'm covered, it hits me for the first time since I've known him that I am only wearing my bathrobe. No underwear of any kind. Nothing but air between us, and no barrier stopping him from getting to me. I clench all over, around nothing, and feel a sense of disappointment at my emptiness.

He puts everything down on my desk and then steps over and yanks me into his body. It's not a hug, it's a grab, and he looks down into my face. His closeness overwhelms me like it always does, and I swear he knows it.

"So, what's my reward?" His expression is playful, but his voice isn't.

"What?" I blink in confusion, distracted by him. Then I remember, and blush immediately. To be honest, he helped a lot. That is not the answer I'm going to give him even if my curiosity about getting eaten out by him is at an all time high. It's flattering and terrifying that he's gotten off thinking about it, but I don't think I'll live up to his imagination's hype.

"I'll let you know."

Tate grins, intuiting my answer, but lets it go. His hands slide lightly over my ass and give it a small squeeze before he steps away to get out the food.

I step back into the bathroom and get dressed quickly - leggings and a hoodie, still no underwear because it's in my room and now I feel self-conscious about going to get it. Tate is already cozied up on my bed and turning on cartoons when I step out. He sticks out an arm for me and I go to him, letting myself lean on his chest like I usually do as he makes me watch *Scooby-Doo* for the millionth time as we eat.

"How'd it go with the vendors?" he asks before kissing my temple. The hand that's resting around me starts tracing circles, giving me tingles even through my sweatshirt as he touches me.

I tell him everything that happened, including when I called and fired the snotty jerk vendor.

"Good for you, Hal. I'm proud of you."

I twist to sit up and look at him. "Couldn't do it without you, champ."

Our eyes snag and the amusement on our faces fades.

Tate's free hand reaches up and tucks my hair behind my ear, and his fingertips linger on my cheeks, jaw, and down my throat. In a quick, unexpected move, he hooks his hands under my knees and yanks me down so I'm laying on the bed. One of my legs is trapped between his as he moves over me, looking down into my face.

My mouth parts slightly when he leans in, nose brushing along mine, lips so close I can feel their heat...but he doesn't kiss me. Instead, he teases and taunts me with almost kisses that steal all the air from my lungs. It does insane things to my body. My legs are clenching around his, my pussy throbbing and turned on, my nipples are hard, my skin is tingling, and my throat feels tight. I want to reach up and grab him and smash his lips to mine, demand with action that he stop this sexual cruelty.

We're playing a game right now, and I can't let him win.

"I want to kiss you so bad, Halle," Tate groans, eyes on fire. It almost feels weird to hear him say my full name, but it's also sexy as fuck in his raspy, aroused tone.

"Then why aren't you?" I challenge, raising an eyebrow.

"You're body is ready, but your mind isn't," he says as he ghosts my lips again. "You said yes to dating me, to trying, but you didn't mean it. Not really." I don't say anything because he's not wrong. I'm holding back, I'm saying what he wants me to say, instead of making the decision for myself and going all in or not. "I'm waiting on you, baby. You'll kiss me, really kiss me, when you're ready."

Tate leans in close. The only thing I can see are his eyes and the only thing I can feel is the barely there brush of his lips against mine as he speaks. "And then I'm going to own those lips, Hal. Kiss you so fucking good you'll moan in my mouth and beg me to finish you off. And I will."

He presses a chaste, closed mouth kiss against my lips. It isn't our first kiss like this – that was New Year's Eve when we were 13. I've kissed him every New Year's since, and a few times at parties under mistletoe. Except those kisses never made me want to shove my hand in my leggings and get myself off. Tate backs off of me and I squirm a little bit as we both sit up.

"Let me take you out tonight on a real date." Tate is so serious and I don't know what to do with it. He's never been this intense about anything. It scares me. "Dinner. Dressing nice, picking you up, the whole thing. Please?"

I hesitate. He's doing so much to my heart and my body that I don't know how to contain it and hold it back. I keep thinking that he'll give up the more I resist, but that doesn't seem to be the case. He wants this so badly and I hate not giving in to him. He keeps giving me options, putting the choices in my hands, and I don't know what to do.

"Yes," I agree before the overthinking spiral can begin. I'll do that after he leaves.

Tate smiles and shifts us back into our comfortable, lazy snuggling position to keep watching cartoons together. We've spent a hundred Saturday mornings this way. Everything he's doing is different yet the same, this other dynamic weaving into what we already are.

Am I wrong about all of this? Has Tate really been hiding feelings for me that effectively for years? Obviously I had and have more than friendly feelings toward him, and my body is definitely attracted to his body, to all of him really, but I always talk myself out of it. There was never enough certainty to risk our friendship. I could not put distance between us while we healed through the awkwardness of rejection because there was always a chance that we wouldn't. I would never do anything to lose what we have for a chance or possibility. What we have is a certainty. It's what makes this dating experiment all the more terrifying.

With every new move he makes I start to wish for the possibilities.

Losing Ray blasted away so many walls we'd all built. Maybe the barriers Tate and I had built for each other were weak now. Maybe weak enough to talk about feelings we've kept buried. I want it to be real. I won't survive it if it's not.

An alarm on my phone snaps us out of our cartoon-induced daze. I'm meeting with Gwen in half an hour to update her on the Founder's Ball. She's the current Steward of the Castle and I want to stay on her good side. She can recommend me for her role next year. I know it's so much more work than I need to be taking on, but I really do want it. The Castle and everyone I met as part of it helped me so much at Elmwood.

I found a place that felt real and true to who I am. Friends that understand me, support me, and even when we're in competition with each other, we're graceful about it. The last two years have been incredible. I never thought I'd feel as accepted as I do with this group of people.

Tate walks me downstairs but when I go to turn away from him, he yanks me back. We're chest to chest and he's looking down at me. I don't know how to handle these possessive grabs and touches from him. They catch me off guard and make me weak, I can't even fight back. As soon as he owns me like that, I'm putty in his hands.

Before I can pull back, he cups my face with one hand and the curve of my ass with the other and gives me a long look, right into my eyes. It takes my breath away. There's so much passion and ferocity that I've never seen before.

"I'll pick you up at seven," he whispers. Then he kisses my nose and steps back, giving me a familiar grin before leaving through the front door.

"Holy shit," Gwen says from behind me, and I turn around in a daze. She's grinning and looks giddy. "I think I win the pool."

"What?" I blink a few times, trying to pull myself together.

Gwen grabs me and loops her arm through mine, and we start walking through the house toward the Steward's office at the back.

"The betting pool for when you two finally come to your senses. It's been non-stop conversation since the second week of your freshman year."

"What?" Is all I can say again. "It has? But we've always been friends."

"No." Gwen shakes her head and unlocks the door to her office. "You've never paid attention to anyone but him, never even realized other guys were hitting on you, and he's done everything you've ever asked for any reason ever. I've never seen a man more devoted when he's not getting sex."

"He was getting it elsewhere," I grumble to myself and sit down. Although thinking about it, I don't know if he's hooked up with anyone all year. He was always with me. "And it's not what you think. It's complicated."

Gwen sits at her desk and rests her chin on her hands. "Tell me."

I trust Gwen, both to keep things a secret as well as her perspective, so I do. How it feels like suddenly Tate's professing feelings for me that I never saw before, how I'm trying my hardest to not give in to the idea of the two of us as anything more than friends, and that I'm worried he's trying to latch on to me because of grief. Even though I did agree to date him, or try, anyway.

"Have you ever felt more for him?"

I raise an eyebrow and she laughs. I expand. "Of course I have, but it's like - he's Tate and I'm me, and it wouldn't be sustainable. It wouldn't be worth the temporary romance to alter my forever friendship. That's a guarantee."

"No risk, no reward, bitch," Gwen snarls at me in her harsh Boston accent. "Why wouldn't it be sustainable? How are the two of you not absolutely perfect for each other?"

"He's popular, outgoing, friendly, flirty, he's everyone's favorite person. I'm quiet, focused, I don't like shallow connections, and I keep to myself except when I'm with him."

"What are you like with him?" Gwen wants to be a therapist, so I appreciate that some of the questions she's asking she already knows the answers because she's seen it herself. She wants to get me to say it.

"Friendlier, easier. I laugh more."

"What's he like when he's with you?"

"At a party?"

She frowns at me. I know what she's asking. What's my private Tate like.

"He's organized more, he thinks ahead."

"So what you're saying is that you fill in each other's gaps, make each other better, and not bitter? That's what you're saying, right?" She sighs. "And it can't be that there's no physical chemistry because a) he has physical chemistry with a bag of potatoes, and b) I saw that goodbye."

"I know." I sink deeper into the chair. "We're going on a real date tonight."

"Good. Follow through on it and explore your feelings. Date the hell out of him until he finally convinces you to let go of your insecurities. That's all this is, Halle. Years of other girls looking at you like you don't count or aren't a threat when it was them that didn't matter. I promise you, Tate is not doing this as a reaction to his grandfather's death. I saw it the first time I met you both that he was wild over you."

"Okay. I'll try to stop being neurotic and insecure and see if this feels real to me too."

"Good. Now, update on the ball."

The change in subject releases some of the pressure in my chest.

Tate and I have always talked about how our opposite ways were why we worked, but I never thought about how I cling to those differences as some sort of justification for protecting my feelings. As if Tate hasn't seen the real me, seen all of me, and still loves me anyway. He's seen me at my absolute worst (the first time I got drunk,) what I think is my best (valedictorian), and what he thinks is my best (Ides Party Beer Pong Champion, 2 years in a row, going for the triple crown this spring.) He's never been anything but supportive and proud of me, sometimes more proud than I am of myself.

It's been the same with me. I celebrated every victory with him and sometimes for him, like when he got a B in Physics and still felt like a failure even though I know how damn hard he worked for it. When he nailed his Economics analysis and got personally called out by the professor for doing such a thorough job. When he got into the Cavalry and the night we celebrated our initiation into two of the Trinity societies.

That was the night I almost kissed him and maybe he almost kissed me, but I was too scared that I had stars in my eyes about feeling like Elmwood was home. Sometimes she fools you into thinking you can have things because of the safe little bubble we build here.

When Gwen and I are done, I get to my room and immediately start tearing through my closet for a date dress. It takes about an hour for Gwen to show up with some other members and their clothes in tow. They know I'm going on a date with Tate, but they keep their thoughts to themselves other than whether or not I look good.

I love them all so much in this moment I almost start crying.

Then I see my ass in a red dress Jeanette brought, and I think it's Tate who's going to be weeping instead. I'm all in tonight, whether or not I'm ready for it.

Tate

I'm actually nervous. I've never been nervous because of Halle in my life.

I'm in my lucky gray suit and a black dress shirt and I wore the cologne she got me last year for my birthday that she said made me smell, and I quote, "absolutely delicious." It was one of the flirtiest things she'd ever said to me, and with this husky growl, too. I got off to recalling the way she said that for about two straight weeks. Sometimes I get hard wearing the stuff because I think about that. Tonight it won't matter. I'll be halfway to hard because I'm with her and with the intention that I get to flirt with her, touch her, seduce her.

Tonight is about making it clear to her how easy it would be to fall in love. It's not like we have to get married any time soon. She can agree now and I'll spend all my time reminding her that it was inevitable. There's never been anyone for me but her.

I park my car and walk up to the Castle house. Before I get to the door it opens, Halle steps out, and stops me in my tracks. I've seen her dressed up before but I've never seen her quite like this. Her thick dark gold hair is in big curls that reach to the middle of her back, and she's wearing a fitted red dress that almost has me biting my knuckles so I don't get on my knees and worship how good it makes her curves look. Her hips, the swell of her ass, the thickness of her thighs...I'm drooling here. When her eyes meet mine her dark lashes flutter, and her cheeks turn pink.

I clear my throat. "You look gorgeous, Halle. Absolutely stunning."

The pink of her cheeks darkens and she looks down before stepping closer to me. When she does, I get a whiff of the coconut oil she uses in her hair and it always makes me think of the beach. Which makes me think of her in a bikini the same color as the dress - a tiny, string bikini that I can untie with my teeth.

She takes my arm and I walk her to the car, holding the door for her. That's not unusual either - I made a point as soon as I got my license that I would always open doors for her. It's habit at this point for her to let me.

When I get in the car, she immediately takes my phone and puts on the music she wants. As soon as I get out of campus and on the road, I reach over and put a hand on her bare, silky thigh. Fuck, she feels so good. I'm a little surprised when Halle puts her hand over mine and weaves our fingers together, idly playing with my hand as she watches the scenery go by. It feels so normal. As exciting as all these new things between us are, it's the way I feel when she accepts them that's the most dangerous. Those are the moments that give me hope.

Direwood, the town closest to Elmwood, makes its money from catering to the rich kid clientele with stores and restaurants. Some people drive down almost every day to get their fix. I made us a reservation at the steakhouse, Block and Catch. It even has valet parking which seems silly in an area so small but I take advantage of it tonight.

I help Halle out of my car and keep her hand in mine, pulling her close as we walk in. I'm jealous of everyone here getting to see her this way. My favorite Halle is still leggings and a sweatshirt, ready to cuddle, but I have to admit that night out Halle is pretty spectacular. I'm almost regretting telling her I wouldn't kiss her until she kissed me, but honestly, the next move has to be hers. Otherwise I'll start feeling like a creep.

The hostess leads us to our table in a dark quiet corner, and if I thought Halle looked good before, putting her in candlelight is dangerous.

"Why are you staring?" she mutters as she looks over the menu. "And what's good here?"

"I don't know, I've never been."

Halle looks up. "I assumed this was where you take dates."

I give her a bland look. "I haven't dated here, and of course I would do something special for you."

She shrugs like that statement has no affect on her. A ripple of frustration goes through me. Apparently, not only am I a player who sleeps around, I also date and woo a lot of women and take them on fancy dates. I feel like those two things don't quite click with each other. I don't know how to fix Halle's vision of me in this side of my life because some of it is correct.

I flirt a lot, I leave parties with women, and I have had sex with some of them. It's not usually more than a one night thing and that's not me, it's them. My personality gave me a reputation my dick didn't earn. Women made assumptions about the kind of guy I was, and sometimes I was willing to indulge their desire for one night, usually when I was so fucked up over Halle that I tried to chase the high of release. It was far fewer people than Halle thought.

Agreeing to sleep with Marin probably fucked that up in a big way. Especially since she won't let it go and I have to keep not only turning her down, but straight up running away from her. That situation just reinforced everything Halle assumed about me.

"Halle," I start, trying to figure out my words. Before I can, the server comes and we go through the chit chat of figuring out what's good and ordering our food. I watch him go until he's out of earshot and then try again, still unsure what I'm going to say, or of what she'll truly believe.

"I'm not what you think I am," I try. "Yeah, I flirt, I won't lie, and I've hooked up, but less than you think. I probably could be that guy, but there's always been something stopping me."

"What?" She sounds anxious.

"You. I can't be the player you think I am because for so damn long all I want is you. Sometimes when it was killing me how much I wanted you, I'd give in and hook up, but most of the time I leave with women and I walk them safely home and then I crash alone in my bed and violate my right hand thinking of you. Always you, even when it hurts, even when I wish I could want anyone else, it's always fucking you."

"Tate." She sounds wounded, and I swear my heart shrivels in my chest. "Why?"

I frown at her. Halle looks a few shades paler and thoroughly shocked.

Not how I planned this date to go but it's a necessary conversation.

"Why what?"

She frowns, eyes darting like she's thinking hard, trying to sort through her own thoughts. "Why me? Why have you never said anything? You get why the timing of this feels suspicious to me right?"

Tears burn in my eyes and I feel like an idiotic asshole. For so many damn reasons, not the least of which is she thinks I'm faking this. That I'd take away a chance for her to find love and happiness, or break our friendship. I want Halle to have the world, and I know that I can give it to her better than anyone else.

"It never seemed like the right time, and you needed me to be your friend. I needed you to be mine. In a way, I guess yeah, I am doing this because of grandpa." Halle flinches but I continue. "It reminded me that life is short so you should go after what you want today. If I had to choose between a lifetime as your friend or one day as more, I'd pick that one damn day to show you everything I feel for you. That I've always felt for you."

Halle shakes her head and looks down. "I want to believe you so badly."

"What reason have I given you not to, Hal?" The anger is starting to settle over me. I'm baring my soul to her and she's still pushing back. "You're my best friend. I think the fucking world of you, without judgment, always on your side. I'm starting to think that's not as mutual as I thought."

Halle's head whips up. "Tate, no. You are my best friend and you're my favorite person in the world."

"And yet you think that I would lie to you this –" I search for the words. "Cruelly? Selfishly?"

"No. No, you wouldn't." Halle reaches across the table and takes my hand, pulling me back down from the heights my emotions are dragging me toward. She runs her thumb over the back of my hand, tracing a line over and over until I'm calm. "I'm sorry. It's a change for me and I'm afraid. I promise, I'm trying, champ."

She gives me a small smile, and my body relaxes the rest of the way. We both take a few breaths, calming down and backing off from that intense conversation. It's not done, but I think we got somewhere.

"What do people talk about on dates?" she asks, trying to bring me into the moment.

"Getting to know each other things - favorite food, colors, movies?" All things I already know about Halle and she knows about me.

"Hm," she thinks and then grins at me. "Let's try it this way - see who knows more about the other person's favorite things."

"Oh, I'll win this, easy."

"Big talk means a big bet. What are the stakes?"

This is easy. "Winner gets to pick the first Christmas movie."

Halle sticks her hand across the table and I take it. We shake firmly and let go.

The game is on.

Halle wins by one question because sometimes she knows me better than I do, and she knew that my favorite Brad Pitt movie is *Mr. and Mrs. Smith* when my first instinct was to say *Ocean's 11*. But as soon as she said it, I knew she was right, and I don't lie to her.

I take her hand as we leave, and she teases me all the way out to the car about which Christmas romance movie she's going to make me watch during our annual marathon. It's maybe a smart move that I don't tell her that I've actually enjoyed some of the ones she's subjected me to in the past. It's a lie of omission but also saves me from non-stop love stories when I'm trying to make my own right now.

Halle talks as I drive, and I enjoy listening to her. She has a tendency to get quiet and hold back around people until she's extremely comfortable with them, and I like being a safe place for her to be free. She's telling me the plot of a romance movie the Castle watched the other night and I'm only half following, lulled by the sound of her voice.

I know that I'm the more social of the two of us, but there's also a weird pressure inside me to perform. To lead the room, charm people, hold their attention. Even if I am a genuine extrovert, sometimes it's less about recharging and more about meeting an expectation. It's who I'm supposed to be, it's who people expect me to be, so I do it regardless of how I'm feeling. I love Halle because I can be all versions of myself with her, and she never points it out or questions it. I just *am* when I'm with her.

There's a stop sign at the edge of campus, and what we do next determines if I go straight, or turn right. No one else is around, I can stay at this spot as long as I need, but I have to present her with the decision. We're falling into a pattern of me asking a question to force her into action. It's frustrating, but I also understand why Halle is so nervous, and I even understand why she doubts me. So I'll keep presenting options until she starts trusting herself, and trusting us.

"Do we treat this like a date and I take you home, or are we us, and you come over to watch movies and hang out?"

Halle frowns and looks down, then turns her head to meet my gaze. I can't read her, and that's unusual. I don't know what she's thinking or feeling.

"Hang out, please."

I laugh because it's weird for her to say please. "Next thing you'll be calling me sir." I start to turn to go toward the parking lot near the Cavalry houses.

"Just don't ask me to call you daddy." She says it with derision, but I can't stop the blood from rushing to my cock as a hundred scenarios wheel through my mind in which I get Halle to say it. To call me daddy while she's begging for me. While she's coming. Halle has no idea how cruel of a statement that was. I adjust in my seat and don't say anything, acting very convincingly like I'm focused on the road, and then looking for an open parking spot. A slightly awkward silence falls when I turn off the car.

Halle's cheeks are pink. "Sorry."

"It's okay. You're not responsible for my thoughts." Before she can respond, I get out and come around to open her door. Relief floods through me when she loops her arm through mine, and we walk to my building. The closer we get, the more the awkwardness fades away and we're just Tate and Halle again, hanging out on a Saturday night.

No one looks twice as we make our way through the building. Some of the guys greet us both and eye her up in the dress she's wearing before catching my glare to look away. They know her by now, and look out for her when I can't. Even though I never overtly told anyone to stay away from her, I think they all knew. No one in the Cavalry ever made a move on Halle, and I know that was because of me. I didn't have to wave my dick around to claim her, they already knew. The only person who doesn't seem to know that Halle is mine is her. For now.

When we get inside my room, Halle slips out of her shoes, wiggling her toes on my carpet. She's frowning again and I wait, leaning back against the door. Something is brewing inside her head and we won't be able to move on with the night until she figures out how to talk to me about it.

"What if a date wanted to come back to your room after? What do you do then?" Halle swallows and I watch her throat, notice her racing pulse, and the slight shiver in her body when I grin at her question. I like the direction her thoughts are taking.

I step closer to her, not touching, but close enough that she can feel the heat of my proximity.

"First, stop trying to compare yourself to anyone I've ever been with because they've all been found wanting when compared to you." I lean in and whisper to her, elated when a flush spreads across her cheeks and her eyes close for a moment before meeting mine again.

"So what would I do if you, my date, came back to my room?" I move, circling around until I'm behind her. She tries to follow me with her gaze but can't. My hands settle on her hips, keeping her where I want her. Close enough to feel me, but not close enough to get satisfaction. It's a tease. I want to tease her until she snaps.

"I'd kiss you," I start, as I nuzzle lightly into her hair. "Work you up with my tongue in your mouth until you're clawing and needy for more. I want to hear you whimper. Say please. Try and rip my clothes off so I'll give you more." Halle shudders in my arms. "I'd get you out of this dress." I run my knuckle up and down along the zipper, ghosting the sensation of it being undone. "Then I'd take those kisses everywhere. Worshiping and pleasuring you with my mouth. I'd fucking savor eating your pussy, wringing every ounce of stress, tension, thought, out of you until all you know is that you need me inside you. Desperately," I draw out the word and Halle whimpers. Fuck, yes.

"I'd give it to you." There's emotion in my voice I can't conceal. On a physical level, I want to be inside Halle so much my cock throbs thinking about it, but on an emotional level I want to connect with her that way. A physical manifestation of how my heart feels entwined with hers. "Make you orgasm so damn hard you see stars before burying myself inside you and filling you with my come. Practice for filling you up with my babies." I grunt, not meaning for that last part to slip out.

"Tate," she moans, her voice uncertain.

I take a deep breath and calm myself, pulling it back in, chastising my dick for being so damn hard. "Then we'd make out in my shower while we cleaned up, and I'd hold you in my bed while we watched a movie, talked about whatever we wanted, spent our time together like we always do." I squeeze her hips. "Nothing would be that different except that I get to make you come and call you mine, Hal. It's still me and you, still us, only more."

I let her go and step further away. Halle stumbles like her knees gave out, and I smother another grin, waiting for her to pull herself together.

"Come on baby, let's watch a movie."

Halle looks over her shoulder at me, eyes dark but conflicted. Then she nods.

I've gotten inside her mind, and that can only be a good sign in my book.

Halle

After our amazing date, Tate pulls back a little. I know he knows I'm a bit overwhelmed. I am seeing a side of Tate that I've never experienced before. This methodical, patient man who seduces me into an achy, torrential heat without even touching me. Who persistently tells me he wants me and doesn't expect anything in return.

I'm starting to believe this is real.

Other than a few nights where I came over to watch TV and ended up falling asleep, we're both busy with school and I also have the Founder's Ball details to finalize. By the time we reach Thanksgiving break, everything is settled except for the setup itself. Everything on my checklist is done. I've stunned even myself with my level of preparation. This year's ball is going to be incredible.

Like always, Tate drives us home. He spends most of the drive stressing about his international finance exam, and I spend it reassuring him that he probably did better than he thinks. The professor for the class has a reputation for grading quickly, so we'll probably know how he did by the time we get home.

Tate pulls into my driveway, stopping outside the front door. We'll see each other tomorrow since our families are doing the big meal together. This year it's my parents turn to host.

"I'm glad it's at your house," he sighs, his head thumping against the headrest. "It'd be too weird to host the first holiday without grandpa."

My heart clenches for him. "You okay? Want to come in?"

Tate gives me a small smile but shakes his head. "No. Get in, relax. I'll see you tomorrow."

Impulsively, I lean across the console and kiss him on the cheek. "Thank you. Come over if you get bored, champ."

He catches me under the chin before I can get away. "Call me when you miss me. I'm dying without you, baby." I watch his eyes dilate and drop down to my mouth. I'm immediately aroused, my panties flooding. He's not usually this direct about wanting me - not like this.

"You know how the holidays turn me on," I joke but it sounds false. He lets me go but there's a hint of a smirk on his face. He knows he got to me. We both get out of the car and he takes my bag to the door. Before I go inside we look at each other, a lingering look that I can't interpret but that makes butterflies explode in my stomach. We're on the precipice of change and I want to trust it.

I steel myself and walk inside the house.

Mom is waiting. She gives my outfit a once over and frowns. I'm wearing comfortable jeans and a turtleneck bodysuit.

"Weren't you with Tate?"

"I'm always with Tate."

I can feel her gaze lingering on my messy bun and unwashed hair, on the lack of makeup on my face, my nails that are cut short and practical. On the way I emphasize my curves instead of trying to hide or minimize them. I'm built like dad's family, instead of overly slim like hers. It eats at her that she has this one daughter who is nothing like her. It's why she pokes at me, scraping away and searching for the weak parts that she can bend to her will. We don't look alike and don't act alike. It makes her feel like she has to take command of me, to fix me somehow.

We stare at each other at a loss, and I take my bag and move around her to go up to my room. As soon as I do, I see that she's cleaned it again. It's nearly sanitized, and I'm relieved to find she's at least left my closet alone. My posters are gone, my office supplies, dishes of pens, and stacks of old planners are not on the shelves where they used to be. I find those in a bin in the closet.There's no reason for this - we have plenty of guest rooms. She likes to remove the signs of my personality.

I flop down on the bed and bury my face in my pillow, wishing that I'd gone to Tate's.

And because I'm an absolute chickenshit, I don't text Tate at all. I only make minimal responses to what he sends me, but otherwise I drown myself in working ahead on my Macroeconomics homework like that's a distraction. I don't even start my early binge of watching holiday movies or bother my parents to start getting out the Christmas stuff.

We hire a decorator to do the rest of the house, but we always do the tree together. Dad jokes that's how we stay humble. Normally I make them put the tree up before Thanksgiving, and then we decorate it on Friday. Right now I have no motivation because I'm off my axis. Everything I thought I knew seems to be crashing down around me, breaking apart and reforming in new pieces that I don't understand yet. I hear Tate and mom's voices in my head, warring for my attention.

What makes it even worse is that Mom only talks about Tate.

We're eating a light dinner and all I get is:

"Is Tate seeing anyone? He's such a catch."

"How is Tate doing? We all miss Ray so much."

"Tate's going to do so much when he graduates and carry on his family legacy."

No questions about how school is going for me, and dad just nods along, as if I'm not also going to Elmwood, or working toward working at his company. It's like I don't even matter. Mom literally called me an asset to bring to the table once, as if my only use was in marrying me off, and I'll never forget the fear that caused. I want to find my own happiness and pushing everything aside to be what they want is the kind of thing Grandpa Ray wouldn't want for me at all. He was always reminding me to be my own person and chase happiness.

I barely speak and leave the table without eating. At some point I fall asleep and I stay in bed all morning. We're doing an early meal this year, everyone coming around noon for cocktail hour and then the big meal at 1:00 P.M.

When I finally leave my bed, I shower, make myself look presentable to my own standards, and wear my favorite short black skirt and an ugly Thanksgiving sweater with a giant turkey on it holding a sign that says "this holiday is a lie." It pisses all the parents off because they won't even have a conversation about colonization and genocide, acting as if history isn't real. They act as if a lot of things aren't real.

The first year I wore it, I knew my parents would be pissed off and so did Tate. He got a shirt made that said "the turkey is right." He's not as good at articulating the conversation, but he listens and believes, and tries to do what's right.

When I walk downstairs, Tate and his family are walking in and handing their jackets to the staff. A light snow is coming down, but I don't think it will stick. Tate hands off his jacket and I should have known that he would wear the t-shirt again. Our eyes meet and we laugh together, some of the tension from the last day dropping away as we fall back into comfortable patterns.

I link my arm through his and we make our way to the front parlor. Immediately, the adults stop talking and stare at us. The pause lingers, bubbling and expectant. I look at Tate trying to assess if he thinks that's as weird as I do, but he's frowning at his dad. Okay, then.

My arm slides away from Tate and I walk across the room to get a drink from the bar.

Tate follows me and leans against it, but keeps a polite distance from me.

I sip from the pre-poured glass of champagne, letting the bubbles dance across my tongue. Tate pours himself water from a carafe, and I appreciate that he has agreed to stay sober without us talking about it. Irritation bubbles across my skin, and I turn around and head to our parents and start making small talk.

Tate's eyes burn into me but I don't look his way. I don't talk to him during the meal, and I excuse myself shortly after dessert. Out of the corner of my eye I can see the hurt on his face. Something about the way our parents have been watching our every move is putting me on edge. I need space from him to clear my head. I'm starting to get paranoid.

I hear their car doors closing as they leave. Tate texts me, but I don't open it or answer.

I fall asleep in my clothes, my stressed heart exhausting my body.

By Friday afternoon, after the world's most awkward tree decorating in which I was talked at for 2 hours, I crack and text Tate.

H: *I miss you. Come over.*

T: *You sure?*

H: *I need you.*

I don't know why I say that, or say it like that, but it's also true. We would normally have spent hours together by now and instead I've seen him for only a handful. We would've gotten a head start on our holiday traditions and started putting things in place for what we wanted to do together over Christmas. Not to mention, I won our bet, and need to pick the first holiday movie of the season.

I'm half asleep when Tate gets here, and he wakes me up by crawling in bed with me and spooning my body into his. I can't deny how good it feels. I sink into him, loving the way his bigger body surrounds mine. Tate burrows into my neck and I don't pull away when he starts pressing soft kisses on the sensitive skin there.

One of his big hands moves up and he palms my breast over my clothes. My back arches automatically and my ass digs into his groin. I can feel him getting hard against me.

An unexpected surge of anxiety rockets through me, and I move forward and scramble off the bed. I hear the sigh Tate tries to silence, and I keep my back to him as I breathe hard, trying to make the feeling go away. I'm wound too tight and I'm pulled in too many directions. I turn to see Tate sitting on the edge of my bed, hands on his knees, something awfully close to fear on his face.

He's afraid he's going to lose me too. I can see it now. Every time I run away from him he's afraid it's going to be the time I don't run back.

My body is overwhelmed for a moment with aching want. So fierce it makes my head light and my vision waver. I want him so much in this moment for being everything that he is, even if he wants me for the wrong reasons. This one moment is going to be mine.

I move quickly to step between his legs, and take his face in my hands before he can catch up and comprehend what's happening. He's so big I don't have to lean down that far to place my lips on his.

Tate's lips are so, so soft. Everything I ever imagined they would be when I really kissed him instead of the brief touches we've done before. I press deeper as he kisses me back, and our lips part for one another. The first time his tongue brushes against mine I inhale sharply, struck dumb by the feeling, before I press harder into him and seal our mouths together. Tate's hands grab my hips and he pulls me close. My arms drop to wrap around his neck and I kiss him with everything I have.

For a second I open my eyes and enjoy the sight of his closed lids, his dark lashes against his cheeks, the way he looks like he's smiling even while he's kissing me. My own eyes close again and I fall into the kiss.

I'm not sure why we stop, but then I'm looking down at him looking up at me. His eyes are hazy with desire, but he's happy, too.

"Why now?"

"I missed you," I whisper, and lean over to press my forehead to his. "But I'm so scared, Tate."

"Of what, baby? Lay it all out for me so I know what I'm up against."

"You have to let me make a PowerPoint or a list first," I laugh. "Off the top of my head it's just going to be an incoherent ramble of anxiety and neediness."

"I can handle your anxiety and I want all your neediness," he growls the last word and his hands cup my ass, pressing my body into his chest. "I can handle all the needs."

"Right now I have needs for food."

"You got it." Tate kisses my nose and then pushes me back so he can stand up. "Let's go get leftovers and then we can watch any movie, your choice."

"No complaints?"

"None whatsoever," he vows with a hand over his heart. I laugh, happy to have my friend back despite the intense moment we shared, and follow him out of my room to go find food.

Halle

Things feel normal but not. We talk like we always do on the way back to Elmwood, and yet, I find myself reaching over the console to hold his hand. It's easy, but also makes my body go crazy with emotion. I'm not sure what we are, but I think I'm taking a genuine step toward exploring it. No more telling him what I think he needs to hear, and I'm tentatively facing the idea that this could be real.

I know that Tate is a player, and I don't think being physical means as much to him as it might to me, but I also don't think you can fake the kind of intensity we had during our kiss. He was so aware of me, it's not like he could have shut off his mind and imagined someone else. It felt like a layer closer than we've been before and I didn't mind it.

I liked it, a lot, and I'm trying not to let that scare the hell out of me.

As usual, Tate walks me to the door of the Castle house.

But this time, he grabs my hand and yanks my body against his, and stuns me with a quick, filthy kiss. His lips are warm on mine in the cold air, and then his tongue is sliding into my mouth, sliding along my tongue in a way that I feel in my clit. Like a hint of things to come.

"See you later, baby." He pecks my nose and hands me my bag.

"Bye, champ," I respond, but it's breathless and woozy. It takes me a minute of watching him walk away before I get a hold on myself and walk into the house. I greet everyone I see on autopilot, respond to questions in a way that must sound sane because no one looks at me weird, and make it back to my room. Tonight we're all getting together to decorate the house for the holidays, and it will stay like that until after Founder's Day.

Before I unpack I make a mental note that we need to pick up candles for the Menorah, as this is the first time in a few years we have a Jewish member of the Castle.

The Winter Solstice party also falls on the last day of finals, so that's going to be insanity too. There's a lot going on in the next few weeks and I'm trying to get in the head space to be excited about it. When I think about the Solstice party, my brain automatically makes it a deadline. I will decide about Tate and I by the party, because then we can go into the holidays and the new year with a clear understanding of what we are to each other.

I try and separate the Tate I know from the Tate that I'm seeing right now.

He's steadfast, attentive, patient, he can kiss so good it would bring me back from the dead. If we had met randomly and he was pursuing me, I'd probably be even more suspicious. I'd also think he was insanely hot and drop my panties in a second because it would be a fuck now regret it later kind of situation. I can't do that with my Tate. My Tate wants it to be fuck now fuck forever, but I'm still not sure he means it. If I merge the two though, if I take everything he's said and done at face value, I have no choice but to give in to wanting him. So that's what I'm going to try and do.

I unpack my room, get a load of laundry started, and read a book while I lean against the warm dryer in the basement of the house. My phone buzzes.

T: *Double date tomorrow?*

H: *With who?*

T: *Colin and Elise. The Sly Remark is having a dinner thing.*

The Sly Remark is a weird institution on campus - the front is a coffee shop by day, kind of a restaurant some nights, kind of a reserved space, and they host nicer dinners or fancy meals for people we want money from. They do have events for students sometimes, and usually it's a fundraiser for a good cause. The food is also pretty good.

H: *Sounds good to me.*

When I lock my phone I see my reflection in the black screen and I'm smiling. I am so gone. Crap.

I walk over to Cavalry 3 the next night because it's on the way, even though I know it will annoy Tate.

I'm wearing black stockings and a black skater dress. It's chilly but I'm comfortable enough. When I knock on the door Tate is the one who answers while he's in the middle of putting on his coat. Immediately he frowns at me.

"I was coming to get you."

"I know. That seemed silly." I shrug. Tate steps out on the small porch, caging me against the wall and radiating cozy heat.

"It's a date, Hal, I should be picking you up."

I roll my eyes and he grabs my chin, tilting my face up to look at him. He's all fire right now and I have to squeeze my thighs together in response.

"I told you things would be different, baby," he leans in close and nips the tip of my nose. "Let me take care of you." There's innuendo in his words, and I swallow slowly, lost in his eyes.

We're snapped out of it when the front door opens, and I'm almost relieved he didn't get a chance to kiss me. I might have burst into a spontaneous puddle right then.

"Hey," Colin greets us both. Elise waves, still a little shy around us when she's sober. I smile at her, and we shift around to face them. "Ready to go?"

"Definitely," I answer. Tate takes my hand rather than letting me hook my arm through his, and we start walking down the street toward the small, odd building that is the Sly Remark. It used to be a house, then the campus bought it ages ago, and converted it into the weird little restaurant that stands today.

"It was built in 1877 and was a private residence until 1918," Elise fills us in without prompting. I'd heard that she was into the history of the campus. It was one of the reasons she was on the short list to be chosen to join the Castle. "The owner died in World War I."

"That's interesting," I answer, and I mean it. Tate and I reach the door first and he holds it open for all of us. We wait at the little host stand and he presses up against my back, pulling me in to lean against his body.

The hostess takes us to one of the tables that's set up for the dinner. It's apparently a Tarot themed evening, as our table is Strength, and there's a card of a woman holding a lion by the head. We take our seats and settle in. The meal is four courses and dessert, so we'll be here awhile. The chairs are deep, padded captain's chairs, so it's easy to sink into them and get caught up in conversation.

We all talk about classes, parties, people although not in a shitty way. Elise is a freshman, I don't want to give her unfair opinions of people she should meet and get to know for herself. It's nice to hang out with people I can relax around.

It's nicer when Tate drops his hand onto my thigh, squeezing me, and then keeps it there. His thumb runs back and forth along the outside and even when I'm focused on the conversation I'm aware of it.

We eat our way through salad, soup, a shockingly good pasta carbonara, and a strawberry chocolate cheesecake, and I don't know that I've ever felt so comfortable before in a public situation with Tate. Usually, I position myself as the silly female foil to his charm, but it really feels like we're in sync right now. The way we're talking and moving, I feel connected to him in a different way.

I've always liked Colin and knew he was a good friend for Tate - I'm happy to see him happy. They both tell the story of growing up together and finally shifting from being friendly to more than friends. They make it sound so easy, but the dynamic of their relationship is so different than ours. I wonder if Tate planned this so they could convince me to be more confident in our own transition.

"I'm happy you two finally got together," Elise says, not knowing more about the situation. She gestures to where Tate's hand obviously rests on my thigh. "Everyone talks about it."

"Oh, we're not," I wave my hand between the two of us. "We're friends. Well," I struggle, knowing that's not quite true anymore either. We are friends, but we're more than that too.

"We're dating, but it's complicated?" I finally finish.

Tate chuckles but there's little humor in it, and I notice the look he exchanges with Colin across the table. Elise turns crimson and I feel bad. Colin rests his arm along the back of her chair and rubs her shoulder.

"I'm so sorry," she apologizes but I wave it off. "I've just heard things."

"Like what?" I grin at her, not upset but entertained.

"Um," she looks between the two of us and then down at her empty plate. "That you're soulmates and there might be a pool about if you'll get married someday."

I sit up straight. "What does the winner get?"

She bites her lip, and I look at Tate and Colin for help. Tate is watching this go down with a mischievous twinkle in his eye. Colin shrugs at Elise.

"You have to follow through and tell them."

Elise sighs. "MC duties at the winning year's Founder's Ball."

I gasp, because that means someone at the Castle is running the pool for that kind of promise to be made and kept. Oh I am going to strangle Gwen for not telling me the pool was more than us dating, but straight up getting married. For all I know she could be the one that started it, considering she's the class above me and has known me for as long as I've been at at Elmwood.

"Wow." I don't know what else to say.

"I mean, if everyone already sees it, you might as well, hey?" Elise's voice is quiet, and I see her give a reassuring look to Tate. Whatever is going on in Tate's head, it appears he's talked to Colin about it, and Colin has talked to Elise. I'm the only one not in on the conversation. Or maybe I'm the one who doesn't want to hear it.

It's dark and chilly by the time we leave. We're one of the last groups to head out, and despite the awkward conversation we fell back into a comfortable flow. It was nice.

We part ways with Colin and Elise at Cavalry 3, and Tate walks me home to the Castle. I'm still squirming and on edge from our almost kiss before dinner, and all the touching he did during it. The question is, what line can we cross without throwing me so far over it I'll never find my way back?

Tate stops at the door to the house, and I tug on the lapels of his blazer, inviting him in close to me. I'm still hesitant to initiate things because it might send the wrong message, but I'll offer an invitation.

It's one that Tate accepts as he leans down to kiss me, his lips and tongue dragging along my own, a deep sensual meeting that makes me weak. I press into him and absorb everything he's giving me in case it's only temporary.

He pulls away and tucks my hair behind my ears.

"Do you want to come to my room?" I ask quietly.

Tate stills. "Do you mean come to your room and watch movies, or do you mean this is the end of the date and you're asking me to come up to your room?"

I take a deep breath. "The second one."

"Let's go, baby." He takes my hand and we walk inside and straight up the stairs. I can feel Gwen and someone else I can't see peeking over the railing, and I subtly give them the finger. Her and I are going to have words, but I don't want to think about that right now.

We walk into my room and I close the door but don't turn on the light. I lean against it and watch Tate with new eyes in my space. A big beautiful man, his shoulders tense as he clearly has some kind of pep talk with himself, before they relax down and he turns to look at me. His eyes drop down and then back up my body.

We keep eye contact as I move around him, closer to my bed. I rest my hand on the skirt of my dress and start pulling up the material with my fingers, slowly revealing more of my thighs to him. His hand was high, but not high enough to know what I was actually wearing under my skirt. Tate's eyes are riveted on me, and when he sees that first peek of skin between the end of the stocking and the start of my panties he groans out loud.

"I think you should kiss me, Tate." My voice is weak, but it's not from fear. It's from want.

"Kiss you where, baby?" His voice is raspy and deep and it makes me shiver. With my other hand I trail a finger up my thigh and then across my hip until my finger rests above my clit.

"Right here." I tap it so he knows.

Tate makes a rumbling sound in his chest and then he's charging toward me. I squeal for a second when he palms my ass cheeks and lifts me, my legs wrapping around his waist. I don't even have time to take a breath before he's devouring my mouth and removing all thought. He turns and stalks across the room to crash us both down on my bed. It groans with the force of it.

He's pressing me down into the bed, his hips cradled between my legs, and I had no idea it would feel so good to be like this. I mean, obviously, messing around feels good, but being like this with Tate? That feels better than anything else ever has.

Tate trails his hands and his mouth down my body, sliding off the bed until he's kneeling next to it. He flips up the skirt of my dress and kisses across my panties, licking me through the material and teasing me before he reaches up and slides them down.

While Tate has definitely seen me naked before, a side effect of being thick as thieves and having impulse control issues when it comes to dares, he's never been up close to my pussy before.

"Fucking hell, Halle. Dream come true," he grumbles. I don't have time to say anything because his tongue parts my folds and he sucks my clit into his mouth. Tate eats me like we're about to run out of time. Alternately rolling my clit with his tongue and then sucking it between his lips. When he slides a finger inside me I start rolling my hips, clenching down on him. He crooks his finger, hitting me just right but it's not quite enough.

Tate slides in a second finger and that's what I need. My body is climbing that hill and I'm almost at the precipice, ready to fall over. He pushes his fingers deep and presses against my inner wall while doing a slow hard swirl of my clit with his tongue. It tips me over, and I ride his fingers and his face as I come. He groans into me, pressing my legs further apart with his shoulders so he can bury himself in my pussy.

When he pulls back his nose, lips, and chin are wet from me.

"You taste so good. Better than my fantasies." He groans and reaches down to adjust himself.

"Take it out. Stroke it while you eat me." My hips roll at the visual, and I lift up on my elbows to watch Tate do what I say. He unzips his pants and pulls them and his boxers down around his perfect ass to free his cock. I've never seen it hard before, but it's big when it's soft and it's even bigger when he's aroused. Long and thick, and I can't look away when he starts to stroke it.

I finally look up to find his eyes focused on my pussy, completely engrossed in looking at me. Tate reaches his free hand to me and uses his thumb to tease my clit, and I moan from the sensitivity. His eyes snap up to mine.

"I'm going to come on your pussy, Halle. That's not a request."

I fall back on my bed in ecstasy when he presses against my clit, and then his tongue takes over. My sensitivity is so high it doesn't take much to work me up again. His fingers are deep inside me, pressing against my spot while his tongue tortures my clit with soft, wet movements. It's exactly what I need.

"You better come quick baby or I'm going to leave you hanging when I paint you with come." He dives back in.

"Tate!" I break and cry out his name and he groans. He stands up over me, still finger fucking me through my orgasm as he jerks himself over my body. I feel his warm release on my pussy, my stomach, and my thighs. There's a lot of it and for some reason that gets me even hotter. We cannot have sex, I'm not ready, but god it's tempting.

Tate collapses next to me, both his hands dirty with our come.

"Marry me. God, Halle, please marry me. I promise I'll do that to you every day. Twice a day. Five times a day."

"I don't take any marriage proposals in the heat of the moment," I weakly slap his chest. "Try again some other time." My head flops to the side to see him and he's already looking at me.

Our eyes lock and his gaze is serious. "I will."

 Tate

I haven't masturbated this much since I first discovered it. The difference now is that my fantasies about Halle are grounded in reality. We haven't done anything else since that night, but it was hot enough to keep me going. Our chemistry was insane. Everything I ever wanted in a sexual partner. I can't imagine how good it will be when we finally fuck.

It's like I know exactly how to touch her, what to say, what she wants from me, and it was intense. If I thought I had it bad for her before, it's nothing compared to how I feel now. Every time we venture into more than friends territory it becomes clearer that we were always meant to be. We were made for each other.

It's unleashed me in a way I didn't know I had inside me. I'm obsessive.

I find her between her classes and back her into corners to kiss the hell out of her, stealing minutes where I can because we're both so busy right now. Sometimes all we do is meet up on the sidewalk to exchange breakfast or dinner - she gets the drinks, I get the entrees. We're taking care of each other even when we're out of time, and even then she'll kiss my cheek or I pull her close and kiss her forehead. I just need to feel her.

She also roped me into helping her with the Founder's Ball by calling people who haven't RSVPed to either confirm them or cross them off the list. She's got to have final numbers before we break for the semester. It's not that many calls and I can see the relief every time we Face Time and I give her updates.

I think she's putting some distance between us, but I also know what her schedule looks like, so I can't be sure. She hasn't slept over in almost two weeks. Finals begin next week, then the Solstice party, and then we're home for the break. I need to see her, and not because I want her, but because I miss my Hal.

It's a Thursday night and I know she's home because I texted Gwen to ask. I got flowers from the on-campus greenhouses, a bag of Skittles, a bag of Reese's Cups. Her favorite study snacks. There's a pre-finals party tomorrow and I want her to go with me.

She's said no to every party, hang out, whatever, even when it's with other people since the night of the double date. I want to spend time with my girl like I used to and I don't know how to find the balance between keeping my friend and pursuing her romantically. Her best friend does not give her space or ask for permission; the guy that wants to claim her as his forever has to do that.

This gesture is a mix of both. Study snacks for my bestie, flowers for my girl, and hopefully a few hot kisses and her agreement to go to tomorrow's party.

I knock on the door and she yells for me to come in.

"Oh! Tate, hi." Halle's face splits into a familiar smile. Real but distracted. It makes something loosen in my chest a bit because I think I'd be able to tell if she was avoiding me based on her reaction right now. Her eyes drop to all the goodies in my hands and it gets bigger. She's genuinely happy to see me right now.

"Are those for me?" She stands up and walks over to grab the flowers. The botany student working at the greenhouse told me they would smell nice, and that was all I wanted. Halle takes the flowers and buries her face in them. "Thank you," she says, her voice and face all soft in a way I've never seen before. She's never looked at me like that.

I step closer until I can set the candy down on her desk, but our eyes are locked, the bouquet pressed between us.

"I miss you," I admit.

Her face drops. "I know, I'm sorry. Stress is making me anti-social."

I cup her cheek and stroke it, loving when she leans into it for support. "It's never kept you from me."

Halle sighs. "You're a little bit part of the stress this time."

I swallow hard, hurt balling in my chest, and I drop my hand. "So you have been avoiding me."

"A little. But I am busy, Tate. I miss you, too, champ." She thumps her forehead against my chest. "Movie night tomorrow? Your room?"

All my plans about the party fly right out the window. Whatever she wants, whatever she needs, as long as we're spending time together.

"I'm also going to preemptively beg for a foot rub." Her head lifts from my chest and she gives me a hopeful look. I can't help but laugh.

"I'm going to preemptively grumble about it and then do it anyway."

"You're the best." She pushes up on her toes and kisses me. When she pulls away we both freeze because that moment was different. That wasn't me devouring her every chance I get, or even the casual touching that's always existed between us. That was the way a girlfriend kisses her boyfriend, a simple act of physical intimacy that's automatic and comfortable. Every time Halle has initiated anything since this started it's been hesitant. There was a surety to that kiss that makes my heart sing.

Her eyes drop to my lips, and I lean in to kiss her again, drawing it out a little.

"Tomorrow, baby."

Halle nods, and I watch her swallow nervously. It's all falling into place.

Tate

I'm standing in line at the on-campus convenience store getting movie night snacks when someone pinches my ass. I turn around and dread pools in my stomach when I see Marin.

"Please don't," I say and turn away from her, trying to end any further interaction.

"So it's true then, Tasty Tate has finally fallen?" She strokes her hand across my shoulder blades and moves to stand in front of me. I shrug her off and take a step back. No one around me notices, and honestly, I don't think they'd do shit anyway. I'm 14 inches taller than this girl, she doesn't look like a threat.

"Maybe I just don't want you touching me, Marin. It's getting creepy."

She pouts, but the words I've said definitely aren't registering with her. "What's so special about this girl? Who is it?"

"All that you need to know is I'm committed, and I'm faithful, and even if I wasn't with her, I wouldn't want to be with you. Seriously," I try and appeal to anything friendly inside her, "please leave me alone."

It's my turn at the till so I step around her and pay for our stuff. While none of the other women that have talked to me have been as aggressive as Marin, it's started getting around campus that I'm off limits. I haven't pulled Halle into it, and I won't until she's ready. The downside to being popular is a lot of people have opinions about your relationships. It's going to come back on her at some point and I want to avoid that. She'll have the protection and support of the Castle and the Cavalry, but that still leaves a few thousand entitled assholes who think their opinion matters.

Or who will make assumptions about her sexual activities because she's the one to "tame" me. I've already heard that kind of talk going around. Our imaginary sex life is much wilder than our actual sex life, but I don't care. I already know that when we finally cross that line it's going to be perfect.

I nearly run down the street to make sure Marin doesn't follow me, and I run faster when I see Halle walking down the sidewalk to Cavalry 3.

"Hi, baby," I bounce to a stop in front of her, and she smiles up at me. She's in leggings and one of my hoodies and it makes my possessive heart purr with pleasure. Halle looks like mine, and she fucking is.

"Champ," she lets out a sigh so heavy I feel it in my own body. Like everything she's been holding in all day has now been let out and is dissipating because she's with me. I know the feeling because it's the same for me when I'm with her. "What are we snacking on tonight?"

We start walking into the house and up to my room. "Well, I was out of popcorn."

"A crime." Halle laughs. I eat popcorn a lot. It's a light snack and I can toss it in the air and catch it in my mouth so it also gets some of my excess energy out.

"Then I was feeling punchy so Sour Patch Kids, Twizzlers, and a box of Raisinets."

"Delicious. And our viewing for the evening?"

I bite my lip as we get inside the room and she immediately starts making herself comfortable on my bed.

"*The Lost City*?" I suggest.

"Like Sandy B and Chan Chan? Yes." Halle kicks off her shoes and then waves her feet at me. "And then you get rubbing."

"Yes, ma'am." We laugh and things fall back into their familiar pattern of me and her. I rub her feet and we talk about the movie as we watch. What's different is that when I'm done with her feet, I crawl to sit behind her and pull her back to rest against me. My arms are wrapped around her like a perpetual hug, and I can run my hands over her thighs, or tease the soft skin of her stomach.

My phone is buzzing on and off all night. I didn't bother telling anyone I wasn't coming to the party, but I also didn't plan for everyone to hit me up non-stop like this. The movie is almost over when it finally breaks Halle.

"What's going on?"

"Just a party." I give the notifications a quick glance to make sure there's not an emergency but it's mostly a variation of the texter asking where I am.

"Tate. You had plans." Halle shifts to look up at me, but doesn't extricate herself from my hold. I weave my hands through hers and pull, as if I could get her closer to me than she already is.

"Plans with you always win, babe."

Halle shakes her head. "Then let's go. We got movie night in, and it's not like the party is ending any time soon."

"Are you sure?" Usually it's a lot more work to get her to agree to a random party. If there's a theme or occasion, she's all about it, but when it's a random just because kind of thing it's not her scene. Halle is my little introverted extrovert. Perfectly capable of being engaging and social but it drains her. It's not how she would choose to spend her energy, and I respect that.

"Yeah. I'm not saying I'll stay long but I think you need to put in an appearance," she elbows me and then moves to crawl off me. I yank her back, grinding my hips into her ass.

"I need to get you ready to go," I whisper in her ear before nibbling down her neck.

Halle stifles a moan. "What do you mean?"

I move a hand under her hoodie before sliding my fingers under the waistband of her leggings, where I learn she isn't wearing panties.

I tsk at her and dive my hand inside to cup her hot, naked sex. "Naughty girl, Hal. Were you hoping something would happen tonight?"

She squirms against the pressure. "Maybe."

"You're going to get it now, sweetheart." I part her pussy lips and gently tease her clit. "I'm going to have to punish you."

"Punish me how?" Her hips grind against my hand, and I let her work herself. It's only going to make the rest of it more satisfying. For me, definitely not for her. Let's test Halle's boundaries and preferences tonight. This is a side of my girl I want to know.

I work her up, feeling every moan in my chest as I raise her toward an orgasm with my fingers, playing with her sweet little clit. One of her hands grips my forearm as if she can hold me in place, and the other reaches back to dive into my hair. Halle pulls my mouth to her neck and I love her demanding what she wants.

"Are you going to come baby? Are you close?"

"Yes," she breathes out the word. "So close. Tate," she moans my name and it almost makes me change my plans.

Almost.

I stop moving. "Now you're ready." I start to remove my hand and she grabs my arm, her nails digging into my skin. I hope it leaves a mark.

"Tate," she whines and it makes my cock throb. It's so fucking needy. Exactly how I want her. I take my hand out of her leggings.

"Naughty girls get punished, Hal. We're going to this party, and your pussy is going to drench your leggings, and you'll be fucking aching for me to finish you off. All night you're going to be aroused and aware of me, wanting me, and we will only leave when you lose your mind and beg me. Beg me to get you alone and make you come, when you promise me you'll be a good girl."

The Halle I know never backs down from a challenge, especially not one between us. Tonight I'm going to see her breaking point and I can't fucking wait.

"You're evil." Her voice is still a whine.

I slap her pussy for good measure. "Let's go, naughty girl."

She groans and climbs out of my lap. I watch with amusement as she adjusts her leggings, and when she steps into my bathroom to fix her hair. Halle's level of not giving a shit is just right for this party. I'm going in jeans and a t-shirt. I stand and wait for her, adjusting my furious cock so it's less obvious until it calms down. My body is real fucking mad at me for playing this game but my brain is all about it.

Deciding she's ready, Halle walks up to me and gets in my space, chest to chest. "And what if I don't beg? What then?"

I smirk down at her and act like a total condescending ass by clucking her chin. "That's cute, babe."

She glares at me like I wanted. "You're going down, champ."

"I fucking hope so." I wink at her and step around her, holding in my laugh at her frustrated scoff. I hold the door to my room for her and she stomps past me.

I take her hand as we walk to the party at one of the student houses that border campus. It's weird to have a neighborhood also be campus, but it works for Elmwood's purposes. We're our only little world up here and it's exactly the way we like it.

Halle doesn't let go of me even when we get inside, and that's unusual. I like it. I pull her closer and put my arm around her, keeping her with me as I'm welcomed with great acclaim. They greet Halle as well, and she knows them too. They all know her well enough to be surprised she's there, but I also see a knowing expression on their faces. The rumors are solidifying into truths.

It's finally happened. Halle and I are more than friends.

Even if we haven't defined what we are yet and things are still in flux, there's a change in us and we can't hide it anymore.

Halle and I cheer on a game of beer pong and call playing the winner. A chorus of groans goes around the room. Halle's reputation is notorious.

"I haven't even had anything to drink yet!" she protests. "I won't even be any good!"

As a result, we both get handed cans of beer and start drinking while we wait. We both get pulled into other conversations, our bodies angled away from each other but my arm is still around her shoulders and hers rests around my lower back. It's so damn easy. It's these tiny changes that speak so much to me.

We touched before, I'd have my arm around her at parties, but she never touched me back. Never held on to me like she had a right to, even though she did.

Every once and awhile I feel her hand squeeze my side, like she's letting me know she's still there and aware of me and it's so fucking cute.

The game finishes and we approach our end of the table. I move behind her and put my hands on her hips, pulling her into me. She shivers when I lean in to whisper in her ear.

"Every cup you hit is another orgasm I'm going to give you." I bite her earlobe and let her go, but she falls back into me and I catch her. She turns her head and speaks into my neck, getting me hard.

"Better give your tongue a rest then, you'll be using it later."

Fuck. If I wasn't already in love with her that would've gotten me damn close to the edge.

Halle steps away from me and immediately sinks her first throw. She turns toward me and winks, and I want to eat all that sass up.

Drinks or not, Halle is preternaturally good at beer pong. This same skill for short range getting balls into holes also applies to mini-golf. We have played easily 50 games of mini-golf together in the course of our friendship and I have never beaten her. It'd be irritating if it wasn't amusing.

Of our 10 cups, Halle is responsible for 6 of them. I can't wait to get to work on her.

I bow us out of the next game. Halle gives me a look because she knows watching her decimate fools at the table is one of my favorite things to do with her, but I've got a pussy to edge.

"Come on, sweetness," I cup her face and murmur to her, "you didn't think it would be that easy, did you?"

Halle's mouth drops open in shock, and it gives me the chance to pull her into the mass of bodies dancing to the thumping music. I press her against the front of my body and wedge my thigh between her legs. Another first for us is dancing like this. Sure we've danced, but not like this. Not when the whole point is to get her and keep her horny, instead of in the past when I was trying to keep my erection from being noticed. I think she'd be surprised how often that's been a challenge.

I palm her ass and keep her close, never breaking eye contact either. Halle balls my shirt up in her fists and tries to resist, but when she's a little tipsy she likes to move. I feel her hips swaying to the music, and every once and awhile I'll pull her harder against my leg to put pressure in her sweet spot.

We're almost nose to nose, one of those moments where it's nearly private because everyone else is so wrapped up in themselves and their moment. We're lost in the crowd of bodies. I inhale her, the familiar scent of her shampoo and her cherry blossom lotion.

"What are you thinking about, Halle?" She only shakes her head in response, denying her want. "My tongue on your pussy again? The way it feels when I fuck you with my fingers?" I reach up to cradle her face. From the outside it looks sweet but it's so she can't look away. "What it's going to feel like when I fuck you? The way you're going to shudder when you break apart on my cock?"

My words are prescient because I feel that exact shudder under my hands. Halle's whole body reacting to my words.

"How wet are you now, baby?" I press a quick kiss to her lips.

"Tate," she nearly cries, her voice a whimper. I'm so close to breaking her.

"You know what to do, Halle."

"Please," the word bursts from her mouth. "God, please, Tate, I need you."

A little further. "Need me to what?"

"Make me come."

Her head crashes down on my chest and out of my hands. I let her stay there and move my hands back to her hips. No one is paying any attention and I start grinding her against me. Halle's head flips up.

"What are you doing?"

I grin at her. "You're going to come apart right here, and then I'm going to take you home and give you the five other orgasms I promised." Even while I spoke, she never stopped grinding her hips, never broke the pattern I have her in or tried to stop me. Halle clings to me more tightly, eyes never leaving mine.

I get to watch them go hazy with her arousal. The way she bites her lip to try and hold back her little cries as she gets closer. Halle's legs squeeze my thigh and she moves in short, jerking motions, pressing hard on me.

When she comes she presses her face into my chest and I feel the hot breath of her moans through my t-shirt.

I lean in. "Good girl."

I guide us out of the party without saying a word to anyone. I put in an appearance and now I'm done. My place is closest so I head back that way. Halle doesn't say anything, but she hasn't stopped clinging to me, leaning heavily into my side. I'm almost worried, but every time I look at her she's got a small dreamy smile on her face.

When I close the door to my room, Halle pounces. She actually jumps up and wraps her legs around me, and I match her energy by grabbing her ass and lifting her a little higher. I only break the kiss to strip her out of my hoodie and nearly rip her bra off. We crash to my bed and in seconds I finally have my mouth on her tits for the first time.

They are fucking perfect. Full and soft with pink nipples that are so responsive to my tongue. Halle thrashes when I suck on one so they're also sensitive. Exactly what I want.

"Tate please, more," Halle begs me so sweetly. I oblige by peeling her leggings down her body. I look up from my place on my knees, my eyes tracing over every naked inch of her. This is my wildest fantasy come true - a fully naked, needy Halle in my bed and mine to fucking devour.

"Brace yourself, baby." Her thighs spread open as I move closer. "Get ready to count to five."

Halle

Tate has me so damn dickmatized that even though it's finals, I sleep in his bed every night. We study like any other time and then it's as if the witching hour strikes and we look at each other and attack, instantly and ravenously horny.

After studying together all day on Saturday, we hit sometime after 11:00 P.M. and lost our minds. He sucked and bit my tits and ground his erection into me until I came on a strangled cry of sensitivity, and then we made out until one of us fell asleep. I'm pretty sure it was me, and I'm pretty sure he didn't care at all.

Sunday we did our usual pre-finals ritual: giant breakfast at the Maybell diner in Direwood, and then a nap. Except when I woke up from that nap, I was a live wire, like I'd been bathing in horny caffeine while I slept. Fully giving in to the sexual side of Tate that I never got to see is hazardous to my control. The fact that he can conquer me physically but also be the best guy I know is confusing. My brain is still trying to merge them, and the more I do the more afraid I am.

If this isn't real for him, I will never be okay. Our friendship, hell, even the multi-generational friendship between our families, will not survive the fallout of this.

Tate's awake and watching me when I open my eyes. The heat I feel in my body is there in his gaze, and I know I'm not alone in feeling this way. He's been unbelievable but the competitive side of me thinks it's his turn to be wrecked.

I roll over and push him onto his back, straddling him and kissing him in one quick move. His cock rapidly hardens under the hot press of my core against him. I wiggle a little, teasing him and laughing at his groan. I kiss my way down his throat, dragging my teeth along his skin.

When my hands wrap around the waistband of his shorts and his boxers, he stops me by grabbing my wrists.

"What are you doing?"

"Having a snack," I answer sarcastically. When I tug on his clothes he lifts his hips, letting me slide everything down and allowing his cock to spring free. I lick him from root to tip a couple of times, and then wrap my mouth around the head, starting to slide up and down on him. I keep my pace slow, going deeper with each pass over his warm erection.

"Fuck, Hal, you look so pretty with your lips around my dick. My best fucking dream." He slides his fingers into my hair but doesn't press or control me. I'm not in a rush. I want to taste him and savor this, learn what drives him crazy the way he's done to me. I go deep, taking him into the back of my throat. Then I stick my tongue out further, teasing the base with the tip of my tongue.

"Holy shit what did you just do?" he groans, his hips thrusting up. I slide him out to the head, then go all the way down and do it again. I keep my tongue pressed hard against the bottom ridge of his cock and he tightens up, moaning as I tease him. Hunger overtakes me and I start moving faster, hollowing my cheeks while continuing to push my tongue against the sensitive underside. The noises Tate makes while I blow him are a huge compliment to my ego and undoing him like this makes me unbelievably wet. If the position wasn't so awkward I'd be touching myself to the sounds.

"I'm gonna come." He tries to move away but I don't let him. I seal my mouth around his cock and press deep when he starts to thrust without control. His come floods the back of my throat and I swallow, tasting only a hint of his warm, salty flavor. While I think blow jobs are fun I've never been a big fan of come, but I love the power of swallowing. I learned fast the farther in my throat they are, the better it feels for them, and the less I taste.

I keep Tate in my mouth and swallow around him, milking everything from him until he's flinching from being too sensitive.

"Holy shit, Hal." He looks stunned when I sit up over him. Tate's mouth opens and closes a few times, and I laugh because he's rendered speechless. Then he leaps at me and presses me into the bed, ripping my pants off and plunging his fingers into my wet, needy pussy. Tate makes me come until I tap out.

Monday night we crack at midnight, getting each other off and then crashing. He has an 8:00 A.M. final, and I'm still in his bed when he comes back, studying for my Spanish 203 final. He kicks me out, afraid he'll get distracted if I stay, but then texts me to come back and sleep with him that night.

Tuesday he wakes me up with donuts, coffee, and his head between my thighs, making me come before sending me to my last final. It's unreal how horny I am at all times for him. Except we also talk like we always have, we help each other like we always have, and it's just like he said it would be - us as we've always been, only with orgasms.

We don't see each other after I leave his room Wednesday morning. I told him I wanted to meet him at the Solstice party. I needed a little bit of time away from him and his sexually talented everything. It's time to think with a clear head.

It's so easy to believe that Tate and I could be like this forever. We've always been best friends, he's always put me before anyone and anything else, and I've done the same. He's my number one and always has been. Yeah, I've definitely been stifling feelings for him all that time, holding tight to denial in order to stop myself from getting hurt. The idea that he's felt the same all along is still difficult for me to trust.

Because I also know him better than anyone else, and I can't believe I would have missed his feelings. I thought I could read him so well and to know he's been hiding makes me nervous. It doesn't help that mom's voice is still in my head, reminding me that I'll never be good enough for him.

She loves me in her way, but she's not happy. My father isn't indifferent to her, but it's obvious sometimes that he doesn't really know her, and it baffles him that after decades together there are things that any true partner would know and he's never heard them before. They love me, but it's like a certain kind of spark is missing from them as people because of who they have to be around each other. I can tell it puts distance between us because I'm a duty she fulfilled at this point, rather than a daughter she dotes on.

Even if I hear it, I've decided that she's wrong. I decided that I'm going to believe Tate because he's never tried to make me be something I'm not, and he's never given me a reason not to trust him. If he's offering forever, he's who I want.

Gwen knocks on my slightly propped door, and comes in. She looks great in a silver jumpsuit, stars in the corner of her eyes, and her hair up in a high ponytail. I turn in place for her to appraise my outfit. I'm wearing a silver dress covered in textured silver stars, and my hair is up in space buns. I've got plenty of silver glitter touches, but my lips are a soft pink. I figured it wasn't worth putting anything on my lips because Tate will only kiss it off.

"You look fantastic."

"So do you," I answer. "I'm telling Tate I'm all in. Today was the deadline I gave to myself, and I want him. I want everything." My voice cracks as I say it and she shuffles into the room on her super high platform boots to hug me.

"That's awesome, Halle. For what it's worth, everyone has been saying he loves you since day freaking one. No one ever really tried anything with him because they knew it was you in the end, even if you didn't know."

"God, I hope so," I send out into the universe. "If he breaks my heart I think it will actually kill me."

"Then lets got get him."

I grab my keys and follow her out of my room. We decompress about our finals as we walk to the party. It's cold as hell outside but I don't feel it, the nerves running through me keeping me warm. We step into the over warm Cavalry house and I start looking around for Tate. Everyone is wearing silver too, and it makes them all stand out against the dark decor of the house.

Gwen stays with me and we greet people and friends as we get deeper into the house.

I see Tate and my stomach hits the floor. I'm frozen.

"What..." Gwen starts, but then she sees it too.

Tate has a girl in a corner, and he's bent over her, one arm on the wall above her head. She's tiny - a brunette in silver shorts and a silver crop top, showing off the toned expanse of her impressive abs and the bright star in her belly button. The girl is looking up at Tate with pure lust, and she looks familiar but I can't remember her name.

I want to throw up when she grabs Tate's face and their mouths collide, and I watch as her tongue obviously slides between his lips. Tate's hands land on her hips, and that's all I need to see. I take a few steps back, and the motion gets their attention.

Tate and the girl turn to see me at the same time. He looks angry, and then terrified when he registers that he's looking at me.

I shake my head at him and turn around to go.

"Halle!" Tate calls my name as he moves to follow me. Gwen takes the hit, stepping in front of him so I have time to get the hell out. I can hear them arguing but not what they say, and in seconds I'm back in the cold. I'm so numb on every level that I barely feel it. It's taking all my control not to cry right now.

I know he's going to catch up to me eventually, but I'm almost home before I hear his footsteps pounding the pavement, and then his warm hand gripping my elbow. I turn at his pull because I can't avoid this conversation.

"It's not what you think," he starts, but I hold up a hand.

"I really can't tell who you're lying to - to yourself, or to me." My voice sounds like it's coming out of someone else. I'm in my body but I'm not, and it's doing things, saying things, without my mind being part of it.

"What?"

"You forget that I know you, Tate, better than anyone. You're trying so hard to convince yourself that you have feelings for me and I don't understand why."

"Halle, it's not like that."

"It is, Tate. How could I not know, all these years, if you'd really had feelings for me? We're together all the time and you expect me to believe you've kept yourself under control, never said a word, never told me this massive secret?" I scoff. "I can't believe that you would destroy our friendship like this."

The panic is real on his face now. He reaches for me and I step back. "I have never lied to you about this, Halle, how can you think I would do that? How can you think that I would ever intentionally do anything to hurt you?"

"That's the fucked up part, you're not actually trying to hurt me. You decided you wanted this, that it was the right thing, and that I should fall in line like everyone else, because it's the shiny new idea. Then we'll get married, you'll realize it was an impulse, and you'll step out on me trying not to hurt me."

"What the fuck, Halle!" Now he sounds mad. Good. Let's fight. "What kind of asshole do you think I am? I'm really that much of a whore in your opinion? Jesus Christ, and you think I'm the shitty friend."

I flinch. "I know your reputation, Tate. How could I ever be enough for you?"

Now he's furious, and I want his anger to take over me like a wave. If he's mad he'll say something that makes me mad back, and I'd so much rather be angry than sad. I'd rather be furious with him than try and sew back together my torn up heart.

"One, because I've fucking said it to you. I've said to your face, looking in your eyes, that you are everything I need." He steps close and I look up at him, swallowing tightly in the wake of his fury. "And two, a reputation is not a reality. If you'd wanted to have that conversation, I would have, but you didn't. I'm not what you think I am. I thought you knew me better than that."

I shake my head, struggling to hear him and believe him, and compare that to what I've seen with my own eyes.

"I don't know what to trust," I barely manage to speak it.

Tate shakes his head and takes a step back from me. "You know what? Fuck this. I have never lied to you, I have always put you first, tried to love you without scaring you, because that's the truth, Hal. I have been in love with you for...ever." He throws up his hands. "I can't help it that Marin won't leave me alone no matter what I say, and you saw her grab me and kiss me. I didn't kiss her back. I pushed her off me. I have no interest in her. But hell, maybe I should let her rip me up again because it would hurt less than knowing you don't trust me."

"Tate..." I trail off because I don't know what to say. I can't reconnect to my body. The second I do I'm going to cry.

"It doesn't matter." Tate's voice is the coldest I've ever heard it. He turns me around and grabs my arm, and we walk the short distance to the front door of the Castle house. He gives me a light push toward the stairs to the front door, and then steps back and away from me. Even furious, he still walks me home.

"I'll see you Friday." I still don't move, but he doesn't wait for me to get in the house before he walks away. The ride home for Christmas is going to be a delight.

My heart is a mess, I'm still covered in glitter, but I slide off my shoes and climb into bed fully clothed, waiting to be ready to cry.

Tate

When I wake up there are calls from Halle, but no text messages. I wish I could say that I slept off my fury, but that's not even close to accurate. I've never been so hurt in my life as when she said she didn't trust me.

The worst part is, she's right, in a way. I am keeping a secret from her, even if it doesn't matter in the end. She has no idea about the will and Grandpa Ray's request. She's not ready to hear it. If I tell Halle about the request, and that it was the impetus for me to pursue her, it will reaffirm her belief this all started with grief and guilt, instead of the push I needed to chase her.

That aside, the fear that there truly isn't trust between us overwhelms me. If that's true, then she could never love me the way I love her, at least not any time soon. I can't think of anything I've done, truly done, to make her question me to that extent.

Yes, I've been with other women. She's been with other men. It doesn't negate my feelings for her, or that I was holding them in, and sometimes fighting them. Which I never explained to her, and maybe I should have. Trying to see it from her perspective, I did spring my feelings on her without any explanation or context. That will be easier to do at home, when I can show her how I've always felt.

I might be mad as hell, but this is not done.

Whatever she might think or believe, whatever she is afraid of, it's ultimately irrelevant. Halle belongs to me. We belong to each other and we have our entire lives. I will make her see it. My chest throbs because I wish I could call Ray. He would know what to say or do to make this better. He'd see the rational, true way to fix things.

I sit up in bed and my gaze is snagged by a bright yellow envelope on the floor inside my door. The stationery is familiar, and my stomach swoops with a mix of love and fear. Halle left me a note.

Then I remember that it's the day after finals. It's a tradition. Something she's done at the end of every year since 8th grade, and the end of every semester once we started college. Halle and I might be fighting, but my girl is still with me.

I pick up the envelope and open it, taking out the card inside. It has dancing cartoon strawberries on the front and says "I'm berry proud of you!" With something between panic and relief, I open the card.

Tate,

I know this semester was hard - harder than we ever could have planned for - but you did so amazing. Every semester your work ethic, your creativity, your intelligence, shine through in everything that you do. I'm so proud of you, and that I get to be with you as you become the man you are meant to be. I could not have made it through this semester without you; between keeping me fed and on a regular sleep schedule, to study hours together and also making me take a break once and awhile. Have I thanked you yet for all the help with the Founder's Ball? I can't wait for every semester we have left when I can make you color-coded flashcards, listen to you practice presentations, and build you up when you need it. I am always here for you. We are the best version of ourselves together and I am so lucky that my lifelong best friend is you, champ.

Love,

Hal

P.S. I wrote this after our fight. Ready to talk when you are.

I was not ready to talk. I'm not sure if it's better or worse that she could tune out the fight we had to still right me a note like this, one that built me up, rather than trying to talk about anything that we said last night. Part of me is afraid of what it means for the type of feelings she has for me, and another part feels like she loves me enough to put aside anything to do what she thinks I need.

My whole life I was an athlete, and as long as I did okay in school no one pushed me to be anything academically. Once I got to Elmwood and I wasn't playing sports, I realized that I truly wanted to learn, but I had no idea how. I didn't know my learning style or how to study, and it took lots of research and exploration, with Halle guiding me, to figure out what worked for me. Even though I learned a lot about myself, it meant I still got insecure about my academics, especially during midterms and finals. I always doubted myself after, even if I went in confident. Halle knows that better than anyone because she's always the one talking me off the ledge and building me up. Honestly, if I hadn't already been head over heels for her, the way she was there for me during all of that would have sealed the deal.

She keeps giving me new reasons to love her, even after a lifetime by each other's sides.

I set down the note, get dressed, and go downstairs to the large shared kitchen in the house. No one is up yet, they're all probably nursing serious hangovers from the Solstice party and since I never even had a drink and was in my bed by 11:00 P.M., I was going to be the only one up for awhile. I make myself a bowl of cereal I don't want and sit at the large island to eat.

The pad of footsteps sounds behind me, and I'm surprised to see Colin when I look over my shoulder. His hair is standing up in all directions and there's a hint of a hickey peeking out of the collar of his shirt. I can't help but smirk and he frowns and readjusts his collar to try and hide it.

"Where did you go last night?" Colin asks over his shoulder as he digs around in the cupboard to start the coffee pot. It's a massive professional grade machine, and it's part of our monthly dues to live in the house to cover the communal pot. We keep coffee going all day almost every day. I don't answer him until he's got everything going, and turns around to face me.

"Marin cornered me, assaulted me with her mouth, Halle saw."

"So?" Colin yawns and crosses his arms over his chest. He blinks a few times and really looks at me. "You didn't explain?"

I sigh and stir my soggy cereal. "I tried. It turned into this huge fight. She said she didn't trust me."

Colin winces. "I get where she's coming from a little."

I glower at him and he holds up his hands.

"I think it's stupid for her to doubt you, not for as long as you've known each other, but to her it is kind of out of nowhere, my man. Everyone else can see it, has seen it for years, but you've never said a thing to her and actively pursued other women, sometimes in front of her. Forgive her whiplash."

I grunt because those are the same points I've repeated to myself during our dating experiment when I was trying to convince her. Maybe the problem is that I got so caught up in finally crossing the physical boundaries I've stuck to that I never bothered to deal with the emotional ones. I treated everything the same except that it's not. It's not our normal friendship plus sex, it would change a lot more than that. That's my fault.

"Do you love her?"

"Of course I do," I snap. Then I shake my head, and Colin nods, accepting my apology.

"Why have you never told her? What held you back?"

I think about my answer, trying to get down to the deepest truth. "I was afraid she didn't feel the same, and that I would lose her. Plus, she needed me to be her friend, her ally, for a long time. It's only recently I realized I could be more and still be what she needed."

"Have you told her any of this? Talked about your feelings and your decisions?"

"No."

"Then you have to - you have to have the heavy, hard as fuck conversation about your emotions. Show her that this isn't out of nowhere. Halle does trust you, Tate, but a romantic relationship is a different kind of trust. You both have to earn it."

What he's saying makes sense, but I'm still mad and hurt, and I have to let that dissipate. I have to find a way to continue the conversation without devolving into defensive mode. I can't face her in person yet.

"What do I do? Send her a text?"

"Maybe," Colin shrugs and turns away from me to fill up two mugs with coffee. He sets one in front of me, knowing I take my coffee black, while he pours in a slightly frightening amount of sugar.

I think about the card from this morning, and remember how much she used to light up when I'd write her notes in high school. They were usually dumb jokes, movie quotes we both loved and things that made me think of her, or a reminder for plans that we made. I don't want to send her a text, but I can writer her a note.

"I'll give a try," I tell him, and then dump my soggy cereal down the garbage disposal and put my bowl in the dishwasher. "Where's Elise?"

"Still sleeping," Colin gives me a satisfied smirk and I shake my head at him before leaving the kitchen. Some guys have all the luck.

When I get to my room, I open a random notebook, grab a pen, and think about what I need to say to Halle.

Halle

I'm pretending to pack to leave for break, but I'm just sitting on my bed surrounded by clothes and thinking about Tate. He's never been mad at me like he was last night, ever. I deserved it. After crying for about an hour until I passed out, I woke up feeling like shit. It was still damn early in the morning, but I had a tradition to follow.

I wrote the note, walked over to Cavalry 3 in the dark just before dawn to slide it under his door, and then cried some more sitting on my bed as the sun came up. There's too much to process about what he said, what I said, and trying to figure out how I feel. There's this whole extra level of pressure and complication added to our situation and I don't think he takes that as seriously as I do. I don't think he understands what he's signing on for.

I know Tate loves me, but that's not the same as being in love with me. Finding me attractive and wanting to be physical with me is not being in love with me. Nothing he's done so far has made me believe that part of it to be not only true, but something that's been true for a long time. We've been us with fooling around, and that's not how relationships are, at least not one that I want to be in. There has to be emotional intimacy too, the kind that happens in a romantic relationship, and that hasn't happened for us yet. It's the thing that makes me doubt.

There's a soft knock on my door and Gwen pokes her head in. Her expression is full of sympathy.

"Tate dropped this off for you." She holds up a plain white envelope. My heart squeezes in pain, but I slide out of my piles of clothes to go grab it from her. "He said he'll see you tomorrow."

"Right." I stare down at it, my name written in his firm block print on the front.

"What happened after you left?" Gwen asks.

"We had a fight. A big one. I don't know where to go from here."

"Go home," Gwen shrugs in response. "Go where nothing can interfere like it does here." She bites her lip and hesitates at the door. "I heard that girl, Marin, after you left."

I wait her out and wave a hand, letting her know I'm ready for whatever she's going to tell me. If it was bad, she wouldn't be hesitating. Gwen likes to throw it out there hard and fast when it's rough, ripping the band-aid right off.

"She said she thought Tate was playing hard to get, but when he chased after you she felt like an asshole because she wouldn't have kept going for him if she knew he was finally going after you."

"That's weird," I answer, unsure how to interpret that information. So this girl didn't trust Tate's no when it was because he wasn't interested in her, but respected it when he said no because he was with me? That's shitty.

"Yeah, well, I think it should also tell you that everyone saw what you didn't. It's getting around that the two of you are finally a thing. It's kind of a big deal."

I groan and smack myself in the face with the note. "I don't know what we are."

"Well start taking steps to figure it the fuck out, one way or another." On that parting note, Gwen closes my door and leaves me to the note.

I sit down on the floor and lean against my closet, where I can sit comfortably in the bright winter sunshine, and read Tate's note.

Hal,

I went about a lot of this wrong, and for that I'm sorry, but I can't lie that you really hurt me last night. All my life, there's only been you for me. Sometimes life itself got in the way, our parents interfered, the expectations they have for us, and the fears that got inside our heads. I was your friend because we needed friendship more than we needed romance; I was always going to claim you as mine. When Grandpa died, for me it was like puzzle pieces falling into place. It was a sign that now was the time for things to change, and that it would be easy, a small change in our dynamic, and everyone would be happy, but especially me and you.

That wasn't the case for you. I made a mistake. We have a lot to talk about, things we should've talked about at the start. I also think you never gave me a chance, not really, so that's what I'm asking for, for the last time.

Let me tell you everything.

Love,

Tate

That feels ominous. Like I'm on my last chance with him, when I probably need more chances than that. When I will probably mess things up between us many times between now and however we end up.

Tate's not wrong though - I was always one foot out the door in all of this. Always afraid or hesitant, always holding back and bracing for the hurt. Some of that is because we never really talked about anything. This forced me to confront and admit my feelings. I gave in and immediately got them crushed. I believe him about last night, but I'm afraid I won't be able to withstand when it happens again.

Because I think better when my hands are busy, I start actually packing. Tate will pick me up tomorrow morning to drive home and that gives us a few hours to sort through some things and figure out what break is going to look like for us. We have so many traditions and rituals, especially around the holidays, and I don't want that to change.

I pause with a handful of underwear because a thought hits me harder than it ever has before.

There is never going to be room in my life for anyone else.

There will never be anyone worth making space for because it's already been claimed. That's one kind of commitment that I've never questioned when it came to Tate. He's always been my number one and I've always been his. Despite the fact that I knew he was with other women, it genuinely never occurred to me to question that I came first. They were always temporary and I never cared about them because they never interfered with the Tate and Halle Show.

The first time my mom threw down the possibility of Tate was the just before the Christmas we were 12. I'd hit puberty, gotten boobs I didn't know how to manage yet, and felt all wrong in my body because I was tall and solid instead of willowy like her.

"If you eat those cookies, Tate will never think you're pretty."

"Tate doesn't even see you as a woman, Halle, can't you be a little more feminine?"

Those were arrows to my chest. I'd spent those few weeks emotionally bleeding all over everything, hating myself, my body, things that I couldn't change. Suddenly I was afraid of being judged by Tate and found wanting. On Christmas Eve, he offered to kiss me under the mistletoe, and I shut him down. It was from both that fear of rejection from my best friend, and that I was now thinking of him like a boy and not like my friend.

A cute boy. A perfect boy. The fear always overruled my attraction. Mom never stopped telling me that if I didn't change I'd never be good enough for him, that I was never feminine enough, that he was always keeping me in the friend zone for a reason. She had me convinced that Tate didn't see me as more, would never see me as more, so I locked all of that attraction in a box and threw it into the deepest, Marianas Trench-deep, part of my heart. I spent so much time believing mom that I can't believe Tate.

Even if I can say yes, I love him, I'm in love with him, I can know that is objectively true, the damage mom has done makes me unable to feel confident about it. I thought I'd stopped letting her ruin my sense of self-worth but I was being deliberately oblivious.

If I'm going to rip open those wounds for anyone, it would be for Tate. Time to start bleeding, because I can't lose him.

I'm waiting outside when he pulls up. My stomach is full of bees rather than butterflies as I wait for him. He's wearing a black hoodie and gray joggers, his favorite white hat backward on his head. It's my favorite cozy Tate look and he knows it. I didn't play fair either - I'm wearing his gray high school baseball sweatshirt and leggings. I look very much like Tate Daniels is my boyfriend right now.

Tate stops in front of me and I look up into his face. He's hesitant, and I'm a second away from crying.

"Shit, Hal, don't do that."

I let out a gasping sob and he opens his arms to me. I crash my face into him, burying my face in his neck where it belongs.

"I have to tell you some stuff," I blubber.

"Me too." He pulls back and kisses my forehead. "Let's get going, and no more tears."

"No promises." I wipe my eyes with the cuffs of the sweatshirt as he takes my bags and puts them in the trunk. He's already got it all done and is holding my door open when I make it down the walkway. The car is perfectly warm and cozy against the cold winter day. Campus is barely awake right now, and we ride in comfortable silence until we're past Direwood.

"I've told you a lot about the things my mom has said to me," I take a deep breath, deciding to get this started. "But I've never told you what she's said about you."

Tate stills, and I think if the car wasn't in cruise right now we would've been screeching to a stop.

"What?"

I take a deep breath and look down at my hands. "It wasn't just pressure to look good for the family, to do what would be best for the family, it was specifically about me not looking good to you. She would use the idea of disappointing you, you rejecting me, to get me to do what she wanted."

"Halle." The fury in Tate's voice is the mirror of the desolation in mine.

"It worked, too. I did things she wanted, but it also made me bury a lot of my feelings about you because I was terrified she was right. That I was wasting time feeling anything but friendship because I was never going to be right for you, and you already knew it."

This time Tate does stop the car, pulling us over to the shoulder. I peek at him for a second, and there are red blotches on his neck and cheeks, his jaw is clenched, and his nostrils are flaring. If it was possible for smoke to come out of his ears, it would've been. He looks down, not seeing anything, and forces himself to take deep breaths.

"Fuck your mom, Hal. And I can't lie, I'm a little fucking furious with you for never telling me before." He looks over at me from the corner of his eye, and another tear falls down my cheek as I nod in agreement. I gasp when I feel his hand on my cheek, wiping it away. "She's full of shit, you know that, right?"

"I do, but I don't think I realized until all of this quite how much damage she'd done. I was really good at burying and rejecting any feelings I had for you that went beyond friendship. It's a change I wasn't ready to hear or accept."

"So what can I do?" Tate asks as he steers the car back onto the road.

"Be patient with me. I have to rearrange my whole view of you, and of us. It's taking me a minute. I realized it's not that I don't trust you, it's that I don't trust myself. My own feelings. If you want to handle all the neediness, reassuring me is going to be a big part of it."

Tate nods, and we fall back into silence. It's not tense or bad, it's that Tate likes to think and process before saying anything.

"I got too excited about being able to touch you that I flew past the talking part. I should've wooed you, Hal, not just seduced you."

I laugh. "Are you going to woo me now, champ?"

He turns his head to meet my eyes for a moment. "Yeah. That's what I want to do over break. I got your body, I need your heart." Tate is so serious when he says it, and I know he means it, but it's still a little bit funny.

"Okay. I told myself that I was going to ignore everything except you and me. This is about us."

"Damn right." Tate reaches over the console and takes my hand. Warmth runs through me as the stress runs out. I'm still scared but I'm ready to push away my mom's bullshit to give Tate what he deserves, and the trust that he's earned.

Tate

The Bridgers are going to be lucky that I don't deck either of them in the face when we get to her house. They'll be lucky if I don't tell her mom off for being an absolute cunt at some point during the break. I knew she put pressure on Halle, but using me to do it is really fucking low.

I know a lot of that stopped toward the end of high school because I finally broke and told Grandpa Ray about some of it. That I was worried about Halle when she was getting morose and frighteningly fatalistic about getting into college and what she would major in. She was talking about the exciting new start of college like it was a death sentence, another way she was marching to her family's drum, and ignoring anything that was what she actually wanted.

I don't know what he said, but they backed off. It's how we ended up at Elmwood together instead of separated at different schools. I was lucky to get in, she was a guaranteed acceptance.

Our conversation turns to regular topics like debriefing our finals, other rumors we'd heard about the events of the Solstice party, and she updated me about the Founder's Ball. Everything was set, nothing needed to be done until the few days before when we'd back back up there to decorate.

We hold hands the entire drive. At some point she's holding mine in both of hers, absently playing with my fingers as we talk. It feels good, and natural. In another world, I made this happen a lot sooner. I told her what I was thinking and feeling instead of putting it off, instead of waiting thinking that there would be a sign it was time.

We're almost to her house, and I can feel her getting tense again.

"So, now what?" she asks. "How are you going to woo me?" I know she's teasing me for using that word, but there isn't a better one.

I bring her hand to my mouth and kiss it. "Get settled, call me. We'll do all our usual things, but I'm your boyfriend now. Touch me, talk to me, ask things of me."

She nods and turns away, thinking as I pull into her driveway.

"Movies?"

"Of course. Call me when you're unpacked."

After parking the car I get her bags out like usual, and then pull her into me for a hug. It feels different holding her knowing part of what was holding her back. My opinion of her mattered that much. Whether or not I wanted her was something that was used against her. She's never been anything but perfect to me, perfect for me, and I have to show her.

"Are you okay?" I ask but don't let her go.

"Yeah." She shifts her head to look up at me. When her eyes drop to my lips, hope cuts through me. After a moment of indecision, Halle pushes up on her toes and connects her lips to mine. I tilt my head to kiss her more deeply, reassuring her with my mouth that this is happening between us. I owe her the words too.

"You're beautiful, Halle. I remember the first time I thought that. We got caught in the rain at the far end of my yard, we were like, 10, maybe?"

Halle laughs but doesn't pull away from me. "When we got covered in mud and your housekeeper threatened our lives?"

"Exactly." I kiss her nose. "We were covered in mud and rain and when she yelled you laughed and put your arms out. I watched you spinning in a circle with your face to the sky and I thought that's my Halle, and she's the most beautiful girl in the world."

"Your Halle?"

"Are you going to pretend like that's not true?" I wrap a possessive hand around her ponytail and pull her head back a little. "Are you going to say you're not mine?"

Halle's face gets serious and the look she gives me hits me in the soul. "No. I'm yours."

I grin and kiss her again. "Call me when you're ready."

She pouts as she steps back from me, and I've never felt happier about it. I stand there and watch until her and her stuff disappear into the house.

Halle

As soon as I get inside, I charge upstairs to unpack. First to avoid mom, and second so that Tate and I can be together and keep talking about some of this stuff. I know he was still angry when he left, although no longer with me, and he needs a few minutes to blow that off so he'll behave when he comes over.

It doesn't seem like anything's been moved or hidden away this time, and I throw all my clothes where they belong, and then start getting out all my extra pillows and blankets so we can start our movie marathon, as well as dragging out the box of gift wrapping supplies I keep for myself. We usually spend tonight wrapping our gifts for our families, and then watch movies until we pass out.

Mom opens the door and walks into the room without knocking.

"Has Tate proposed yet?"

I still and look at her as if she's hit her head. "What?"

"You know what I'm talking about, the will request. Has he convinced you it's the right thing to do yet? I mean you can't expect him to stay with you forever but I think you owe him this."

My insides freeze, and I take a deep breath before turning to look at her and try and figure out this absurd conversation.

"It's the engagement that matters, but I think a wedding right after graduation will be fine. His parents are quite firm on following through with the wedding."

"Right." I agree with her and sit on the end of the bed.

"Imagine, Ray telling him he'll delay his trust until he's 40 unless he gets engaged to you," Mom turns to me with a sneer, her eyes lingering on my hips, then my stress bitten nails. "His little follower in the friend zone. I don't know what Ray was thinking, but I send a prayer of thanks up every day." She walks over to my closet and starts flipping through the clothes I brought home, judging each piece that she hasn't seen before.

I'm sitting stunned on the end of my bed and she hasn't noticed at all. Tate never mentioned any of this. He didn't say anything about the will other than that Grandpa Ray left him a note. A note that made him emotional, and also had his behavior toward me turning on a dime. I was wrong that this came from a craving for safety in a sea of grief, but right that this happened because of Ray's death.

The fissure working it's way through my heart is like fire. I can't breathe.

"Halle?" Mom finally notices that something is wrong. My hand thumps against my chest as I try to get my lungs to start working again. I see her feet come over and stop in front of mine.

"You didn't know?" Her voice is a whisper and I think she feels sorry for me, but when I meet her gaze there's something more like amusement there. "Did he tell you he had real feelings for you? That all this time he's wanted you?" She shakes her head, pity dripping from every pore. "Halle, really."

"I need to talk to Tate."

"You do, but to be clear, you will get engaged. You will marry him. That's not optional."

Without another word, she spins on her heel and leaves the room.

I'm so uncomfortable in my own body right now. I've been backed into a corner I never wanted to be backed into. Doing something because my family tells me I have to, choosing to give into their demands over doing what feels right to me, or giving up my dreams because they have something to hold over my head. I never thought Tate would be part of that, especially when he knows how I feel about this kind of stuff.

Why wouldn't he tell me? Why would Tate think it was the right thing to keep this from me?

In one short, brutal conversation with mom, everything that Tate has said for the last two months is tainted. Every time he promised me that his feelings were real is now thrown into doubt. I have to ask him about this. His response will tell me everything that I need to know. The knowledge of this has made it crystal clear to me: I'm in love with Tate. I've always been in love with Tate, and it might actually kill me if he doesn't feel the same. We will be ruined forever.

I send him a text that I'm ready to hang out. The truth is, I'm not ready for anything at all, but I have to finish this. I have to know.

 Tate

It only takes me a few minutes to unpack when I get home, and I go off in search of my parents. Dad should be home, not sure about mom. Christmas Eve will be with Halle's family, and Christmas Day is being held over here. Mom is probably out handling the last minute details and making sure it's all perfect even though it's a small amount of guests. Every occasion must be done with gusto. Sometimes Halle reminds me of my mom in that way, and it's one of the things I love about them both.

I find dad in the library. He looks up and gives me a tight smile when I come in.

"How did the semester end up?"

"Good, I think. Grades will be out in a few days."

Dad's eyes drop back and forth from the desk to me, nerves clear. "And things with Halle?"

"We're dating." It feels amazing to be able to say that. Officially.

The nerves on his face don't dissipate. "Does she know?"

It's my turn to feel nervous. "No."

"Tate," his voice is full of disappointment. "And suddenly you're going to ask her to marry you?"

I shake my head. "No. It was the push I needed to go after her, but I don't care about the request. You can't enforce it anyway, my trust doesn't actually change, but I get the thing I want most. I get her."

"I trust you're doing what you think is best."

My mouth is dry and I realize that my time is up to come clean about more than my feelings with Halle. Before we can talk any further, my phone buzzes and it's Halle telling me to come back over.

I say bye to dad and head straight to the car, ready to spend basically the next 18 hours wrapped up in her until we have to separate to get ready for Christmas Eve. I'm always going to remember this one especially, the one where I finally made Halle mine.

I'm grinning like an idiot when I walk into her house, and pull up short when her mom gives me a semi-manic smile as she walks through the front hall. The smile falls from my face and it takes everything I have not to tell her to fuck off. I can't fight Halle's battles for her, even if I was used as a weapon, but I can make my distaste clear.

"Tate!" She comes toward me and moves to hug me but I step back. She's never been a hugger, it's weird to start now. Something in her expression is off though, between annoyed and nervous, and I don't like it.

"Halle is waiting for you upstairs. I'm happy to hear you two are taking Ray's request seriously." My stomach drops to the fucking floor. Dad told them. Of course he did, Mr. Bridger is his best friend. It would also logically follow that he would then tell his wife, considering it involved their daughter. Knowing now all the pressure her mom put on her because of me, I'm sure Mrs. Bridger lost her mind with joy. I have to hope that she didn't drop this information as casually to Halle.

"Yeah." I put my hands in my pockets, still frowning, and don't say anything else as I move around her and head up the stairs. I feel as if I'm walking to my doom because there's no way Mrs. Bridger didn't throw this in Halle's face somehow. It's such a perfect, sharp weapon to wield that Halle will be bending to the will of our families, instead of what it really is: that I finally found the balls to tell her I love her.

Halle's voice is hollow when I knock on the door and walk in. Everything is set for our usual movie marathon around her room, except she's not bounding across the room to drag me to her bed, she's sitting on the end of it, looking at the floor.

"Did Ray's will demand that you and I get engaged?"

My chest cracks, my lungs empty, and I nearly drop to my knees. Fuck. Halle's voice is so empty, like the hurt is beyond what she can express, and

I don't blame her.

"Yes." There's no point in lying, even if there's more to it than that.

"Why didn't you tell me?" I can hear how hard she's trying not to cry.

"Because it didn't matter."

At that her head snaps up, gaze meeting mine, and oh god I didn't think I could hurt more for hurting her. I've never seen her look so devastated and furious. This time I do drop to my knees, kneeling in front of her.

"It's not enforceable."

Her brows furrow. "What?"

"It's not legal for him to demand I marry a specific person or I can't get my trust. I'll still get it when I'm 25 regardless of what the will said or if we're engaged."

"Then why would you do this?" Halle's face crumples. "Why?"

"I've been waiting for a sign that you were ready for things to change between us, and Ray left me a sign. That I was letting fear hold me back instead of showing you that you belong to me, with me, beside me." I take her hands in mine and feel relief when she lets me. "I have loved you in every possible way for my entire life. I've known I wanted to marry you since I was 15 years old and asked Ray if I could have my grandmother's ring when I proposed to you."

Tears stream down her face. "What?"

"He said yes. It's in a lock box in my bedroom, has been since then."

"I want to believe you. I want to be with you."

"Then believe me. Be with me." Tears are in my eyes now too but I don't let them fall. I feel like we're holding my heart between us and she could rip it apart right now with her next words.

"I'm scared." She squeezes my hands. "I literally can't live without you, and if this isn't real, if it doesn't work out..."

"That's the risk everyone takes, isn't it?" I take a deep breath. "Halle, do you love me?"

"Yes." She closes her eyes.

"Are you in love with me?"

Halle nods, and I reach up to wipe the tears off her face with the cuffs of my sweatshirt.

"That's all we need. You, me, love." I move closer to her, and she lets me kneel between her legs, and doesn't move away when I let her hands go and wrap my arms around her waist. She's so close, and so far.

"What can I do to prove it to you? Propose anyway, even though the deadline doesn't matter? Because I will."

Halle laughs and something loosens in me a little bit. "The opposite. I'll be with you, but I won't get engaged to you. That will happen on our timeline, if we're ready."

"When," I correct her. "You're mine."

"Make me yours," she whispers as her hands slide up my arms and then wrap around my neck. I yank her closer so I can't see anything but her face. Even tear-streaked, she's fucking gorgeous. The most beautiful woman I've ever seen. My woman.

"What do you mean, Hal?" I think I know exactly what she means, but I want to hear her say it. I want her to tell me.

"You're inside here," she puts a hand over her heart, then slides it down to grab my wrist. I watch as she drags my hand to her warm center. "You need to be inside here."

In seconds, I've got my hands wrapped around her thighs and I'm picking her up to throw her down on her bed. Pillows fall over all around us and I shove them away, attacking her mouth with mine. Halle writhes beneath me, rolling her hips to meet my instant erection, moaning when I press into her.

Both our hands are everywhere, tearing at clothes and desperate to get our hands on one another's skin. I love when she uses her hands and her feet to strip off my joggers and boxers, the way she squeezes my ass and digs her nails into me. The way she moans when I kiss across her collarbone after removing her shirt. Watching her grab her tits and pinch her own nipples when I slide off her bra.

I start to kiss down her stomach, heading for a taste of her when she stops me.

"I need you now, Tate. Don't play with me."

"Anything you want, Halle."

She moves away from me and opens the drawer in her bedside table. I see a flash of hot pink that we'll be exploring another time, but then she tosses me a condom. I sheath myself and crawl back over her. Bracketed by Halle's strong thighs, I tease my tip through her slick, wet pussy and she lifts her ass, trying to catch me. Begging with her body for me to fuck her.

"Kiss me," she begs, and I oblige. While our tongues are tangling together, she reaches between us and lines me up. I press inside her and groan into her mouth at how hot and tight she feels. Halle whimpers but holds my face to hers, kissing me as I stretch her pussy. When I'm fully inside her, I break away, looking down at her to make sure she's okay.

There's a red flush across her cheeks, her eyes are still wet with tears, but she's biting her lip like she's holding back. I've seen her do it when she's trying not to scream when she comes.

"Let go, baby." I whisper and then kiss her nose. "Let me in."

Halle nods and focuses her eyes on mine.

Halle

Tate is looking at me with so much love and intensity it makes my heart feel like it's stopped. He came here and didn't hold anything back. There'd been no intention for him to hurt me, and he owns that he did. Tate doesn't lie to me, this is the closest he's ever came.

I want this, I want him, and it feels like a huge weight lifted off my body to know that I don't have to bury or ignore my feelings anymore. I've mined my heart and unearthed what was so blatantly obvious for so long. Tate is part of my soul.

I roll my hips and love watching the arousal flash across his face. Tate has me by the nape with one hand, holding me close, unable to move, while the other has my hip in a hard, nearly bruising grip. The first glide of his hips, slowly dragging his cock out of me, is sinfully delicious. I brace for the hard thrust inside me and cry out when it comes.

Tate keeps an agonizingly slow pace, making me feel every inch of him drag in and out of me, working me up in a way I didn't know was possible. Even in my sex life I'm efficient, and like to get to the good parts. With Tate, I'm learning that the act itself is the good part. The pleasure moves across my body, building toward something incredible.

I reach down to grab his perfect ass, loving the feel of it flexing as he moves. My nails dig into the curve of his cheeks and he groans, dropping his forehead to mine.

"You want to mark me, baby? Go ahead." He starts to pick up the pace a little, and I drag my nails from his ass up his back and he thrusts into me so hard and deep that I gasp and see stars. "That's my girl."

"Tate," I moan, clenching around him as he starts fucking me harder and faster, teasing all the best places inside me.

"Mmm, yes, say my name, Halle. I've waited so fucking long to hear it." He grinds his hips at the apex of my thighs, putting pressure on my clit the way I like. Tate has played with me so thoroughly it doesn't surprise me he knows how to set me off during sex, even the first time.

"You're taking my cock like such a good girl, Hal, so damn pretty spreading your thighs open for me." Tate lifts from me but keeps his hand behind my head, tilting it up as he continues to move. "Look at us." My eyes drop to where his thick cock slides in and out of me, and I flex and and whimper at the sight. Tate's eyes drop shut for a second.

"You like watching us, huh? Seeing me own you. I always have, I always will. You're mine, Halle. Forever. There's no escaping this." My eyes flick up to his and the darkness inside them sends a thrill through me. "I've been waiting my whole life to have you." He groans again and collapses over me, dripping sweat onto my body as he fucks me faster. "I hope your pussy is ready baby, because I have so much time to make up for."

That does it. My back arches and I hold in a scream, holding my breath, as I start to come. My hips pump, meeting his thrust for thrust as he rides me through it. I gasp when he pinches one of my nipples, sending another ripple of pleasure through me.

When I come down, Tate backs off and flips me over, then yanks me up onto all fours. I feel spread open and exposed but in a way that makes me excited. I clench around nothing, dripping wet and needy still.

Tate grips and massages my ass cheeks, then spreads them apart before sliding back inside my pussy. I let out a moan and then shove my face into the comforter. The chances of anyone hearing us are low but not zero.

"Fuck, I love your ass." He starts to pump into me, and reaches around to massage my clit as he does. "Loving seeing it move as I fuck you. God if I could fuck you and bite it at the same time, I would." With another groan he pulls out of me and I cry out when I feel his teeth dig into the thick flesh. It hurts but I also really, really liked it. He sucks on the spot, dragging the skin deeper between his teeth. There's going to be a hickey on my ass and I love it.

"Tate," I whimper. "I love that, but please don't stop fucking me."

He lets me go with a growl. "I'll get the other cheek next time." Then he slams back inside me, slaps my pussy before returning to torturing my clit with his fingertips, and I come in three more thrusts. I scream into my blanket, slamming my body back into his as he relentlessly pounds into me.

"Soon I'm going to come in you bare, Halle."

I moan at that and his hips start moving in quick, jerky thrusts as he almost reaches the edge. If this hadn't been so impulsive and we'd talked about it, he probably could have gone bare. I've never not used a condom, but I love the idea of our bodies meeting in the raw, of feeling him dripping out of me.

"Give it to me, Tate. Please."

His hips thrust so hard against me it almost hurts as he groans and finds his release. We collapse onto the bed and I'm caged in his arms, his front surrounding my back as he holds me tight to him.

"I love you," I tell him, looking back over my shoulder as he lifts his head.

"I'll never let you stop. I'll never give you a reason to."

"I trust you." Tate's eyes light up and the last of the tension he was carrying around about this dissipates. I do trust him. More than anything, or anyone. This is where I was always meant to be, and how we were always meant to be. I let fear and stupidity get in the way of that. The only person who has no motive other than to love me is him, I know that now.

Halle

Tate tortured me by not staying over, and leaving me with nothing but a soft lingering kiss. By the time his family arrives for dinner, I'm wound up and impatient. Now that I don't have to hold back, it feels like I'm honestly unable to.

As soon as he walks into the front hall, I'm on him, leaping into his arms and wrapping my legs around his waist. We hadn't really talked about how we were going to tell our families but I guess they'll know now.

"Hey, baby," Tate whispers into my neck and sends shivers straight to my pussy.

"Hi, champ." I lean back and kiss him, squeezing him with everything I have. "I missed you. You're staying tonight."

"Yes, ma'am." He would even without my demand, it's another one of our traditions. Has been since we were 6 and were first starting to doubt the existence of Santa Claus. Our parents agreed we could stay together and stay up late, waiting for the bearded man in the red suit. We stayed at the Daniels house in a nest of pillows and blankets in the back family living room with their personal Christmas tree. Right in front of the fire. I remember falling asleep holding Tate's hand as we guessed what our presents might be.

We never saw Santa, and Tate's cousin officially ruined it for us the next year, but it became something we did every Christmas Eve.

A throat clearing has us both turning our heads to see everyone we've ignored for the last few minutes. Both our parents and my grandparents.

His parents look amused, my grandmother looks slightly appalled at the excessive display of affection, and my mother looks like she swallowed a lemon.

"Do you have something to tell us, kids?" Mr. Daniels asks.

"We're dating," Tate answers. "And no, we're not getting engaged."

Mom gasps, horrified. "But - your trust, Tate."

Mr. Daniels snorts. "You know nothing about estate law, do you Miriam? It's unenforceable. Engagement or not, he gets his trust at 25."

"Oh," she frowns. "Then why are you dating?"

I stiffen and Tate pats my leg. I slide down and stand next to him, comforted by his arm around me. The furious determination on his face should scare me, but I also know he'd never put me in a position to make things worse between mom and me.

"Because she's the best, most beautiful person I know, and I can't live without her anymore."

"Tate," I nearly whimper at how sweet that is. He turns to look at me and a blush creeps over my cheeks and down my neck.

"I'm going to marry her," he's looking at me but saying it to them. "But when we want. Not on anyone else's timeline."

"That's great, kids," my dad steps forward and shakes Tate's hand. "You know you're already family to us." He claps his hands together and looks around, trying to dissipate the lingering awkwardness of mom's bitchiness. "Let's have drinks before the hors d'oeuvres are out."

We start to walk toward the lounge but mom stops me with a touch to my wrist.

"Nice job, Halle."

"As politely as possible, fuck off, mom." She gasps and puts a hand to her chest. "This isn't a trick or a trap or a strategic move. Just be a human being and be happy for me."

I walk away before she can say anything else, and when I look over my shoulder, her and dad are talking close and quiet. I'm oddly pleased that she looks upset because I'm finally letting her see the consequences of her actions and comments. How much she's pushed me away and hurt me over the years. I love her because she's my mom, but I need to let go of getting her approval.

Tate and I are inseparable during the cocktail hour, and while we're eating dinner he keeps reaching over to touch me. Everything is driving me crazy. I'm squirming in my chair and nearly panting for him.

Dad excuses us from the table. The adults usually wander off to talk and keep drinking, and Tate and I retreat to watch movies and eat way too many cookies. We're walking down the dark hall toward the back off the house, and I yank him into a corner.

Tate crowds me against the wall, meeting my demand immediately. He kisses me, tongue wet and filthy against my own. My hips press into his and in seconds he has his hand up my skirt, sliding my panties to the side, and his fingers against my wet, desperate pussy.

"You need me, Hal?"

"Desperately," I murmur against his mouth.

"Better be quiet. I'll take the edge off until I can fuck you later."

I moan and he swallows it with his mouth and starts working me with his fingers. Two slide inside me, pressing hard and deep at my front wall as his thumb presses and circles my clit. My hips thrust as I work myself on him, desperate to come for him.

"That's my girl," he lets me go and whispers to me. "Come and give me something to eat later." I squeeze his fingers and he knows I'm close because he slides his tongue into my mouth and swirls it with mine, and the sensual feel of it sends me over the edge. I hold my breath but still let out a small cry, muffled by his kiss. Tate slides his fingers out of me but slides them along my sex, helping me ride out the last ripples of pleasure.

I watch in a daze as he sucks his fingers and closes his eyes in ecstasy. It gets me worked up all over again, but he shakes his head at me.

"Movies. Come on." I follow him to the living room and we snuggle up on the couch to watch *Elf*.

"What did your mom say?" he asks as he runs his fingers through my hair, causing tingles to cover my scalp and body.

"She said nice job. Like you were a fish I caught, or a con I pulled."

"I'm sorry, Hal. I'm so fucking sorry."

"It's not your fault," I turn into his hand and let him cup my cheek. "I'm not letting her taint us anymore."

"Good." Tate pulls me against him so my head is resting on his chest, right where I like it.

"I love you," I murmur into his sweater.

"You better," he answers, and focuses on the movie.

I've never been happier.

Tate

3 Weeks Later

"They're going to be looking for me," Halle moans, her voice is breathy and desperate.

"You can't wear a dress like this and not expect me to fuck you in it," I groan, pounding into her from behind. The dress in question is on the floor in a pool of blue satin, leaving her in a lacy bra and thong. I've got the thong pulled to the side and I groan again as I watch my cock sink inside her wet pussy.

"Better come quick, baby," I push her. "They might catch us otherwise."

"Fuck," she whimpers, and her pussy clenches. I think she's got a bit of an exhibitionist hidden in there. "Please."

"Come quick and milk my cock. I want to know you're walking around all night with me dripping down those delicious thighs." For good measure, I slap her ass, and she squeezes me again. I groan, holding back as best I can even though this is the hottest thing I've ever done, and it's so much hotter because it's with her.

We're in a closet in the hall near the ballroom. The Founder's Ball is in full swing, and in a few minutes she's going to be introducing the MC for the night who will convince people to give us their money and further fund Elmwood.

"You're so fucking beautiful, Halle. A vision. Look at what you did tonight, how perfect it is, how much you accomplished," I praise her. "Come for me baby."

"Tate," she lets out a strangled scream and comes hard, pulling my cock in with her walls and triggering my orgasm. I groan as I pound into her hard and deep, filling her with my come. We're both breathing hard as we come down. I slide out of her and put my dick away, enjoying the fact that it's sticky with our come. I'll make her suck it off later.

I move Halle's thong back into place, already deciding that I'm going to steal it when I peel it off her before fucking her later. It's going to smell like heaven after she walks around in it all night, dripping come.

She straightens up and stretches, giving me a fantastic view of her body. Halle steps back into her dress and pulls it up and I do the hidden side zipper for her. It's something she called a mermaid dress – it's fitted to her curvaceous silhouette until the knee when it flares out in a puff of material. It's an icy blue color that makes her skin glow.

I take her hand. "You really are perfect, and I really am proud of you."

She wraps her arms around my neck and stands on her toes to kiss my nose. "You helped me so much. You always have my back. Thank you."

"Always, Hal. I love you."

"Love you, champ."

With that, we sneak out of the closet and back to the ball. It's crowded but everyone seems to be having a good time. The tables are filled, the food is moving, the decorations are out of this world. Halle went with a winter space theme – there's fake glittery snow, drifts of material across the ceiling and along the walls, then it's dotted with stars, as well as huge printouts of the sky on the walls and ceiling peeking through that makes it look like we're floating in space. It's ethereal.

Halle gets up on stage and introduces this year's MC, who immediately congratulates her on a gorgeous ball. The room thunders with cheers and applause, and she's blushing fiercely when she steps off the small stage and takes my hand. I guide her over to our table where our friends are sitting.

Colin and Elise are deep in conversation with Rome and his girlfriend Cyn. Colin vouched for Rome, and Cyn is Elise's roommate, so it was a no brainer to have them at our table with us. Despite Rome's dark and broody reputation, he actually has a sharp sense of humor. The girls are conspiring for a triple date already.

"This is awesome," Elise compliments Halle as soon as we sit down. "I want to throw this someday."

"Get into the Castle and I'll put in a good word for you," Halle teases. We all know there's no question about Elise getting in.

When the music starts, I pull Halle out onto the floor and behave myself as we dance.

"I think you've got Steward of the Castle on lock," I murmur against her ear. Not too far from us, Gwen is dancing with a donor, talking his ear off. She gives us both a nod.

"I better," Halle grumbles. "Gwen won the pool. She owes me."

I laugh. "You didn't tell me that."

"Yeah. She had the end of fall junior year that we'd finally crack. Gwen even had by Christmas. Got it to the damn day."

"Wouldn't change a thing," I lean back and kiss her.

Halle smiles at me, her face lit up with true happiness. There's so much stress and tension that's melted away for both of us since we've been together. Our lives fell into place and shifted as easily as we thought, but the effects it's had on us are more powerful than we imagined. The energy we spent keeping it platonic is now spent on better things, and we have each other, always.

Halle

Weeks Later

Tate is up to something. He went home for the weekend without me, which was as miserable as I expected even if I did get ahead on homework without him around to distract me, and I had a girl's night with a few of my friends from the Castle and had Elise and her friends join us. I like all of them, and I feel such immense gratitude that I ended up at Elmwood because of who I've found here and who it's help me become.

That it was the safe space that Tate and I needed to figure out our shit and finally be together. It's been amazing. Everything has changed, and yet so much of it is the same. The sense of possession I feel over him, and that I know he feels over me, gives the things we've always done for each other more meaning than before. I take care of him, he takes care of me, and I feel like I can do anything.

I'm going to be the next Steward of the Castle, and Gwen and I have already started working on recruitment. The Founder's Ball raised millions, which is to be expected, but we continue to get compliments and requests for information about our vendors and planning. I couldn't have done it without Tate.

It's really cold today, and the groundhog did see his shadow, so we've got 6 more weeks of winter ahead at least. Before Elmwood, I wasn't superstitious, but the more time around the magic, traditions, rituals, and idiosyncrasies of this place and it can turn even the most skeptical person into a believer. Rome Dwyer is perfect proof. The Dark One has become one of mine and Tate's closest friends in the last few weeks, much to all of our surprise. He's the most grounded, logical, scientific person I've ever met and even he's a believer when it comes to Elmwood.

Tate had Rome deliver me a note that told me to meet him at the campus greenhouses, which are on top of the science building. I'm not sure why he couldn't send a text, but when I asked Rome, he just shrugged and told me to follow instructions.

Knowing that Tate is a fan of surprise dates, I wear tights and a black dress, even if I go with practical flat ankle boots because it's icy as hell right now. The damp, earthy smell of the greenhouses reaches me even through the cold air.

Of the four that are up there, the door to one is propped open a little so I head toward it.

It's a hothouse for flowers and I am greeted by a riot of color. Tate's sitting on a bench in the back, wearing a black button up so I'm glad I dressed nice. When he hears me he looks over his shoulder and smiles.

I walk along the soft dirt covered spaces between flowerbeds to get to him. He pats his thigh and I perch on his lap, something I'm not entirely comfortable with yet but know that he loves. Tate wraps his arms around my waist and tugs me closer, pressing a soft kiss to my neck where it's exposed by my coat.

"The deadline passed yesterday."

I freeze for a moment, and then force myself to relax. "How do you feel about that?"

Tate shrugs. "It's irrelevant. But I needed you to know that. I need to tell you that I don't think I let anyone down. All Grandpa wanted was for me to finally tell you that I love you, so request complete. I told you. I have you."

"Yeah you do, champ." I kiss his nose. "So are we celebrating?"

"Sure," he grins at me, but it's a little tight. Something is still going on in his head. "But first I want to give you something."

"Tate," I groan. He's constantly giving me things, surprising me with anything from candy to clothes to office supplies because it makes him think of me, or he knows it'll make me happy. Tate was always a stellar gift giver but I learned he was really holding back when it came to me. It's like his brain is my Pinterest board because he always knows what to get me, even when I don't realize I wanted it.

Tate takes a small velvet box out of his pocket.

"What are you doing?" My voice is a breathy whisper.

"The deadline is done. I'm going to give you this because I want to," his voice is quiet and his gaze is reverent. I can't look away. He's more vulnerable and soft than I've ever seen him. "It seems fast, but it's not, not when you think about us. I will love you for the rest of my life and I've always known I was going to marry you, so this is me asking, and if you say no, I'm going to force you into it somehow."

Tate reaches up and tucks my hair behind me ear and I inhale sharply, so mesmerized by him that the touch catches me off guard.

"Halle Bridger, will you marry me?"

I take the box from him and open it. Inside is a platinum ring with an emerald cut diamond, and smaller diamonds on the side. It's classy and Art Deco, and I love it immediately.

"Is this the ring Ray gave you?"

"Yeah," Tate nods, swallowing thickly. "Do you like it?"

"I love it." I take the ring from the box and hand it to him. "I love you. I've always loved you. I will always love you. There's no choice for me except to marry you."

"Damn right." Tate kisses me as he slides the ring onto my finger. It fits perfectly.

Tate

A year and a few months later...

Halle walks into my bedroom and throws a giant binder at me. Papers go flying everywhere, spreading across the bed and cascading onto the floor. When I pick one up, I see a checklist for what appears to be wedding things, at the bottom it indicates that this is page 3 of 7.

"I can't put them off anymore. Our mothers have descended and are demanding decisions."

"What do we need to decide?"

"Everything, and then they don't listen to me anyway." Halle swipes all the papers off the bed and then crawls up it to straddle me where I sit against the headboard. I pause my game and toss the controller away, wrapping my arms around her and pulling her close.

"I hate this."

"Marrying me?" I tease her.

She slaps my chest. "Having a wedding." Halle flops her face into my chest and I hold her and rub her back, feeling the tension in her body. We've been graduated for a few weeks and I have noticed that the moms keep cornering her, and asking both of us pointed questions about setting a date. While I promised Halle I'd be involved, they don't seem to share that same sentiment, and keep springing things on her when I'm not around.

I don't want to get to our day and have her be so stressed out from planning and organizing that she doesn't get to enjoy it. That we don't get to celebrate committing to each other. I don't want her to be so exhausted it's a chore to get through. Halle is a planner and an organizer;

for something like this she would never give it anything less than her all, even if it runs her ragged.

That's not what I want for her, or for us.

"Let's elope."

Halle sits up quickly, looking at me like I'm crazy. "What?"

"Let's run off and get married. Fuck them and their social event of the season shit. That's not us, it never will be, and I don't care what they say or what they want. I want you, I want you happy, and I want you to be so hopped up on how much you love me that we'll fuck for about 8-10 hours straight."

Halle wiggles against me and I start to get hard. "How? When? Where?"

"As soon as possible. We have our wedding rings, and we're rich. Let's grab our friends and go."

"Go where?" She's totally with me on this, and I love the glee on her face. That's what I want to see when we're talking about our wedding.

"Elmwood. Duh."

Her face breaks out into a huge grin but her eyes are glassy with tears. "I can't tell you how much I want this."

"Then lets do it. Friday. We can get a license today, we have to wait 24 hours per the law, and then we can get married. Everyone is up there except Colin, and we can grab him on the way."

"Yes." Halle grabs my face and kisses me hard. I try to take it deeper but she pushes off my chest. "Stop it. Start making calls." I grin as she climbs off of me, grabs her phone, and gets to work.

I'm standing in a clearing in the hedge maze dominated by a Cupid statue. It was Elise's idea for us to use this one, and while it's on the nose, it's also beautiful. The flowers in this part of the maze are roses in a riot of colors, and since we're all wearing white we contrast well against the dark green hedge and the deeply hued flora.

Colin and Rome are standing with me in one corner, and Gwen is our officiant. We're waiting for Elise and Cyn to walk Halle to me. These are our witnesses, our best friends, and the people who know us for exactly who we are, individually and as a couple. Better than our families ever could.

The parents suspected nothing, although I did tell Halle's grandfather. I think Grandpa Ray would want him to know, and I think he'll help with the fallout of what we're about to do. He seemed entertained, and that's a good sign. Cyn even found us a photographer, one of their friends, to document the event so the moms can run with the "elegant, intimate ceremony" line instead. Except that's exactly what this is, and feels exactly right for us.

When the girls come around the corner and I get my first glimpse of Halle, I breathe in sharply. She's wearing a simple white dress that clings to her figure and swirls around her feet as she walks. The smile on her face etches itself into my heart because she looks so incandescently happy, and I vow to myself that I'll try and keep her feeling that way every day. No matter how hard, no matter what we struggle with, at the end of the day that smile is for me and I'm taking responsibility for it.

I reach for her hand when she's close enough, and our friends stand at our sides as Gwen marries us.

Something slides into place within me, like the reality and the security of this moment are the final piece. Halle is my best friend, the love of my life, and with the pronouncement that I can kiss her - she's my wife.

BEGUILED

Maeve

My Maeve,

Do you know what it's like to desire something you can't have? The idea that I will never touch you or tell you how I feel because you belong to someone else drives me into darkness. I see you and I smile. I miss you even when I'm with you, not that you'd know it. This is all I can give you. All you can give me.

–P.C.

The first email came a month into my first year at Elmwood. An anonymous email, signed with initials that aren't familiar to me. I came here with a mission and a plan, and one stupid, wayward email distracted me.

I was supposed to get here, work hard at my classes, do my volunteer time with the admissions office to get myself recruited to the Magistrates, and have a little bit of restrained fun until I graduate and have to get married. To someone whose name I'm not allowed to know because of an agreement signed when I was born that put restrictions on my life.

It's fucking weird when at 13 your mom sits you down and explains that not only has your husband already been chosen for you, but you have to remain a virgin for him, or the deal is off. It clearly pained her to tell me and I know my father felt weird about it, and the fact that they apologized about the agreement all the time is probably the only reason I followed through on it all. That I kept myself pure for an unknown man who was likely out there being a whore. But I was told it would end a feud, and I liked peace.

Another email came when I didn't respond.

My intoxicating one,

Please. This is all I can have of you. My mouth waters at the thought of tasting you. My nails bite into my palms because I have to curl my hands into fists to stop myself from touching you. Give me something. Anything.

–P.C.

It was flattering, I can't lie. So I wrote back. At first, I wrote back with facts about animals because it was something silly and innocuous. Except they responded and the conversations evolved until we were talking about our days, our dreams, what we were doing or watching. Based on their responses, I knew they were another Elmwood student. Someone who knew me, but wouldn't reveal themselves. They flirted and I tentatively started to flirt back.

Some of the emails we sent were outright sexual, and I shared things with them that I never thought I'd put in writing. About the things I watched, the ways I touched myself. The way I feared being with a person who didn't care about my pleasure so I made sure I learned how to get it for myself.

We emailed when classes frustrated us, when grades got us down, when professors annoyed us. I had a safe person to talk to who never judged me for anything. I was falling hard for someone I knew almost nothing about it, while simultaneously knowing everything.

It wasn't breaking any rules. My heart was my own even if my body wasn't.

I knew they loved pistachio flavored anything, that they like gray, the ocean, had a fascination with pumas as a child, and their favorite superhero was the Flash. I knew they didn't like spiders and that the old buildings on campus meant constant confrontations with them. I knew what movies they had seen and loved and hated, what TV shows they quoted (*New Girl*. Often.) They knew the same things about me.

P.C.

Tell me something true.

–M

My Maeve,

I'm half in love with you. Every time I see the notification that I got an email from you, it lights me up inside. I wish...

-P.C.

I wish, too. The emails continue all through the fall semester. I tell them about my friends, my family, we talk about my marriage agreement like it's not the only thing standing in between us. In a weird way, they actually reassure me that I'm doing the right thing. For some reason, that hurts, but I also know they are right.

Long before I was born, there was a fire. It's kind of family legend more than truth at this point but we all grow up knowing the story. There was a group of families that were working together to build an empire, one of them being mine, the Keans. They were doing well, and had been for a generation. The bonds between them were tight, some formal through contracts, and some through marriages.

No one really knows what happened, but one night they were meeting in a hotel. It was the patriarchs and their heirs, everyone who mattered in one place at one time. The fire started, the hotel burned, and not everyone made it out. The families lost either a patriarch or an heir, the leaders of their business, and one family lost both. It was devastating.

It hurt the company but it didn't go under.

For reasons no one will explain, the Keans were blamed. My great, great grandfather, who died in the fire, was the one who picked that location. Therefore, it was our fault.

Over the years, peace and settlements had been made with all of the families except one. The history is intentionally obscured by previous generations. Even my father wasn't really aware of where things were at and what was happening until a lawyer showed up shortly after I was born.

The last act of peace was a marriage.

The agreement was apparently ironclad, and heavily on the side of the other family.

My father knows who they are now, and has put all the pieces together, probably like his father did and his father before him as every generation promised something in order to make amends for a loss from a hundred years ago. He won't tell me a thing, and I get it. I do.

In the age of technology, I'd find my future husband in minutes. I'd know everything about him before meeting him. I'd have preconceived notions and biases, I'd think I knew him without ever giving him a chance. Father has been very adamant that when the time comes, I give him a chance.

I know it's the right thing to do. It's the last one left before my family can leave the painful past back where it belongs. I'm ending something, and I know the value of that.

Just before we leave for break, P.C. changes the game.

My Maeve,

Give me one night. Take this one thing for yourself. Please.

-P.C.

P.C.

If I know who you are, I'll never be able to let go. I can't.

-Maeve

My intoxicating one,

I'll wear a mask. Meet me at the Founder's Ball. I'll be wearing a black suit and this. *photo*

-P.C.

It's a picture of a black mask with black and silver glitter on it, fitting the space and stars theme of the ball. It would cover all of someone's face except their eyes and their mouth. The appearance should be threatening, but instead it feels protective. The hand holding the mask is masculine, the nails broad and cut short. It seems to confirm my theory that my secret admirer is a guy, in addition to the detail that they'll be wearing a suit. That one could go either way though.

I want to meet them, regardless. I need to meet them. For closure, if nothing else. If only to end things.

P.C.

I'll be there, but I'm not promising anything more than a dance with you.

-Maeve.

My Maeve, my one, my queen,

It's enough.

–P.C.

 Maeve

I'd been nervous since winter break. It made for a very subdued holiday, especially when my parents told me that over spring break I'd finally be meeting my future husband. As if my anxiety wasn't already staggeringly high. Change was hurtling toward me and I was desperate to grab for any sort of control.

I almost didn't go to the Founder's Ball. I almost backed out.

But all my friends were going, and it would look good to the Magistrates. I knew I was a solid recruit, especially since I'd already started to get invites to their events, but in my mind there was never enough. There were only so many things in my life that were my choice, especially now, and taking advantage of everything I could at Elmwood was one of them.

When I was here, I was safe. On campus I could get lost in the library, wander the campus paths, dip into the woods and disappear. I could find a hidden nook or cranny to read, or sit with my thoughts. I knew the history of our campus. I loved it.

It's why working in admissions and doing tours and recruiting was such a perfect fit. I was a third generation Elmwood student. This was my happy place.

So the Founder's Ball felt safe, even if I was anything but.

I'd found a dress that matched their mask. It was strapless black glitter, clung to my curvy body, and went all the way to the floor. If I walked right I looked like I was gliding or floating rather than taking a step.

I was waiting on an outside edge of the dancing when I felt heat at my back.

"My Maeve, you came." The voice was male and deep, and I could tell he was changing it to talk to me, in case I recognized it. Another sign that I knew this person, and knew them well enough that I might recognize their voice.

I turned around and had to tilt my head up slightly to meet his eyes through his mask. They were startling in their darkness, but I didn't mind. Their depth caused a shiver through my whole body. He was tall and fit but not broad or overly-muscular with dark hair. The suit fit like it was made for him and it probably was. My eyes lingered on his mouth because I couldn't help it - I had wondered about it too much. His lips were pillowy and dark pink. They looked well-bitten and I wanted to bite them too.

He groaned. "Don't look at me like that, I'm trying to be good."

I stepped closer. "I don't want to be totally good."

One side of his mouth lifted in a smirk. "Whatever you want, my queen. But first, dance with me."

We stepped out onto the dance floor and I braced myself for the heat of his touch. He pulled me close, our bodies lining up perfectly, his hand on my lower back pressing me close to him. He moved and I followed, trusting him to guide us without hitting anyone, even though we never took our eyes off each other.

I couldn't deny that I was attracted to him. Devastatingly. Catastrophically. In a way that should have had me running from the ball like Cinderella at midnight because whatever happened tonight was going to mark me for life. I would always know that this kind of electricity existed with someone out there that I couldn't have.

I'd crave the way my body felt when he touched me, even innocently, for the rest of my life.

"You feel it too," he asked. I could only nod. He pulled me closer until we were cheek to cheek so he could whisper in my ear. "I want you. I want to know that someday when you're trapped, you'll have this to remember. I want to know that no matter what happens, you took this one thing for yourself."

I couldn't breathe. I pulled back so I could look at him. There's something tortured in his eyes, and I wouldn't have doubted that it's the same look that I had in mine. Misery and desire.

"Okay."

"Okay?" That one-sided, small smile came again. It made me wonder what he was keeping from me and if telling me would have revealed his identity. We recognized the struggle inside one another and it was clear there was something he was using this for too. I didn't doubt his attraction to me, but there was more on his mind and I'm his escape. I wanted to be his escape.

"Okay," I said again. "I want you. I want something for myself."

"Good." He got a hard look in his eyes and guided me out of the ball and into the hallway. He looked around for a second and then took off, looking back and forth until he found a small room around a corner. It was empty except for some wayward furniture.

As soon as the door closed, he took my face and kissed me. It was a hard, desperate kiss but I parted my lips for him and moaned at the taste and feel of his tongue on mine. I leaned back on the door and let myself be devoured as I ran my hands over his body.

I palmed his erection through his pants and he pressed into me, desperate and groaning into my mouth. I didn't want to wait anymore or I might back out. I wanted him and I wanted him now.

I pushed him away and moved to lay on a small couch in the room. He followed and knelt next to it, sliding up my dress and exposing my body to him. I was curvy but I was fit. I'd played sports all through high school and still worked out. I had the thighs and ass to prove it.

He groaned again as he exposed the small black thong I was wearing.

"So fucking gorgeous."

I shivered as he teased his hand along my thigh until he cupped my core, then teased and aroused me through my panties. I was already soaked, and the material slid over me easily.

"Promise to keep your eyes closed?"

"What?"

"If this is the only time I get to have you, I have to taste you, my queen.

Let me worship you on my knees with my mouth."

"I promise," I answered, and started sliding off my thong. He growled and ripped it down my legs, the string on one side snapping and breaking off. I squeezed my eyes shut and let my head fall back, and a second later I felt the wet warmth of his tongue on me. He knew I'd never done anything other than kiss before. All my other firsts were going to be his.

I cried out when he slid his fingers inside me and moved as he tried to find the places inside me that felt good. It all felt good. It all felt amazing as he sucked and licked my clit, as he made me feel full in a way I'd never felt before. He hummed against my sex, the vibrations starting a chain reaction I couldn't stop. My hips pumped up into his face and he held on as I rode him through the best orgasm I'd ever had.

I kept my eyes closed even as he slid his fingers out of me and pressed a soft kiss to my pussy. I heard him slide his mask back on.

He cupped my face and I smelled myself on his skin. I loved it.

"Look at me."

I opened my eyes. His were somehow even darker. Lust had caused them to dilate to almost full black.

"Do you want this?"

"I want you," I nodded. "Please."

He looked conflicted for so long that I thought he was going to stop us.

Then he knelt between my still spread legs and I watched as he unzipped himself and reached inside for his cock. Before I could see it, he leaned over me, my gaze trapped in his. I felt the heat of his head push against my entrance, and gasped as he slid inside me.

He watched for every reaction, slowing and moving based on my face, until he was pressed right up against me. I wasn't a virgin anymore. I was so fucked, in so many ways. I had taken this for myself and with the way he was looking at me, I couldn't regret it.

"My Maeve," he grumbled before leaning forward to kiss me, and then he started to move. It felt incredible, and I could do nothing but hold on for the ride as he pounded my body in a way that loved it. Every inch of my skin was singing as he fucked me on this random couch in a random room, hidden away from a party we were supposed to be attending. Doing something that could ruin my whole future.

"Shit," he paused. "Condom."

"No," I grabbed his ass and stopped him from moving away. "I'm on birth control."

"You trust me that much?" he sounded honestly bewildered. I shrugged, and he didn't seem to like that answer.

I gasped when he pulled out of me, and breathed hard as he shuffled around. I heard the tearing of a package and his sigh. Then he was over me again and I got lost in his eyes. He kissed me and slid inside me and I was nothing but feelings and sensations again.

He let my mouth go and pulled away so he could slide a hand between us. I felt the graze of his rough fingers as he played with my clit.

"Please," he begged. "I want to feel it. I can't come until I feel you."

It was so desperate and needy, and I loved that he was feeling that way too. I moved my hips, meeting his thrusts, grinding my clit into his fingers, until I felt my insides start to flutter and clench. I cried out as I came, squeezing his cock and feeling something entirely new and powerful. An orgasm when I had something to grip was an incredible experience. I squeezed him with my inner muscles and it increased my pleasure.

"Fuck," he grunted before burying his masked face against my neck, the glitter scratching my skin, and he pounded deep as he came.

We stayed like that for a long time. Mostly dressed, thoroughly fucked, both feeling a sense of impending doom.

After a moment he moved off of me. He looked around the room for a second and on a shelf he found a box of napkins. I watched as he wiped away the mess between my legs and didn't miss the smear of blood there either.

"Thank you," he said, his voice weary. I sat up and adjusted myself, knowing that my panties were a lost cause, and I couldn't even find them.

"For what?" I asked.

"Giving me a night. Giving me you."

We both stood up and fixed our clothes. Time stood still when we looked at each other, and I ached in my chest knowing that this was all I'd get.

"Come here." He pulled me to him and kissed me. He kissed me and kissed me as tears fell down my cheeks, as his breath stuttered when he tried to stop, until my phone started buzzing in my purse because people were looking for me.

"My Maeve," he whispered reverently against my mouth.

I swallowed a sob, and left the room.

 Bennett

Maeve left me in the closet, and I felt like the world's biggest asshole. I had lied to her, manipulated her, and now it was my job to humiliate her. I would have to break that girl over a feud neither of us had been alive for, to get money neither of us cared about.

I was supposed to marry her.

I'd known it for years. I was told her name when I turned 16 so I could familiarize myself with my bride and her family. Before I'd ever sent her a single email, I knew more about her than she could imagine. It had been a borderline obsession for years. My obsession was encouraged, even, as it would make things easier when we had to take the final commitment.

When my grandfather died, it all changed.

Dad didn't want the settlement. For some reason, he took blaming the Keans personally, and he wanted the contract broken. He wanted to get more from them and marrying Maeve Kean didn't get us more. He saw it as the Silars backing down from what we were owed, instead of putting the past to rest.

The contract was only void in two circumstances: Maeve's death, or if she had sex prior to her marriage. If Maeve died, it would be another generation's problem. While my dad is an asshole, he's not a complete monster, and he wanted it broken, not put off. He wasn't going to murder her.

Instead, he went the path of seduction. I wasn't even the first person he put in my future wife's path, but she resisted them all. Maeve was genuinely disinterested and clung to the contract. There was a lot of physical fun that could be had other than sex, but other than one of his hires getting her to kiss him, she'd never engaged. Never even been tempted.

They didn't know her.

His plan really started moving when he found out both of us would be going to Elmwood. That's when the seduction of Maeve Kean became my duty. I would seduce and fuck my future wife and when I had the evidence of it, I could show that she was a "morally weak" woman and break the contract. Our family was getting millions in the marriage deal, but we'd get millions more in the event of the contract being voided by her actions. That's what dad wanted. More of their money.

Not like we needed it, but greed grows greed.

She walked right into my life. So damn easy.

It was odd at first to get used to this girl I knew from photos on my phone suddenly being around me. In one of my classes. Working together. Living in the same building as me. I learned her in a way I hadn't been able to before, and everything I needed to know to capture her revealed itself to me. I was in her life and she didn't even know it.

I seduced her mind until she was so gone over me it was easy for her to give me her body.

Tonight had been hazardous to my sanity. While I didn't want to marry someone I didn't choose, I couldn't deny that I was attracted to Maeve. She was sassy and smart, and her body was one I'd have jerked off to regardless because she was sexy as hell. I'd seen her doing squats in the gym once and I got so mesmerized by her ass I had to leave.

Kissing her was dangerous. The sex had been incredible. I don't think I'd ever come as hard as I did while inside her. In a weird way, she was mine. She'd always be mine, no matter what happened with the contract.

It was all so fucked.

I moved around the small room that I'd set up for this moment. I'd made sure that couch was there and placed just so, right in the view of the small camera I'd hidden in the shelves across from it. I took my small stash of hidden supplies and collected my evidence: the camera, her panties, and the napkin with her blood on it.

I looked at her panties that were still damp with her arousal and I could smell them. The scent mixed with the knowledge of what this would do made me sick, and I barely held myself back from vomiting. I gathered my things, changed my clothes, and left the ball.

I got drunk in my room, hating myself, at war with what was right for my family and what was just...right. I couldn't help but think that I was utterly in the wrong.

Maeve

Spring semester is a fresh start. New classes, new school supplies, new goals to make and achievements to check off the list. Priority number one, still: getting recruited to join the Magistrates.

While I have zero interest in student government, I do love rules and organization, and I love the idea of shaping what future classes of Elmwood students are like. It made working for the admissions office my dream job. I got to sell people on why they should come here.

Recruiting at Elmwood isn't like recruitment anywhere else. It's a much more intensive process before you even fill out an application. People can't just call and schedule a tour at Elmwood, they have to apply. They put in a request along with information they feel makes them a viable candidate, and then they get approved or not. We also send out invites to prospective applicants that meet our criteria, and pre-approve them for a tour.

Anyone that gets approved gets to schedule a tour. We try not to do tours in groups but with individuals, to address their individual needs and questions. It's one of my favorite parts of the job. I get to walk someone all over campus and instead of generic information that's a sales pitch, I get to have a straightforward discussion with them about what they're looking for and how they can achieve it at our elite, but amazing, institution.

In between classes and studying, I'm at the admissions office. I can't help it.

It's located in this tiny wonky brick building that used to be the on-campus post office. It's got columns in the front and a banner with our school name stretched across the front. It's a warren of little offices and cubbies, of random swag that we give out to prospective students, and its own small computer lab for us to review candidate applications.

Most days it's perfect.

Then there are days like today.

"Oh, be still my heart, my purple princess is with me today." Bennett Silar clasps his hands over his heart and pretends to swoon. I want to punch him in the face. I have dark hair and for the last few years I've added a purple tint to it. I love it. I love the way it makes me look and feel, and I found out one of the meanings of my name is "purple flower" and it felt right. For some reason, Bennett fixated on that, among other things, and calls me some variation of purple or dark blue at all times.

"Fuck off, problem child. I'm not in the mood today." I started calling him that when I found out he almost went to juvie for joy riding. He claims it was just the one time and he learned his lesson.

"You're never in the mood," he scoffs and gives me a slight sneer. First semester I did my best to ignore him but he's so damn good at getting under my skin. The fact that he's so perfectly my physical type only makes it more annoying - tall, dark blonde hair, dark eyes that are constantly twinkling with mischief, a constant smirk, and arms that I want to grip or sink my teeth into. The veins in his forearms and on the back of his hands make me clench my thighs together. He's on the lanky side, but those arms? Delicious.

Of course he would be my shallow catnip on the outside but be a complete douche on the inside. The worst part is that our schedules line up this semester so that we'll likely be working together all the time. He wants to join the Magistrates too, and it seems he's taking a similar route to get their attention.

"I'm never in the mood with *you*, Bennett. Get it right."

That's a total lie. It's not just about Bennett. In fact, he might be a needed distraction. The semester starting makes spring break's approach feel real, and I'm scared. I confirmed with my parents that I don't have to get any medical certification of my virginity, and the belief that I'm still a virgin on my wedding night is up to my husband. It's even grounds for annulment if he declares that I'm not.

It was so gross to think about.

At least I'll have something good to think about while it happens. As good as the sex felt, I think about P.C. kissing me the most. The feel and taste of him haunt me in my dreams, and the thoughts of him have been the source of so many orgasms since then. It's been almost a month. The ache in my chest hasn't gotten any better, but I do feel the sense of closure that I promised myself I would get if I saw P.C.

I'll always want him, but I get some comfort knowing I had him.

Whoever he might be.

"Maeve. Baby."

I whip a pen at Bennett's head as I take my seat at my usual computer to start reviewing tour applications. "Call me baby one more time."

"No, no, it's "hit me" baby one more time. The Millennials are going to get you for that."

"Ugh," I groan and squeeze the tiny llama stress squeezer that stays at my station for exactly this purpose. I bought it online specifically to get my annoyance out so I don't either murder Bennett, or kiss his stupid perfect mouth to shut him up. It would shock him so fiercely he might be quiet for a few days, let alone in the moment. He's trying to break me, and I swear I won't let him.

"I can hear you thinking from over here."

"At least one of us can think."

"Are you still jealous of my grade on that psych paper?"

"Get over yourself." I grab another pen, debating on throwing it at him, when our boss comes shuffling into the room. Mallory Tilden is normally one of the most put together people I've ever seen, and right now she looks frazzled. Bennett and I both stand up and go to her, recognizing that something is wrong.

"We have a problem."

"What can we do?" I ask, immediately volunteering Bennett as well.

"The flyers to the pre-approved recruits need to go out by tomorrow, but the box with the flyers didn't get to us until today. I need them stuffed, stamped, and stickered by tomorrow at 10:00 a.m."

"I can do it," I reassure her. "I don't have anything planned for today and I don't have class until 2:00p p.m. tomorrow."

"Really?" Mallory clutches my arms like I'm saving her actual life. "I'll get you food and drinks but I can't stay - Roy is out of town and it's just me and Lily." Roy is her husband and he does recruiting for Elmwood sports teams. Lily is their 2 year old.

"Of course."

Bennett clears his throat. "I can stay too. Don't worry Mal, me and mauve Maeve have got this for you."

"Great. Well do your usual hours for now, and I'll get everything ready for you. If you need to run any errands or anything just be back here by 5:00 p.m. so I can lock the doors."

She gives us a distracted wave and leaves the lab. I couldn't exactly deny Bennett's help, and it wasn't up to me, but the idea that I am now spending an entire night locked in this building with him does not sound like the good time I was imagining. I thought I'd set up a little assembly line, pop in a podcast, and go to town while guzzling coffee like it's water.

I could probably still do that but I know Bennett will want to talk to me.

I know that instead of finding a personal distraction to keep him awake and motivated, he'll utilize me for that purpose.

Without another word, I go back to my station and start reviewing applications. I leave with an hour to spare to run across campus back to my dorm room. Tati is sleeping so I sneak around quietly and send her a text where I'll be in case she wakes up and gets worried. I change into comfy clothes, grab some of my own snacks, and my personal stash of coffee pods to use in the admissions office break room coffee machine.

I'm still oddly looking forward to tonight. There's something satisfying about being in a place after hours, with only a few lights on, and working through the night. I like the idea of being awake when everyone else is asleep, being productive while everyone else is resting. It keeps my mind whirring with the possibilities. There's so much potential in that kind of stillness and alone time.

Hopefully Bennett isn't too much of a disruption.

I get back to the office with plenty of time to spare and get myself set up in the work room. I take a stack of invites and a box of envelopes and start working.

Mallory comes in with Bennett and they're carrying pizza boxes and a bag of 2 liters of soda. She sets it up on an empty table.

"Do you two need anything else?"

"Nope." Bennett answers, and I shake my head.

"You have my number if you do, otherwise, have a good time. Behave." Mallory seems much less frazzled now, and gives us a wink as she leaves. The lights in the other areas turn off, and we hear the thunk of the front door locking.

It's just me and Bennett now.

He sets his stuff down and gets comfortable, and I watch with confusion as he walks over and hands me a little pink box.

"What is this?"

"Conversation hearts, my amethyst amor. It's Valentine's Day tomorrow."

"Oh." I take them and see an orange heart right at the front that says 'kiss me' and I blush. "Thank you."

Bennett winks. "Looks like you have a plan. Want me to stamp, or should we get everything stuffed first?"

"Stuffed."

Bennett nods and makes a setup like my own on the other side of the table so we're facing each other. We work in silence for a long time. The repetitive motions lull me and I start to droop a little. I'm not tired, more like I'm hypnotized by picking up a flyer, sliding it inside, pulling the strip off the envelope, and the slide of my hands along the flap as I seal it up, then putting the sealed envelope into a stack.

I come back to myself when Bennett slaps his hand on the table and makes me jump.

"What the hell?"

"I called your name three times. We should eat before it gets too cold."

"Right," I swallow thickly. It's only been an hour, but if I don't eat now I'll forget.

We walk over to the table and Bennett slides one of the boxes over to me. "I remembered you like mushrooms, so you and your fungi can have a pizza to yourselves."

I roll my eyes at him, but also feel oddly touched he remembered that. It was something that came up at a pizza party the staff had early last semester. It didn't even occur to me that he'd been paying attention. Stupid Bennett being all cute.

"Thanks," I finally answer and move away from him. Proximity to Bennett will soften me and I cannot do anything except be annoyed by him. I'm not good at forgiving people. My annoyance is still pretty thick with Cyn's boyfriend Rome even though he's made it up to her ten times over. I stay on guard so she doesn't have to, and for that same reason, I will always guard myself against Bennett.

Something about him picks at me, but I can't let myself think about it.

It takes us until nearly 4:00 a.m. to finish all of the letters. I would have sat in silence, but Bennett has to talk. I enjoy it more than I should. It's about everything and nothing, and I don't think I've ever communicated so easily with anyone. Face to face, anyway.

"You're 100% wrong," Bennett throws his hands up. "Math is blue, social studies is yellow, English is red, and science is green."

"English is green."

"NO! Science makes the most sense as green. We studied green things."

"No, science is red because that's the color of blood."

"Whoa, Maevy, morbid much?"

I laugh. "At least we can agree math is blue."

He narrows his eyes at me. We fall back into silence and keep working.

"Do you want to have kids?" I ask.

Bennett waggles his eyebrows at me. "You offering to be my baby mama?"

"Absolutely not."

He doesn't look at me and keeps working. "Yeah. I want to be better than my own parents." The silence that falls between us is heavy, and I wait him out to see if he'll say more, but he doesn't.

Shortly after midnight, we're both dragging hard. My hands are fumbling and I got a stinging paper cut that slowed me down. Bennett found the first aid kid and insisted on putting on the band-aid himself. I flinched when he leaned in and kissed my finger when he was done.

"We need a break. Nap? Half hour?" He's already standing up and moving over to the couches in the corner of the room. I follow him, unsteady on my feet. They're set up in an L-shape, and he lays down on one and I lay down on the other, our feet pointing toward each other at the corner. I watch as he sets an alarm.

"Sweet dreams, periwinkle princess."

I stick my tongue out at him and close my eyes.

A soft finger is moving over my cheek, then down my nose. I blink awake and see Bennett. The expression on his face catches me off guard, but when he sees my eyes open it's as if a mask drops down over him. I shiver, and sit up. We get back to work, but we're tired and much more subdued.

By the time we finish, we're both a little drunk on being tired. The work is all done and in the post office bins to be driven for mailing. I'm on my third or fourth wind, where now I'm giddy and silly, as we pack up our things to head to our rooms.

We let ourselves out of the building, and Bennett checks that the door is locked. I texted Mallory to let her know that it was done and we were going home to get some sleep.

Campus is covered in a cold fog and the sidewalks are a little icy, so we move slowly and carefully toward the other end of campus where the halls are. I almost slip and Bennett grabs my arm, keeping me from landing on my butt or twisting my knee. I try to move away but he doesn't let go, looping my arm through his.

"You know this means if one of us goes down, we both go down."

Bennett shrugs. "I'm pretty steady."

I shake my head. "Well don't blame me when you break a leg."

"I've never broken a bone in my life, I don't plan to start now."

"Never? Like not even a toe?"

Bennett shakes his head. "Some of us are just lucky. We're born with natural agility."

"Excuse you, I was a nationally ranked softball player. I have agility."

"Sure," he says as he pats my hand with condescension. This is why Bennett drives me insane. He'll do things that seem nice or thoughtful, but then he falls back on this habit of looking down on people. Especially me. It's like he lives to get my fur up and make me hiss at him. That's not a person who is good for me, I know it.

I move to pull away from him and head into Harwood-Locke, but he follows me.

"You don't have to walk me to my door, I'll survive."

Bennett stops and looks at me strangely. "I live there, too."

"You do?"

"Yeah..." he trails off like he's disappointed or hurt that I don't know that. "Have the whole year."

"Oh." I have no idea what to say to that, and we get inside and take the most awkward walk up the stairs of my entire life. We part at the third floor as I continue up to the fourth.

"Happy Valentine's day, my mulberry mistress." Bennett blows me a kiss before going through the door to his floor, but doesn't miss me giving him the finger. I can hear his sharp laugh before the door shuts and cuts him off.

I wish I hated his attention.

 Bennett

I miss Maeve.

Which is probably why I volunteered to stay up all night and stuff envelopes with her even though I have a class at 8:00 a.m. I couldn't resist the chance to be alone with her for hours. To pick at her and observe her. God, just to inhale her.

It's amusing to me that while Maeve fell hard for the person in the emails, she can't stand the me she interacts with regularly. I haven't figured out why she overreacts to my teasing, but the fact that I get such a big reaction almost every time gives me satisfaction. It's getting something from her she doesn't give to anyone else, and I want that.

Instead of going to sleep, I open my computer and login to the email I used to talk to her. She never sent another email after the Founder's Ball, since we agreed that was the end of things for us. I haven't either, although it's tempting to keep that connection going.

I scroll down and open a random email.

P.C. -

Sometimes I feel like I've never taken a breath. I've been holding everything in my whole life, being beyond careful, making sure that no one has a reason to question me or my integrity. Until Elmwood, I never went out. I never partied. I never even had friends until the ones I have here. What if I had feelings for someone? I didn't want to set myself up for heartbreak. Not until you.

-M

She has no idea how badly I'm going to break her heart.

But when the agreement is broken, she'll be free. She can find someone to love. She can choose someone to belong to, even though pieces of her will always belong to me. I've accepted the reality that Maeve is going to hate me someday but I've also accepted that I'll deserve it.

If my dad gets off my back, maybe I'll be able to make decisions about what I want for the first time in my life. He'll have his money. I'll have my freedom. That's what Maeve and I both want more than anything, and I have to break us to get it.

When I first started sending the emails we kept things surface level, but more and more she started opening up to me and telling me so much more than she realized.

I learned a lot.

Some of it made me feel justified in breaking the agreement, even if it had nothing to do with my father's reasons. I wanted to break it for Maeve, and this was the only way forward.

It never occurred to me how much she had to shut down her life. I could do whatever I wanted as long as I understood that I was going to get married to a girl from a contract I didn't sign. It had never bothered me because until that point where I had put an engagement ring on her finger, I could live a normal life.

I lost my virginity at 15, and dated that girl for a year. I dabbled in drugs like any rich kid does although nothing serious, and I partied with my friends on weekends. I had a few one night stands. After I knew Maeve's name I felt weird getting into any relationships, but that doesn't mean I curbed my needs either. I wasn't holding out for her even though she intrigued me.

I never really thought about how much pressure it would be on Maeve to remain a virgin. Sure, she could have dated, but eventually if you fall in love or really care about someone, you'll cave to giving them what they want. Maeve had to cut herself off, and even held herself back from friendships. That sucks, and I hated that for her.

I didn't notice it when I was looking at her Instagram back in my stalker days, but in hindsight, knowing what I did after our emails, it was easy to see her life was lonely. The photos were always either her sports teams, selfies, or her dog. There was no her and her bestie photos until college.

The entire tone of her page changed when she met her roommate and her other friends. There were photos of Maeve at parties, in costume, dressed up to go out, eating and drinking, playing stupid games, and a million of her at campus events with her arms around her friends, a real smile on her face. Elmwood transformed her, and I hoped she wouldn't lose that.

I wish that I could be her friend in person, but I think if I spent too much time with her, I'd want her again. I'd want to tell her the truth about about that night, and I would be too selfish to let her go. I'd want to take as much as Maeve could give me, even though we're hurtling towards pain.

Not a day goes by I don't think about that night at the Founder's Ball.

That I don't get hard at the memory of her tight, virgin pussy and the way she looked at me and kissed me. For that one night, she was wholly mine. My Maeve, my queen, my intoxication. I got to be someone else that night, and he was the one that got to have her.

 Maeve

After sleeping like a disaster for a few days, I'm mostly back to normal. I still need coffee to function but not at terrifying levels. This semester is going smoothly, and I'd like to keep it that way. I'm generating momentum and I want to enjoy the ride.

Tonight there's a recruitment meeting for potential Magistrate members. I got the invitation in my email and nearly danced with glee. While the Castle and the Cavalry have more more subtle, secretive processes, the Magistrates are a lot like a job interview. A lot of work goes into being a member and they have to make sure you're up for the challenge.

I walk into the meeting and wave to a few people I know, other recruits as well as Cyn's boyfriend's bestie. Del gives me a wink and I smile back at them, relieved that someone I know is one of the people running the meeting. Tonight they're going to outline the timeline and process for all the potential recruits to make sure we know what we're getting into, and expectations for our first year of membership.

If I could float with excitement, I would be.

I take a seat and get myself settled. Someone sits next to me and they are way too close. I look up to protest and ask them to move, but then I see it's Bennett, smirking away, just waiting for me to snap.

Instead, I huff and cross my arms, staring straight ahead. I'm not going to give him the satisfaction.

Bennett takes it as an invitation, and puts his arm along the back of my chair.

I ignore him as the meeting gets started, led by Del and another Magistrate.

They talk and I try very hard to listen to every word said even though I already know most of this. I picked Del's brain last semester and they got me fully prepared, as well as gave me solid advice about making myself a prime recruit.

Bennett is playing with the ends of my hair.

I ignore him and in the notes section of my phone I type out the dates that they say and what they are, pretending that he isn't occupying any of my thoughts. When the presentation is over, the floor is open for questions, and the room relaxes and gets chattier.

Bennett leans over, further into my space.

"What are you going to do when we're Magistrates together, purple princess? You won't be able to avoid me."

"Sure I will. It's a big society."

I listen as people ask questions and then the meeting is dismissed. With every bit of swiftness and agility I have, I dart between people to get out of the house and down the street and away from Bennett.

At first I think I've succeeded, but then his heavy arm falls around my shoulders. I frown up at him and move away. It's cold as hell and it was very warm tucked up against him, but I won't give in to the temptation or give him the satisfaction.

"What's the matter, violet vixen? Afraid you'll get hot for me?"

"As if," I snort. "I wouldn't touch you with a ten foot pole." I walk faster to stay a few steps ahead of him.

"Then it shouldn't bother you at all if I want to snuggle up and keep you warm."

"What's your deal Bennett?"

"Just proving that you're a sweet little prude. So pure you can't even let a boy put his arm around you."

"You're not a boy you're a toad."

"Why don't you kiss me and see if I turn into a prince?"

I stop abruptly and turn to face him. He isn't expecting it and pulls up short, our chests bumping each other.

Before Bennett can register what's happening, I slide a hand over his nape, push up onto my toes, and press my lips to his.

His lips are as perfect as they look, soft and warm, and it's only a second before he's kissing me back and his hands are resting on my hips. I give in for way too long before breaking the kiss and taking a big step back from him.

Bennett is frozen, his hands still out where he was holding me and his eyes wide and surprised when they meet mine.

"See? Still a toad." I'm breathless when I say it, but manage to hold it together as I whirl around and march straight to Harwood-Locke.

My heart is pounding because I felt...everything. Bennett is my foil and my perfect match, and that's why I push him away so hard. If I was free, I'd be all over Bennett. He'd have no choice but to be with me because we drive each other crazy in the best way. I have to convince myself every day that I hate it, that what he does and says gets under my skin and I don't like it. That he's annoying.

Because I can never have Bennett.

I get upstairs to my room and Tati isn't there. I throw my coat on my bed and cross the hall to Elise and Cyn's room. They aren't around as much either because of their boyfriends, but I'm hoping tonight the universe is on my side because I have to tell someone.

I knock and Elise opens the door, a huge smile on her face. She blinks when she sees the shocked expression on mine and opens the door wider so I can step inside. Cyn is wearing her magnifying glasses and holding a pair of tweezers, working on some sort of intense paper craft. Her hugely magnified eyes blink in shock as I stand, dumbfounded, in the middle of their room.

"I kissed Bennett."

Cyn whips the glasses off her face. "YOU WHAT?"

"I thought you hated him?" Elise asks softly.

"I do? I don't know. He taunted me and I snapped." I tell them what happened and appreciate that they laugh with me. It makes some of the tension slip away inside me.

"It was just a kiss, Em," Cyn says as she wraps her arms around me. "You didn't do anything wrong." They don't know about the Founder's Ball. It felt too special and private. They don't know that I've already done the worst thing I could possibly do. I know they'd be on my side, and probably even be happy that I owned what I wanted, but I want to keep P.C. to myself.

"I know. But I kissed Bennett."

"You like him," Elise says. "You don't want to like him, but you do."

"Yeah. That's why I've always kept away from people, especially guys." I fight the tears springing to my eyes. "You're my first real friends since I was a kid. Your guys are my first guy friends, ever. The first guys I can trust." I even mean Rome in that statement because I do trust him, when I'm being sane.

"That had to be lonely. Now you're just bursting with people." Cyn starts to rock us back and forth trying to soothe me, which is funny because she's so much tinier than me, even though we're about the same height.

"Do you think Bennett likes you?" Elise asks.

"I have no idea. I can't tell the difference between him being an asshole and him flirting with me. It might be both. Plus, it doesn't matter. Bennett could tell me he's in love with me and it wouldn't change a thing. I have to keep my distance." I can't hurt my heart twice like this, especially since I'd probably never get the closure with Bennett that I did with P.C.

"We need ice cream." Elise moves to get her keys. I follow my friends, beyond happy that I have them.

 Bennett

Things return to normal. I see Maeve in admissions, I give her crap, she snaps back at me, and all is right in our world for the time being. I can't believe she kissed me. I can't believe she wanted to, and if she'd done it for a few seconds longer I would have lost all control and taken her mouth the way I did at the Founder's Ball. She's always surprising me. It never occurred to me that our snarky banter was appealing to her.

That she might like this part of me, too, and not just the guy in the emails.

Fuck fuck fuck.

My dad is going to murder me.

It's hard to explain to someone how damaging emotional manipulation and financial abuse can be. The way he's so good at pressure and guilt, at getting me to do things that I would never choose to do because I'm afraid of the repercussions. I'm afraid of him yanking my future out from under me, of penalizing other members of my family, or isolating me from them as a punishment. Dad holds the purse strings and therefore he holds the thread of our lives. If financially cutting me off didn't also mean I'd be blocked from my family, I would have walked away from this a long time ago.

As it is, I keep moving ahead, trying to find a way out without losing everything.

It's a lot to carry.

The first day of March is one of Elmwood's newer traditions, but no less important or fun. It's Scream Day.

March means midterms are coming. It means we're itchy for spring break. It's the time when the students who are about to graduate start getting twitchy and lose motivation. We feel the wait of the year ending, of secret society recruitment, of finding internships for the summer. We need a release. Even though there are a lot of other spring traditions ahead, we all need this one.

I'm helping organize the event, as is Maeve, and I can see her at the other drink station across the concrete mall from me. She's smiling and chatty, although she keeps giving exaggerated glares at her friend Cyn's boyfriend. Not sure what that's about, but I know it's a cover. She loves them, and I like seeing her happy. I like watching her smile when she doesn't know I'm looking.

More and more people are crowding into the mall, and all I can see are heads and bodies in every direction. From 11:50-12:00 there are no classes. On this one day, at 11:55, everyone leaves whatever building they are in or going to, and we scream. It's a way to get out the energy and tension of the semester so far. It's something silly and obnoxious that provides catharsis.

The Dean of the college gets up on the little platform and uses her megaphone.

"3...2...1...SCREAM!" She blips the siren on the device and it's like I hear everyone collectively take a deep breath before they start screaming.

I'm doing it too, but I only have eyes for Maeve.

She's got her arms away from her body, her head tipped back, and she's screaming with everything she has. I can't look away, and my heart jolts when twin tears track down her temples and into her hair. Why is she crying? Did something happen I don't know about?

The Dean blips the siren again, and we all stop. People immediately start shuffling and moving, and I get distracted handing out water to my fellow screamers. The campus clears fast with people rushing to their class or back to their halls.

I steal a water for myself, and try to catch a glimpse of Maeve. Her station is already packed away and she and her friends are gone.

My phone buzzes when I'm hours deep into my calculus homework. When I see it's my dad calling, my stomach pits and I have to take a few deep breaths before I answer the phone. Luckily, my roommate isn't here. I love the guy, but I know the way my dad and I argue makes him uncomfortable. Liam is not good with confrontation.

"Dad."

"Bennett. How are things?"

"Fine. School is good."

Silence falls between us and I wait for him to cut the crap and tell me the real reason he's calling. It's usually not for anything good. He's a busy man so I know making time to talk to me just because isn't a priority. There's money to be made, who cares about his kid?

"Is everything ready for the meeting at the end of the month?"

I feel a wave of nausea and think about the things stashed in the small safe in my closet. The proof that Maeve violated the contract, and evidence of her virginity up until that point. The animal in me loves that I own it. The human being hates that it exists, that I did it, that I am using anything against her.

"Yeah. Are you sure we have to do this?"

"Do you want your freedom taken away like this? Do you want someone to take away your choices about your future?" Dad snarls. He always talks about it like that, as if it actually has any impact on him at all. He's never directly asked me if I don't want to marry Maeve. It's always framed about freedom and penalties. If we get married, he gets money. The family gets money. Maeve and I get what can only be labeled as a fuckton of money. The money goes everywhere.

It's the fact that he wants to deliberately fuck over the Keans for that money that makes him so dedicated to this plan. It has nothing to do with me or my freedom.

"Do I need to cut you off again?" He threatens

"No," I answer quickly. He blocks me from being able to talk to the rest of my family because he cuts off my phone, warns them not to speak to me unless they want consequences, and he blocks my access to money. After the last time, I squirreled away cash so that I at least had something in case I managed to piss him off again.

"Everything is ready," I reassure him. "It's fine."

"It better be. The Keans never paid for what they did, and I'm going to be the one that finally stands up to them."

"Right," I agree.

"Good." Dad hangs up the phone.

The rest of the families involved in the original fire don't hold this same grudge. They work with the Keans and make deals with them all the time. Literally the only person still stuck in the past is dad, and it's a past that had nothing to do with him.

I dig through my desk until I find the business card I'm looking for. It's for my grandfather's lawyer, and he's the one who facilitated the contract for my union with Maeve on behalf of my grandfather. I've always taken my dad's word for it what was in there, and now I think I need to see it for myself.

I need to understand what's worth ruining an innocent girl's life for.

I need to know the exact words that got all of us into this situation.

My dad is not to be trusted, and my future is at stake.

Even though it's late, I call the direct number written in slanting handwriting on the back of the card. Denton Stilworth worked with my grandfather his entire career, and he's old but still young enough to be working. Apparently he's a shark of contract and estate law.

"Stilworth," he answers.

"Uh, this is Bennett Silar."

"Bennett! How are you?" We only met a few times, and one of them was at my grandfather's funeral. He seemed nice, and I liked that he had a sharp sense of humor and didn't bother asking how I was doing.

"I was wondering if I could see the contract between the Keans and the Silars, the one that arranges my marriage."

"Well," Stilworth clears his throat. "I don't see why not since you're a party to the contract even if you didn't sign it. Let me check the legality, make sure I'm not getting either of us in trouble, and I'll get back to you."

I give him my email and thank him for his time.

It's not like I have a lot of hope this is going to change anything, but I think knowing more provides clarity. All I want is to understand, and this is an important first step.

Maeve

My next chance to ingratiate myself with the Magistrates is the Ides Party. Instead of bewaring the Ides of March, we throw a giant toga party, hand out gloomy predictions, and host a massive beer pong tournament. This year is a big deal, apparently, as a junior is going for her three-peat as Ides Beer Pong Tournament Champion.

We're getting ready in Elise's room. I bought a sheet with big obnoxious purple pansies all over it and Cyn is currently doing some cutting and pinning to get it to tie over my body. It's still pretty cold but we'll all be okay with the body heat of everyone running through and crowding in the hedge maze. I've got leggings on underneath but otherwise it's just a sports bra. I feel comfortable and Cyn is kind of amazing at the knot-braid something that she made to hold it together.

Her own sheet is a classic cream and pinned with a giant gold badge. Elise is wearing black, and Tati's sheet is neon pink. Cyn tied her sheet so there are long braids hanging down the side that swing when she walks and whip around when she dances. We all look amazing.

I pull everyone together and hold out my phone.

"Smile!" We all grin big into the camera, and I love seeing them surround me. I love seeing that they share my excitement for all things Elmwood. Tati doesn't want to be here, but she never misses a chance to have fun with us. After taking the picture I immediately post it to Instagram, and then tuck my phone into the pocket in my leggings underneath my toga.

Lights are flaring from various places in the hedge maze and music is thumping. We can hear and see it before we even get close. Elise is an expert in the maze, and leads us toward the largest clearing there the beer pong competition is already starting. This is one of those times where the administration turns its head but tells us that if we don't party responsibly, they'll take the party away. Since it's thrown by the Magistrates, I doubt there's going to be a problem.

I can't wait to part of it next year from the inside.

We lose Elise the second she sees Colin but we knew that was coming. It doesn't take long until there are cups in our hands and we're drinking. Cyn sticks with me since Rome won't show up until it's time to take her home and do unspeakable things to her, and Tati disappears at every party but shows up in time to get me home.

Cyn and I wander through the maze, trying to find the other drink stations and the games and fortune tellers. The first clearing we come to has people in matching costumes wearing gold masks.

"Come to hear your fate?" one of the masked people booms. Cyn and I giggle and head toward the group. I move toward the one who spoke and is staring me down.

He looks down at me through the mask and I think of P.C. for a long moment. This guy's eyes are blue, but it still make me miss my own masked man. Cyn is with a girl in a mask who is similarly staring at her. It must be part of the gimmick before they read your fate.

"Maeve Kean," the guy says, and I jump because he knows my name. After a second though, it's kind of flattering, since it means I must be a known entity to the current Magistrates. "Do you want to see beyond the veil to know your fate?"

"I do," I giggle, nervous.

He closes his eyes, opens a large leather bound book and runs his fingers along the edges. His hand stops, and his fingers slide between the pages until he opens to where his hand stopped.

"You will face a great betrayal, not once, but three times. If you can let go of your anger, you will find your peace."

I gaze up at him with my mouth slightly agape. I know the tradition dictates that the fates and fortunes are almost all negative, but I can't stop the chill that races over my skin. There are so many secrets I'm keeping that the opportunities for betrayal are ripe. It scares me.

The masked guy lets out a booming laugh, then hands me a tiny bottle of liquor.

"To fate," he offers. I toast him and down the shot.

When I walk over to Cyn, she's blushing furiously.

"What was your fate?" I ask.

Cyn giggles. "I will be taken in the darkest places, and I will do it willingly."

I stop in my tracks. "Your fate was anal?"

Cyn laughs so hard it distracts her from asking about my fate. We go to the next clearing and stay there, sipping our way through multiple drinks until we are solidly drunk. It relaxes my whole body and I feel good. Cyn starts talking to some people from her classes and in my happy, floaty mode I start walking through the hedge maze, turning and twisting on the paths and walking past other revelers.

Suddenly I feel like someone is watching me, and I whip around to catch whoever it is.

Bennett is standing a few feet behind me, leaning against the wall with his arms crossed, as if he wasn't following me a second ago. My eyes meet his and hunger flares in my stomach. His arms are bare and he's wearing a golden laurel on his head that shines with his golden hair. Bennett is a god among us tonight.

My eyes drop to his lips, and his raise in that smirk that I hate-love.

He walks toward me and I know he's drunk because his movements are almost too smooth. His body is insanely relaxed and it's like being approached by a panther.

A sexy panther.

I want to bite him.

"Mauvy Maevy," he whispers as he gets closer. "Are you lost?"

"No," I swallow thickly. "Just wandering."

"Alone?"

I wave my hand back in the direction we came, and he nods like he understands what I mean. We're both a little drunk right now, and it makes it easier to talk than it has been for the last few weeks since I kissed him. I haven't been embarrassed, exactly, but I also don't want him to think of it as an invitation. It was a mistake.

Bennett reaches out and tucks my hair behind my ear, then his fingers trail down my jaw. His eyes keep bouncing from my lips back to my eyes, and I gasp and take a step back when he moves closer.

"I was looking for you," he admits, not letting me move away from him.

"Why? No one else will listen to your bullshit tonight?" *Stay in control, drunk Maeve.*

"Nope. I save it all for you. I know you can take me." Bennett winks and the urge to shove him and run away overtakes me.

"You're ridiculous."

"You're beautiful. Extra purple," he nods vehemently and takes a long blink. Bennett bends at the waist to close the space between us. "I'm thinking about kissing you, Maeve."

"I don't think you should, Bennett."

"Don't you want to find out if I can turn into a prince?"

"It's safer when you're a toad."

"Where's the fun in that?"

Feeling out of control, I move around him and walk back toward the clearing. Bennett follows me but doesn't try anything. I'm not entirely sure where I'm going, but I know I've been walking toward the clearing I left for longer than I walked away from it. Okay, so I'm drunk and lost and being trailed by a boy who wants to kiss me.

There's light ahead but when I step out into the clearing, we're back with the fate readers instead of where I left Cyn. But maybe I can get back there from here. I start heading toward a different opening, but Bennett grabs my wrist.

"Wait."

 Bennett

I can't let her walk away. She stands still and crosses her arms, and after I stare at her for too long, she makes a gesture toward the fates. She thinks I'm waiting to get a prediction.

Okay, then.

I walk over to one of the open fates, a short girl in a mask.

She stares at me for a long time, then runs her fingers along the pages of her big leather book. I'm kind of mesmerized by the sound and the movement, and it seems like she goes in slow motion when she finally flips it open.

"You know you're on a dark path and set toward destruction. Will you be strong enough to change direction?"

I glare at the fate and turn away. They're generic and intentionally have a negative bent, I know this, but it doesn't mean that didn't hit close to home. Everyone listens to dad and he knows that cutting me off from my family will penalize me. He knows they won't defy him and speak to me. All the power is with him.

Maeve is waiting for me, and her frown deepens when she sees my face.

I stomp out of the clearing and this time she's the one who follows me. I don't move so fast she can't keep up, but I take her deeper into the maze and away from the party.

"Bennett," she calls softly, and I come to a stop in a dark corner, right near an alcove in the hedge. "Are you okay?"

"No," I sigh and turn to her. "I'm not okay. I..." There's nothing for me to say, not right now. Not that will make any sense to her, or that won't destroy any chance I will ever have to repair the damage I've done. Looking at her right now, her face open and caring, I know that I won't be able to do this to her.

I'll find another way to break the contract. Exposing her and what we did is too much. The price is too fucking high.

"Maeve." I say her name like a prayer, half moan, half pain.

Her bottom lip trembles, and I can't stop myself from reaching for her.

The astounding thing is that Maeve reaches back, her body meeting mine with enough power to knock me back a step. Her arms are wrapped around my neck and our mouths meet, wet and hungry as we open for each other. I'd forgotten how potent it was to kiss her.

She tastes like something a little bit fruity, and I lap at her tongue to get to her flavor. The taste that is only Maeve. I groan into her mouth and pull her closer, running my hands over her strong, thick body and feeling her in a way I didn't the first time we were together.

"So good," I murmur over her lips before kissing down her jaw and neck. Maeve shudders and holds me tight against her, and I know I've found a spot she likes. I groan into her throat when she scratches her nails through my hair and I pull us back into the alcove. I turn so she's shielded by my body, further in the dark.

My hands fumble with her toga but I find where it splits open and slide my hands under it. I love it when I touch the bare skin of her stomach, and don't hesitate to reach for the waistband of her leggings. The tips of my fingers are beneath it when she pushes back and stops me.

"We shouldn't. I...you know my situation." I know her situation better than she can possibly imagine. I'm her situation, whether she knows it or not. Still, she's right.

I press a soft kiss to her lips and start to withdraw my hand, but she stops me.

"This can't mean anything."

"I know." I press my face back into her neck and lull her back into arousal with soft licks and sucks of the skin there. Maeve pushes her hips up and toward my hand, but I wait.

"Touch me, Bennett," she whispers into my ear. It goes straight to my already throbbing cock. To hear her say my name in that sexy, needy voice. I slide my hand under her leggings and straight to her core, since she's not wearing panties.

"My sweet orchid," I murmur, "going commando?"

She laughs. "I usually am."

"Fuck, that's mean."

"Right now it's not." She ends on a gasp as I slide my finger between her pussy lips and tease right to her clit. Maeve is so wet and I wish I could taste her again, but there's no good way to do it here and I think if I tried to get her somewhere else it would break the spell we're both under right now.

I move so that I'm cupping her face with my other hand and lean back enough that I can watch her as I play with her. Every expression and reaction that teaches me how to touch her and where she likes it. I press a little harder, pinching her clit between two fingers and she groans, her body grinding against me.

"Bennett," she whimpers my name and I know she's close. I rock my hand in opposition to her, my hand and her hips smacking together as she chases an orgasm. She lets out one sharp cry and then buries her face in my chest as her pussy gushes on my hand. I keep moving until she's clawing at me to stop.

Maeve's eyes flutter open and she watches with rapt attention as I lift my hand to my mouth and suck her flavor off my fingers.

She surprises me again when she dives up to kiss me, swirling her tongue with mine, tasting herself while tasting me.

Then she drops to her knees and I'm sure that I'm dreaming.

"Maeve," I stop her and step away, pulling her back to her feet.

"People are doing worse. There are probably people fucking on the other side of this hedge wall."

"Do you want to be one of them?" I tease her, testing how far she'd go, and how much she likes this me, Bennett, me.

"I do," she lets out a frustrated moan, "but I can't. I'm sorry."

"No," I cup her face in my hands. "No sorry."

"I want to taste you," she says so quietly I almost miss it, and even in the dark I can see the deep flush that runs over her cheeks. Maeve is so rarely embarrassed that this is a moment for me, barely dimmed by the fact that she wants to suck my cock.

"You sure, my amethyst amor? I'm not the kind of dick that's going to act like you owe me for getting you off."

"What kind of dick are you?" Maeve palms my cock and it's another flashback to the first time I was with her, even though it's brand new to her. "I think I should find out."

She drops to her knees again, and this time I don't stop her when she opens my toga and reveals my boxers. They're straining to keep me in place, and she slides them down my legs a little. My cock bobs free and I hiss when her hot hand wraps around the base.

I know for a fact Maeve has never done this before, and I also know that unless she chooses to bite me, whatever she does is going to feel fucking amazing. I can't look away as she wraps her lips around the head and starts to slide me along her tongue and deeper into her mouth. My eyes are on her, but hers are on my cock.

She starts to move back and forth, taking me deeper with each stroke, and then I feel her press her tongue along the bottom ridge and I thrust uncontrollably. It feels so good. It takes everything I have to keep my body from reacting and pounding into her hot, wet, perfect mouth.

I can't take my eyes off her.

"Hottest blowjob of my life," I moan as I feel my head hit the back of her throat, and the reality that I'm about to come down it gets me close to the edge. "You're perfect Maeve. So damn perfect."

She moans around my cock and I barely have time to warn her.

"I'm coming," I groan and let out something almost like a scream when that makes her take me deep into her and hold there as I start to explode into her mouth. It's so deep I can feel her swallow around me, pulling my come down her throat.

Maeve slides off me and looks up.

"Holy shit," I murmur. "That was…"

"You're welcome," she smirks at me and stands up. I don't care about anything except getting my mouth on that smirk. Maeve makes a little sound as I yank her back into my body and I swallow it with my mouth. We taste like ourselves and like each other and I devour her until she's a boneless puddle in my arms.

"Come home with me," I ask.

"We live in the same building," she answers. The sounds of the party have faded, and it's got to be late if Ides is ending.

"You know what I mean." I want to go to sleep with her and wake up with her and I want to not hate myself. I want to give this girl world and I want to set her free, but I also want to chain her to me, to my body and my heart, and never let her go. There's no way for me to win this. Every path is a dark path for me, right or wrong.

"You know I can't."

I hold her to me and feel bad for putting that pain in her voice. "I know. I'm sorry."

"Me too."

We hold each other for awhile like that, and then she steps out of my arms.

"Bye, Bennett."

"Bye, my periwinkle princess."

I get one last giggle from her before she disappears around a corner.

 Bennett

I have a little over a week until the hammer falls.

Maeve is all I can think about.

I break in the worst way.

My queen,

See me again. I know your time is running out and I need to say goodbye one last time. I'll wear my mask again. Please don't say no.

-P.C.

She writes back in less than a day.

P.C. -

Okay. Tonight. 7. By the old chapel.

-Maeve

I wait for her in the semi-dark, mask obscuring my face and hat obscuring my hair. For the ball, I colored my hair so she wouldn't recognize me. Maeve steps out of the small patch of trees they kept around the chapel, and her eyes lock with mine.

I can't breathe.

She walks toward me with sorrow in every line of her expression and I hate that I'm responsible for it in so many ways.

When she gets close, neither of us knows what to do.

"I have a week," her voice breaks. "A week."

I open my arms to her. I borrowed Liam's cologne tonight in case she would recognize me by my smell. God I have to be so stupidly paranoid about this because I couldn't help insinuating myself into her life. Interacting with her too much, too closely, until it's going to break us both when she finds out the extent of my betrayal.

Maeve sobs in my arms and I wish I could tell her it's all me, and I'm going to get us out of it.

A tiny spark of hope springs at the most terrible thought I could have: *maybe she'll find out it's me and she won't mind.*

"It's going to be okay," I reply roughly. "It's going to be okay."

I tip her head up to me and move to kiss her but she stops me. Her soft fingers resting over my mouth and putting a barrier between us. The rejection hurts more than it should.

"I can't begin to tell you how grateful I am for what you've been to me. You started my heart, but now it doesn't know how to stop."

"What are you saying?"

"I have feelings for someone else." She sighs and steps out of my arms. "And even though I can't be with him either, I'd rather stay true to that feeling."

My heart swells because I know she's still talking about me, even when she doesn't.

"I kept away from people for a reason. I kept my heart closed for a reason." Tears stream down her face. "I let my friends in. I let you in. I can't shut it anymore. I try but I can't."

"I'm sorry."

Now Maeve smiles. "I'm not. I'm sorry if I'm hurting you, but I'm not sorry that we talked, or that I met you, that I gave you something I probably shouldn't have." She laughs and shakes her head. "I don't regret a second of it, no matter what happens."

I lean back against the chapel and stuff my hands in my pockets to stop myself from grabbing her. From tearing off my mask and my hat and revealing myself to her.

"Who's the guy?"

"Not telling," she shakes her head. "I still don't know how you know me, and I need to keep it to myself."

"Fair enough."

We stand in silence and she moves over to lean on the chapel next to me.

"I'll still be here if you need me. You call, my queen, and I'll answer."

Maeve rests her head on my shoulder, and doesn't say anything. She won't need me, and soon enough she won't want me either. I turn and kiss the top of her head, and say goodbye.

Maeve

Spring break is torture. Everyone else is going on trips or excited to be going home. I feel like I'm walking to my own execution.

I promised father that I'd keep an open mind. That I would give this guy a chance. I know that he's as trapped as I am by this but his life was his own. His body was his own. In a way that makes my skin crawl, a guy I've never met owns mine. The most personal, private part of me has belonged to this faceless stranger.

I don't think I'll ever truly trust him, my future husband.

My parents are anxious as hell. My family lives in New Hampshire a lot of the year, and mystery man and his parents had to fly in. Dinner is ready to be served, the house is impeccable, and I'm wearing a dark purple dress that I kind of hate but also makes me think of Bennett.

He sent me a text as break started. Even though he knows about my marriage contract, he doesn't know I'm meeting him for the first time over break. He said he missed me. It hurt, but I also kind of loved it. I didn't reply. I know he'll understand.

"Wait here. I'll talk to them, and then we'll let everyone meet at once." Father gives me a look and waits.

"Okay." I take a deep breath and stand in the front lounge by the bar. I wish I could have a drink but my parents are strict about the underage drinking thing. They were strict about everything even though I never gave them a reason to be worried that I wouldn't hold up my end of the bargain.

Even though it turns out that I didn't.

The front door opens, I hear voices. My parents leave the room and I shake with nerves. Footsteps sound in the hall and get closer and closer. I take a deep breath and turn to watch them walk in.

First, a woman with dark blonde hair and tired eyes comes in. She's made up perfectly, but I can see through the show. Next, a man with dark hair and dark eyes and a barely controlled sneer. I don't like him at all. His eyes flash over me and the sneer deepens. I do my best not to roll my eyes and let my future father-in-law know that I give zero fucks about his opinion of me.

It's the next person through the doorway that almost brings me to my knees.

It's Bennett.

"Hey, Mauvy Maeve," he smiles at me. A smile I know so well. A smile that gave me butterflies and now feels like a lead weight in my stomach. At first I'm at a loss for words, struggling to accept what I'm seeing. There are so many things I could ask, but only one comes to mind.

"Did you know?" I don't care that our parents are watching this play out, and that I'm clearly emotional and not entirely in control of myself. No one exists for me right now except him.

"Yeah," he nods, his smile more forced than before. "I knew before we ever went to Elmwood."

"Oh my god." My chest cracks and I start moving. At first, I'm sure they think I'm moving toward him because I see Bennett take a step like he's going to meet me halfway. I hold up a hand to ward him off and charge out of the lounge. I feel trapped and I have to escape. I need to get away. I cut through the dining room and into the kitchen, then out the backdoor.

I know they're talking behind me, but the world is spinning around me and I think I might be sick. I'm thinking about every interaction Bennett and I ever had. My mind lingers on the maze at the Ides party. Just over a week ago I had my future husband's dick in my mouth and I didn't even know it.

He knew.

Thank god I hadn't been weak enough to have sex with him right then and there or I'd be in so much trouble right now. I pace on the back patio and try to pull myself back together, and decide what this means and what I'm going to do about it. If there's anything I can do about it.

"Maeve."

I don't turn toward him. I can't look at him. I stop pacing and turn my back to the house. I focus on the yard like it's the most interesting thing I've ever seen. The trees. The gray, overcast sky.

Because the hurt and the truth aren't heading in the same direction. Bennett betrayed me. He kept something monumental from me and for all I know everything that happened between us was a play of some kind, or a test to see if he wanted me or not. That's the hurt.

The truth is that I want Bennett, and once I get over being hurt, I don't have it in me to fight the way I want him. It would be so much easier for me if I genuinely wanted and liked the person I have to marry. If they lit me up inside the way Bennett does. Even when he annoyed the hell out of me I couldn't stay away from him. I don't want to stay away.

Bennett steps up behind me and puts one hand on my hip, pulling me back into him so he can talk quietly. Talking so only we can hear.

"Surprise." I try to pull away but he pulls me back. "It's not the only one I have for you, either. It was so easy to find my way into your life, Maeve. So easy to watch you and know what I needed to do to get to you. You're an open book, my lavender love. My Maeve." His voice drops and my heart falls to my stomach. "My queen."

A sob rips out of me as I put the pieces together because only one person has ever called me that. It's another betrayal, one deeper and more deadly than the first. I could have gotten over Bennett knowing he was supposed to marry me. I would've understood that everyone was being particular about me knowing, and we could have moved past that.

"P.C.?" It's the only thing I can think to say right now. I will not be able to get past the fact that he misled my heart and manipulated me into something that only has gain for him. Bennett knows I'm not a virgin because he took care of that himself. He has all the power to keep or end the agreement.

He has all the power over me.

More power than I ever imagined my future husband would have because I never could have imagined it was someone who had worked their way into my life so thoroughly. Who had manipulated me on every single level, in every possible way, until I am owned by him because I have no other choice.

"Problem child," he has the audacity to chuckle as he says it.

"I'm an idiot."

"No. You were lonely." There's condescension in his voice, that special tone he always saved just for me that made him get under my skin when we worked together. I realize now it's full of pity, and it's always been pity that he gave me.

"Now," he clears his throat and continues, "we're going to go back in the house and our families are going to have dinner. You're going to say you reacted poorly to the surprise but you're delighted that it's me."

"If I won't?"

"Then I'll have to tell mommy and daddy how much you loved my cock at Founder's Ball, and how good it felt to come down your throat, when was that, last week?" He tsks in my ear. "We can talk more when we get back to school."

The only thing I can do is nod. I move away from him and walk back into the house. Bennett follows but doesn't try to touch me. I move back into the lounge where the parents are standing, waiting and confused.

I put on a good show. I make my excuses. I meet Bennett's parents.

We sit down for dinner and I look like I'm eating when I'm dying inside. I've never felt so hollowed out. Ruined on every level.

I think back to the fate's prediction at the Ides party: I would face three betrayals. Two of them came today in the form of Bennett being my intended, and Bennett being P.C. It was like he found ways to hurt me on purpose.

To make matters worse, he keeps smiling at me across the table, playing it up like this is great news. Like he wants to marry me. Like he has even an inkling of the feelings for me that just an hour ago I still had for him.

Why would he text me to tell me he missed me, if he knew he was going to see me?

My heart hurts.

When dinner is over, they give us another moment alone as my parents walk Bennett's to the door.

"I'll see you soon, my queen."

"Don't call me that." I want to sound angry, but I only sound hurt.

Bennett steps close and tucks my hair behind my ear. "You are my queen. You are mine. Don't forget it."

He forces my lips to meet his and they automatically soften, already used to his kisses, his scent, his taste, and it takes a second before I can get back in control of my body and pull away. Bennett just grins at me as he takes a few steps back, and then leaves.

I flee to my room before my parents can try and speak to me. I don't know what I'd say.

 # Bennett

Spring break ends, and I head back to Elmwood. While I was home, I met with Stilworth in person and we went over the details of the agreement together. It was why I was such a dick to Maeve when we met - I need her to stay away from me. I need to not give in to the temptation of her until I know how to take the next steps.

What I learned in that meeting is that my dad was full of shit. It had never occurred to Stilworth that dad wouldn't let me see the agreement that signed a part of my life away, nor that dad would lie to me so spectacularly.

We had all the power. The Silar family was the lead in this situation, and what happened with the settlement was entirely up to us.

We could call off the deal at any time, for any reason. We had the power to determine the matter settled, and go our separate ways in peace. Dad could have denied the marriage years ago, we'd still have gotten a payout, and I never would have had to do anything to Maeve at all. We could always have picked the money over the marriage.

The virginity clause was there, but it wasn't what it looked like either. Not the way that Stilworth and I both read it: "If the bride is determined to have morally compromised herself and engaged in relations with anyone other than her intended, the contract is immediately void." Then it detailed what the payout would be for her side violating the agreement. It's more, but not that much more, than what we would get for just calling the whole thing off.

But the most important detail, to me at least: I'm her intended. She can have all the relations she wants with me. I'm not sure dad read it that way,

I don't think any of them really did, because it probably seemed easier to tell Maeve to stay a virgin than to tell her she can only fuck me. Not that I would have minded her knowing who she belonged to as soon as possible.

She belongs to me, but I have to let her go. I have to step up.

The part of the contract I think dad is worried about is the mingling of businesses. If we go through with the marriage, I get a place on the board of her family's company, and someone from her family, if not Maeve herself, gets a place on mine. We get voting power and decision-making authority for each other. Dad loves nothing more than control and knows he'd have to relinquish it. Someone from the outside would see how he runs things, and that would only be bad for him.

Dad took the cruelest route possible to try and end this. He didn't only want the contract void for the payout, he wanted to humiliate the Kean family. I was used in his game to hurt a girl I can't stop thinking about, who crawled inside my head and won't leave, and I broke her because he held the threat of cutting me off from my family over me. Fuck the money, I want my mom. My brother. My cousins. He knows that separating me from them is the biggest weapon he wields.

Then again, if they love money more than they love me, maybe I don't need them either. When all is said and done I might end up alone, but maybe I should. I let him convince me to do the unthinkable to someone who didn't deserve it.

I broke down in Stilworth's office and told him everything. My grandfather had been a great guy; he thought the marriage would provide me stability, but I guarantee he would have called it all off if I'd asked. I know without a doubt he'd be furious at what dad did and is doing knowing that there were so many other options. Stilworth was horrified, but determined. What dad was doing was illegal. It was fraud.

That gave us options.

I got together all the documentation I had of what he'd asked me to do. Everything he'd said to me over text about the contract, and the role I was supposed to play. Dad didn't even try being careful. I don't think it ever occurred to him that I would turn against him in this way.

The only thing more powerful than my fear of my father is the feelings that I have for Maeve. I don't know if it's love, but it staggers me what I would do to keep her safe. What I would be willing to give up and change if it meant I never hurt her again.

Stilworth is handling filing the fraud and breach of contract paperwork. My father will be served, and Stilworth is going to give me as much warning as possible. He also reminded me that there's a morality clause for my father's job, written by my grandfather. I might bring him down in even more ways, and I can't help but feel it's what he deserves.

We all deserve to be free of him.

There's a knock on my door and I wonder if Liam can't find his keys after the break.

"What would you have done if I wasn't here?" I yell as I open the door. I start to say something more but it's not Liam. It's Maeve.

"Maeve." I try to drop into the sarcastic asshole mask that I wore at her house, but I can't. I'm worn out. Stilworth and I talked for almost an hour last night and my brain is struggling to get back into school mode when this is hanging over my head. All I'm doing is working to protect her.

"Bennett." Her voice is heavy and it hits me in the chest. "You said we should talk when we got back. I'm back. Let's talk."

I move aside and she steps into my room for the first time. Maeve looks around and immediately knows which side of the room is mine. She steps over to my bed and fingers the dark gray comforter, and her eyes flick up to the poster on my ceiling of a coral reef. She looks sad more than anything, and I hate that too.

"So some of it was real."

"It was real." My voice is raspy. I shouldn't say it.

She turns to look at me now. "But that wasn't the plan, was it?"

"No," I admit. I don't want to lie to her about anything, ever again. "I didn't mean to fall for you."

Maeve flinches. I can't help myself so I move closer to her, backing her against my bed. "Making you fall for me was a double-edged sword because I fell too. I know you can't stop the way you're feeling because

I can't either." My body is pressed up against hers now. She's trying to stand firm and stand against me and act unaffected, but I know her better than that.

"I don't want to stop it either," I whisper as I slide my hand around her waist. "All I want is you. I even dream about you." Maeve sways slightly, and I drop down to my knees in front of her. She sighs when I press my face into her stomach and then slide lower toward her core.

"It doesn't matter," she murmurs, voice weak.

"Nothing matters except you," I tell her honestly. I reach up under her hoodie and to the edge of her leggings. Maeve doesn't stop me when I pull them down, and like she told me the night of the Ides party, she's not wearing panties. When I lift her hoodie, her pussy is bare and waiting for me.

I move closer and she falls back onto my bed. I waste no time following, and spreading her legs open so I can get to her. Maeve moans when I lick from her entrance to her clit, my tongue diving between her lips to taste her.

"I want you," I tell her as my fingers tease along her slit. "I always want you."

Two of my fingers glide easily inside her. "But I won't make you stay with me. I'll find a way out. For you. If that's what you want." I'm saying one thing but I mean another - I will find a way out, but that doesn't mean I'll let her go.

"Bennett," she moans when I curve my fingers against the front of her, and I return to working her clit with my tongue. She moves like a wave beneath me, sliding up and down my fingers, her hands clawing into the comforter, and I can do nothing but watch and lick and suck until she comes apart for me.

Maeve screams into the room, and I play with her through her orgasm until she pushes me away.

I'm surprised when she grabs me and yanks my mouth to hers, pulling me onto the bed with her and climbing on top of me. It's borderline violent as she pulls at my clothes and removes her own. Maeve takes off her hoodie and bra and I barely get a chance to look at her before her hard nipples are dragging across my bare chest as she bites and sucks at my skin.

Maeve yanks down my pants and boxers, then stops, chest heaving. "Condom."

It almost hurts that she asks, since our first time, when she didn't even know who I was, she was willing to fuck me without one. I open the side table next to my bed and grab a condom from the drawer. Maeve steps down and removes her leggings and I can't look away from her even as I roll on the condom.

Her breasts are small and tight with dark rosy nipples and I want them in my mouth. I want to know how she'll react. If she likes it. How she likes.

When I have the condom on, she pushes me down again and mounts me. I watch as she lines my cock up with her body and have to work to keep my eyes open as she slides down on me. Maeve moves slowly, carefully, and I can tell it hurts a little. It's only her second time. She lifts up and down until I'm fully inside her. It's hot and tight and I use all of my control not to move.

This is her taking something from me. I feel that, and I'm going to let her.

With a deep breath, she starts rolling her hips. Adjusting her movement, her speed, until she finds what feels good. I tentatively put my hands on her hips and she lets me keep them there. I follow her lead and grind against her, thrusting deep and burrowing into her core.

"Bennett," she moans, moving faster. I hold on tighter and move her, pulling her harshly onto my cock to get her over the edge. Maeve cries out, her nails digging into my chest, and watching the ecstasy on her face is what I need. I groan as I pound inside her and see a flash of white as I come.

Maeve looks down at me, and her gaze is still so sad.

"I want to forgive you," she says quietly. "But I can't."

My heart falls, and I nod. Maeve slides off me and I feel cold and vulnerable. I've never felt that way in my life, but I know she pulls emotions out of me that I've never felt before. It's pathetic the way I sit there on my bed as she gets dressed.

"Bye, Bennett." I feel like she's saying it for more than just now, this moment. Like she's saying it forever.

I have to fucking fix this.

 Maeve

A show I watched once had a moment that should've been sexy, except the character later said that it was a moment of perfect misery. That was me going to see Bennett. I needed to feel as close to him as possible and burn myself alive in my feelings for him. I needed it to hurt. I needed the wound to go so deep it severed the nerve.

We didn't have any classes together this semester, and he changed his schedule with admissions so we didn't cross paths. It didn't matter though. Elmwood is small. We lived in the same hall. We saw each other all the time.

I could feel his eyes on me even though I never looked back. If I met his eyes, I'd break. I knew that I would, and I couldn't afford that. He told me he was going to find a way out. In the single text he'd sent me since I left his room after spring break, he reiterated that promise. He was going to let me go. It was only a matter of time.

The darkest part of me wanted him to fight to keep me.

When my friends all got back from break, they took one look at me and knew something was really wrong. I broke down and told them everything. Not just about Bennett being my unknown fiance, but the truth about P.C. and the emails, losing my virginity at the Founder's Ball, and that I'd fallen for Bennett while working together in admissions. I even told them about our drunken adventure in the hedge maze at the Ides party.

"That hedge maze is the horniest place on campus, I swear," Elise said as she massaged my scalp before braiding my hair.

"My prediction was that I'd be betrayed three times - I'm just waiting for the third."

"Those predictions were crap," Tati reminded me. "Totally generic."

"I know."

"But it feels real, doesn't it?" Cyn asked softly. "Like life aligned to fit it."

"Yeah." I closed my eyes as Elise began to braid my hair. "What do I do?"

"He said he's working to get out of it. Make sure he does." Tati shook her head, disappointed in it all. She had always been the one most bothered by the marriage agreement I'd been trapped in, and the fact that I might be able to get out of it was a relief to her.

"That's fine, but what do I do about the feelings?" I fought back my tears.

"If we knew, the world would be a very different place," Cyn said and sat close to me. "It's going to be okay."

The call I got at 7:00 a.m. two weeks after spring break made it very clear that it was not going to be okay. It was going to go to the deepest depths of hell.

"Dad? What's wrong?" I answer the phone and sit up. Tati groans and puts her pillow over her head.

"Sweetheart. Mr. Silar sent us a video." I have never heard my father sound so shaken in my life. "It's of you. And a boy."

"Okay..." I'm still waking up, so it takes a long time to compute.

"Having sex," mother's voice comes through the phone and I can tell she's been crying. "He's using it as proof you violated the agreement. The settlement is done."

"Oh my god." I didn't know emotional pain could feel like this. I didn't know that I could feel as if I'd been forcibly pushed out of my body in order to disconnect from the power of the pain and betrayal I'm feeling. It's as if I'm looking down at myself and watching this happen to me. The world waves around me, bile burns in my throat, and tears burst from my eyes. How could Bennett do that to me? To us? That moment was special and private. I had thought his manipulation of me didn't get any deeper.

This was it. The third betrayal.

"We were so close, Maeve. What were you thinking?"

"That my life had been hell," I snap, so far from control that everything I've felt since I was 13 comes pouring out of me. "That I had to stay isolated and in absolute control so that we could keep to this disgusting, archaic agreement that was a result of an incident a hundred years ago. That someone else that I didn't even know owned a part of my body but all of my future. Did you not see that I didn't have friends growing up? That I never made connections with anyone so I didn't get hurt? How could you not see how fucking lonely I was, and how much it wrecked me?"

"Maeve," my father chokes out, and I know that this hurts him. I know he hated this deal. He could've paid us out of it, but he always said it was the principle of the thing, and ending the last debt to the last family.

"I hated my life. I hated never really knowing anyone. You want to know the worst part, dad? You know who it is in that video?"

Silence.

"It's Bennett."

"WHAT?" he roars.

"Pay them. End this. I'm done." I hang up the phone because I can't talk about this anymore. The Silars are getting their money, Bennett and I are both free, and I will probably spend the next 30 years of my life never trusting anyone. I'll let our family name die with me. Move to a cabin in the woods and adopt a puma.

I twinge and think of Bennett. I wish I could ask him about the pumas.

That's such a stupid fucking thought.

But if I think about how he filmed us together, how he did this to me, seduced me knowing he was going to collect evidence to ruin me, I might never stop crying.

"That was brilliant," Tati mumbles, moving the pillow away from her face. "I'm really proud of you for telling them off."

"Bennett filmed us having sex."

"WHAT?" Tati roars like my father did and springs from the bed. "I'm going to kill him."

"No. I want to forget he exists." I stand up and grab her, squeezing her until she looks at me. "He's dead to us now. Promise me."

"Yeah," Tati nods, calming down. She yanks me toward her and hugs me, and I let her. I can't fully give in because I'm still afraid of what will happen if I start crying. "What do you need?"

"I have all of you. I'm good."

I'll keep saying that to myself until it's true.

 Bennett

Stilworth calls me in the middle of class. That's unusual since he and I don't often connect during business hours, so I quietly step out and take the call.

"We have a problem."

"What's going on?" My stomach drops to the ground.

"Your father got the video and sent it to the Keans. He got in touch with me to start the arrangements for the contract being violated."

I sink down to the ground and put my head in my hands. Holy fuck. I never gave him the video. I never gave him anything. The camera uploaded the video to my private cloud, but the rest of the evidence is still in my safe in my room. I was supposed to give it all to him over spring break, but I claimed I'd forgotten.

"I never gave him the video."

"He accessed it somehow, and he used it. The agreement, as far as he knows, is done."

I swallow thickly. "Do the Keans know it's me?"

"No, and even if they did, I don't think it matters considering how they viewed the expectation for Maeve."

"Fuck." Maeve's parents would have called her by now. Not only would she know what I'd done, but she'd think this was how I got us out of the agreement. I'm sure I was blocked on everything already, and unless I found her in person, alone, she'd never hear me out about what really happened.

"What do I do?"

"Well, I'm prepared to file the paperwork on the fraud against your father, as well as submit the documentation to trigger the morality clause of his contract. Are you ready for that?"

"Yes. Do it."

"Good," Stilworth sounds relieved. "If I were you, I'd call her father. Explain everything. Whether or not the contract is done and how it's done is up to you. Have him give me a call if he has any questions."

"Thank you. For everything."

"I might be a lawyer, but I still believe in right and wrong, and I think your grandfather would want this for you. I owe him more than you will ever know, and I feel like this is me making a dent in the debt."

We end the call and I go back to class. I don't hear a word from the lecture but I'm with it enough to make note of the homework. I don't have anything else today, so I head back to Harwood-Locke, head on a swivel in case I run into Maeve.

I don't.

I sit down on my bed and stare at my phone. I have the number for Maeve's house in New Hampshire, where as far as I know her parents are at the moment. Then again, if I call and they aren't, I'm sure someone will put me in touch. If the Keans do know that it's me in the video and that I recorded it, I deserve whatever her father wants to say to me.

With a fortifying breath, I hit send and call the Kean house.

"Kean residence."

"This is Bennett Silar. I'd like to speak to Mr. Kean."

There's a long, heavy pause. Whatever they know, the whole damn household knows it.

"Please," I add. "It's...it's important."

"One moment."

The phone starts to ring again, and then a gruff voice answers. "You've got a lot of nerve calling my house."

"I know. I'm sorry." I swallow. "It's not what you think. None of this is what you think."

I take another breath, reminding myself that legally I'm an adult, I'm a party to the agreement, and I should have done this as soon as I knew I had the power to end it. This is the last day my father will ever have power over me, and hopefully the last time he has any power over anyone at all. I'm destroying my father for Maeve, and I doubt she'll ever know that it's because of her I was finally strong enough. I couldn't do it for me, but I could do it for her.

"My father is not a good person, Mr. Kean." I lay out the threats he made against me, that he tried before to have other people seduce Maeve, that I did get close to her and I did film the two of us together, but I never intended for that video to be used or seen. I told him about the complaint I'm filing and gave him Stilworth's information to verify everything that I was saying. And even though I die a little inside talking to Maeve's father about our sex life, I tell him everything about the interpretation of the contract too.

"She didn't violate anything, and I have the authority to end it. We'll go with the initial payout, and be done. I'm so, so sorry Mr. Kean."

I hear him sigh on the other end of the phone. "I don't think you're the one who should be sorry. It took a lot of integrity to call me."

"Maeve didn't deserve this."

"Hm. I don't think we helped the situation any either. I'm not going to accept your apology Bennett, because I'm not the one that needs to hear it. Talk to Maeve."

It's hard to talk around the lump in my throat. "I don't think that's going to happen."

"Tell her everything you told me. Put it all on the line. See what happens."

"It sounds like you're trying to get her to forgive me."

He laughs. "She could do worse than you."

It's a weird time to feel accepted. Mr. Kean and I talk through some logistics, and he tells me he's going to call Stilworth to resolve and dissolve the agreement.

I found a way out.

So why do I wish I was still stuck?

 Maeve

Bennett texts and calls.

I haven't had the guts to block him.

I asked Mallory for a week off from admissions, which is stupid considering I'm right on the brink of recruitment. My last official Magistrate interview is next week. It's the only positive feelings I've had about anything since father called and told me about the video.

Father followed up with an email explaining that he was working with an attorney, and the contract was concluded. I was free.

I felt like I was drowning instead.

Other than class, I haven't left my room. One of the girls brings me food, and they don't even try to press me to go out and do things. Not yet. I love them for how well they know me, and truly feel how well we know each other. They know that I need quiet and peace to recover and heal.

If it was Tati or Elise, we'd be surrounding them in distractions and taking them everywhere. With Cyn, it'd be never leaving her alone. With me, it's making sure that I get to hide in my bubble, and they're doing all they can to keep me cocooned inside it.

At least I can do school on auto-pilot.

Someone knocks on the door.

"Maeve," Bennett calls through the wood. "Please. We need to talk."

I don't say anything.

"I'm not giving up. There's so much you don't know."

Still nothing. He can't be sure I'm here.

"I'll wait if I have to, my queen." I walk toward the door as quiet as I can and rest my forehead against it. It's as close as I'll let myself get to him right now. "My Maeve. My intoxicating one, my soul, my heliotrope heaven." That's a new one. I feel myself smile and immediately hate it. "When I get to see you face to face again, I'm going to tell you that I love you."

I gasp and Bennett stops. I can hear him breathing on the other side of the door. It's heavy enough that it almost sounds like he's crying.

"I'm going to tell you that you are my orchid obsession, my lavender love, the purple pansy that grows in my heart like you had on your toga that night in the maze. I'm going to tell you that from the moment I laid eyes on you, the real you, I was yours." He sighs again and there's a soft thump on the door. His voice sounds closer when he speaks, and I get the feeling if the door wasn't between us we'd be forehead to forehead right now.

"Please."

My heart throbs, but I'm not ready. "No."

I know he hears me. "Okay."

I stay at the door and listen to his footsteps as he leaves.

I'm afraid he's going to come again, and I'll weaken. It's time to pull out the big guns.

After class on Friday I race to Elise before she heads to Colin's for the night.

"I need a place to hide."

She narrows her eyes at me. "How hidden?"

"More than the library, less than the old hospital."

"I think I know the place. Let me get my stuff and I'll take you there on my way to Colin's."

I go back into my room and grab my phone and charger, pack my backpack with my homework, laptop, laptop charger, and snacks. At the last minute I also stuff a fleece blanket inside. I don't know where I'm going to be, but I'm not against hiding there all night. Maybe even all weekend.

Elise knocks twice on the door and I follow her out. She links her arm through mine and we compare what we can about our recruitment processes. It's the only thing that gives me any energy lately. Being recruited for the Castle sounds as intense as it does for the Magistrates, only with less interviews.

She had to prepare a party budget. That sounds more fun than the Elmwood citizenship test I had to go through that was all about how to make rules, policies of the campus, and historical traditions. Okay, I'm lying, it was fun, and it was easy. I'm not letting what happened with Bennett take away my enthusiasm for this place.

Not all memories can be good.

We make it to Manderly and go up to the second floor. There's a random door at the end of the hallway and when she opens it, there's a small study room inside. It's nothing but windows, a roaring gas fireplace, and a few overstuffed couches. It's perfect.

"No one is ever here. And please don't tell anyone."

I offer her my pinkie. "You got it."

She hooks her pinkie through mine. "Text if you need anything, okay? We're all here for you."

"I know."

She lingers for a bit as I get setup, like she's double checking that all I'm doing is plugging in my laptop and settling in. After a few minutes she gives me a wave, another reminder to text if I need her, and she leaves. I brought my homework but I already know that I'm going to binge watch something on Netflix.

When I pull up the website, it advertises *New Girl.*

A pang of hurt goes through my chest. Despite the fact that Bennett as P.C. quoted it all the time, I've never watched the show. How much do I want to hurt myself tonight? That's the real question.

Before I can hit play, my phone rings. It's my father.

"Hi," I answer, shifting the computer off my lap.

"How are you?" he asks.

"Fine." It's not that I don't talk to my dad, or catch him up on my life, it's that when he calls out of the blue and not at a time he schedules, it's because there's something specific he wants to talk about. "What's going on?"

"Have you talked to Bennett?"

Didn't see that coming. "No. Of course not."

"I think you should."

"Did you hit your head?"

He laughs. "No. I want to make sure you understand what Bennett did for you."

"What are you talking about?"

"Search his father's name."

I pull my laptop back over to me and do what my father asked. A series of articles comes up about his father being removed from his position with their family's company saying that the morality clause was enacted but the specifics are being kept confidential.

"I don't understand."

"Then talk to Bennett."

"Maybe."

He laughs again, and I'm shocked that despite recent events not the least of which is seeing me in a sex tape, he's got any sense of humor at all. "I'll take it."

We end the call and I snuggle into the couch I was on to watch *New Girl*.

Bennett

My phone buzzes with a text, and my heart lifts when I see that it's from Maeve.

What it says when I open it is far more confusing.

M: *"I'm not like you! I don't just jump in the potato sack with the first potato I meet with diabetes!"*

It takes a second for me to place why I know that, and then I can't help but laugh.

B: *Are you watching* New Girl?

M: *Yes.*

B: *Do you want to talk?*

M: *Maybe.*

I don't know what to say to that, so I don't say anything. The next move is hers to make. For the next half an hour I pretend to read the textbook for my sociology class, but I'm bouncing my leg so hard my whole desk is moving and I'm staring at letters but not seeing words. I might as well be reading a different language.

"What's going on?" Liam interrupts my staring. He's focused on his video game but I know he's still weirdly attuned to everything around him and could probably hear and feel my anxiety and excitement.

"Maeve texted."

"Whoa. Was it a threat?"

I laugh, and it feels like the first time in a long time. She reached out. Possibility and hope are racing through me.

"Shockingly, no."

There's a knock on our door before he can ask anything else and then it's pushed open. Liam's best friend Hayden and his twin sister Heidi walk in. Hayden gives me a nod and flops down on Liam's bed. Heidi gives me a tight smile and walks over to Liam.

He's focused on his game but looks away for a second to smile at her.

Heidi reaches up and runs her fingers through his longish blonde hair, moving it away from his face. She's looking at him with unabashed want, like she does every time I see them together, and I have no idea how both Liam and her brother are oblivious to it. Heidi is desperately in love with her brother's best friend. Given how long Hayden and Liam have been best friends, Liam is probably one her best friends too.

She catches me watching and snaps her hand back. I give her a look of sympathy and she shrugs, moving away.

My phone buzzes again.

M: *Meet me in the maze.*

B: *Where?* I answer immediately.

M: *Find me.*

It's a challenge, and I'm going to rise to meet it. I stand up and yank on a hoodie while also reaching for my socks and I start to fall over. In my haste, I swipe my textbook onto the floor and knock over my desk chair.

"Where's the fire?" Liam throws over his shoulder.

"Maeve wants me to find her in the maze."

"Shit, dude," Hayden bounces off the bed and grabs my socks off the floor, throwing them at me, followed by my shoes. "Go get her."

I grin at all of them while finishing getting ready, then grab my phone and tuck it in my pocket.

"Good luck," Heidi calls softly as I run out the door. The fact that any of them are still speaking to me when I told them what happened is a testament to their kindness, and belief that my father is deserving of ruin. Heidi's been a little distant, but I understand why, especially after Liam explained her own history with being recorded.

I don't stop running. I run down the stairs and out of the building, following the path past the other halls, the office buildings on the edge of campus, then past the old hospital until I get to the gardens. I'm out of breath when I reach the hedge maze, but I head right inside and start heading for the center.

I have a feeling she's going to be in the clearing where the fate predictions were, and I try to follow what I know of the maze to get there.

"Maeve!" I call her name.

"Getting warmer," I hear her call, but still far away. I move through the maze and call again.

"Warmer!"

I take a turn and call. "Colder, wrong way."

I turn around and try again, moving toward what I think is the clearing before I say her name again.

"Hot. So close."

I keep walking down the path I'm on, and the clearing opens up in front of me. Maeve is sitting on a bench off to the side, buried in a hoodie with her legs tucked under her.

"Maeve."

"Burning up," she replies quietly.

Her eyes don't leave me when I walk across the clearing and sit down next to her.

"What don't I know?" She gets straight to the point, which is something I always liked about her.

So I tell her everything. I tell her more of the story than anybody else gets to know, even Stilworth. The fucked up dynamics of my family, the way my dad manipulated and controlled us by separating us from each other, the things he did with the contract, and the way that he lied to me about what it actually said. Even the detail that I didn't discuss with her father in specifics, which is that the payout doesn't go to the Silar family, it goes directly to me. I was financially free of dad the second the lawyers approved the wire transfer.

Then I tell her about Stilworth, about what I told her dad about the real interpretation of the virginity clause, and about what's happened because I turned my dad in for fraud as well as violating the company morality clause. My mom and my brother still aren't speaking to me, but I think they have to be careful because dad lives with them. I'm going to be patient and forgiving when the times comes that they feel safe enough to reach out.

"You were put in the middle of something, and I didn't protect you," I end, and I can't look at her. "I failed to do the right thing."

"No, it just took you awhile to do it."

"I know." I stare down at my hands. "I want to tell you that I'll let you go now, but it's a lie. I can't, Maeve." She stills beside me. Fuck it. I move so I'm in front of her and get down on my knees. Now we're face to face and eye to eye.

"I love you. I'm in love with you. I spent two years kind of obsessed with the idea of you and when I met you? Hopeless." I shake my head and see her lip lift a little. She's trying very hard to keep a mask of neutrality, but I can tell I'm getting through to her. "I will never give up on getting you to forgive me because I know we work. You've seen every side of me, even my worst, and every single version of me was hopelessly in love with you."

"Then why break the contract?" her voice stutters.

"I want you to choose me."

Her mouth drops open in surprise. I take her face in my hands and she doesn't pull away. If anything, she sinks into me.

"Do you want to know the moment I knew I was in love with you? That I knew I was going to tell my dad to fuck off?"

She nods in my hands.

"When we met at the chapel and you wouldn't let me kiss you. I was sure you'd choose the idea of P.C. over the reality of me, and you didn't."

"Bennett," she murmurs.

"Give me a chance to earn your forgiveness, and then I'll work on earning your love."

"No." It's said quietly, but it may as well have been a knife straight to my heart.

My head drops and all the air in my lungs wheezes out of me.

"You already have both."

I snap my head up to look at her. She's smiling tentatively, and I move closer.

"If I kiss you now, you're mine, my queen. Forever."

Maeve pushes forward and presses her lips to mine. I don't know how long we kiss. We kiss until it's full dark and we can see our breath. Until our noses and the tips of our fingers get cold. By the time we're done, she's straddling me on the bench and even though we're freezing, I don't want to let her go.

"I love you," she says against my mouth. "Take me home."

 # Bennett

6 YEARS LATER

"Faster," I grunt as I grip the dashboard of my brother's car.

"If I get pulled over, it will take longer," Ford reminds me. About a year after everything went down and when Ford finally turned 18, mom divorced dad. Neither of them have really spoken to him since. Mom and I have a long way to go on fixing our relationship, but Ford and I patched things up pretty quickly.

He joined me at Elmwood and when we graduated, we took over Silar Shipping together. It feels good to fix what our asshole father broke. It also helped that I had Mr. Kean to help guide us through some of the biggest transitions. My father-in-law is the only person I call dad these days.

"First births take a long time," Ford's fiance reassures me from the back-seat. She squeezes my shoulder and I appreciate the gesture. Maneuvering New York traffic when your wife called to say she went into labor is perhaps it's own level of hell. We aren't far, but I don't want to be away from Maeve for any of it.

We hadn't planned on getting pregnant, but were delighted to find the other was ecstatic when it became our reality. I loved the idea of the two of us blended together to make a human being that I will love more than anything in the universe. Aside from its mother.

We decided not to learn the sex of the baby.

My phone rings and Elise's name flashes on the screen. Thank god she was visiting and with Maeve when everything went down. The baby is coming over a week early, and her parents weren't planning to get in for a couple more days. They're on their way from New Hampshire now.

"What's going on?" I ask, flustered and trying not to panic. I'll hold it together when I'm with Maeve, but right now I'm losing it.

"They got her all checked in and hooked up to a million machines. The baby's heartbeat sounds great. You have plenty of time to get here."

"Right."

"You do. I promise. I went through all of this with Rosie. Maeve is doing great."

"Right."

"You're still freaking out, aren't you?"

"Yes."

"You're going to be such a great dad," she says softly. "Everyone is fine." She reassures me for a little bit longer, and then we end the call.

Ford focuses on the road and gets me to the pull in for the hospital front doors.

"Congratulations and good luck, daddy," he grins at me. "I expect a call when all is well."

"And when we can visit!"

I nod at them both. "Thanks." Then I run into the hospital like I did the night Maeve told me to meet her in the maze. I anxiously check in at the desk and then race to labor and delivery. The floor is eerily quiet, and I accidentally scare a nurse.

"You must be Bennett. Come on, she's waiting for you."

I follow her to a room and then I see nothing but my perfect wife, her big round belly exposed with a strap across it monitoring the baby's heartbeat. She's smiling and talking to Elise, positively glowing even as she prepares to push out a whole new person. Then her face scrunches up and I run to her side, taking her hand in mine and sliding the other around her nape like she likes when she's tense.

Maeve breathes and then relaxes. Her eyes move to mine and her smile returns.

"Hi."

"Hi."

"I'll see you after," Elise says, and we both wave at her without looking away from each other.

"We got this," I tell her.

"Yeah we do."

After an apparently short 15 hours of labor, Violet Kean Silar arrived.

She was tiny and perfect and I loved her immediately.

I stretched out on the bed next to Maeve because she didn't want me to be far from her as she held our sleeping little girl in her arms.

"Am I finally a prince?" I tease her.

"Give me a kiss and I'll let you know."

CONSTRAINT

Note

The primary incident that sets this story in motion is an act of dubious/non-consent in which the victim is heavily under the influence of alcohol. It's not necessary to the understanding of the plot to read the first chapter when the event occurs, and from the perspective of the person it is happening to; however, the rest of the story is built on this event, and parties engaging in CNC and restraints as part of their exploration of sexual desire. One of the main characters experienced abuse throughout their life and finds their interactions to be helpful.

Most of the other Elmwood stories are on the lighter side.

This doesn't start that way, even if it moves in a lighter direction. If this kind of sexual engagement is difficult for you, then this will be difficult for you.

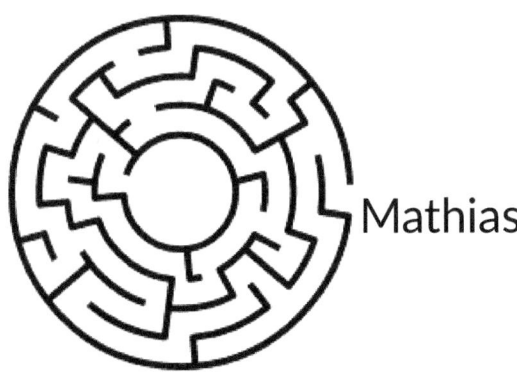 Mathias

I'd been sober for 131 days.

Since Halloween, I hadn't touched any substances. I wasn't an addict; I didn't need it. According to my therapist, I'd been self-medicating to distance myself from my thoughts and emotions.

It was fucking hard being sober, but not harder than accepting that I was a monster. That I'd drowned myself in liquor and the occasional drug instead of confronting my father, my trauma, or taking medication that would have actually helped. I was a survivor with shitty coping skills, but things had been better since Devil's Night last fall.

My father was dead and my mother was dead to me, and I was finally finding a way to move on that wasn't destructive or dangerous. My head was clearer than it ever had been, I was building trust with Dr. Stanton, and it felt like I was experiencing things in ways I never had before. I was no longer clawing out of the grave in which my father had buried me. Now I was hopefully wandering around in the dark, certain that I could find a light.

Things might get worse again before they got better, but I knew what my low looked like. I'd never get there again.

Without the shadow of my father or the weight of my mother, I'd made it through. I spent the holidays with my best friend Wyatt and his parents and none of them questioned why I didn't drink. I even made it through Founder's Ball. Then every party every weekend once the semester started. To some that doesn't seem like a big deal, but having to be present in my own head with my own thoughts, feelings, and memories, meant I spent the majority of my days convincing myself I didn't want to die just to make them go away.

Convincing myself that I no longer wished I'd never been born. That my life was my own. That I didn't need to lash out to feel control.

I kept up the outer facade of who people expected me to be - I went to class, I fought for good grades, I attended meetings for the Cavalry, I helped with events, and I showed up where people expected me to be. None of it touched me, but I was there. There but not part of it, on the periphery while I figured out what my existence should look like without fear and expectations from anyone except myself.

Until the Ides party.

It was my favorite event every year. The ominous fortunes, the drunken ramblings through the hedge maze, the costumes and masks, the disconnection from reality. Dr. Stanton told me that if I felt like I was drinking for fun and not to forget, he didn't see the harm in me doing something I'd previously enjoyed. The Ides party was an untainted thing that brought me joy. Something that was purely Elmwood.

So here I was in a blood red toga, wearing a green laurel crown on my head, and finishing the drinks that kept appearing in my hand. I wasn't entirely sure where they were coming from but every time I threw out one cup, soon enough another would be pressed into my hand. That was normal for Ides.

I was drunk, and I was okay with being alive.

That was progress, in my estimation.

It was almost the end of the school year. As much as I loved Elmwood, I needed to get out of here. It had been a hell of a year, and if I wanted to survive, I needed to process everything that had happened and find a way to move on. Find a way to apologize and make amends.

Find a way to be honest. Especially with Dr. Stanton.

He couldn't truly help me if I couldn't tell him everything. It was hard to fight the idea that if I didn't say the horrible things out loud then they weren't real. If I breathed them into life that made them concrete. I wasn't ready for that yet.

I stood alone, watching everyone else live while I existed.

A girl was watching me.

She was wearing a black toga that was oddly sexy. It was twisted and crossed over her chest, leaving the skin on the sides of her torso exposed. When she turned around I saw that her back was bare, and the idea that her breasts were free, nestled only by the soft material, was oddly erotic. It was a tease.

I didn't notice shit like that. I didn't care about women or sex; didn't have the time, energy, or inclination for it. The fact that I was physically drawn to anyone was enough of a shock even through my intoxication that I tried to pay attention.

Her hair was light blonde and long, a tangled mess that went to her waist. There was black paint around her eyes, tracing along her skin like spreading dark veins. Everything around me was blurry but I felt like I knew her.

She kept looking at me. I kept looking back.

I didn't do that. I didn't look or pay attention. I didn't want anyone's flirtation, attention, or intentions. I might as well be a statue for all I wanted sexual or romantic attention from anyone, but I couldn't stop fucking looking. My head would turn and my eyes orient themselves to her.

Time to walk away.

When I stumbled walking through the maze to the next clearing, that was the sign that it was time for me to leave the whole party. I was a little bit disoriented, but I'd find my way out eventually. Once I was out of the maze I could figure out where I was on campus and make my way back to the Cavalry houses and eventually to my bed.

Hands landed on my arm and I flinched. I didn't like touch without knowing the source.

"This way," a soft, feminine voice said. I turned and there she was. The girl in black. Ethereal, a little terrifying when the world was wobbly, but beautiful. I didn't react like this to anyone. It should have felt frightening but instead I felt curious.

"I know you," I said stupidly. She stared as if waiting for me to figure it out, and then tugged on my arm when I didn't.

I followed her, tripping along as she twisted and turned within the hedge maze until I saw the dim light of an exit. When we stepped out into the dark night we were on the far side of the maze, near the residence halls.

The girl took my hand and started walking deeper into that side of campus, farther away from my bed. I went. I was too drunk to question anyone or anything. I wasn't all there. For some reason, it felt good to be with her. I wanted to go wherever she led me because that's what I was supposed to do, according to my drunk brain.

My memory was fading in and out.

I would blink and we would be further into the dark side of campus, farther from the maze, the party, from civilization. Ahead of us, I could see the old chapel surrounded by scaffolding, and the graveyard that spanned around it in all directions. No one had been buried there in years, and it had an air of haunted neglect no matter how much the school tried to care for it.

It probably was haunted. Wasn't everything?

The girl confidently held my hand and pulled me between the stones. We stopped at what seemed to me an arbitrary place.

"You look good in the dark," she said, her voice barely above a whisper.

"It's the only place I know," I tell her honestly. "Who are you?"

"You'll remember," she says, and then our mouths are sealed over one another and I can't see anything but I can feel her. The sensation of her tongue on mine is overwhelming. Her body is warm pressed against me and my hands rest on the bare skin of her waist. I want to touch her everywhere.

I never want to touch anyone.

I haven't had sex since my father forced me to lose my virginity when I was 14. Other than the fucked up things I did to try and prove myself to my father, and some very forced and awkward kissing, I haven't done anything sexual with anyone.

I thought I hated kissing but I'm wrong because I like kissing this girl. My body loves it, and the affects of her ripple across my skin, through my veins, and my cock gets rock hard. The last time I reacted to anyone this way was in high school and that...well, that was a feeling and a person I'd never get to be around again. A part of me that I thought was dead is alive under her touch.

This girl, woman, goddess, ghost - she arouses me.

I had forgotten what that felt like. Genuine attraction and desire.

When I lost the only person who'd ever brought it out in me, it was another set of feelings to lock in a box and bury away, never to be considered again. Now I'm drowning in them, unable to process what I'm feeling, I am nothing but want.

The next thing I can feel is that we're on the ground, the grass is dry and cold on my back but I don't care. Her legs are squeezing my hips and I can't keep the groans inside as she grinds down on me.

I'm too drunk to catch what's happening when she lifts my hands over my head, and I'm too uncoordinated to stop her or fight her with any success when she ties them together. I blink as she stills over me and assess the situation.

It isn't good.

I am on the ground in the middle of the graveyard, and I am tied to a grave. I can move but not enough to free myself. There's a woman looking down at me like vengeance embodied, someone familiar but not familiar enough. She's obscured herself from me.

The worst part is that even though I know I am in a bad situation, I'm still hard for her. I don't think anything good thing is about to happen, but I don't think I'll try that hard to stop it, either.

"Mathias Talmidge, you deserve what's coming to you."

She's right, I do.

I watch as she takes a knife out of the grass. She must've put it there before. This was all planned. It makes it feel even more justified somehow.

I resign myself to pain, but instead she uses the knife to cut off my toga. I'm nearly naked on the ground. When she goes to pull off my boxer briefs, I lift my hips to help her. Now I'm a hundred percent naked, cock a steel rod pointing up and weeping for her, leaving a sticky spot on my stomach. I don't think she wants me to want this, but I do.

God, I am so fucked up. This woman is clearly trying to hurt me, and I'm turned on by it. Dr. Stanton is going to shit an actual brick.

The ghostly goddess in black stands up and slides her panties off from beneath her black toga. The knife is in one hand, and there's a condom in the other.

She's going to fuck me.

"Don't," I ask, my voice barely there.

I react the way I think I'm supposed to, rather than they way that I want.

I try to turn away from her when she kneels down and opens the wrapper. I hiss when her hand wraps around my cock, panicked and pleasured at the same time, and I try to get away as she slides the condom onto my length. I can't believe I'm even staying hard between my own hang ups and the alcohol, but this ghost...under my skin...I want her even if it's like this. I want this so fucking badly that I tell my brain it's okay to give up the pretense.

It's okay to be taken.

I'm weak and my hands are starting to go numb. She presses me onto my back and straddles me, positioning herself over my groin.

"Don't," I ask again, but I don't mean it. I'm not even sure this is really happening.

"Oh, do you not like it when someone takes from you? When you get fucked without consent?" I move again, bucking my hips, trying to make something happen, but when my cockhead is at her entrance and I move it thrusts my dick inside her wet, tight pussy. My hips drop and she comes with, impaling herself on me and sliding along my length until I'm balls deep.

I groan and try to control my breathing, try to come back to myself. As much as I have convinced myself that I am indifferent to sex, I can't deny that this woman feels like ecstasy. I twist my hands and grab the rope that's binding me, and hold on as she begins to move.

Her hips roll, sliding me out to the tip, and then gliding back down. Over and over she fucks me, and eventually I fuck her back because I embrace that I *want* to fuck her. My hips move to press deep, and it is pure pleasure.

I don't know who she is and I don't know why she's doing this, and on one level I know it's really, really fucking wrong.

But I like it.

In a way I don't understand, I need this.

"You take and take, Mathias, and this time I'm taking from you. You can fight me, you can say no, but you're going to get fucked right now. And the best part? You're going to come. I'm going to take it from you."

That shouldn't turn me on either.

Except the idea that she wants to make me come and take it from me, gets me right on the edge. I am more turned than I ever have been in my life. I'm being punished and I want it. I deserve it. Control is being taken from me in a way I never expected to work, but fuck if it doesn't. Submitting to this woman is everything. I will do whatever she wants. I will give her everything. I want this.

She places her hands on my lower stomach and starts to grind hard and fast, her fingernails digging into my abs. I can feel her cunt squeezing me, clamping around my cock. This might be an act of vengeance, but it turns her on, too.

"Do whatever you want to me," I grunt, pressing into her, willing her to come so I can feel it. "I deserve it. Do it. Oh, fuck, make me come." I'm begging, and she throws her head back and cries out right as she tightens around me. I hold back my own release somehow, and watch as she orgasms.

When her head whips down and her eyes meet mine, clarity strikes me.

"Willow," I groan her name, and my orgasm rockets through me. I pulse inside her tight pussy, filling the condom between us, staring at the face of someone who was once the center of my existence. Someone who left me behind when I wanted to keep her.

A tear streaks down her cheek.

The world goes black.

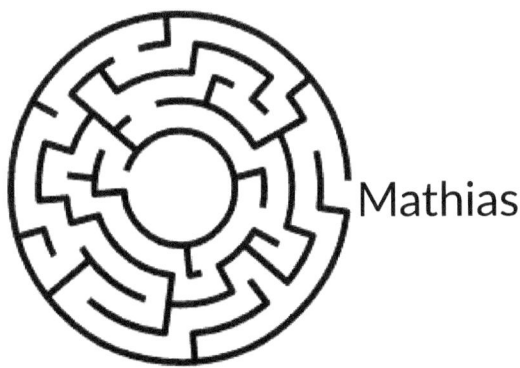 Mathias

5 Months Later

Elmwood doesn't look the same. In the three years that I've come here, everything always felt dark. There was always a shadow.

I know now the shadow wasn't over Elmwood. It was over me. The darkness was over my eyes, and now it's gone. I have one year left here, but it's the first year where I feel like myself. Where I'm present and sure of who I am.

I spent most of the summer at an intensive in-patient therapy retreat. It took what happened after the Ides party for me to finally admit to Dr. Stanton the extent of my father's abuse. He'd suspected, but until I was ready to talk about it, he wasn't going to push it. The summer, as corny as it sounds, was cleansing for my soul.

I'm not ruined unless I want to be.

That's the fucking mantra. My father didn't break me, my mother is an unnecessary blood tie that I can ignore, and the ghost in the graveyard who unlocked something inside me was my savior. My ghost gave me a chance to reconnect to parts of my body and myself that I had chosen to ignore. Parts of me that I was sure no longer remained came back to life.

I've gone no contact with my mother. If she needs something, she talks to my lawyer. She knows that if she tries to get in touch with me directly, I will slap her with a restraining order and make sure that everyone knows about it. I will make it my mission to destroy her. While I will no longer seek out hurting other people because I'm hurting, I won't hesitate to get revenge on the people who got me to that point.

At least my father is dead. I'm safe now, cut off from his manipulation and control, cut off from the hell he dragged me down into, and recovering from the years of damage he inflicted. The damage he pushed me to inflict on others. It's no one's fault but mine, even if I can see the threads of his influence that led to my actions.

So I'm going to start making amends.

I've finished moving back into my room in Cavalry 4. It's the smallest of the houses and on the other side of the courtyard, right up against the woods, and I like it that way. This is going to be my quiet year. Head down, finish my coursework, meet my Cavalry obligations, and then figure out what I want to do with the rest of my life.

I walk across the courtyard and into Cavalry 3. I get a weird look from Tate Daniels for being in their house, but he doesn't say anything as I go up the stairs. I saw Elise leave earlier, so I know she's not around. I'm careful to avoid her - have been since the shit I pulled while I was unbelievably fucked up last year. It makes me sick to think about it. That I traumatized her again.

"It's open," Colin responds when I knock on his door. I don't open it, and knock again because I'm not walking into his space unless he knows it's me. After a second the door whips open and Colin freezes when he sees me.

"The fuck do you want?" he snarls at me.

I hold my hands up. "To talk. Please."

Back when we first moved and I got to start at a new high school, I wanted to be friends with Colin. We sort of were and then my father got involved and obsessed. Colin became my measuring stick, and the reason that I was punished. The reason that things were done to me because I couldn't beat him. I hated him, and he never deserved it. He wasn't responsible for my father's fixation. Except his fixation infected me and my choices, and it led to things I can never take back.

Colin holds the door open and lets me step inside. He closes the door, then crosses his arms and waits. I don't know where to start.

"I'm here to apologize. To you, and to Elise if you think it would help her to hear it."

"I'm listening." He looks suspicious, and that's valid. I would be too.

"My father abused me. In ways that I don't think you want to imagine, and for reasons that only made sense to him. In high school, he made you my enemy. If I didn't beat you, do something better than you, take something that you had or wanted...I would be punished for it." Even though I've said some version of those words out loud many times - the safe, sanitized version of my life - it still makes me sweat. Makes my throat dry with discomfort.

"Punished how?" Colin steps back and leans on his desk. His expression hasn't changed and his arms are still crossed, but his shoulders drop. He's not bracing for a fight anymore.

"Do you really want to know?"

We stare each other down, and for the first time in years I'm not glaring at him. I feel nothing but regret and shame when I look at him. I want to make sure he sees that I'll tell him, but he might regret asking.

"Yeah, I think I do. I need to understand. We were friends, and then we weren't." It almost hurts that he saw us as friends too. That in an alternate world, we would have been. In an alternate world, I would never have hurt him, or the woman he loves.

"Mostly he was physical - beating me, breaking bones and leaving bruises most of the time. He would starve me, or force me to eat food that had gone bad. He'd save it just for me. I would be forced to run or lift until I either got hurt or passed out. He'd make me sleep outside, or standing up in a small closet in his office. One of his favorite punishments was not letting me sleep at all. You have no idea how many days I'd come to school and hallucinate from lack of sleep." I cross my arms protectively and shake my head.

Colin's brow furrows.

"It had been going on all my life, and I would have done anything to avoid punishment." I take a deep breath, swallowing the horror and the flashes of my nightmares. "I'm honestly not here to make excuses, but I thought explaining might give you both closure. In high school, and here,

I was not mentally well. I was paranoid, anxious, and broken. I did things to avoid being punished. I hurt Elise because I was fucked out of my head and she represented absolution to me. It was like I believed that if I could get her before you, my father would finally leave me alone.

"I know that I'm the enemy, and I'm the villain in your story, and I accept that. I deserve that. I owed you, and her, more than anyone else, an explanation. I'm not asking to be friends, I'm just asking for peace."

"Okay." Colin nods and stands up. "I can give you that, as long as you stay away from her."

"You probably don't realize how hard I worked to stay away from both of you, until last fall. Things were better once I came to Elmwood, but then..." I trail off. "I spiraled. I really am sorry, as little as that matters."

"I mean yeah, things seemed fine, both of us being here, so what happened? Why the fuck did you come for us during the Hunt?"

"My father died the week before. As much as I hated that bastard, things were worse in my head. That's...that's how the Hunt happened. Fuck, I don't even remember some of it." I massage my temples, as if it would bring back more of my memory. "After that night I started therapy. Realized I was a fucking monster and I didn't want to be like him. I didn't want to be what he'd made me."

I'm not ruined unless I want to be, I remind myself.

"You can tell Elise whatever you want, but I'd appreciate it if you didn't tell anyone else."

"I won't. We're good."

"Thanks." I step back and don't say anything else.

"Hey," Colin stops me before I leave. "I'm sorry that happened to you. I can't say I'll ever like you, but no one deserves that."

I nod because I'm not capable of speaking, and leave.

That was beyond embarrassing and painful. The person that I held responsible for so much of my pain was now privy to the source of it. To the role he unintentionally played in it. My father had hurt him too and he didn't even know it, not until now.

Every step I take away from Colin's room leaves something behind. The memories and the shame dropping away from me, as if I'm physically letting them go from my mind.

It feels good.

Fuck.

I walk back to my room and lock the door, embracing that lighter feeling and knowing where my mind will go next.

Because whenever I think about how much better things are getting, I think about *her*.

Willow Talbot, my ghostly goddess of vengeance, who took from me, punished me, and I don't even know why. Even though it was probably the best thing that's ever happened to me.

I know I'll feel guilty for it later, but I lay down on my bed and use the handcuffs there to attach my left hand to the headboard. Being restrained has become a thing for me, even that little bit I can do by myself. I'm already half hard, reliving our time in the graveyard in my mind.

With my free hand I shove my shorts down, spit in my palm, and start to stroke my cock as I think about her. How tight her pussy felt, the way her screams echoed as she orgasmed, the feeling of her mouth on mine and the lingering taste of her on my tongue. The way she took from me, fucked me against my will but I liked it, wanted it. Wanted her.

It doesn't take long for me to get to the edge, and I suppress a groan as my come shoots up my abs. My body relaxes immediately.

Part of my recovery is reclaiming my control and my desire, and that includes masturbating. Something I did rarely before my encounter in the graveyard. I was so disconnected from my body I didn't want sexual contact. Even from myself.

It still feels kind of weird, and I don't think Dr. Stanton would be enthused about my spank bank material. He did explain to me that some people engage in consensual non consent, or like being tied up and used, because giving up control is a form of control in itself. I know he's concerned that I'm into it, but he can't argue with the results.

My body trusted Willow when my mind couldn't catch up.

I haven't sought her out. I didn't even know she'd come to Elmwood.

When she cut me off I let her go, because even being on the periphery of her life was too painful. Enough things hurt me, I didn't want to put her in that category too.

What happened in the graveyard spurred me into action, and was what finally got me to go all-in with fixing myself.

I wanted to be better before I tried to find her. I wanted to be in a different, healthier place when I confronted her and asked her why. Willow was the one who abandoned me, and I never got an explanation. I think she thinks I was too drunk to remember it was her that night because I've been radio silent, and I look forward to the moment she realizes the truth.

I woke up the next morning naked and cold, my wrists burned from the rope. Everything was gone except my sliced up toga. The only proof that any of it had happened.

Dwelling on her is getting me half hard again, and I shake my head as if I could clear her out of it. I hit the release on the handcuffs and rub my wrist.

This year is going to be different. The only person I will let ruin me is her.

Willow

Moving in this heat is exhausting. How can a place that gets so deeply cold by November be this humid and sweltering in August? Sweat is dripping from under my arms and in a line down my back as I drag boxes up the stairs.

Georgia wanted to live in this creepy old Victorian on the edge of campus, and talked the rest of us into living here with her. It wasn't hard, exactly, but she had spent too much time telling us she believed it was haunted that now we're all unsettled. However, we got enough of us together that the entire house is made up of people I either consider friends or trusted acquaintances.

The freedom from being in the residences after two years also feels good. Like I can really let go now. We might be renting the house from Elmwood, but at the end of the day, it's ours. Together.

I put the last two boxes on the floor inside my room and look around. It's got high ceilings and it was built well. The family of one of the Elmwood founders built the house and lived here. My room has big windows, a fireplace that I will never use, and one corner is the second floor of the front turret. It's going to be a cozy reading nook for me. The overstuffed, cozy chair I bought just for it is arriving tomorrow.

This year I'm going to try and leave things behind.

For the last two years, I've stayed quiet and hidden. I didn't want to run into Mathias. When I ghosted him after he and Lola broke up, that was what I needed. After her and I talked more about their breakup, and some of the questionable choices she made afterward, it became imperative to stay away from him. No matter how deep my feelings were, Mathias was not only my sister's ex-boyfriend, but apparently, a monster.

I don't know what got into me last semester when I decided to go after him. To make him hurt the way he'd made other people hurt. To punish him for the way he made me hurt.

I don't let myself think about it. About him. About what I did.

Or at least I try not to let myself.

I'm not hiding from him this year.

He probably doesn't even remember what happened he was so drunk. But it felt like vengeance to me, and that was all that mattered.

He shattered my heart. I needed to take something from him.

I shake my head to clear it of those thoughts and start setting up my room. I can hear everyone else thumping around their various areas. When the school bought the house and renovated it to be functional for students, they were not messing around. Even thought they tried to keep as much original architecture and details as they could, some things just need to be updated, and they made it kind of amazing.

They kept the ground floor as living space - there's a kitchen, a living room, and one huge room that's a library and study area. Then two floors of bedrooms, four people per floor, and then the two attics. One attic was converted into a living space where we've tucked our resident nerd, Liam, and the other attic was staff quarters. It was converted into small, private study rooms. I doubt we'll use them, and right now our plan is to each call dibs on one for storage.

I'm on the third floor with Georgia, as well as Lachlan and Moss. Luckily, they added two bathrooms to each floor as well so we will not have to be sharing with the boys. The second floor is where we stuck Bronte and Gus, who rented individual rooms even though it's impossible to separate them. Bronte brought her friend Goldie, and Gus brought his brother Felix into the fold as well. Goldie is reserved, but I think we might need some of that energy here.

I already love living here. Surrounded by people that make me feel good, in a room that feels like a fresh start. I've purged myself of the guy I couldn't get over and now it's time to move on.

I'm just finished putting together and making my bed when my phone buzzes.

It's Lola, because her timing is impeccable even when she's a few thousand miles away from me in California. Sometimes I think my older sister is psychic, or that we're somehow spiritually tuned to one another.

"Hi, babe!" she chirps. "How's the big creepy house?"

"Gorgeous." I flop back on my bed and stare up the ceiling, at the molding around the chandelier that dimly lights the room. "I have a fireplace. Jealous?"

"Of the decor? Maybe. Of the possibility of ghosts, no."

"For someone getting a degree in applied physics it's kind of weird that you believe in ghosts."

"I believe everything is a possibility until proven otherwise."

I laugh and feel a tug in my chest. We were born barely a year apart - 387 days. Lola was on purpose, I was an accident, and we'd been living our lives accordingly. Our parents love us both for exactly who we are, but it's always funny to me to think about how close we are even though we are like opposite ends of a spectrum.

My big sister is goal-oriented, planned, focused, likes to take endless notes and has the memory of an elephant. She's always been high-achieving and wants to make sure people know it. She also dresses like a Stepford wife with a love of pastels, plaid, and keeping her blonde hair pin straight.

Then there's me. Same blonde hair but in constant disarray, same green eyes, same genetically perfect eyebrows. I'm more on the creative side, never sticking to one thing for too long, and only holding onto the details I find the most interesting, or the most personal. I love knowing things about people. I love their possibilities, secrets, and celebrating the things that matter to them. While Lola is going to remember your birthday, I'm going to get you the best gift. I also spend most of my time in leggings and an increasingly bizarre collection of t-shirts.

The t-shirts are how I made friends with Georgia.

I was walking through campus on one of my first days in a black shirt that had a skateboarding grim reaper and said "hang dead." It's still one of my favorites because it's super duper soft even though the white print is fading. She walked straight up to me and said that she liked my shirt and we were friends, and that's been true ever since. I brought in Bronte, who was my randomly assigned roommate, who brought Goldie. When Bronte started dating Gus at the end of our first year, we got our guys through his friends.

If you'd told the isolated outcast that was me in high school that this was what my life would be like, I wouldn't have believed it for a second.

In high school, I had Lola. For a small window of time I had Mathias. Otherwise, it was just me.

Now I rarely had a day to myself, and I loved it.

"WILLOW TREE TALBOT GET OUT HERE NOW!" Georgia bellows from the hallway.

"Gotta go," I laugh, and it's like I can feel Lola smiling as she says goodbye. She was worried about me a lot when I first left, but we're both happy exactly where we are.

I groan as I move off my bed and walk out into the hall.

Georgia is wearing a black, high-neck dress with no sleeves. Her tattoos are on display and make her look especially witchy today.

"What?"

"You're the last one to finish your shit, we're going to Direwood for groceries."

"Okay." I take two steps backwards into my room, put on my flip flops, and follow my best friend down the stairs. Everyone else is waiting at the entrance and Gus is dividing us into cars, while Bronte and Lachlan are making final decisions about the shopping list. They're the cooks out of all of us.

"Where's Liam?" I ask.

"Gaming, duh," Felix answers. "He added to the list."

I shake my head as we all pile out the door and into our assigned car to fill up our over-sized kitchen with food.

Going to Direwood to go grocery shopping turned into going to dinner turned into wandering around downtown and going to whatever store someone said they wanted to go to.

By the time we get back to the house, the temperature has cooled and I'm sweaty but not as uncomfortable. I am, however, completely exhausted.

I call dibs on the shower and hurry through it so I can crawl into my bed with fresh, cold sheets.

My head barely hits the pillow when Lola calls again.

"What? It's midnight here."

"Whatever. You good?"

"Yeah, why?"

"I dunno. A feeling."

"Maybe you're getting the vibes of one of the ghosts through me."

"Shut up," she laughs. "Have you seen Mathias this year? He sent me a text the other day."

My entire body stiffens up. Lola dumped Mathias during the first half of her senior year of high school; I remember hearing them fight but not what they were fighting about. Their relationship never really made sense to me, but whenever I would ask Lola about it she'd tell me things were fine.

When he left the house after the fight and she told me they were done, I asked her why. The answer she gave me haunted me: "He took too much." The look on her face, the hurt and fury I saw there, told me everything that I needed to know. Mathias was a complicated figure in my life, but it became pretty uncomplicated when I realized what he'd done to Lola. Then a few months later there was a situation with him and a sophomore at a party, and I didn't need to ask Lola for more. Not unless she wanted to tell me.

Back in the present, I ask Lola, "What did he want?"

"Well, he said he wanted to say hi, but when I asked him if he'd ever run into you at Elmwood..." Lola trails off, her voice teasing. I'm surprised she's talking about him so easily, and with such lightness. After they broke up, we both seemed to decide he was a totally off-limits topic, even though we never said it explicitly. It was like he never existed to us.

Even if he dominated my mind for years.

Even if he still does.

"We haven't." I lie, voice clipped.

"He said he hoped to see you this year. You'll have to tell me if you see him."

"Sure," I lie again. When it comes to Mathias, I always lie to Lola.

You can't exactly tell your beloved big sister you were in love with her high school boyfriend, especially not knowing that he hurt her. I also definitely can't tell her that I tied him up and assaulted him to get revenge for the women he hurt.

The conversation fades out for me and I make the appropriate noises until Lola gets the hint that I'm tired and wishes me goodnight.

I can't tell Lola anything when it comes to him. Not about the past in high school, not about last year, and I'm going to try and genuinely pretend he doesn't exist this year.

In high school, he'd come over to our house with Lola after school. She'd go to her room and study, but he would sit with me at the kitchen table. We did homework, sure, but most days it turned into the two of us talking about anything and everything. I'd sit next to him and lean close while we shared videos with each other on our phones, or we'd play games against each other and earn bragging rights over the other.

While we weren't friends at school, he always acknowledged me and never let anyone mess with me. Most people didn't see me but if they tried, he stepped in. It was always under the cover of me being his girlfriend's sister, but I liked to think it was about me. About the thing between us.

They were together for 8 months but it only took me 2 to fall hopelessly in love with my sister's boyfriend. Who only saw me as a friend. Despite the fact that at least four days a week we were together for hours while Lola did her own thing. She got him in public, and I got him in private.

She got the brooding, icy Mathias that intimidated people with his good looks and muscles, with the snark and arrogance he never stopped slinging. The one who was mean first and asked questions later. He was popular purely because he was too beautiful to ignore, even when people weren't sure they even liked him.

I got the Mathias who smiled, who laughed when he beat me at a game, who drew cartoon faces in the margins of my notebooks. That wrote down the dreams he had the night before on post-it notes so he could tell me about them and we could look the meanings up in my dream dictionary. The guy who practiced tying different kinds of knots with me because I got curious. That learned to french braid my hair when Lola refused, and I can still feel his fingers on my scalp and the way he'd trail them down my neck and across my shoulders. Even when we both knew he shouldn't touch me like that. I got the Mathias that told me he loved my mind and never got tired of talking to me.

Now I wonder which Mathias was real.

I'm not the same girl he used to know.

In my bed in the dark, I can think about after the Ides party. I can stop denying the thoughts like I do in the daytime. In the dark, I'm the girl that got vengeance. That got what she wanted.

Even though I'd planned it, I didn't think I was going to go through with it. I was a little bit drunk, and I think that's where I got the courage. When he didn't recognize me, that made it a certainty. It made the hurt fresh. I was going to take Mathias.

Heat pools in my belly when I think about it. When I acknowledge the darkest truth: I liked what I did to him, and how he responded to me.

I liked having Mathias at my mercy. Bound and helpless, taking from him, but especially knowing that I was also giving him pleasure. The sounds he made, the way his body moved against mine, that he was begging me to make him come by the end. The fucked up but beyond delicious orgasm I had while riding him. It felt incredible.

I was doing to him what he'd done to others, but I had also gotten something I wanted. I'd gotten him.

God, he could kiss. I hadn't planned on that part, I wasn't going to kiss him, but then we were connected and I couldn't stop. Once the entire thing was in motion there were parts that I hadn't been in control of at all.

My hand slips inside my sleep shorts and I'm already wet when I start teasing my clit.

I taste the memory of his tongue in my mouth and grind against my hand. I think about how badly I wanted to put his dick in my mouth and taste him like that too, but I couldn't wait any longer. The ghost of the feeling of his hips slamming up into mine, of the relief on his face as he orgasmed after saying my name.

Remembering the agony in his voice when he recognized me is the thing that breaks me again.

I grab my pillow and hold it down over my face as I cry out into it, coming on my own hand, thinking about the man I pretend not to love saying my name before he came.

As I come down, I send a prayer out into the universe that I never see him again because I don't know if I'm strong enough to stay away.

Willow

Today, I'm back at the scene of the crime.

The graveyard next to the almost-done-being-restored campus chapel.

This semester I'm in a preservation and restoration class even though I'm getting my degree in psychology, but it meets my required lab course. I have to do some grave rubbings and identify some markers that might be in need of work. It's purely by chance that I have to come here. Dr. Cunningham put all the options in a jar and we picked them out at random.

So here I am.

Wandering through the rows and looking for a marker with an interesting design or name, one that's in decent condition for a rubbing so I have some sort of progress to show in class tomorrow.

We're a few weeks into the semester but the temperature is dropping rapidly. I regret complaining about the heat in August. The grass here is already dying and crunches beneath my feet.

I stop next to a stone in decent condition with a design of vines and roses on it. The name says Elizabeth Van Dyne. Looks good to me.

I kneel down in the grass and get my paper and charcoal ready. I use blue painters tape to affix the paper to the stone, and then softly rub with the charcoal. To my surprise, the design comes through clearly, the roses well and deeply carved into the stone. It's lovely.

I'll have to look Elizabeth up when I get home tonight. The graves on either side of her also belong to Van Dynes, but I've never heard of the family before. My curiosity makes me question again if I should be focusing on history instead of psychology, but I think I'm just as interested in the minds of people in the present as I am the stories of those from the past.

I do another rubbing on the stone of her name and the dates of her life, and when I rub the epitaph below it becomes legible: *a true believer.*

In what, exactly? It's almost creepy. Now I'm even more excited, and I bet that I can rope Georgia into researching her now too. She's up for anything dark and spooky, and especially if it might tie to the history of Elmwood. While a lot of us come from more cosmopolitan and far-flung backgrounds, Georgia is one of the few Elmwood attendees that could be considered a townie. An affluent townie, but still someone who was born and raised in Direwood. She's already on track to graduate and take over the county records and archives which includes Elmwood and its history. Her family has been curating county history for generations.

Sometimes it's like Georgia appeared from the roots of the forest, a dark spirit that watches over it all. If I hadn't met her parents I would genuinely believe in that theory. Despite her broody exterior and generally cloudy mood, she has genuine enthusiasm for every single tradition on campus, and tries to do everything at least once.

She's been writing the fates in the premonition books for the Ides party since her first year. I swear it's the reason they recruited her into the Magistrates at all. I love it. I love being macabre and weird with her, and that she is the most supportive person I know. As long as it makes you happy, no matter how random, Georgia is down to support you. With a frown on her face, but it's not personal.

I roll up my rubbings and store them in the cardboard tube I brought with me, before sliding it and my other tools in my backpack. If I head back now I can probably meet up with my housemates for dinner.

Then I hesitate.

If I walk around the other side of the chapel, that's where it happened. The chapel blocked us from sight than night.

It was me, Mathias, the dark, and the stars.

The grave I'd picked was a short obelisk, easy to tie him to.

It belonged to a man named Elliot Renault, and his epitaph was simple and appropriate: *the lover.* It had a detailed skull design with vines and a small heart with the initials M.B. inside it. I hadn't looked up his story yet either because I had a feeling it would make me sad. He was associated with my own sad love story now.

Every grave in this yard was known. When the preservation program started cleaning up the graves they also created a repository of every person buried here and all of the information they could find out about them. Electronic biographies were available through the library website, but actual artifacts and photos were available in the library itself as well.

Damn, this was place was awesome.

Decision made, I walk around the chapel to head to Elliot's grave. I'd been back a few times since that night because I wanted to remind myself that it was real and I did that. I'd carved into a piece of myself to try and fix what was hurting. Like extricating a love tumor.

Usually, the shadowed corner was empty and quiet.

Today, there was someone sitting with their back resting against the stone. From my angle all I could see were long legs in dark denim. I stop in my tracks, ready to turn around, except I step back on a rock and start to trip.

I catch myself but not before a startled "oh!" has already left my mouth.

The person sitting on Elliot's grave turns at the sound and even before I can see more than legs, I know who it is. He came back too.

Mathias turns his head to peer around the stone and his ice blue eyes lock onto mine. Eyes of angel in the body of the devil. He looks as startled as I feel, until recognition has his expression dropping into something full of heat.

He stands quickly, a faint blush I've never seen before spreading across his cheeks as he wipes the dry grass from himself.

"Willow," he starts, and takes a few steps toward me. He holds out his hand like I'm going to come forward and take it.

Other than a little light, long distance stalking, I haven't been this close to him since the night I punished him. I'd almost forgotten how insanely beautiful he is. Nearly white blonde hair, piercing blue eyes, a face that's all cruel sharp lines but still manages to be sensual. Tempting. Even from this distance his size and power draw me in like they have their own gravity.

There's a tug behind my belly button like a string is yanking me forward to respond to his outreach. Like I am meant to put my hand in his.

"Willow," he says again, and this time it holds a hint of that same agony that makes me orgasm every single time I think about it, and heat rushes to my core.

"No," I say, not sure what I'm denying but I know that I need to, and then with absolutely no dignity whatsoever, I turn on my heels and run. I don't listen for him to follow, I'm too worried about tripping on another rock and taking a header into a gravestone. By the time my feet hit the sidewalk, I'm panting.

If I still lived in the halls, I'd be able to hide behind their brick walls and electronic doors, but I don't. Now I have to keep walking through campus and past buildings and through a neighborhood to get to my lovely haunted house.

When I brave a look behind me, Mathias isn't there. I hate that I feel something like disappointment that he didn't follow me.

It's cool and dark inside the house, and it doesn't sound as if anyone else is here. They had talked about going to the dining hall for dinner, and even if it's a little early they probably went already. I lean against the heavy front door and shut my eyes.

"You okay?" a soft voice asks. I jump and open my eyes to see Goldie standing at the top of the stairs looking like a ghost. She's in a short white dress and her auburn hair is down, which is unusual, and it reaches almost to her hips.

"I don't know," I answer honestly.

Goldie walks down the stairs. "Everyone else went to dining but I was going to make ramen. Want some?"

"That sounds great." I leave my bag at the bottom of the stairs to take up later and follow her down the hall to the kitchen at the back of the house.

When I move to help, Goldie stops me with a wave of her hand. "I need to feel busy right now. Sit. Tell me what's going on."

She blinks at me as she starts filling the pot with water and I take a seat on one of the stools at the kitchen island. The island is massive, and has the sink, a stove top, and the dishwasher all built into it. We have double wall ovens and too many cupboards. It was designed by one of the donors for the house renovation and she had a very particular idea about what things should look like.

"Have you ever had feelings for someone you shouldn't?"

Goldie gives a sharp bark of a laugh. "You have no idea."

"Okay, now I kind of want an idea."

She shakes her head and puts the pot on the stove top to boil. After a second she nods to herself like she made a decision.

"There's a guy, and he got kind of...obsessed. I shouldn't like it but sometimes..."

"Sometimes you do."

Goldie looks down at her feet. "Yeah. The obsession isn't all bad but I keep telling myself I'm wrong for liking it. For liking him."

"Can I be blunt?"

"Sure," she grins.

"That's bullshit. Just because other people might not understand or think that it's wrong isn't enough of a reason not to go for it if you want it. It's your mistake to make, but it's better than not knowing."

Goldie nods and puts two packets of ramen noodles into the now boiling water.

"That's a good point. Can that same advice be applied to you?"

Solid question. Mathias recognized me right away and he didn't seem angry with me. Does he remember that night? Does he remember that it was me? I won't know unless I interact with him. That's the only way to know for sure but what I don't know is if I want to have any kind of conversation or confrontation with him. That's utterly chicken shit of me but it's also the truth.

I thought I was punishing him but in the end, getting to be with him was only a punishment for myself. I thought it would be enough, and it wasn't.

"Before, maybe, now...no."

"Who is he?" Goldie stirs slowly and looks down at it, intuiting that I wouldn't want to look her in the eye when I say it.

"My sister's ex-boyfriend."

"Oof."

"Yeah."

"Is she still hung up on him?"

"Not even a little."

"So..."

I shrug. If it was that simple then yes, I could go for him. If that was the only barrier standing in the way of us, I could get over it. I even think Lola would understand because she always teased me about how close the two of us were, and asked if I was interested in him as more than my friend. No matter how close we are, I was not the kind of person to admit to having feelings for the guy she was with, even if I didn't understand their relationship.

"It's complicated."

"It's always complicated." Goldie adds the two flavor packets and mixes the seasoning into the noodles. It smells amazing. This whole conversation has been very soothing, even if it didn't give me any answers.

"Does he go here?" She asks as she gets bowls and starts dividing up the noodles.

"Yeah."

"Do you have reason to believe your feelings are reciprocated?"

"Maybe?" It always seemed like he felt the same thing between us, and his reaction today wasn't what I was expecting.

"A lack of information leads to an incomplete decision."

"You're a fortune cookie now?"

"Maybe." She takes the seat next to me and slides my bowl over. "But I'm also not wrong."

I have to understand the way Mathias looked at me today.

If the opportunity appears, I'll take it. For now, I'm going to keep running and hiding.

And fantasizing.

 Mathias

At first, I chase Willow out of instinct. Like a rabbit caught in the sight of a fox, she turns and runs so I have to capture her. It takes a few minutes for me to come back to my senses and stop. Willow ran for a reason, I'm not going to catch her when it was clear she wanted to get away.

I've come to the grave a few times. Mostly in the late afternoon. It's a nice, shadowed place and Elliot Renault is a good listener. Our conversations happen inside my head, but since he was witness to one of the most complicated, erotic moments of my life I feel like he can provide me perspective. Ghosts talk.

Willow has never come before.

At least, not when I've been here.

I was relaxing in the fading light when I heard the noise, and when I turned my head I was sure for a second that I'd imagined her because everything about her was what I pictured. Even though I could have, I didn't look her up. I've never had social media and part of me was afraid I'd get obsessive if I found her. Willow was a whirlpool and if I got caught in the edges she would pull me in.

She'd cut her hair since last semester. It was still messy but just past her shoulders now. Her green eyes were lined dark, and it made them stand out and glow even more than usual. Did she realize she was wearing the shirt I got her for her birthday? It looked well-worn so maybe she'd forgotten. It was dark purple when I got it for her but it had faded to a soft purple gray and has a cartoon cat skull that says "I regret nothing" underneath.

As always, Willow lived in black leggings, and she was wearing purple high top Converse. I watched her feet move when I stopped chasing her.

Why had she come back? Did she come there too, and I'd missed her every time? Was this a place that meant something to her?

It was overwhelming to me to see her in person.

It was more than I imagined because even that brief glimpse showed me she was still my Willow.

In high school, she was the girl I couldn't have because I didn't want everything I was to taint her. I would have done anything to protect Willow, and the biggest thing I had to protect her from was myself, and all the darkness that came with my life.

Everything had changed now. My father was dead, no one could make me do anything I didn't want to do, and everything in me wanted her. I wanted her to tie me down again. I wanted her to take what she wanted from my body, from me, and I wanted to keep her. I wanted to know what she was like now and how the woman of today lined up with the girl from back then.

I couldn't love her then like I can now.

Standing among the graves, yards away from where she fucked me for the first time, my brain plays out a different fantasy of our encounter today.

One where Willow steps toward me and takes my hand, where I get to kiss and taste her again. Flashes of all the things we could do together, that I want to do with her, overtake my brain and flash like lightning through my mind and body. Willow kneeling on my arms and sitting on my face, holding me down and smothering me with her pussy. Her skinny hands wrapped around my wrists, stopping me from touching her as she rode me.

I was rock fucking hard and surrounded by dead people. God damnit.

I decided I didn't give a fuck. I stepped back toward Elliot Renault's grave, knelt on the grass, and freed my cock. I brace myself with one hand on the stone, and with the other I jerk myself rough and fast. In my mind, she has her hand around my throat as she rides me, those dark lined eyes flashing with triumph and power. It doesn't take long for me to orgasm, spilling into the grass and groaning out her name.

With everything I've been through in my life, I have never been mentally well, but Willow opened up an unhinged side of me I hadn't even known existed. There was a horny, fucked up monster that would only be satisfied by her. It continued to surprise me how much I physically wanted her, and the way my body still ached for her now that I knew we were in proximity to one another again. My heart and soul had always known there would be no one but her.

When I lost her, when things imploded with me and Lola and our secret, it broke me even further. Willow stopped talking to me, dad punished me, and then that fucked up party happened with Elise. Whatever Willow wanted to punish me for, I wanted to let her.

Forcing my body to relax, I work my way around the chapel and back out to the campus proper. My best friend Wyatt sends me a text message to come to dinner, so I head that way instead of back to Cavalry 4.

Wyatt is one of the only people who knew about my father prior to his death, and even though our friendship is real and deep, both of us wish we could undo how he found out.

He was my ride back to Elmwood freshman year after winter break. I didn't want to deal with having my car, and it would be a good reason to never go to my parent's house because there was no way they'd make the effort to come and get me. I was all set to go, and then my father decided he no longer wanted to take my word for it and looked up my grades.

I'd gotten in A- in my Human Geography course instead of an A.

His fury took over and he started to smack me around. I didn't fight back, hoping that the less resistance I put up the faster his energy to hurt me would die out. Wyatt arrived shortly after my black eye was beginning to show and my lip was split and bleeding. Father had always been careful of my face when I was a minor but after I graduated high school, that didn't matter anymore. He could tell lies about me being aggressive and getting in fights and most people would believe him.

Wyatt saw him sweaty, red, and heaving, and didn't ask questions. He grabbed my bags and told me to get in the car without saying a word to my parents, which was considered rude and unheard of in our world.

He could've ghosted me. Instead, he stood by me, and asked me for the truth in a way that made me trust him. I never went back again because he made sure I never had to; he's not only my friend, he's my brother. I would die for him.

I suspect he told his parents the situation, because they pulled me into their family without ever asking about my own.

After my father died, Wyatt was the one who got me back to myself, and made me see all the destructive shit I was doing. He gave me a black eye trying to snap me out of it, and I've never been so grateful to be hurt. For him to get to that point I had to be really fucked up.

I'm an only child and so is he, but we're each other's family at the end of the day. He made me feel normal for the first time in my life. He helps me feel normal every damn day.

Wyatt is waiting in the dining hall seating area with two trays full of food. He grabbed whatever looked good and was waiting for me like usual. What was unusual was that he was smiling at his phone, but if he wanted to tell me, he would.

He looked up as I approach and his expression drops.

"Are you okay?"

"No?" I answer it as a question because I honestly don't know.

"What happened?"

"I saw Willow Talbot."

"That's awesome, did you talk?" Wyatt knows about my situation with Lola and Willow in high school, and that I had feelings for her. He knows more than Willow does, at least I'm assuming unless Lola finally caved and was honest with her family.

"No. She...ran."

"That's weird." Wyatt shrugs and starts eating a burger.

"Remember how I came home kind of fucked up after Ides?"

Wyatt laughs. "Yeah you were naked and covered in dirt. Why?"

"I have to tell you something." And for the first time, other than Dr. Stanton, I tell someone what happened last March. I tell him everything I remember and I don't back off from telling him that I liked it. Wyatt and I have had more out of pocket conversations than I can count, and Wyatt is honest to the point that he should probably consider having a filter. Although sometimes I believe that's the key to our friendship - Wyatt never hesitates to say what he's really thinking about something that I do or say. He keeps me in check that way, especially when my worst thoughts start dominating my mind.

"Mathias. That's assault."

"Yes and no," I toy with the pasta on my plate. "I knew why we were leaving the party. I can't entirely say I didn't want it before it happened and during it I definitely did. Then knowing that it was Willow...it's all I can think about."

"Kind of fucked up." Wyatt finishes his burger and wipes his hands. "What do you want to do?"

"Talk to her. I want to know why she did it, what she was punishing me for, and I want...I want her. Physically, yeah, because you know what it's been like for me, but completely. I never got over her."

"Are you sure she felt the same?"

My heart stutters at his question as doubt creeps in. If she didn't, if she doesn't, I'll survive. The chance that I'll ever find someone else who makes me feel the way that she does is low, but I'd rather finally have a chance to be honest with her than keep it inside forever. Even if she rejects me. Willow knew me at my worst and still became my best friend. I had to treat her like she didn't matter in public even when it felt like I was flaying my own skin to push her away, and she never called me out on it when it was the two of us.

I owe us both to try and talk it through.

"Listen, I'm going to try not to judge how you feel about this and what you want, so my advice is this: she clearly thinks you did something shitty so if you want to talk, find her in public, where other people are around, so she feels safe."

"We've been here together for 2 years and I never saw her before the Ides party. A miracle would have to occur."

Wyatt grabs an apple and crunches into it, licking juice from the corner of his mouth, and then he shrugs. "What's meant to be finds a way."

Willow

For two days, I ignore thinking about my encounter with Mathias in the graveyard.

The problem is that suddenly I'm seeing him everywhere. Because I'm so attuned to watching for him, I see him before he sees me and successfully avoid him, but it's making me jumpy and paranoid. I can't shake the feeling that he was happy to see me, or at least that he wasn't angry with me.

I don't understand.

It makes me feel like I'm missing information. After Lola told me why they broke up, I refused to talk to Mathias even when he tried, and Lola never tried talk about him so I didn't bring him up. The only reason she's talking about him now is because she likely assumes enough time has passed that it wouldn't bother me anymore. What I want to know is why it doesn't bother her...

That's where I have to start.

I text Lola and ask her for a FaceTime conversation later tonight. It's a Thursday so her classes are done by 4:00 P.M. and if I give her time to eat dinner that means we're looking at 9:00 P.M. my time. There are so many times we've set up calls and gotten the time difference wrong, or forgotten about conflicts we have because I was talking in my time so she was thinking about hers. It's very annoying, and this is important, so I'm extra careful about the time.

Lola calls at 9:00 P.M. on the dot and as soon as I answer she starts talking about the class she got out of before dinner and the success she had in the lab. It takes her a solid 10 minutes before she realizes that I'm not replying much and that something is wrong. Between the two of us, I'm not usually the one that needs to talk, so I don't blame her for not picking up on it right away.

"What's going on?"

"I saw Mathias."

"Okay…" Lola trails off.

"How are you not upset? After what he did to you?!" My voice is high and louder than I want it to be. Lola pales and stares at me for a long time, and I see her take a deep, slow swallow. Her mouth opens and closes a few times, and then she shuts her eyes and takes a deep breath through her nose. I am used to Lola's calming techniques, and it makes me feel slightly better that she's not acting like nothing is wrong here.

"What exactly do you think he did to me, Willow?" Her voice is very quiet. Almost shaky. I've never heard her sound like this before.

"He raped you," I answer, my voice nearly as quiet.

Lola covers her mouth with her hand and squeezes her eyes shut. "Why would you think that? Is that why you acted the way you did when we broke up?" There's an emotion in her voice that I don't understand, and tears are welling in her eyes.

"You said he took too much. Then you got weirdly hypersexual, and that thing happened with Elise Manning, and it made sense."

"Fuck." Lola's voice breaks and she drops her head into her hands. I can't do anything but wait for her to say more because I don't even know what I'd ask right now.

"Mathias never…he never did anything like that. He fucked up with Elise, and I ripped his head off for that, but that…oh my god, Willow. Oh my god." Lola is crying now, tears dripping down her face. "There's things you don't know about him, about us…what I meant by he took too much was like - he was taking too much onto himself. He was putting up with too much. I got angry with him, and I got angry with him about you."

"Me?" I'm floored. My head is spinning and I think I'm going to be sick.

Lola pulls back abruptly and wipes her eyes. "I can't talk about this. I can't…he never hurt me, Willow, not like that. I have to go." The screen goes back to her contact when she disconnects the call.

It's not that Mathias didn't still deserve punishment for what he did to Elise Manning, because he did, but everything that I chose to do was about getting revenge for my sister, and for myself. Now, I might have been even more in the wrong than him.

I distanced myself from him back then for nothing. If I'd stuck around or reached out, could I have stopped what happened later? Could I have pulled him back?

No, I can't take that onto myself. I'm not responsible for his bad decisions. I'm responsible for making assumptions and doing something...terrible. I need to talk to him, but I don't even know how to start that conversation. Based on what Lola said, I'm starting to think there's more I don't know about him.

Once again, the Mathias I knew seems to be a mask or an illusion. A person he was only with me, and I don't know if it was real, or a game. I don't know anything.

I toss my phone aside and burrow into my pillows.

It buzzes and I pick it up.

It's a text from Lola: *what did you do?*

Me: *what do you mean?*

Lola: *I texted him. He said you had a confrontation last semester and he's been trying to talk to you.*

A confrontation. Ha. That's cute.

Me: *I paid him back for what he'd done.*

Lola: *You need to talk to him.*

Me: *No I don't.*

Lola: *I gave him your number.*

Before I can respond that she shouldn't have done that, and she doesn't understand, a new text comes through from a number that isn't saved in my phone.

Unknown: *Hi*

I don't reply. I send Lola a huge block of the middle finger emoji and go back to staring at the other text thread. What do I say? Where do I start?

Unknown: *I've been thinking about you.*

Unknown: *Actually, I never stopped thinking about you.*

Unknown: *I'll see you soon.*

It should be ominous but instead it's kind of sexy? What the hell is wrong with me?

I've been asking myself that question more than ever lately but all of the answers I come up with make me feel increasingly like a monster.

I wanted him, and I took what I wanted.

I can come up with a hundred other explanations and justifications but at the end of the day, that's the truth. If it was less of a violation because he wants me too, it's irrelevant. His feelings on it didn't matter in the moment. I punished him with our bodies for breaking my heart, and for the fact that three years later I still love him as if it no time had passed at all. Even if I've also been denying that truth.

Love made me a monster. An animal.

I don't know how to move past this.

Willow

We've reached the start of October, and one of my favorite dumb traditions of the Elmwood year: Castle Cookie Day.

The Castle orders thousands of cookies and hands them out all day long. You can come back as many times as you want for a cookie. They also set up stations with water, coffee, and hot chocolate, no matter what the weather is. It's a delicious, silly Sunday to keep us going for another week.

But basically, campus is one big party.

I've been feeling like crap since my conversation with Lola a week ago, and we've barely talked in between. She knows I did something and she blames herself for not being clear with me. We'll get over it, but I can't stop thinking about seeing Mathias. What I'd say, or what he'd say. The unknown number I'm pretty sure is him has texted me every day. Sometimes just to say good morning or good night, sometimes a comment on the weather.

This morning they sent a message saying they liked my shirt. It's navy blue and has a huge goose on it that says "world's silliest goose." I'm wearing my favorite heavy gray sweater over it, since it's pretty chilly today.

My housemates and I have commandeered a concrete planter all to ourselves while gorging on cookies and coffee. I'm sitting soaking up the weak sun with Lachlan's head on my lap while he tries to explain how to scientifically prove the multiverse theory to me and Liam. I'm only half listening.

I'm more amused by watching Liam try and talk himself into going to talk to a girl across the mall from us. She's surrounded by other girls and they're all wearing the same outfit, so I'm guessing it's an a capella group. They perform on and off all day at things like this.

"Are you going to go talk to her?" I ask, and Lachlan doesn't even notice we're not listening.

"No. No. I'll go after the performance."

"Who is that?"

"Heidi. My best friend's twin."

"I didn't know Hayden had a twin." I look between him and her. "Something there."

"I wish," he grumbles, but then shakes his head like he could make that statement go away. "He's gone this semester, I have to look after her."

"Sure thing," I laugh. Liam sighs and shrugs, ending the conversation, but still keeping his eyes glued to Heidi.

Bronte wraps her arms around my neck from behind. "What are we laughing at?"

I open my mouth to tell her, but Liam shakes his head vehemently. "Nothing." I shove a piece of cookie in her mouth to distract her and she moves away from me to perch on Gus's lap like usual.

They're kind of disgusting if they weren't so cute. She's all short with wild curls and he's a little on the gangly side but can literally make her disappear inside a hug. They're the busybody mom and dad of our group, so I kind of get why Liam didn't want them to know anything.

Lachlan sits up now that he realizes we're not listening, but something catches his eye. "Someone is staring at you," he leans over and whispers to me, failing to be subtle.

I follow his gaze and jolt when my own lands on Mathias.

He's leaning against one of the light poles, his hands in his pockets, talking to a guy but staring at me. My eyes can't seem to let his go, even when he straightens up and starts to walk toward us. His friend follows. My friends have gone silent, watching the approach of my beloved blonde demon. Whom they have never seen or heard about before, ever. Not even Georgia.

"Hi," he says and gives me a small smile. I don't think I've ever seen him smile in public before. Let alone look pleasant. His eyes dart from mine to my friends, who are staring at him. Bronte's mouth is open. It's embarrassing. "I'm Mathias, I went to high school with Willow."

Oh, is that all it is? Is that how we know each other?

Silence falls again.

"I'm Wyatt," his friend holds up his hand and waves. "I'm going to leave now." He turns around and does just that, and the awkwardness grows.

"Can we talk?"

"We are talking," I reply automatically, shifting into sarcasm mode as I panic.

"Alone?"

Lachlan immediately pushes at me until I slide off the planter and have to stand. "Go. Talk to him. Leave. We don't want you here." Then he swipes the rest of my cookie out of my hand. Traitors, all of them.

Mathias didn't move when I was forced up, and there's barely any space between us as I steady myself and look up into his face. No matter how horrible and guilty I feel, the first urge I have when I'm this close is to kiss him.

My eyes drop to his lips before I can catch myself and when I look back into his eyes, there's heat there. Like he's thinking about kissing me, too.

"Walk with me," he says, and I follow him as we weave through the crowd. We're near the library, and he leads me around the building until we're at the entrance to the walking path through the woods. It circles the campus and doesn't go too deeply, so I feel pretty safe in terms of being able to run away as well as it being private.

"I'm sorry," I blurt when the silence becomes too much.

"For what?" It's a question but it doesn't sound like he's really asking.

I stop walking and squeeze my eyes shut. It's the only way I'll get this out.

"I thought you'd raped Lola and you broke my heart and I was so angry with you for so long and I wanted to punish you for what you'd done and so I got you drunk and assaulted you. I didn't - Lola told me that's not what happened and I'm so sorry, I'm still mad at you and you still did shitty things but that…"

I trail off as I open one eye to see how he's reacting to all of this. There's no anger on his face, mostly sadness, but Mathias is just standing there taking my verbal explosion with hardly any reaction.

"I wanted to punish you," I finish, barely able to make a sound.

"I deserve to be punished," he replies, and takes a step toward me. "I was a mess when you knew me before, I did terrible things, I hurt people, but I never, ever intended to hurt you. Willow," he starts and then stops, looking at me with desperation in his eyes.

"What, Mathias?" I don't know what I want him to say. I don't know what *I* want to say. "I hurt you. You hurting me didn't give me the right to do that."

"It did give you the right. God, you have no idea…"

He turns his back on me and I watch his shoulders heave, desperately wishing that I could touch him. Feel his lungs and ribs expanding beneath my hands, his warm skin, his smooth muscles. Even knowing there was no justification for what I did, I still want to touch him. Hold him down. Press him up against one of these trees and feel the perfect ways our bodies line up. I want to take and take from him until I have all of him. Until he doesn't exist except inside me.

It's psychotic and obsessive and I can't seem to stop.

"I liked it," he says and it's so quiet and unexpected that I think I imagined it.

"What?"

He turns to me and takes a step closer so I have to tilt my head back to keep contact with his eyes.

"I liked it. While it was happening. Being controlled, tied down, fucked by you." I jolt when he says fucked and I feel it like a slap to my clit. It makes me wet immediately. "When I recognized you? It was even better. My Willow, taking what she wanted from me, the only person I'd ever be willing to give everything. My pain, my soul, my penance." He takes another step closer and I can feel our breaths pushing against each other.

"My love. My come," he drops down to a raspy whisper and I let out a sound somewhere between a gasp and a cry.

"You can do whatever you want to me," he whispers, agony and ecstasy in each word. "Give me what I deserve."

I don't know why that's what makes me snap, but I shove him back. He stumbles for a second but I follow until he's backed up into a tree on the side of the path. The way he's leaning against it drops his height enough for what I want.

My body presses against his, forcing his back against the rough bark. I wrap my hands around his neck to hold him where I want him when I take his lips with mine.

Mathias groans into my mouth and I sweep my tongue along his, devouring him as if stopping will kill me. I don't know how long we lose ourselves in the kiss, it never gets less intoxicating or exciting as I learn the shape of him and drown in the flavor of his tongue. One of his thighs ends up between mine and I can't stop my hips from grinding on him.

I bite his bottom lip and suck on it as the friction gets me close to the edge.

"Take everything," he grunts, gripping my hips and moving me faster. "Take anything you want." Mathias buries his face in my neck and moves me faster. The heat and sound of him, his begging, undoes me.

I cry out into the woods, my head flying back as my hips work and my thighs squeeze his leg as I orgasm. It's a long wave of pleasure and I cling to him to survive it.

We both lean heavily against the tree, and Mathias keeps his arms around me.

"You didn't do anything I didn't want, especially from you," he murmurs into my hair. "I never stopped thinking about you. I can't stop thinking about you now," he admits. "That night was a turning point for me, in ways I want to explain to you. I want to tell you everything, but if I do..."

I pull back and look at him. "If you do?"

"I don't think I'll ever be able to let you go, and I know that what I have to say is going to make you run."

I extricate myself from his hold and adjust my clothes. He stands up and brushes dirt and bark off his legs.

"I can't say I won't run."

"I know."

We stare at each other.

"Give me time," I finally ask.

"Of course."

Without talking about it, we turn around and walk back the way we came. When we emerge from the trees, it's like a switch flips in both of us. We talk about school things, where we're living, innocuous things that we'd have updated each other on if we were really old friends randomly running into each other.

It's amazing to me that we're out in public and he's so close to being like my Mathias. The one that laughs, talks openly and easily, that smiles without hiding it immediately. The tiny hopeful part of me wants to believe it's because the real him was always who he'd been with me, but the practical part wants to reserve judgment.

He doesn't hate me for what I did.

There's clearly some kind of sexual tension between us that needs to be worked out.

I need to talk to my sister about the fact that I fucked her ex-boyfriend and I'm pretty sure I'm going to keep doing it, no matter how she feels about it. He's a different person than who I knew before, and I want to know everything.

We stop at the corner where I need to turn to go back to the house.

"When can I see you?" he asks.

"Text me," I respond. "Then we'll see."

Mathias grins at me and then steps close to plant a kiss on my temple. It makes butterflies riot in my stomach, and I quickly squash both them and the desperate hope inside me that this is going to be something.

"God, I missed you," he whispers, then steps away. He waits until I start walking. Every time I look back, he's still standing there, watching me go, until I turn down my street and out of his sight.

 Mathias

Me: *What are you wearing today?*

To anyone else that would sound like a suggestive question, but we both know better. I'm asking about her t-shirt. I always loved her silly t-shirt collection and added a few entries of my own whenever I had an excuse to give Willow a gift.

We've been texting casually for a few days, and I don't know about her but the tension has been building for me. First because I'm turned on every time I think about her, and second because I feel like we have more air to clear and I want the chance to do it. The hard part is that some of it isn't my secret to tell.

My phone vibrates and I see a return message from Willow. It's a photo.

She's wearing a purple shirt that looks like an entry on the periodic table, except it says "Ah! the element of surprise." I would laugh because it's a good one, but the photo she sent is suggestive. It's taken from above and she's holding out the bottom of the shirt so it's legible. She's on her knees and her legs are bare and spread open. It makes it look like she's not wearing anything else.

After a long moment a text pops up.

W: *Do you like it?*

Me: *The shirt, or that hot as fuck photo?*

Three dots appear, disappear, and then reappear.

W: *You think that's hot?*

Me: *It looks like you're only wearing the t-shirt.*

After a long moment she replies.

W: *Want to find out?*

Damn, my little Willow is all grown up if she's getting this suggestive with me. While I was always wildly, unexpectedly attracted to her in a physical way, it's the way she made me feel that had me so hung up on her. I could be myself with Willow without judgment. A gentle side of me that I didn't know existed came out around her. Smiles were easy. I could breathe with Willow, and I wanted to keep that feeling forever. No one and nothing mattered more than her, and if my father had known she was my weakness he would've used it any way he could.

I couldn't let him hurt her, so we never got to be anything more than secret friends. A secret Lola kept for me while we played fake relationship and kept each other's business out of other people's mouths. I disagreed with Lola about her fears, but she was willing to put on a show that kept my father at bay. Lola knew how bad it was, and finally lost it on me about never standing up to him. It's why we finally gave up the dog and pony show.

I couldn't watch her lie, and she couldn't watch me be hurt and hurt myself.

I always wondered why Willow dropped me after the break up, and eventually convinced myself it was because my feelings were one-sided. We were only friends, and she would always have chosen her sister, no matter what.

Now, I know there's more to the story, and I know she wants me now.

Nearly every night I dream about her rising above me, riding my dick, taking us both to the edge of sanity and pleasure. It's never happened to me before.

Me: *Find out how?*

Willow sends a photo. It's a side profile of her body in the same position, only her shirt is pulled up to just beneath her breasts. There's an unbroken path of smooth skin from her toes, all the way up to her waist. I can see the muscles in her calves and thighs, and get to admire the soft curve of her ass. My cock is throbbing in my shorts and I reach down and squeeze it for some relief.

Me: *You can sit just like that, right on my face.*

W: *Have you earned that?*

Fuuuuck.

Me: *I want to taste you, love. How can I earn that?*

W: *Show me you want it.*

It sounds like she's asking for a dick pic. I've never sent one before, and I understand that rule that they are not to be sent without being solicited. I switch over to another message thread.

Me: *How do I take a good dick pic?*

Wyatt Wyatt West: *Holy jesus I don't know. Take a few and send what looks good.*

WWW: *How have you never done this before?*

Me: *Shut up.*

WWW: *You're better off sending a video.*

With that thought in mind, I pull my shorts down and maneuver my phone until I like how I look. While she's had my dick inside her, I don't know how much she really looked at it, and it's different. Pussies are pretty - all soft pink skin, but dicks - not so much.

I hit record and stroke myself. It did not escape my notice in the past that Willow liked my hands, so I make sure to flex and show the veins on the backs of my hands and up my forearms.

"I want it, Willow," I rasp her name, end the video, and send it before I can talk myself out of it.

It feels like forever until she responds, but it's a voice message.

W: "Okay, you earned it, because you made this happen."

The last seconds of the audio are the unmistakable sounds of Willow playing with her very wet pussy. It makes my mouth water.

Me: *When can I have it?*

W: *Are you sure?*

Her hesitation kills the mood, but I'd rather be certain that she knows how much I want her than fuck it up. I hit the call button next to her name.

"Hello?"

"Hi." I smile like an idiot at the surprise in her voice and that she's still a little breathy, worked up from our chat. We're silent for a second, so I start the conversation.

"I want you, however I can have you."

"How do you want me?" There's a tease in her voice that releases some of the tightness in my chest.

"No, it's how do you want me, love? Because I want to serve you. I want you to tie me up again and use me however you want. Whatever will get you off. I'm yours."

"Mathias," she nearly whines. "Is that wrong?"

"No. Not if we both want it. Do you want to control me again? Do you want to know I'll do anything you say if it makes you feel good? To have you ride my dick and scream my name and know there's nothing I can do but take it?" While talking to her I reach down and free myself, my erection having returned talking about how I want to be with her. I stroke myself slowly. "Tell me what you want."

"I want," she pauses to audibly swallow. "I want to sit on your face until you have to tap out. I want to tease you until you beg me to let you come."

"Yes, love, suffocate me with your pussy. Are you touching it now?" My words nearly slur I'm so drunk with being turned on.

"Yes," Willow admits softly.

"Tell me what you're thinking about. Get me there with you."

I can hear her heavy breathing over the phone. "I want your hands tied above your head. I want to hold your wrists while I ride you and know that I'm in control of it all. I want to look into your eyes when I come all over you," she gasps again. "I want to hear you say my name when you lose it. I want you to say my name when I break you." Willow cries out in my ear, and my hand works faster than ever to finish with her.

"Willow," I groan as my hips flex and I come in hot spurts over my hand and stomach.

"Just like that, Mathias," she moans and I listen to her stifled gasps and cries as she comes too.

We listen to each other breathe on opposite ends of the line. I wish I could hold her. Clean her up. Tell her how amazing she is, how precious, that I love her dirty mind and soft body. That I'm not exaggerating when I say I would do anything to please her.

For a lot of my life, all my choices were careful and calculated to avoid punishment. It was never about what I wanted but about what I could have that wouldn't put me in danger, or that would make my father happy enough to leave me alone.

Willow was my exception. I let myself have her as safely as I could.

Now that nothing is stopping me, I want to choose her.

I want to move forward with my life, free of abuse and working through my trauma, and I want to be the man I always should have been for her.

"I want you," I tell her again. "Whenever you're ready."

"Okay," she huffs. "Goodnight, Mathias."

"Goodnight, love."

I stay on the phone, breathing with her, until she ends the call.

Willow

Mathias is coming over tonight.

The rest of the house is going to a party, so we'll have it to ourselves for at least a few hours. I'm nervous to see him like this. For this. I messaged him yesterday with a time and my address. He responded with a smiling devil emoji, which I've always associated with him, and I think it means we're going to try this.

Whatever this is.

The only person I can trust to help me is Georgia because she'll keep it to herself. She doesn't know the details of our previous...encounter...but she knows he's coming over for sex. She knows he's my sister's ex and finds that hilarious.

I step out from behind the screen I keep near my closet and show her the lingerie I picked to wear for him. It's not like I had a lot of options, but I also want to look sexy. Most of the time I'm pure comfort, but I want to look on the outside the way he makes me feel on the inside.

Like a conqueror. Someone he would get on his knees for.

I'm wearing a black lace bralette with no lining, so my nipples are just barely visible beneath the pattern of the lace, and a high-waisted black thong. It's comfortable as heck which is why nearly all my panties are made by the same company, but I also like the way it sits on my hips and frames my ass.

Georgia whistles, then growls. "Yes."

"Am I crazy?"

"No." She shakes her head vehemently, her dark braids shifting. She looks like Wednesday Addams if she incorporated black sequins into her wardrobe. "If anything, you're repressed. Let your inner dark goddess out."

I smirk at the term because it's how I felt that night in the graveyard. It's definitely what I want to channel now. With a firm nod in her direction, I take my bathrobe off the hook and put it on. Georgia hops off the bed and lights the candles I put on a stand in the fireplace, and I turn on the LED lights I put along my baseboards to a soft purple. I can see fine but it takes all the edges off.

This is like every stupid fantasy I had in high school, except now I know what I'm getting into and exactly what I want. Back then, it was all imagination and feeling, I had no real experience and I would have had no idea what to do. All I knew then was that my body wanted him, it just didn't know how.

I'm still unsure about the dynamic between us, but at least I have experience in how to have a good time having sex. Still, this is something else.

It's going to feel different to be with him when he knows it's me the entire time. When I'm going to be controlling the way I was that night, but in a situation where we are both completely present. I'm nervous and excited. I did a lot of Googling about what I might want to do, what he might like, and how to do it without accidentally killing him.

Part of me still wants to hurt and punish him, but I want him to be alive to feel it all, and feel it with me. I think it's what he wants too.

We were pretty up front with each other in our texts about what we wanted to experiment with. I want to be in control and make him give in to me. He wants to be restrained, and he wants to feel like had no control at all.

Georgia gives me a kiss on the cheek and leaves me to stare at myself in the mirror above the dresser as I contemplate my life choices. Mathias will be here in 15 minutes, and I listen without moving as she wrangles the other housemates out and to the party. She even got Liam to leave, but he was acting weird when we talked about it, so I don't think she had to try too hard.

As soon as the house is dark and empty, I go downstairs and sit on the bottom step to wait. It isn't long before there's a soft knock on the door.

I lose all my air when I open it. Mathias is pure temptation. Black t-shirt that accentuates the muscles of his upper body, fitted dark denim, and a motherfucking leather jacket like a rebel without a cause. His blonde hair is pushed back away from his face, and one glance tells me that he's as anxious about this as I am.

His light gaze gives me a quick once over and his eyes dilate when he absorbs the robe I'm wearing before they pop up to meet my own.

"Hi," he says softly.

"Hey. Come in." I back up and step aside. There isn't a single light on downstairs, so I take his hand and pull him with me until we get up to my room. We're the ghosts haunting this place tonight and I like it.

I wait for him to step inside and then close and lock the door. It feels oddly intimate to watch him look around the dim room with all the things that are me laid out before him. He was never allowed in my room all those years ago. We had the kitchen table and our homework, the notebook we shared, sometimes the back patio when the wind was right. Now it's like he's having a look inside my mind after years of being one of its primary occupants.

Mathias has always been my obsession. The only thing that changed was my own perspective on it. There was a time I didn't mind my unrequited love for him. Then it became a curse. A penance. Loving him was a form of self-flagellation.

I don't know what it is now.

He approaches the fireplace and looks at the pictures on the mantle. I wince because Lola is prominent but then panic when I realize what else is up there.

"Willow," his voice is so soft, like someone might hear us. He turns to me, and I can't see him well enough to read his expression. "You told me you didn't take one."

"I lied."

When he'd come to pick Lola up for Homecoming during the school year they dated, I asked him to take a picture with me before they left. It was near the end of their relationship but our friendship was stronger than ever. We were close, and I was in love. Lola was busy talking to her friends, it was just the two of us like usual, only he looked extra beautiful in a navy suit with a white shirt, unbuttoned at the collar without a tie. He looked every inch the insouciant asshole playboy he wanted people to believe he was.

I'd leaned in close, our cheeks nearly touching, and moved to take a selfie. Mathias didn't smile but his face relaxed in a way I liked to believe I caused. I don't remember why but right before I took the photo we'd ended up looking at each other.

That's the picture. A younger us, trapped in a moment of connection in perpetuity. We're looking into each other's eyes with an intensity I tried to deny, but I remember how it felt too. I remember the world fading away as we looked at each other, as I thought about his mouth, about wanting to feel his lips smile against mine. That rare, special smile that only I got to see...I wanted to feel it on my skin.

Someone had called for him, and he stepped back. Before going he'd made me promise to send it to him. I didn't. I told him I'd never pressed the button, that we got interrupted before I could take the picture.

"You've been hurting me for so long, you have no idea," he grumbles. Mathias steps toward me and takes off his jacket, then slides out of his shoes. This is getting real.

Steeling myself, I take a deep breath and remove my robe, letting it drop to the ground. Mathias lets out a sharp breath of air as he looks at me, head tilted, eyes leaving a slow, blazing trail over me.

He drops to his knees and I shiver, aroused at the sight. It's what I wanted and I didn't have to tell him.

I step closer and he leans his head back to look at me. I take his face in my hands.

"Do you want me to restrain you?"

"Yes."

"Hurt you?"

He swallows. "I think so."

I nod. I don't know enough to go too far with that, so I won't do much. We're both too uncertain here. This is the start of it. We don't have to do everything all at once.

"Is it the restraint you want, or the resistance?"

Mathias drops my gaze and I shake him a little so he looks back up. "I want to resist. I want you to force me."

"Then I will. You can move, fight, say no, say stop, and I won't listen to you."

"Fuck," he sighs. "Please."

"We need a safe word. In case."

"Sharkbait."

I smile, I can't help myself. "Sharkbait." It's my turn to swallow hard. "Anything else?"

Mathias reaches up and wraps his hands around my wrists, holding me to him, as if communicating with his touch how much he needs me to keep our eyes connected.

"Unleash yourself on me. Do whatever you want, whatever you think I deserve, I want it all from you. I am yours. Use me, hurt me, drive me to the edge until I'm in agony. As long as it's you, I want it."

Mathias drops his hands and sinks more deeply onto his knees, submitting.

I slide one of my hands into his hair, finally touching it's slick softness for the first time. The sensation is unbelievable. Without conscious thought I bury both my hands in it, then grip it tight and pull.

"I want you in agony," I whisper across his lips as I lean over him. "I want you to hurt over me the way I do over you."

He swallows and tries to nod but I'm holding him too tight. I take a step back and he shuffles on his knees to follow me, never taking his eyes off mine. When we're close enough I tug up and he moves until he's standing.

When I slide my hands under his shirt he shivers, and I don't stop myself from grazing and touching every inch of him that I can as I remove his shirt. He's beautiful in this light. Almost unreal with his pale skin glowing, his eyes almost translucent.

I undo his button and fly, and shove his pants and boxer briefs down. He's naked and vulnerable in front of me. And he likes it.

His cock is hard and weeping already.

It doesn't take much effort to push him back on the bed, and he moves to lay on the pillows. I straddle him and lean close, sliding one of my hands underneath a pillow and grabbing the first restraint.

I get it hooked around his left wrist before he realizes what's happening. Mathias bucks under me as I reach for the second restraint, one of my hands holding his right wrist down roughly, squeezing until I get him tied down. I figure he can have his legs this time.

When I sit back up and look down, his eyes are wild, his hair disheveled, and his hips are rolling, grinding his bare cock against the soaked gusset of my panties. I'm so aroused I catch my own scent when I move.

"Don't," he murmurs like he did the first time, but now there's more desperation.

"You'll take it," I assure him, and shift my body down so I can reach between us and stroke his cock. "I'm going to take what I want from you. I don't care if you beg me to stop. I'm going to soak you with my come until you break and fill my pussy up."

"Oh fuck," he grunts in response, bucking his throbbing erection into my eager hand. I'm so wet I don't need to work myself up, I'm ready.

Pulling my thong to the side, I slide his head through my entrance. He asked if we could do it bare, and after a lot of negotiation and sharing of medical documentation, I agreed. Mathias used to be a mystery wrapped in secrets, but now he's slowly revealing them all. Nothing is secret, private, mysterious if I ask it of him. He's stripping it all away to show himself to me.

"No, stop, wait," his mouth says but as I press my opening down on the head of his cock he pushes back, plunging himself inside me until he's so damn deep. I shift and angle forward so I can grab his wrists and pin him down further. My hips start to roll and he tries to buck me off and move away.

"Time to get fucked, baby," I croon, and pick up the pace. Mathias's face is screwed up in pleasurable agony, his eyebrows drawn together but his mouth open and relaxed.

"I don't want this," he huffs out.

"Don't lie to me," I reply. "I know what you want."

Mathias lets out a groan, and I file that statement away to think about later, and pull apart why he likes it and what else I might be able to say.

"Guys like you want it rough, want what they want, take without caring," I hiss at him. I want him to hurt now, and tilt my head until I can bite the top of his right pec. My teeth grab flesh and he grunts, his hips pumping up into me harder when I suck the skin in deeper, leaving a mark on his body.

"I'm going to mark you as mine, my toy, and when you wear my mark you can't say no to me. You give me what I want." Now that's what works for me. I can feel myself clench around his cock, getting close to the edge. Looking down at the mark on his chest fills me with satisfaction.

He's mine. I marked him.

Mine mine mine.

Losing my mind, I start biting and sucking across his chest, and even leave one low on his neck that has him nearly whimpering with pain and pleasure.

"Almost there," I gasp, grinding down harder on him. I balance on his body and dig my nails in.

"Fuck, please," he cries out, and I tip over into pleasure. I cry out, my pussy getting wetter and wetter as I squeeze his thick cock and come all over us both.

"Now give me yours," I command.

"No," he shakes his head, but I can see the strain in his neck.

"Yes," I laugh. "Break and come for me, Mathias."

"Willow," he groans out. Then his body bows and he pulls tight against the restraints as he comes inside me.

I've never had sex without a condom before and the feeling and knowledge that not only was his cock bare but I'm also now full of his come, is incredibly hot. It gets me all worked up again.

After a few moments of heavy breathing on both our parts, I look down at him. He looks somehow both relaxed and tormented. I lean over and kiss the tip of his nose.

"You can give me more," I declare, and start grinding on him again.

"Please," he begs, but I don't stop.

I don't stop for another hour, multiple orgasms for me, and one more for him. Until he calls sharkbait because he needs water.

When I release him, I cover him up and rub his wrists, and then for some reason I brush his hair. We come down together with his head in my lap, my favorite brush running through his locks, teasing his scalp, until I can tell he's back to himself.

Mathias rolls over to look at me.

"Are we fucked up?"

I laugh. "Yeah, but not because of this. From the sheer amount of things I found on the internet, we're not fucked up for liking this."

He nods.

"Why..." I start. "Why do you want this?"

Mathias knows what I'm asking, but doesn't say anything. "Can this be an I'll tell you when I'm ready thing?"

"Yeah."

He sits up and I think he'll get dressed to leave. He got what he wanted from me, and I got any piece of him that he was willing to give.

I'm surprised when he turns his head toward me but won't meet my eyes. "Can I stay?"

"Overnight?"

He nods.

My heart swells and my belly swoops. "Yeah."

I pull down the covers and slide underneath. Mathias joins me and surprises me again when he burrows into me, pulling my body against his and cradling me to him. One big, strong arm bands across my stomach and the other slides alongside mine under the pillow.

There's a ghost of a kiss on the back of my head, and then I'm drifting off to sleep.

 Mathias

When I told Willow I wanted her unleashed, I didn't realize it meant she'd put one on me instead.

But damned if I'm not wearing a collar and the reality of being on a leash for her isn't driving me insane.

It's 3:00 A.M. and we're both covered in sweat and come, lost in each other and trying our hardest to be quiet so we don't wake her housemates. She still smuggles me in like a secret.

Willow is bent over her bed, the leash wrapped tight around her hand so I can't move away from her, and I can't even fake trying to pull my cock out of her tight pussy. She's rippling around me and I can tell she's close to another orgasm. My fingers are gripping her hips to a bruising degree, alternately pushing her away and pulling her further onto me. The constant resistance and submission lights my brain and body up in a way that I've never experienced before.

"Give it to me," she growls, then yanks on the leash. I fall forward, my stomach pressed to her back, hands braced on the bed.

"No," I answer, barely able to keep it together and fight her.

"It's mine."

"Never," I grunt, my hips rocking against her ass as she slides back and forth on me.

"You don't have a choice. You're mine," she moans, and I love hearing her say that. Love that I can believe in this moment that it's true. We've been going at it like this every chance we get for about 2 weeks now, but she still panics if we interact outside the walls of her room.

In here, we fuck, cuddle, talk, do it all again, and empty everything that we are into each other. We're as close as two people can possibly be, and I'm getting to know my Willow for who she's become, the person in this moment, and everything about her is perfect.

"Mathias," she gasps out as her orgasm overtakes her, and the collar pulls tight on the leash until I have no choice but to bend until my face is buried in her hair and my breath is huffing across the sensitive skin of her neck. Willow strangles a cry as she reacts to me.

When she says my name again, her voice as desperate and needy as I feel, my own orgasm bolts through me and I press deep into her, spilling my come inside her.

After breathing hard, we disconnect and I drop to my knees on the floor. This is the first time tonight she's let me come inside her, and based on some of our dirty texting from this week I think I know what's next.

Willow rolls onto her back and puts her feet up on the bed, spreading herself open for me. Just seeing my essence dripping out of her, and the glistening slick of her come on her pussy lips, her ass, and down her thighs, starts getting me hard again.

She tugs the leash until my mouth is centimeters from our mess.

"Clean up."

"No," I pull back, my cock almost back to completely hard, my pulse beating inside it.

"You want it. Taste us, Mathias." Willow gives a harsher tug and my lips land right over her clit. She stifles a whimper as she tries to maintain control. The tip of my tongue slides out to circle it, taunting her, before I move lower to her entrance. I take wet laps of her with the flat of my tongue, cleaning up our come. It's a little salty, mostly sweet, and when I think I've teased her enough I suck on her clit until she's writhing.

"That's it. Show me what a liar you are, Mathias." Willow pulls the leash and digs one hand into my hair, holding me where she wants me. "Your words say no but your filthy mouth can't resist. Eat our come."

I've come three times tonight and yet every word she says gets me harder, and has me ready to go again. I pull away from her.

"Please." Our eyes meet and she grins. It's so deviant.

Willow lays back and pulls me with her. She's so fucking wet and I'm so damn hard that I slide inside her easily. I don't even have to line myself up, it's like my cock finds her all on its own. He knows home when he feels it.

I brace myself over her body and watch as I pound her pussy like we haven't been at this for hours already. Her perfect, gorgeous tits are bouncing with how fiercely I'm slamming into her. Willow's hand trails up the leash until she tucks her fingers under the collar and yanks me down.

We're face to face, sharing air. I want to kiss her so badly.

She won't though. Or at least, she hasn't since we started fucking. On my cheeks, nose, forehead, any part of my body except my mouth. Like she knows as well as I do how much it changes things.

Willow's body is tensing beneath me as she gets close to cresting the wave.

Her head lifts and her lips find mine, trapping our mouths together with her grip on the collar. I open our mouths and our tongues glide and swirl. I taste her and I taste us and it's delicious.

Willow starts to come, crying out into my mouth. I smother the sound with my lips and tongue, pressing more deeply into her. I'm not going to orgasm again, no matter how hard I am or how good this feels, but I can fuck her through it and enjoy the taste of her and of us.

As she comes down I grind slow and deep, never taking my mouth off hers. I won't until she tells me to stop, taking advantage of the moment. Our kiss slows, becoming softer and more sensual.

It makes me want something I can't have. A feeling of nostalgia for something I never actually experienced, and that I won't get to, even if this turns into the relationship that I want from her.

It's the way I would have kissed her back in high school. Making out for hours because we connected and it felt good without ever needing to take it further. Simply holding her would have been enough for me.

It occurs to me that in addition to my father's abuse and obsession, maybe I got so fixated on Elise because Colin could have had her if he'd pulled his head out of his ass sooner, whereas I couldn't be with Willow. His chance was right in front of him and he didn't take it, and it fed my anger. I took it out on them when I never should have; I punished them for my own pain. All I wanted was Willow, and fear of something terrible happening to her if my father learned that I cared about someone kept me away. Colin was held back by his own pride.

Willow closes her mouth and ends the kiss, but I don't move far. Just enough to see her eyes.

"Are you going to stay tonight?" I try to decipher in her tone if she wants me to; so far after we play I stay with her. Based on my own internet searches, I think needing to be close to her like that is something I need for my aftercare. The one time I tried to leave I spiraled really fucking hard and she found me sleeping on their porch the next morning. We haven't risked it again after that.

"Is that still okay?"

She reaches up to brush my hair out of my face. "Of course."

We get up and I sit on the bed as she removes the collar and touches my neck, soothing me both physically and psychologically. Willow rubs the rest of me - my shoulders and upper back, down my arms, and then each of my hands and each finger. I'm not sure what she feels when she does that, and how she always knows how to give me exactly enough.

Willow keeps one of my hands in hers. "Shower. We'll have to be sneaky."

I wear her bathrobe and she wears a giant t-shirt, and we step carefully through the dark hallway toward the bathroom that she shares with Georgia.

Who slaps on the bathroom light and steps out to us, pointing a finger in our faces.

"Stop hiding. We can all hear you!" she whisper shouts.

Willow jumps back into me, startled, and I hold her to me on instinct.

"Okay," Willow answers, still processing. I laugh quietly.

"I'm Georgia, you're Mathias, clean up and get some sleep you whores." She gives us a wave and walks to her bedroom.

"How long do you think she was standing in there waiting to scare us?" I ask.

"Knowing her, at least half an hour. She's got that level of commitment."

I kiss the crown of her head and we step into the bathroom.

That was good. Important.

I've got Willow's body, but now I've got to work on winning the trust of her heart. I know she still has feelings for me the way that I do for her, and now I have to convince her that I'm worth taking a chance on. I have to give her my demons and let her decide how she feels about them. If I'm worth trying. Worth loving.

I hope I am. I'm not always sure.

Willow

I needed some distance to figure out what I was feeling. We were all over each other the second we were alone and by the time there was physical distance between us, I was too exhausted to think about my feelings and what any of it meant, and what I wanted moving forward. Getting confronted by Georgia seemed to pop the bubble of obliviousness I'd been operating inside. As long as no one knew about us, or not really, I could do whatever I wanted without thinking about it too hard.

Life gave me an assist when I got my period the next day. It was the perfect, vaguely painful, excuse I needed to tell Mathias we couldn't hook up this week.

Then that jerk showed up at our door after dinner with candy, my favorite coffee, and a heating pad that looked like a little black teddy bear that could be warmed in the microwave and then held over my cramping tummy.

It gave my heart concerning flutters.

No flutters should be involved. What I felt for him was dark and greedy, unhealthy even, and I wanted it to stay that way. Dark love only. None of the pink dreamy butterflies and happily ever after fantasies of the past. That's how I get my heart broken.

Before leaving, Mathias kissed my forehead, my nose, and then gave a brief, so quick it was basically stolen, kiss to my lips.

So there I was, snuggling with a warm teddy bear and reading my psych textbook, actively resisting letting myself think about my fuck buddy. That I'd been in love with for years.

It only got worse.

He started showing up to eat lunch with me and my friends. Waiting outside the building of my night class to walk me home. Sending me texts that weren't only sexy, and I so easily fell into the habit of texting him about my day or whatever random thought came across my mind. I didn't let him hold my hand but he always found an excuse to touch or hold me. It was unraveling me and the boundaries I had put in my mind between us and something real.

Between us and the possibilities that would ruin or crush me.

Even on the weekends, he'd invite me to study with him in the library, or the intense, fancy study rooms that the Cavalry had for their members and members' guests. We hadn't had sex in over a week, and he didn't even ask about it. All he ever seemed to want was to be around me.

Interacting with each other again had been under the guise of hooking up , but it was becoming clear we both had ulterior motives. I wanted him however I could have him but I'd put a limit on what I was allowed to feel. It never occurred to me that he'd have feelings for me beyond enjoying the sex. We could be friends again, and I'd unlocked a kink door for both of us, but part of me would always see myself as his girlfriend's little sister, as someone he hurt and left. As someone that wasn't worth a second thought to him. I'd outworn my usefulness once before; it was bound to happen again.

Yes, we were close. Closer than he was with a lot of people but I had always assumed it felt platonic on his side. Now I wondered. Mathias and I needed to talk but I was afraid to have that conversation.

So instead of talking to him, I sat down to call Lola.

It took her a long time to answer and she immediately requested FaceTime.

"Your face tells me everything I need to know. Spill it." She was laying down on her all white bed that contained a frightening amount of pillows.

"I've been hooking up with Mathias."

Lola stills, her eyes getting huge, and her expression frozen.

"I know that's weird because he was your boyfriend and now we've had sex with the same guy but I try not to think about that part but it's really intense and I'm so confused because my feelings in the past are overlapping with the present and I don't understand what he wants from me, what I want from this. What do I do? Tell me what to do."

It takes her a few seconds after I stop talking, but Lola nods slowly as if processing everything that I said.

"You're having sex with Mathias?"

"Yeah. I know it's weird, I'm sorry."

"No," Lola waves her hand, a habit when the conversation is going in the wrong direction. "You're having full on, his dick inside you, fucking?"

I feel confused. While talking about experiences is not overshare territory for either of us, this is getting a little weird. "Yeah...I mean, it's more intense than that, but yeah."

Lola points at me. "We're coming back to that. But holy shit, that's a huge deal."

"I'll stop, if it's weird for you."

She laughs so hard her face leaves the view of the camera. "No, god no, he was always in love with you. Still is from the sound of it. It's why we broke up."

My insides freeze. "What?"

"Fuck," Lola puts her forehead in her hand. "Listen, Mathias and I never had sex. We never did anything other than kiss, and that was only in public, mouths closed, for appearances. We had the high school equivalent of a relationship for PR purposes."

My heart thumps once, hard and painful, in my chest. "Why?" There's barely sound, just air. This conversation is heading off track, and I know already it's going to rewrite my understanding of the history between the three of us.

If he was supposedly in love with me, why date Lola? Why is the fake nature of their relationship something I'm only learning about now? That's an insane level of deception, and on top of that is the fact that I believed for years that they'd broken up because he assaulted her.

My body hurts like I've been hit by a truck, every part of me aching from how tense I got over the course of about 10 seconds.

"Some of this isn't mine to tell, Will."

"Then tell me your side," I snap. "Why would you do that? And if you knew he had feelings for me, and it's not like my feelings for him were a secret...why?" I'm starting to hate that word.

"We became friends, as much as anyone could be with him, and we both needed our parents to leave us alone about dating. Mom stopped bugging me, and his dad felt I was good enough to date his son. Even when he talked shit about me I didn't care, because I wasn't invested beyond dating until we graduated. We wanted to be left alone to do our own thing, and I didn't mind if Mathias stayed around us so he didn't have to go home."

While he never acknowledged it directly, I knew Mathias had an awful father. It was clear when he talked about some of the things he did and why he did them, it was because it was an expectation he lived under and not something he wanted. I'd seen the marks and bruises when he wasn't as careful about hiding them.

The first time I came into the kitchen and he was doing homework at our table, he'd been touching a bruise on his side. I didn't ask about it. I sat down and started my own homework.

That's how it started. The two of us sitting quietly, side by side, until one day we started talking and then we never stopped. Not when we were alone. The more relaxed version of him even came out around Lola after a time. I think that's was when he knew he was safe in our house. Safe with us.

I wanted to ask then but I didn't know how.

"I realized there was something between you..." Lola sighs. "I came downstairs once and saw him watching you. The look on his face was peaceful and happy, and I'd never seen him look that way. It was like you existing within his sight was all he needed. I kept pushing him to end what we were doing, to be with you, and then he took me to his house for dinner for the first time, and I understood." Lola shakes her head and she's begging my forgiveness and understanding with her eyes.

"Even though I was deemed good enough, his parents were cruel and passive aggressive. I could take it because I didn't care, and he let it happen because he didn't either. But you? They would've seen the difference and ripped you to pieces just because you made him happy. Because you would have been an aspect of his life they couldn't control. He told me they would've found a way to hurt you."

"You talked about me?"

"Yeah. We got in a huge fight and I said a lot of mean things to him. When I told you that he took too much, I meant he took too much from his parents, too much pain and abuse, and I wanted him to stand up and do something for himself. It was absolutely unfair of me to demand that, but I wanted you to be happy."

"Instead you hid your lie, kept things vague, and I believed the worst of him. I punished him for it, Lola. I'm punishing him for it now."

She frowns at me. "What did you do?"

"It doesn't matter. Nothing matters." I can hear myself fading away as I say it, disconnecting from my emotions until I have the energy to process it.

"It does. The idea that the two of you are finally together, that he's healthy enough to be with you…if the two of you had met under any other circumstances, this would still have happened. Like magnets, you're drawn together. A rule of physics."

"Why me?" More fucking whys. I lay back on my bed and put the phone down. I don't care that Lola is staring at my ceiling. It's a pretty ceiling.

"I don't know." I hear her sigh. "What are you going to do?"

"I don't know."

We stay in silence, existing together on opposite ends of the call. If we were together in person it would be the same, the two of us lying side by side on the bed, lost in our own thoughts but not alone.

"So…what do you mean by intense?"

I laugh, some of the tension broken, and a lot of my anger already dissipating. While it takes a long time for my hurts to heal, I've never been good at holding onto anger.

"I don't think you actually want to know."

She snorts. "Try me."

"Do you know what consensual non-consent is?"

Silence. "Okay, I don't want to know, but damn I had no idea you were that kinky."

We laugh together and I know that eventually, this will be another thing that I move past, and we'll be fine.

Mathias and I...I have to decide if I want us to be fine. If I want us to be good.

If I want more than our dynamic and can open myself up to a real relationship, despite the revelations about our past. I have to decide if they even matter, or if who were now is all that matters.

 Mathias

Willow is trying to push me away but I won't fucking let her. That is unacceptable.

While I might have gone to terrible lengths to get what I wanted, or to avoid punishment, in the past...I'm trying to practice slightly more restraint here. For the first time in my life, I might be genuinely addicted to something.

Her presence. Her existence.

I didn't realize that I craved it back in high school, or recognize how much I shaped my feelings around the way she made me feel. Now I do. Now I know that she brings out a piece of me I was sure had been killed by my father. It's like I get my innocence back when I'm with her.

Not sexually. She took some of that innocence from me herself, not that she knows that yet.

It's emotionally, spiritually, even. I am restored in her presence. I feel safe with her. I couldn't articulate the feeling before, but this time around I know that's what it is. Maybe because in the time after losing her I met other people who made me feel safe - Wyatt, Dr. Stanton, a few of the guys in the Cavalry. People who view me as a person, not a commodity.

Like right now we're laying side by side on her bed on our stomachs and watching a TV show together. I keep looking at her more than the screen, but it's more fun to ask her what's going on and have her explain it to me anyway. I love the way she reacts when something makes her happy or sad, or when she doesn't like a plot point or a character.

I move onto my side and start running my hand up and down her back, gently pulling on the ends of her hair in a way I know she likes. Willow shifts down and lays her head on her arms, eyes on the screen, and I watch her body melt. Not the way she does when she orgasms which is a lack of energy, but in a way of true relaxation.

Willingly sinking into the mattress, relaxing next to me, trusting me to be by her side. We've come so far and I wish she could see it. Willow's eyes flutter like she's fighting to stay awake.

It's been over two weeks since we had sex. I miss connecting with her, but we're also sort of dating in reverse. We started with the intense kinky fucking, and now we're hanging out and dating. I see her every day, we text all the time, and she's stopped acting surprised when I join her friends for meals. Half of them have my number and invite me to things because they want us to be around each other. I make her happy, but I don't think she'd admit that.

I know she talked to Lola the other night and things have been weird since. Not a wall, but a barrier for sure. I want to ask her, but Willow takes her own time with things. When she's ready, she'll say what she wants to say to me. All I can do is wait, show her I'm not going anywhere this time, and make her believe that I'm the love of her whole damn life.

She's the love of every life I might ever live. Willow makes me laugh. Makes me pause and look at the world. Willow helped me reconnect my mind and my body. Even Dr. Stanton thinks she's good for me, even though he was unsure at first given our whole dubious graveyard encounter.

Part of the reason I haven't even tried to have sex with her is because he advised me not to - it's easy to tie emotions to physical intimacy, and he wanted me to test where we were at without it. He did say that when we cross the physical line again, I should see if I'm comfortable engaging with her when it's not play or a scene, but the two of us. He wants me to see how that makes me feel.

Even more in goddamn love, at least on my side.

I'm a horrible person. I've done horrible things. I will endure any punishment, for eternity if I have to, as long as I get to be next to her. Even if all she wants from me is friendship. I'm hoping for more, but being realistic that I don't deserve it.

The laptop screen pauses to ask if we're still watching, and when I focus on Willow I realize that she's drifted off to sleep. I stop petting her and try to shift off the bed without waking her up, but before I can get all the way off her hand reaches out and wraps around my wrist.

"Stay?" she murmurs sleepily.

"Okay."

I get off the bed and move around the room, shutting off the main light and blowing out her candles. I plug her laptop in on her desk so it's not dead for class tomorrow. Willow is vaguely awake when I check on her, and I take off her socks because she hates sleeping in them, before I lift her up and put her the other direction on the bed so she can slide under the covers. Then I take off my jeans and slide in beside her.

Most nights we sleep together, I pull her into my body, gripping her tight like she's going to disappear on me. Afraid she'll do to me what I did to her.

Tonight, Willow rolls onto her side facing me and throws her leg over mine, winding her foot around my calf. Her nose burrows into my shoulder and after a few long breaths on my end, she lets out a small snore.

She held onto me.

It's the encouragement I need.

Even when she hints at wanting to hook up, I put her off for another week because I've got a plan. I'm going to woo her, dammit.

It starts with bringing her coffee in the mornings because she's usually too tired to make breakfast or go to the cafeteria. Being a night owl means she is definitely not a morning person. I say nothing as I walk her to class, but I change it all up by kissing her goodbye. I've started kissing her more in general, especially in public and in front of her friends.

And no tame we've been a couple forever pecks, I mean I lean into her and own her mouth, tease her with my tongue, and leave her flustered and vaguely aroused. The kinds of kisses that mean she's going to be thinking about me because the feel of them will linger on her swollen lips.

My theory is that if I act like I'm her boyfriend, then it will eventually be true. I'm manifesting this shit.

Wyatt is sitting with me outside the building where her night class is as I wait for her to finish.

"I swear, my mother hates me."

"She doesn't hate you."

"Then why does she want me to get engaged?"

"That's how it works for rich people?" I suggest.

"I'm just going to find someone cool to take to the party who is willing to bullshit mom, and then give her a solid story about how we broke up and I'm brokenhearted and can't possibly date anyone new."

I snort. "That will definitely work." It will not. His mom is one of the most perceptive people I've ever met in my life. As much as I love her and how they've been there for me, I am a little bit glad she's not my mom because it doesn't come with the same expectations that she has for Wyatt. She can love me without a concern about family legacy. Wyatt does have some strings attached when it comes to his mother's love.

I'd never tell him I think she has a point about him needing to focus a little because my life has been a disaster and I have made so many destructive decisions it is a shock I'm as intact as I am. I'm a glass house and I'm not stupid enough to throw stones.

Plus, even if I agree with his mom, I'm team Wyatt. That's what best friends are for.

"Got anyone in mind?" I ask him.

He looks thoughtfully into the distance and that's somehow more dangerous. "Maybe."

People start exiting the building and I start to watch impatiently for my girl.

Willow steps out and her gaze locks on mine, expecting me. I've been here at the end of her night class for weeks. This isn't the first time Wyatt's waited with me either. Since I'm so swept up in Willow we aren't hanging out as much, but we've had some good chats here. He calls it our bitching bench.

"Hi," she smiles at me. "Hey, Wyatt," she smiles at him too and it makes me want to glare at him, same as every damn time.

"Know anyone who'd be willing to be my fake girlfriend and fake destroy my heart?"

Her eyebrows draw together. "I mean, probably, but I think I need more information."

"The Gift from God can fill you in," he says as he slaps my shoulder. "Make a list." He points at me, dead serious. "I'm going to win this one." Wyatt puts his hands in his pockets and walks off whistling.

Willow stares after him looking perplexed, and I stare at Willow. She turns to look at me.

"What the hell?"

I take her hand in mine and give it a tug so we start walking toward her house.

"Gift from God?"

"It's what Mathias means. Wyatt was seeing this girl who was really into that stuff and he never let it go."

"And the fake girlfriend?"

"It's a lot to explain."

"You have a lot to explain to me already, we probably shouldn't add to the list."

I stop. "What?"

Willow sighs and bites her thumb. She pulls me this time and we resume walking.

"Lola told me the truth about your relationship in high school."

"Oh." How much else did Lola tell her?

"She wouldn't tell me much else. I was really mad at first, at both of you. Do you know how horrible I felt for that year you were together, not only because I was madly in love with you but because I was coveting my beloved sister's boyfriend? Do you have any idea how I tortured and hated myself when I wasn't with you? It was like I forgot all of that the second I was in your presence and it would hit me so hard the second you'd leave.

"And it was all bullshit. Both of you knew how I felt, knew how you felt, and all we did was hurt. I keep telling myself you had a good reason to do it and I've been waiting for you to talk about it. To say anything, explain anything, about how we ended up here."

I swallow thickly because Willow is right. It was ultimately my responsibility to confess everything, and I had been avoiding it out of fear. With how close we'd gotten again, I don't think there's anything I would tell her that would make her reject or walk away from me.

But it would change how she saw me, and I wasn't sure I was ready for that.

How do you tell someone who always saw you as strong and impenetrable that you were weak and a coward? That you were manipulated and abused even when you knew you should fight back or stop it? How do I tell her that my own mother let it happen and pretended like it didn't?

I stop us in the middle of the sidewalk and turn us toward the other end of campus. I can't have this conversation with her inside. To keep me calm, I need open air. Even though it's chilly, we're both dressed warm, so I think we'll be okay. Willow follows my change in direction without questioning it, and I have so much gratitude for her trust.

"The way Lola and I became friends, and came up with our plan, is more about Lola than me, so she'll have to tell you that part."

"Okay..." Willow trails off. She looks around and realizes where we're headed, I can see it in the way her jaw tenses, but she doesn't stop me.

"My father beat me."

She stops. I tug her arm and we keep walking, through the small line of trees that block the graveyard. Not letting go of my hand, we weave together and apart around the stones until we arrive at our dear departed friend, Elliot Renault. We sit down and lean against the stone, the chill of it seeping through my jacket but also making everything around me clear and cold. Exactly what I need to be able to talk about this.

"I don't remember a time he didn't. As I got older, he liked having excuses for what he did, so there were always expectations. Always someone I was supposed to beat, something I was supposed to accomplish, but even when I did it wasn't enough. The goalpost was always moving because he felt better if he had a reason to hurt me. He could tell himself it was how we was raising me to be a man. Covered in bruises and scratches but it was so he could make me tough.

"Everything I cared about was always taken away from me. The one time they let me have a dog he gave it away when he saw it gave me comfort. I was 11." I sigh. "He had a very specific idea of the kind of man I was going to be, so when I was 14 he paid a sex worker to take my virginity. It's not that weird in wealthy circles but it meant I had almost no interest in it like most guys did as we got older. It was another thing for him to invade, to judge, to force on me, so I kept my distance. I did everything else he wanted, I went to parties, I insinuated that I was hooking up, but I wasn't."

"I'm sorry," she whispers, and pulls our entwined hands into her lap, cradling mine in both of hers. Willow's fingers trace across my knuckles and I close my eyes, falling into the sensation of her.

"I was a monster because I was treated like one. I lost my connection to myself, and I would do anything it took to prove myself to him so he'd leave me alone. It's how all that shit happened with Colin." I open my eyes and turn to look at her. "I forgot who I was for so long until you. My father started putting pressure on me to be seen with someone, and Lola and I happened upon each other. She met his standards and I had a reason not to be at home, and then my reason for doing anything at all was to get to the end of the day to be with you."

"Then why wouldn't you be with me? If that's what he wanted, why wasn't I good enough?" Her voice breaks and it's a knife to the chest. I've hurt her so much that she should never forgive me. The way I acted, the way Lola and I both did, gave her a fucking complex. That's on me.

"Lola wasn't hurt by my father's shit talking, and I felt no need to defend her. If I'd been with you and he spoke to you the way he did to her, I would have killed him. If he'd tried to take you away from me, or found a way to hurt you in order to punish me, nothing in the world would have stopped me from destroying both my parents. No matter the consequences. I couldn't let him near you. Couldn't let him know you even existed, or I would have lost my goddamn mind out of fear."

"I would have put up with it for you." Willow sniffles and I pull my hand away so I can tug her into my body. She burrows her face into my chest.

"I don't mean emotionally hurt, I mean he would have found a way to physically hurt you, the same way that he hurt me."

Willow looks up at me, pale and furious. "Why?"

I shake my head. I don't know why he was like that, why my father got so much enjoyment out of hurting me. Why he hated me so much. Any other father would be proud - I was his spitting image, good looking, athletic, good grades. I was as close to perfect as I could be but it was never perfect enough for him and his demands. He wished I'd never been born and I don't know why; I never will.

Willow nods and then leans her head back on my chest. I feel her take a deep breath and I wait for the next question.

"What happened when you and Lola broke up?"

The events that led to the real end of our fake relationship are ugly, and everything I did afterward is ugly too. It started off the worst year of my life, not only because I felt more alone than ever but because I gave in to the monster. I gave in to wanting everyone around me to hurt the way that I did. Even when I'd find ways to break out of the dark spaces, I would also find myself back there.

"I needed to go to the hospital so I called Lola. It was the worst he'd ever..." My throat closes up and I swallow. "She told me I needed to report him and I said no. After she took me home, we kept fighting about it on the phone, she said she'd turn him in herself. I ended it."

"She said you took too much and I thought..."

"That I hurt her. How could you think that?" I don't want to be hurt because I did take too much from someone in the end, just not Lola.

"I was hurting and irrational, and I doubted it, but then what happened afterward..."

I was basically an asshole for months, got even pissier when Lola hooked up with Colin at a cabin weekend and told everyone, and then I started drinking and couldn't seem to stop. Willow refused to talk to me and wouldn't tell me why, and even though my father had been careful since the beating when he broke my ribs and and gave me some internal and external bruising, I was standing there and taking it from him every single night. No one hated me more than myself, and I leaned into that.

Watching Colin watch Elise and the way he denied them both got through to me. I didn't have any intentions to hurt her when I started talking to her and flirting with her at her locker. The party where I assaulted her I was out of my mind on liquor and a borrowed opiate. I deserved more than what Colin did to me that night, but it did help me mentally check out, and everyone left me alone for the rest of the year. I could slowly kill myself in peace, without the pressure of the facade.

I try and explain where my head was at to Willow, without ever denying what I did. That I hurt someone in a way that should never be forgiven.

Willow pushes away from me and puts an inch of distance between us.

"How does any of that explain last fall?" It's a valid question. There hadn't been any interaction between Colin, Elise, and me for years at that point. It hadn't mattered to me that he was here and I'd worked hard to avoid him. I'd known Elise was at Elmwood and made no move to be near her either. Until Devil's Night. Until that fucking week.

"My father died. The weekend before."

"Oh." She waits for me to explain.

"I'd escaped him. I only went home when necessary, I was doing well. Then I was summoned home for him to tell me on his deathbed how much he hated me. How I'd failed him. How he was going to haunt me for letting him down, and that I'd never know a moment's peace."

"What the hell."

"He died less than a day later. I didn't stay, I came back to Elmwood. It was almost Halloween, I wanted to escape, and I did but I was not well. I was manic and I was drinking. It's the only explanation I have for falling back into old patterns, like if I could do this one thing that I'd failed at, he wouldn't haunt me."

"Jesus, Mathias." She sounds appalled but I don't think all of it is directed at me.

"I stayed sober for a bit after that, started seeing a therapist, but I held back a lot." I look at her sidelong, watching for her reaction. "Until this girl got me drunk at a party and tied me to a grave to fuck me."

Willow stills.

"It broke something inside me. Not in a bad way," I tell her quickly, "but I got a lot more honest with Dr. Stanton after that. I'm here today, not whole but well, because of you. In more ways that you could ever imagine."

She looks up and stares at the darkening sky. "What you did was really fucked up, Mathias. I know you were hurting, but she didn't deserve that."

"No, she didn't, and I've come clean with Colin. We'll never be friends, but I needed him to know I'm not a threat to her. The villain, yes, but not a threat."

Willow turns to look at me, eyebrows lifted in surprise. "You did that?"

"They deserved to know. I deserved worse."

We sit together in silence, pondering that, and Willow shifts so her body is pressed up against mine again. Eventually, her head leans onto my shoulder and we watch the cloudless sky, breathing in the dark, becoming part of it. I could sit like this with her forever, living our entire lives in this moment on this spot, until hundreds of years from now someone finds our skeletons entwined like this. Holding each other's bony hands, her skull perched on my clavicle. Until we become nothing but dust, indistinguishable from one another.

"I didn't know it then," I start quietly, nervous as fuck, "but I was in love with you. I'd never felt it before so I didn't realize, and by the time I did it was too late. Then you came to me, darkness and sensuality, and I should have known sooner that it was you. I only ever reacted that way to you."

"What way?" she murmurs.

"Turned on. Desperate."

Willow laughs. "Yeah, okay."

I take a deep breath. "That was the first time I'd had sex since my first time."

Willow scrambles up so she can look me full in the face. "What."

"I told you, I wasn't interested. Until you." I reach out and cup her cheek.

"Not just sex but...intimacy. Touching. I wanted to be close to you all the time. I thought about you, obsessively, in every way, every day."

"I was obsessed with you," she admits and looks down at her hands. "But I...assumed you moved on."

"If you're feeling guilty for having sex with other people, stop it right now," I laugh. "I want you. Only you." Did I want to kill them? Yes. Would I? No. I had her, and they'd never have her again. It was all that mattered.

"I don't want anyone else," she admits after a long moment of looking into my eyes like there's more answers there.

"Are we okay?" I ask, my stomach fluttering at her admission that she wants me. It's not her agreeing she's my girlfriend, but it's progress. It's her finally owning her feelings.

"Yeah," she gives me a small smile that says more than a big grin would. Willow stands up and offers me her hand. I take it and stand beside her, gazing down at her before we start walking to her house.

Willow

The revelations Mathias shared with me were both expected, and heart-breaking. I knew about his dad theoretically, but never enough to be sure. I'm less mad at Lola because I know she takes keeping secrets too seriously, and especially one that made him feel humiliated. I wish they'd both been more open with me.

Part of me is still angry with him. I know that it's not reasonable, and I can't blame him for the things that were done to him, but I feel like he should've known better once he got older. Once he had people to rely on and have his back. Instead, he kept hurting others until he hit his own rock bottom.

I want to believe he's changed. I need some sort of sign.

Except every time he's close to me, all of my thoughts go out the window. It feels so good to be able to touch him with affection, lean on him, fall asleep and wake up beside him. If I had my way, I'd be around him every second of the day so I never had to think about anything else.

It's hard because I like his friends and he likes mine, and our worlds are becoming so mingled that I need to decide what this is and what we're doing or it's going to get more complicated than I want to deal with.

He's all I ever wanted, and I wish I understood what was holding me back.

Instead of figuring that out, we're at the annual Halloween party.

In couple's costumes.

This year, the party is being held in the old infirmary. Elmwood finally got the funding to fully gut and renovate the spooky, looming building and agreed to let us basically destroy it before they rip everything out of it. Of course the theme this year is Infection.

Mathias and I are a zombie football player and a zombie cheerleader. I was never a cheerleader, but the costume is fun and oddly comfortable. The fake blood is sticky and it's gotten everywhere, but overall I'm having fun.

He won't leave my side.

The party is spread out over the whole building – the first floor is where the music is blasting, the second has games, and the third has areas to sit and relax. We're on the second floor, cheering on a giant chess drinking game that I don't entirely understand. Wyatt is with us but he's got his eyes on someone across the room and I can't figure out who, but the rest of the people with us are my friends.

Gus and Bronte are, of course, a zombie bride and groom, while the rest of my housemates are in various zombie costumes. Except Liam. He disappeared somewhere as soon as we got here and I hope it's because he's with Heidi. She's been coming to the house a lot, although I think the only person who knows is me because I'm as much of a night owl as they are.

Mathias has his hand resting on my bare lower back and it's starting to drive me crazy. I'm so horny right now but the boundary I made was that we weren't going to have sex until I figured out if I could forgive him, and truly be with him. Even though he hasn't said that outright, I know it's what he wants.

The sex we've had, the *kind* of sex we've had, is now like a barrier between us. We let each other inside a dark, vulnerable space so quickly without doing a lot of the trust building that we should have. Neither of us was honest about what we wanted from our dynamic, and even though at the of the day the thing we want is each other, we let our desperate, deprived libidos take us somewhere our hearts weren't ready to go. Not the way we did.

No one has seen my dark side but him.

No one brings it out of my like he does.

There's never been a part of me that he's turned away from, but I can't say the same. I can't deny being disappointed in him, or being ashamed of his actions. I told him that, outright, and all he did was nod and accept it. He didn't try to defend himself or make excuses, and I think that's why I want to forgive him. I've never encountered anyone who owned their fuck ups and their damage that way.

"Wanna go dance?" he murmurs in my ear.

I nod and signal to Georgia and Goldie that we're going downstairs. They nod and before we walk away, I check that my phone is still in the little pack strapped to my thigh, just in case. Safety first.

Mathias leads me out of the crowd to the staircase, his hand clinging to mine. As we're heading down, other people are heading up. I jolt when I register that one of them is Colin. And behind him, tucked against his back, is Elise.

We all pause for a second, everyone's eyes darting to each other like some kind of stupid moment in a movie. Elise looks at me, curious, but then with understanding as she recognizes me. I don't know what to make of the interaction. Colin and Mathias are looking at each other.

Colin gives him a brief nod, and Mathias tugs my hand so we resume our way down the stairs. His eyes meet mine and he nods at me too, before turning and talking to Elise like all of this never happened. As if time didn't freeze for an awkward moment. Elise didn't seem scared and Colin didn't seem angry. The only people who should hate him acknowledged their indifference to him.

It makes something click inside my chest, and anxiety slides through me.

Mathias has wanted what we've done as a form of both pleasure and punishment. I was punishing him for what had happened, what he'd done, and how he dealt with it. Now that so many of the things that made him chase that feeling are resolved, what if his feelings for me fade? What if he doesn't need me anymore?

What will I do if he leaves me again, like before? I don't know how to survive the kind of hurt that will put on me. The decimation of my heart. It beats for him. He's inside every inch of me. Even when I hated him and avoided him, I never got over him. There was never anyone else who ever came close to mattering the way that he did.

No one else ever felt like my own special secret, a door that only I could unlock.

When we get to the bottom of the stairs, I pull my hand away from his and start walking toward the front door. I need air, I need space, I need to think.

I move away without saying anything, and hear Mathias call my name a few times but I don't stop. The closer I get to the door the faster I move, pushing through people until I burst out into the night and down the stairs. For a moment I pause and take a few cold, deep breaths, trying to stop my mind from spinning out.

Mathias calls for me, loud and clear, and I know that if I look back I'll see him coming for me. I'll see him worried. If I meet his eyes, he'll see too much.

So I book it and start running.

The good thing about being a zombie cheerleader is that I'm wearing sneakers. No tottering around on heels for me.

The bad thing is that sneakers or not, Mathias is faster than I am and he runs as part of his workout so it won't take him long to catch up with me.

That makes me run faster.

I'm all out sprinting, breathing hard, pushing myself as fast I can go as I dart into the trees. My feet are pounding on the packed earth of the path, the sound oddly loud since the night is dead quiet and even the rumble of the bass from the party is fading. I get free of the treeline and stumble into the graveyard, my body moving of its own accord to the back corner.

My back corner, my hiding spot, until I brought Mathias here and made it ours.

"Willow," he calls to me, moving closer as I stop over Elliot Renault's grave. I wish he could give me advice about love right now because I just know it would be good.

When I finally looked him up so I could learn who MB was, I discovered that they'd been in a star-crossed Romeo and Juliet kind of situation.

MB was Marianna Bernard, and her and Elliot's fathers hated each other. They'd even been involved in an actual duel. Since Elliot's father "won," he demanded Marianna's hand in marriage...for himself. Shortly after that, Elliot and his father died under "mysterious circumstances" that were very vague in the library records. I have my own theories. I want to believe Elliot tried to take out his father to get the woman he loved, and ended up dead himself. I want to believe that he and Marianna loved each other so much that he would have done anything to be with her or save her. Even to the death.

Marianna never married.

I can hear and feel Mathias step closer to me, but he stays a few feet away, giving me space. I still can't look at him.

"Listen," he sighs, so defeated I almost turn to him. "If you want to end things, I understand. I'll always be there for you. Always be anything you need. I get it. I expected this."

"Expected what?" I snap, not understanding him.

"That you might not be able to move past what I've done. If you realized that you can't be with me, I'm not going to argue with you. I'll let you go."

"Just like that?" It comes out strained and painful. "Without a fight?"

"Willow, please," is all he says, and it's that agony in his voice that pulls at me. I finally turn around and he looks more broken than I've ever seen him. Mathias isn't looking at me, he's looking at the ground, his face tightly controlled in a non-expression. His shoulders are down, his entire body dragging toward the ground in defeat. There's no fight in him at all. Nothing but hurt.

"I'm afraid that you'll leave me when you realize you don't need me anymore."

Mathias snaps his head up, confusion furrowing his brows. "What are you talking about?"

"What we've been doing - it's your punishment. For what you've done. When you don't need to be punished anymore, you won't need me."

He steps closer to me and I don't back away. As he watches me, reads me, his face smooths out.

"That's why you ran?" I nod and he swallows thickly. "You honestly think that any part of me being with you has anything to do with them?"

"I..." I look up at him and he's fighting a smile. There's affection and desire in his gaze and it makes me lose my train of thought.

"As if I needed any reason other than everything about you to want you? To be fucking obsessed with you?" Mathias takes another step closer and slides his hand along my neck until he's cupping my nape. The move makes me gasp, my entire body reacting to his touch.

"Like I haven't loved you and existed for you, even when I didn't have you, for actual years?" He shakes me a little and moves even closer. I can't see anything but him. "Willow, I'm yours. I'm not going anywhere unless you send me away."

Then his mouth is on mine and I can feel tears tracking down my cheeks and they're both happy and sad. I sink into his warmth, wrapping my arms around him and holding him close.

I almost melt when I feel him sigh happily, and feel the curve of his smile against my lips, like he can't stop himself. It's the thing I always wanted. I wanted to feel his smile on mine, and know that I caused it.

The kiss changes eventually, getting deeper and needier. I don't know which of us makes a move first but his hands are under my skirt and squeezing my ass, and mine are under the ripped up football jersey he's wearing, groping his abs and the smooth contours of his lower back.

"Should we go to your house?" he asks me between kisses, neither of us able to disconnect for longer than a few seconds.

"No," I answer, and direct his mouth to my neck. I cry out when he bites me and my hips thrust into his. "Right here. I want you right here."

Mathias pauses and then lifts me up so my legs wrap around his waist. His mouth is back on mine as he drops to his knees and gently lays me down on the grass. We grind on each other, his hard cock pressing against my panties, driving me crazy with need. I slide my hands under his pants and push them down as I reach to squeeze his muscular ass. It's one of my favorite parts of his body and I get distracted by it before I remember I'm trying to get him naked.

He pulls away from me and sits up, reaching under my skirt to quickly yank down my underwear, then moves his pants down enough to free his throbbing erection. I reach my arms up for him and he comes back to me, our chests pressed together, our mouths constantly seeking one another, and he reaches down to line himself up and press inside me.

I feel full immediately, and lift my hips to take him deeper. We're not even moving much, not in a hurry, not trying to get anything from one another except this exact feeling. Our bodies rub and slide as we kiss and touch one another. I love the way he keeps coming back to his hand cupping my face, thumb stroking my cheek, before he trails it down to feel all over me again. He touches me like I'm precious, and I feel the same way about him.

Before, when I first fell for him, I only had pieces because he was broken. I can feel how much work he's done to put himself back together, and I want to help him get the rest of the way. I want to find a way to be whole with each other.

My orgasm is building and every time he drags his tongue across mine it gets closer and closer. I'm moaning into his mouth, my body moving on its own as it chases the high. Mathias is moving faster, pressing deeper, and I feel like we're trying to meld our bodies into one. Nothing will ever be close enough, but this will have to suffice.

"Willow," he moans into my mouth, the sound echoing down my throat until it meets my own cry of pleasure. My entire body clenches as I start to come, squeezing him tight with every muscle in my body.

We're no longer really kissing, just connected by our lips and sharing breath as we find our release with each other. Mathias stills, his cock buried as deep as it can go, and holds there as he fills me. There's so much from both of us I can feel it dripping down my ass cheek.

He keeps kissing me, soft and slow now. I can feel him trying to stop but every time he gets pulled back to me. I don't mind.

I glide my hands up into his hair and run my nails over his scalp the way he likes, and he finally stops. His nose brushes mine and he stares into my eyes.

"I love you, Willow. I always have."

"I love you, Mathias. I don't know how to stop."

"Then don't," he smiles, presses one last peck to my lips, and then we both groan as he moves his cock out of me. "Let's go to your house and talk."

 Mathias

When we get to her house, we shower off our extremely smudged zombie makeup. It's tempting to change the tone of things as I wash her body and get off the fake blood she can't see and make sure her face is clean, but this silly, innocent teasing as we clean each other is nice too. It's always tempting to get sexual with her but I have to remember how amazing all of these moments feel, too. How much I need them.

After we get out, we crawl under her covers, still damp and naked.

I pull her into me, leaving enough room that we can see each other's faces.

"What are you afraid of?" I ask softly. I want to make sure that she knows it's all about her. That leaving her is never going to be an option for me.

"That you're going to get bored. That if you don't need me to punish you, you won't need me at all." Willow's voice is small, but she doesn't look away or hide from me.

"I won't lie and say I don't enjoy it, but it was never about needing you to punish me. It was about needing you, however you would let me. It's never been about anything except you. Even saying I'm in love with you doesn't feel like enough."

Willow's cheeks turn slightly pink. "So...you still want to do it though? You want me to dominate you?" She bites her lip and I laugh.

"Hell yeah." I yank her close and grind my hips into hers, half hard from proximity alone. "But not every time. Sometimes I want to be you and me, and that's enough."

Willow nods. "I want that, too."

We stare at each other, both smiling like idiots, owning that we're in love. Then her smile falls.

"I don't feel good about how it started."

"I know, but I do. You broke me when I needed to be broken, and I don't think we'd be here if you hadn't. Without you, the monster would have won eventually. It would've been all that was left of me."

"I'm sorry."

"I'm not, but if you need it, I forgive you." I run my hand up and down her back, soothing her as we talk.

"I don't forgive me," she says, and then squeezes her eyes shut. "Even if you wanted it, I set out to do something against your will. It's one thing when we play at it, when I know you're all for it, but...it gets to me sometimes."

I press a kiss to her forehead. "Then we'll talk to someone about it. I'm sure Dr. Stanton would love to unpack it with us both."

She laughs then and burrows into me, her forehead nestled against my neck and her lips pressing kisses across my clavicle.

"You're not alone in this. You'll never be alone again," I promise her. "But you need to sort out your kink from your guilt. I had to do the same."

"Is that why you were holding out on me for the last few weeks?" she huffs and then laughs.

"Yeah. I wanted to make sure you knew I wasn't with you only for the sex we had. That I wanted to be around you, just you. Even if we never played like that again, I'd be satisfied."

I reach down to tip her chin up so I can see her. "You know that, right?"

Willow's eyes search my face and then she gives me her small, real smile. "Yeah. I know."

Yeah. She knows.

Willow

3 Years Later

We decided to take a trip in March this year - our own celebration of Ides and when we finally crossed lines with each other. We did have lots of conversations with Dr. Stanton and I think it helped us both understand each other and our needs. It made me feel less ashamed until I didn't feel it at all anymore.

Until I could fully enjoy who we are and how we got here.

Mathias the man is more like the boy I met in high school. He's so much more open now than he ever was before, and we have never been happier.

This year, we rented a tree house in North Carolina. It's gorgeous and isolated, and after cooking way too much food over the fire because it was fun, we've been laying on the bed in the loft, staring at the sky through the skylight.

"I love you." He takes my hand and kisses my knuckles. "Are you ready?"

I turn my head and look at him. His face is relaxed, his blue eyes twinkling with mischief, and he's in need of a haircut.

"If you really don't want to, we don't have to."

"I know," I answer. I roll onto my side and watch him. "But if I dish it out, I should see if I can take it, right?"

Mathias laughs and gets up. "Call my name when you're ready." He goes down the steep, winding staircase to the first floor of the tree house to wait for me. I'm nervous but excited at the same time.

The bed is already setup, so now it's about me. I get up and remove my clothes, and then debate over the lingerie I brought with me. None of it feels right, so I decide to stay completely naked. I climb back on the bed, and arrange myself in a way that doesn't make me look as nervous as I am.

In all the time we've been together, I've dominated Mathias, or things have been mutual and with no dynamic at play, but I've never let him dominate me. I've never been tied up or held down, he's never been the one playing with me the way that I play with him. Never been edged or teased, never got punished or rewarded. I got him, however I wanted him, and after teasing me about it I decided I needed to try.

It was fun to read about in sexy books and in the videos we watched, but my interest in being submissive had always been passive. We both agreed I should try, and that we'll stop if it doesn't do anything for me. The thing I didn't say to him was that of course it will get me off, because it's about him, not what we're doing, but we'll see.

"Mathias!" I call his name and hear him start moving up the stairs a few seconds later. He's stripped down to his boxers and when his eyes land on my naked body, his cock jolts in his briefs. I grin at it.

"Interesting choice," he purrs at me. His fingers trail up my leg, over my hip and belly, teasing the tip of my nipple, and then he takes my wrist and lifts it. The bindings are soft, and my stomach clenches before I talk myself down. I take a deep breath when he does the same to the other one.

"You good?" he checks in with me.

I nod and bite my lip, trying to anticipate what he'll do next.

"Safe word?" he prompts.

"Sharkbait."

Mathias grins at me and then goes to the end of the bed, where he starts kissing his way up my leg, teasing me with his lips and his hands. Watching him work toward my center is pleasurable agony. My hips move on the bed, seeking relief.

"Did you want something, love?"

"Yes," I answer. Part of the game we setup today is that I'm only allowed to say yes or no, unless I'm using the safe word.

"Does this feel good?"

"Yes." I squirm again.

Mathias grins and resume his tease of kissing, touching, and licking, getting closer and closer to my soaking wet core. I gasp when he inhales sharply and then lets out a breath, the air making me jolt from the sensitivity.

"Should I eat your pretty pussy, Willow?"

"Yes," I whine.

I feel him spread me open and my hips thrust up when he presses his tongue to my clit. Mathias settles himself between my thighs, legs resting on his shoulders, and buries his face against me to eat me out. It doesn't take long for me to come, and I actually like having the restraints to hold onto and brace myself as my pleasure breaks.

"Yes," I pant over and over, body rolling with my orgasm. Mathias never stops. He moves with me, keeping the attention on me as I cry out.

He sits up and wipes his mouth with the back of his hand.

"Should I stop?"

"No," I shake my head vehemently.

Mathias reaches a hand between my legs and slides two fingers inside me, then curves them to press against my g-spot. The muscles in my thighs twitch and I clench around him with pleasure.

"You were such a good girl coming on my face," he murmurs to me, and I clench again, reacting to the praise. It surprises me, but I'm glad I like it. "All tied up, ready to be eaten...oh, Willow. My love. My soul. Do you want to cry from coming so hard?"

"Yes," I beg. I've never begged before. He works his fingers inside me, driving me close to the edge.

"Will you come over and over for me?"

"Yes!"

"Do you want me to fuck your pretty, wet pussy?"

"Yes!"

"Are you going to come all over my cock?"

"Yes," I gasp out, barely able to breathe from how good it feels as he fucks me with his fingers. I'm getting close but he's not giving me what I need to go over the edge.

"Will you be a good girl and take all my come?"

"Yes."

"Will you scream my name, love?"

"Yes!"

He starts moving a little faster and my sanity is racing toward a precipice.

"Will you marry me?"

Mathias curves his fingers and I explode, fluid gushing out of me as I come all over his hand, orgasming harder than I ever have in my life. I hold onto the restraints like they're the only thing tethering me to the earth as the pleasure goes on and on. I squeeze his hand, trapping it between my thighs. He stops moving his fingers but doesn't try to move out of me.

I take a deep breath and look at him.

"Yes."

Also by Ashley Mack

The Senses

The Sight of You

The Taste of You

The Sound of You

The Feel of You

The Scent of You

Companion Novellas

Look at Me

Savor Me

Silence Me

Heart Series

Take to Heart

Elmwood College Tales

Offerings

Preservation

Transfigured

Beguiled

Constraint

Obscured

About the Author

Ash lives in the Midwest with her husband, two girls, a dog, and a cat. She reads during every spare moment. She hopes that her characters go in new directions with terrifying, strong women who go feral for their men, and that sometimes the men are the damsels in distress who need saving. Connect on Instagram and Tiktok at @totalsassreads